TANK & FIZZ

THE CASE OF FIREBANE'S FOLLY

LIAM O'DONNELL

MIKE DEAS

ORCA BOOK PUBLISHERS

Library and Archives Canada Cataloguing in Publication

O'Donnell, Liam, 1970–, author
Tank & Fizz : the case of firebane's folly / by Liam O'Donnell;
illustrated by Mike Deas.

Issued in print and electronic formats.
ISBN 978-1-4598-1261-1 (softcover).—ISBN 978-1-4598-1262-8 (pdf).—
ISBN 978-1-4598-1263-5 (epub)

I. Deas, Mike, 1982-, illustrator II. Title. III. Title: Tank and Fizz.
IV. Title: Case of firebane's folly.
PS8579.D646T33 2018 jC813'.6 C2017-904526-1
C2017-904527-X

First published in the United States, 2018
Library of Congress Control Number: 2017949716

Summary: In this illustrated middle-grade novel and fourth book in the Tank & Fizz series, a goblin detective and technology-tinkering troll get wrapped up in a scheme from the Dark Depths to take control of Slick City using the infamous Crown of Peace.

MIX
Paper from responsible sources
FSC® C016245

Orca Book Publishers is dedicated to preserving the environment and has printed this book on Forest Stewardship Council® certified paper.

Orca Book Publishers gratefully acknowledges the support for its publishing programs provided by the following agencies: the Government of Canada through the Canada Book Fund and the Canada Council for the Arts, and the Province of British Columbia through the BC Arts Council and the Book Publishing Tax Credit.

Edited by Liz Kemp
Design by Jenn Playford
Illustrations and cover image by Mike Deas

ORCA BOOK PUBLISHERS
www.orcabook.com

Printed and bound in Canada.

21 20 19 18 • 4 3 2 1

For all the little monsters with big ideas.

—Liam O'Donnell

For Faye, Annie and Nancy. Love you.

—Mike Deas

CHAPTER ONE
Field Trip Foul-Up

Principal Weaver was ready to burst a silk gland.

"Fizz Marlow!" she barked through her megaphone. "You. Are. Late!"

I hated to admit it, but the old web-head was right. My spider-principal swung alongside the little yellow bus pulling away from the school gates. A bus I was supposed to be on.

The name's Fizz Marlow. I'm in the fourth grade, and I solve mysteries. It's a living. I'm a goblin. I'm also very late for the bus taking me on my first overnight field trip.

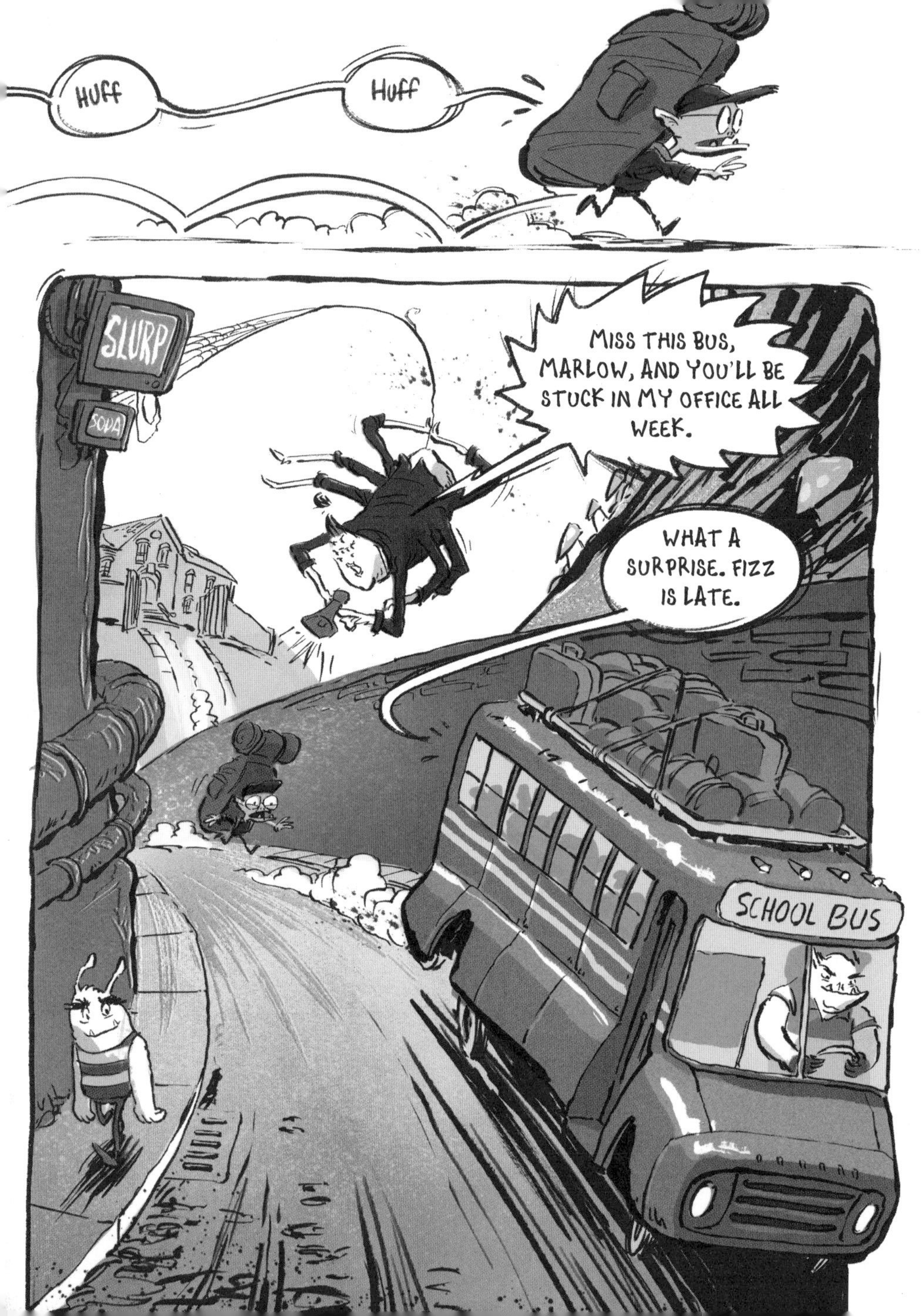
HUFF
HUFF
SLURP
SODA
MISS THIS BUS, MARLOW, AND YOU'LL BE STUCK IN MY OFFICE ALL WEEK.
WHAT A SURPRISE. FIZZ IS LATE.
SCHOOL BUS

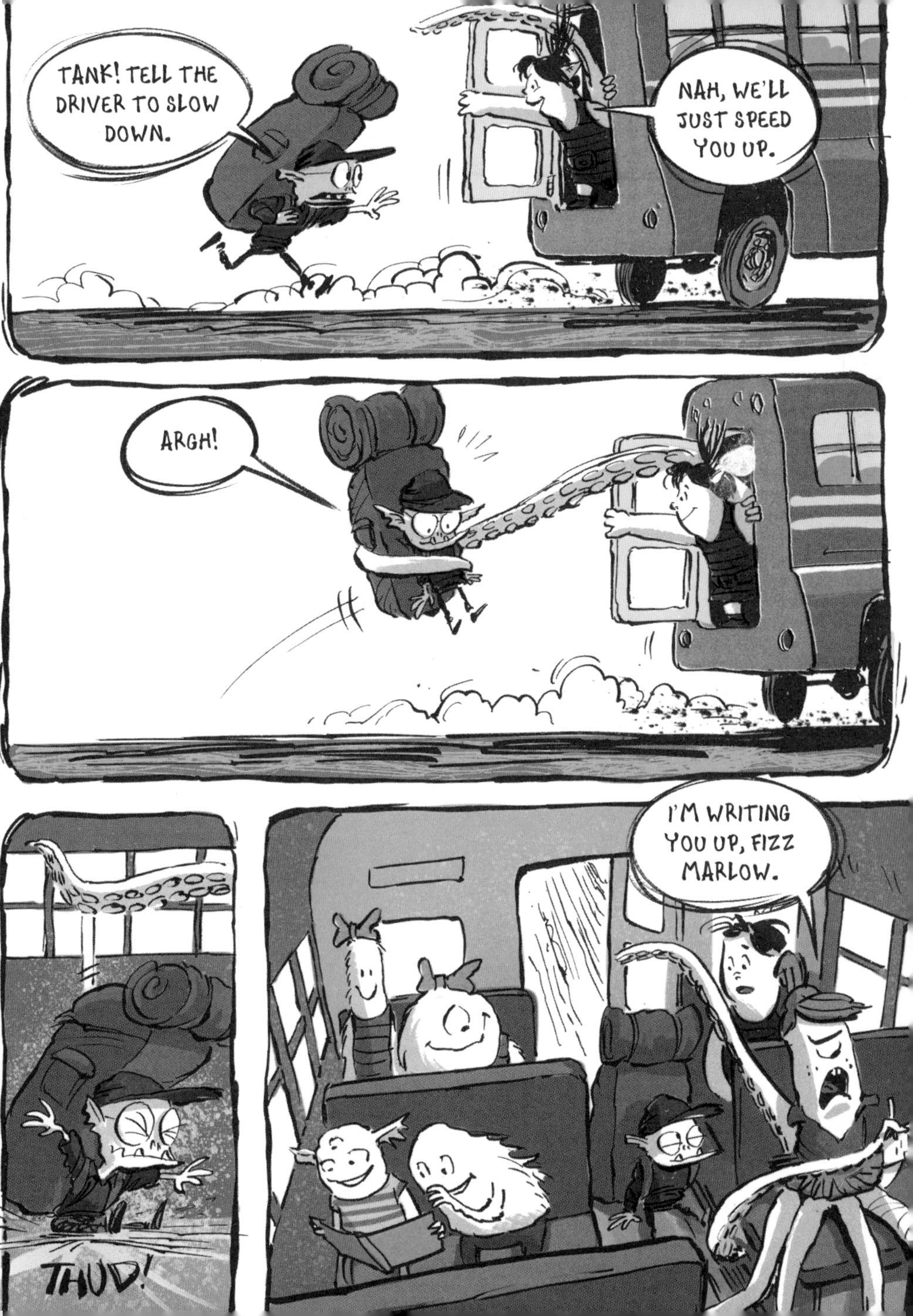
TANK! TELL THE DRIVER TO SLOW DOWN.
NAH, WE'LL JUST SPEED YOU UP.
ARGH!
THUD!
I'M WRITING YOU UP, FIZZ MARLOW.

Tank helped me to my feet.

"Take it easy, Henelle," she said. "He's just a little late."

Henelle glared at me with her one large eye. A shiver ran down my scales. The octoclops was student captain of our field-trip group. She might be half cyclops and half octopus, but she was *all* bossy pants to her classmates.

"Late will get you killed in the Dark Depths," she growled.

"We're not going to the Dark Depths," I said. "We're visiting the Glowshroom Glades, remember?"

"The glades are on the farthest edge of the Shallows," Henelle said with a sigh. "One wrong turn and you're in the Dark Depths, home to the deadliest monsters in Rockfall Mountain. You would know all this if you read the field-trip information package I created for the class. But I guess reading is a little too much to ask for *some* of us."

Henelle gave a final whip of her arms and stomped to the front of the bus.

I let my backpack fall to the bus floor. It landed with a *thud*. At the front, the driver looked back at me through the rearview mirror. The reflection of the ogre's stare cut into me like a hatchet and made me want to jump out the back door again. Instead, I slunk into my seat beside Tank.

"You're welcome, by the way." My best friend was focused on her phone. She had taken off the back and was poking at the wires inside with a tiny spinning-screwdriver thingy. Tank was always poking at technology. When you're a troll, tinkering with technology is what you do. And Tank was the best tinkering-troll detective partner a sleuth like me could ask for.

"Thank you for getting me scooped up and tossed onto the bus," I grumbled.

"I told you not to be late for school today. It's a long drive to the glades."

"I wasn't late," I snapped. "The driver left early!" Hatchet-Eyes looked back at me again. Had he heard me? I lowered my voice. "What's the deal with the driver? Where's Ms. Yallo? I thought she was taking us on this trip."

"Ms. Yallo is sick. This guy said his name was Mr. Ravel or something. Anyway, it doesn't matter who drives us." Tank's ears wiggled. "For the next few days, our classroom will be the majestic forests of illuminated fungi known as the Glowshroom Glades."

"You sound like a tourist brochure," I said.

"That's because it *is* from a brochure." She pulled a folded paper from the pocket of her tool belt and handed it to me. "The glades are the only place in Rockfall Mountain where you can find over three hundred varieties of glowshrooms."

"Fascinating." I yawned. Spending the week in Principal Weaver's office was sounding more exciting every second. "Wake me up when we get there."

A buzzing came from the front of the bus. A blaze fairy the size of an ogre's tooth flew up the aisle.

"Fizz Marlow!" the fairy barked.

"Now you're in trouble," Tank muttered and doubled her focus on her phone's circuit board.

Miss Blinx, Gravelmuck Elementary gym teacher and three-time Slick City weightlifting champion, zipped closer.

"Henelle tells me you were late, Marlow," she sneered. "I will not have any students go missing or get eaten on this trip. That would create far too much paperwork. This is your only warning."

Miss Blinx buzzed back to the front of the bus before I could think up one of my amazing comebacks. It was probably for the best. For the next few days

Miss Blinx was in charge. She might be small enough to fit in a troll's pocket, but you did not want to make that fairy mad.

Near the middle of the bus Mr. Mantle hovered above his seat, flipping through the pages of a book. He is my math teacher, and he looks like a floating brain with a mustache and wispy tentacles for arms. When your teacher is all brain and loves numbers, you know you're in trouble. Mr. Mantle and Miss Blinx were our chaperones for this field trip. Our whole class had been planning it for months. We had held bake sales and raffles to raise enough money, and now we were on our way. I wasn't a huge fan of spending a week looking at glowshrooms, but anything was better than looking at the walls of a classroom.

Beside me, Tank quietly tinkered with her phone. The other kids around us laughed and chatted excitedly, bouncing in their seats with each bump in the road as the bus rolled through the outskirts of Slick City. Outside the window my hometown whizzed by as the driver steered us deeper into Rockfall Mountain. From mystery-loving goblins like me to fire-breathing dragons, Rockfall Mountain was home to a vast underground world of scales, tails, fangs and fur.

I had never been this far outside of Slick City, so you'd think I'd be excited. Instead, it felt like something was missing. It had been weeks since Tank and I had solved a mystery. And even then, it had only been finding Mr. Mantle's missing monocle. Excitement overload on that case. There wasn't much chance of finding a new mystery in a field of glowshrooms, so there was nothing I could do about it now. I guess even scaly detectives need a holiday from crime solving every now and then. I closed my eyes and tried to have a nap. It had been a busy morning, what with me rushing to get to school on time and all.

I must have drifted off to sleep, because when I opened my eyes the bus had stopped. Monsters were getting out of their seats and grabbing their things.

"Restroom break," Tank said. "We're at the Sparkling Falls rest area. Mr. Mantle says the falls are a *sight to behold*. Whatever that means."

"Let's see what makes them sparkle." I climbed out of my seat and shook the sleep from my tail.

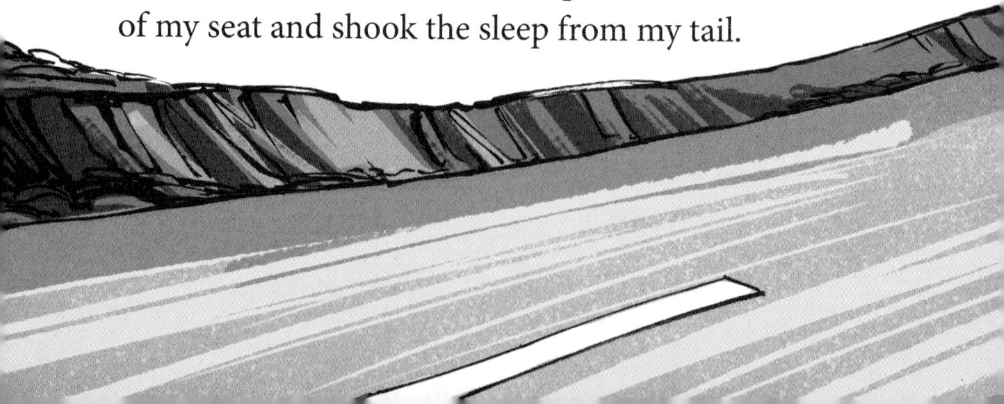

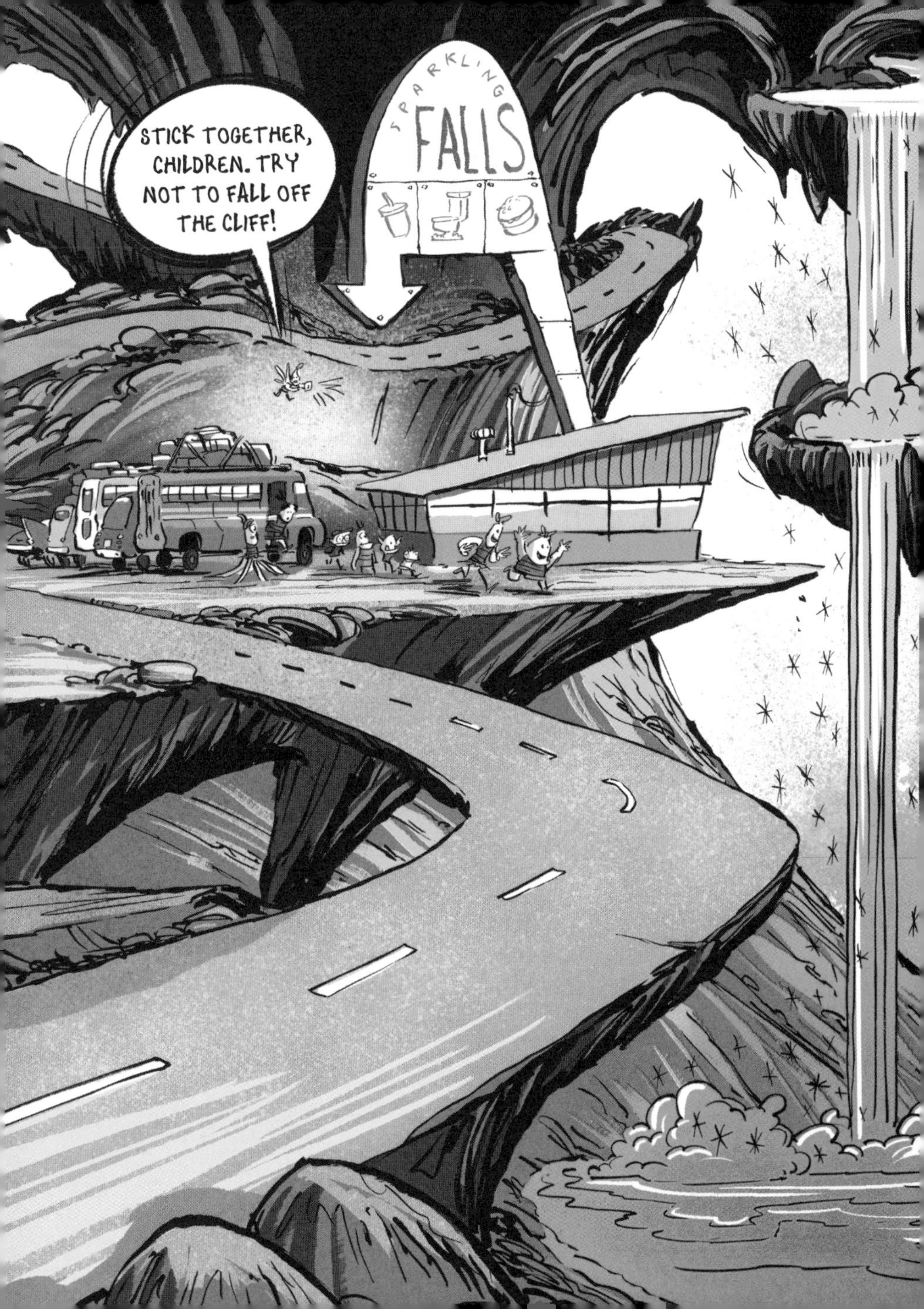
STICK TOGETHER, CHILDREN. TRY NOT TO FALL OFF THE CLIFF!
SPARKLING FALLS

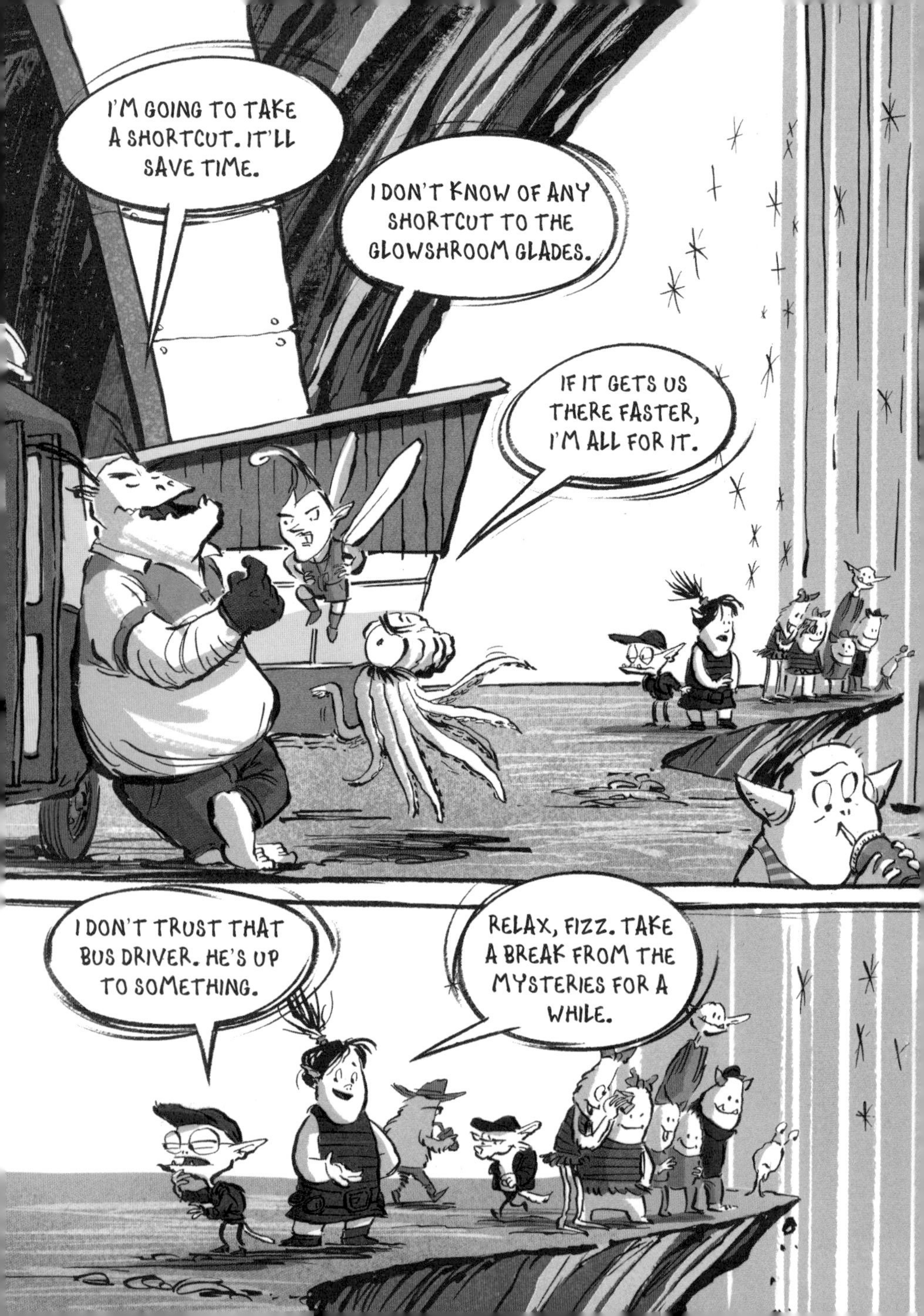
I'M GOING TO TAKE A SHORTCUT. IT'LL SAVE TIME.
I DON'T KNOW OF ANY SHORTCUT TO THE GLOWSHROOM GLADES.
IF IT GETS US THERE FASTER, I'M ALL FOR IT.
I DON'T TRUST THAT BUS DRIVER. HE'S UP TO SOMETHING.
RELAX, FIZZ. TAKE A BREAK FROM THE MYSTERIES FOR A WHILE.

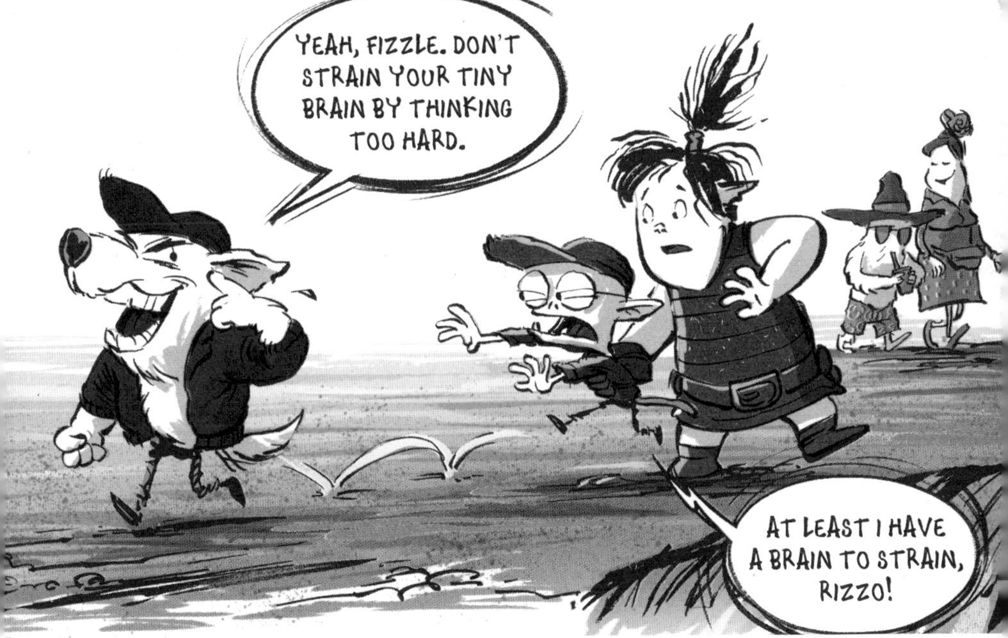
YEAH, FIZZLE. DON'T STRAIN YOUR TINY BRAIN BY THINKING TOO HARD.
AT LEAST I HAVE A BRAIN TO STRAIN, RIZZO!

"Nice comeback." Rizzo Rawlins chuckled and headed to the washrooms. The kobold had been handing out wedgies and dishing insults since he was in diapers. Rizzo got under my scales just by showing up to school each day.

"Hopefully, Rizzo will get locked in the bathroom and we'll leave without him."

"Forget about him." Tank sighed. "Just enjoy the field trip, Fizz."

My friend was right. I couldn't let bullies like Rizzo Rawlins get to me. I watched the sparkling water of the falls rush from the rock walls and plummet into the blackness below. The roar of the water soothed my frustration. Pretty soon I had forgotten all about Rizzo Rawlins. I stopped worrying about Hatchet-Eyes the driver too. I even felt okay about not having a mystery to solve.

After a while Miss Blinx ordered us all back on the bus, and then we were rolling once again. The rest of the ride was pretty quiet. Most kids put on head-phones and listened to music or read their books. Seeing water sparkle really takes it out of you, I guess. The scenery now was just rock, rock and more rock.

Suddenly Tank jabbed me with her elbow. "You've got to see this." Her eyes were glued to her phone's screen. "Something is not right." There was a map on the screen. A flashing dot moved across the map. Tank pointed to the dot. "That's our bus traveling along the road."

"So what's the problem?" I said. "You think we're lost?"

Tank shook her head. "No, but we're taking an interesting route to the glades." She moved the map with her finger. It sent our little flashing dot off the screen. It was replaced by a large splotch of yellow. "Those are the Glowshroom Glades."

"We're driving away from it," I said. "We're totally lost."

"We're not lost." Tank's fingers dragged the map back down again. The flashing dot returned and slid to the bottom of the screen.

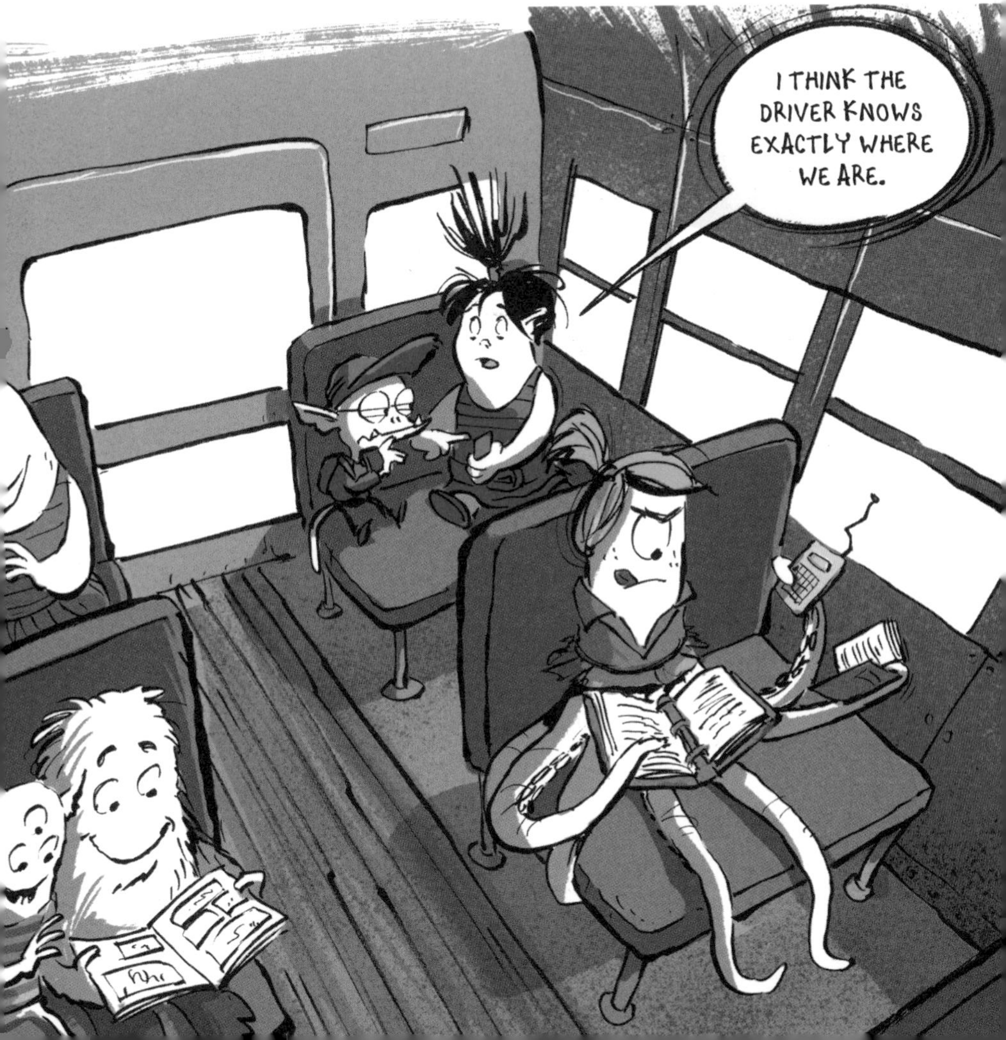
I THINK THE DRIVER KNOWS EXACTLY WHERE WE ARE.

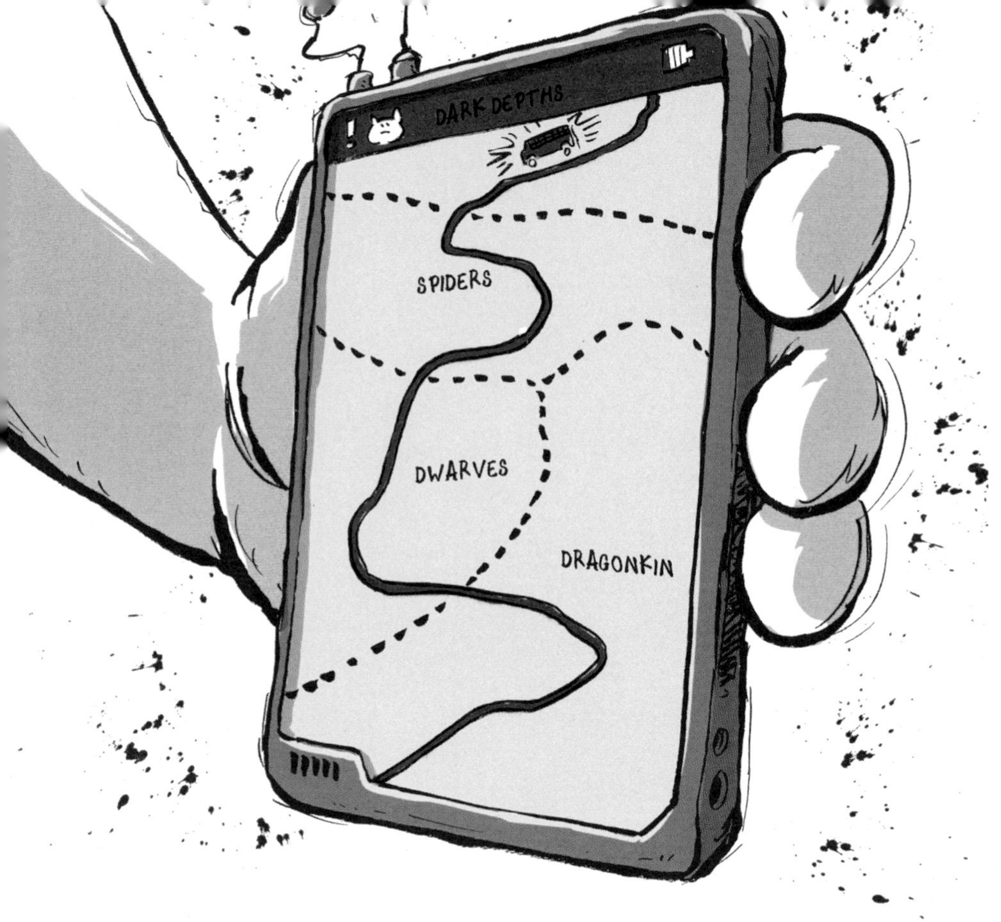
DARK DEPTHS
SPIDERS
DWARVES
DRAGONKIN

"The Dark Depths," I gasped.

Tank's ears were trembling. Our bus driver's shortcut was taking us into the most dangerous place in all of Rockfall Mountain.

Suddenly I wished I had missed the bus that morning after all.

CHAPTER TWO

Dark Depths Disaster

The region known as the Dark Depths was bad news.

The massive cavern lay deep underground, at the very bottom of Rockfall Mountain, and was crawling with monsters too wild to be allowed in Slick City. The Dark Depths was divided into three lands. Each land was ruled by a different group of monsters.

DWARVES
SPIDERS
DRAGONKIN

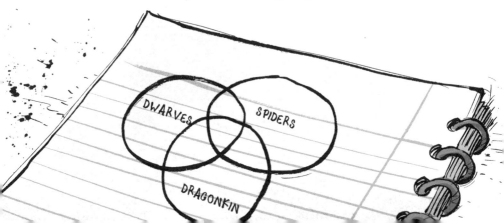

One land was home to deadly spiders who lived in a city made of web. Dwarves controlled another vast region rich in gems. The dwarves did not trust other monsters and only ventured out of their mines to trade the precious jewels they mined from the rock. The third region was the land of the dragonkin, ruled by the ancient dragon Firebane Drakeclaw. With dangerous spiders, mysterious dwarves and a dragon as old as the mountain, the Dark Depths was definitely not a parent-approved destination for a fourth-grade field trip.

"We have to tell Mr. Mantle," I hissed.

At the front of the bus, Mr. Ravel's hatchet eyes locked onto me in the rearview mirror. My body went as cold as a rockslipper fish. I slunk down in my seat.

"The driver knows we're on to him," I whispered.

Tank slunk too. "How do you know?"

"He keeps looking back here."

Tank sighed. "He could just be keeping an eye on all of us, not just you. Relax."

"Relax?" I hissed. "He's taking us toward the Dark Depths. They eat goblins for breakfast down there! We have to tell Mr. Mantle."

I wriggled out of my seat.

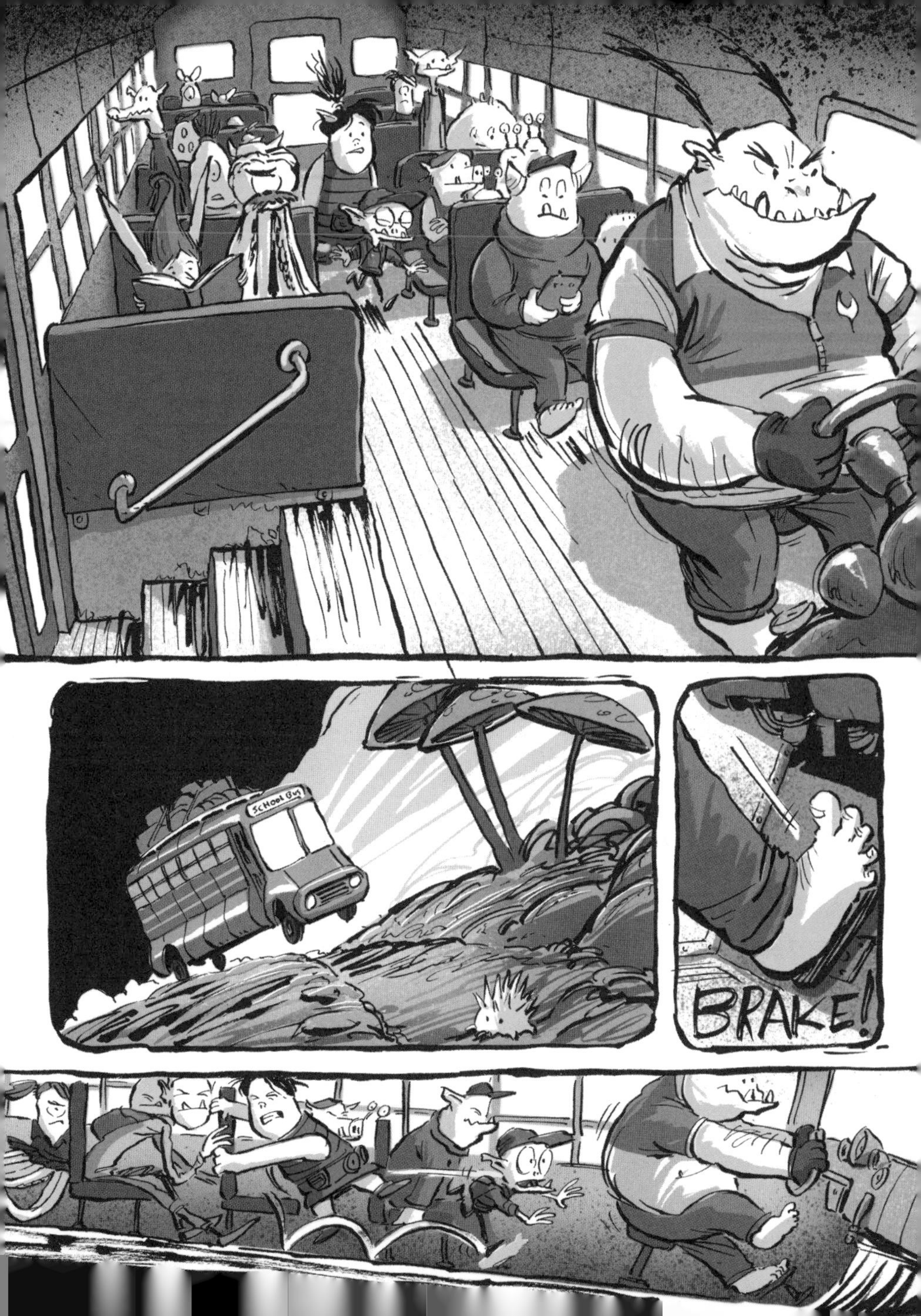
SCHOOL BUS
BRAKE!

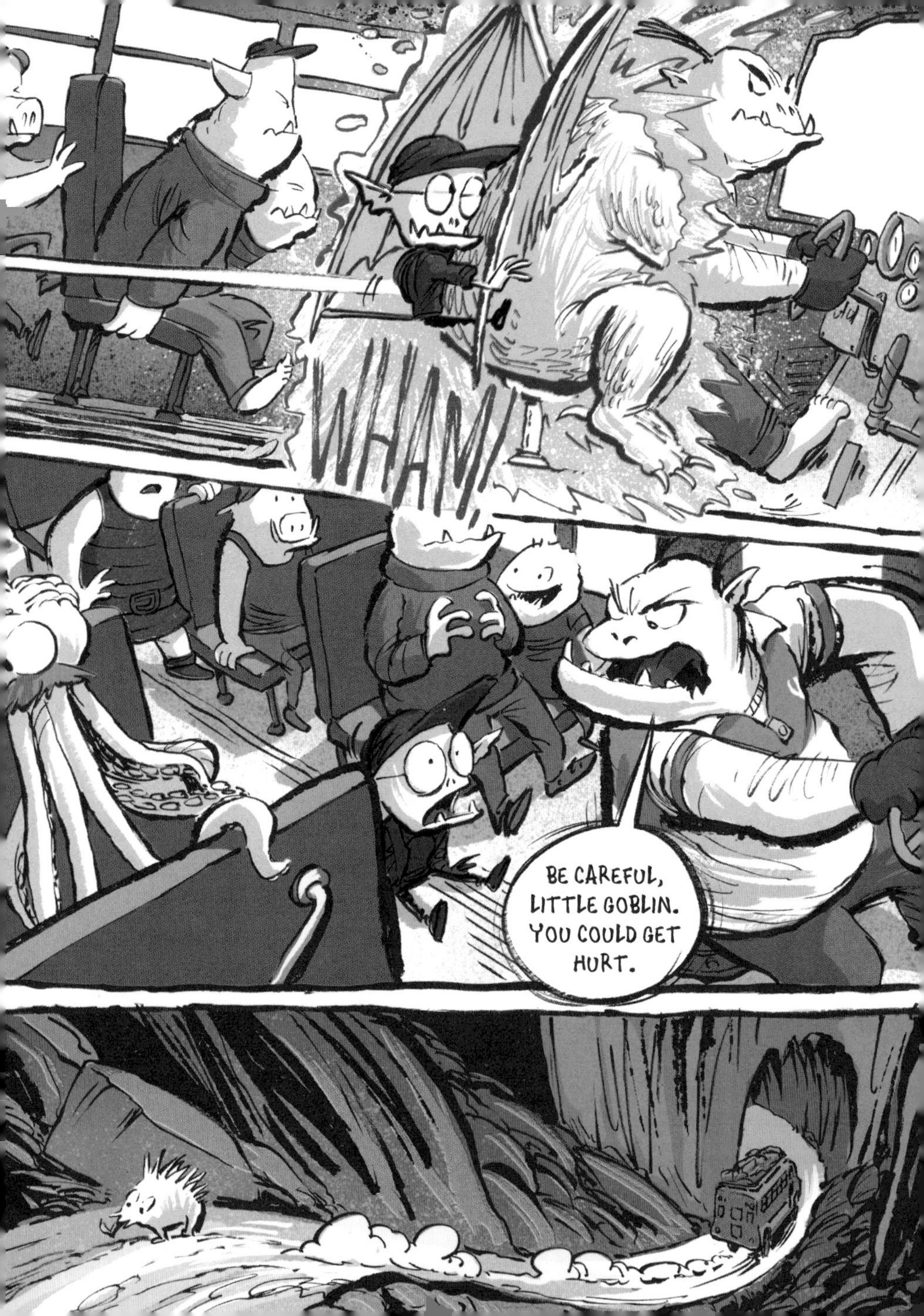
WHAM!
BE CAREFUL, LITTLE GOBLIN. YOU COULD GET HURT.

The ogre's gaze returned to the road. I scrambled to my feet and rubbed my eyes. Mr. Ravel was still very much an ogre driving our bus. I stumbled back to Tank, still not sure what I had just seen.

Tank was showing Mr. Mantle the map on her phone.

"There must be some mistake." Tentacle-Head's mustache twitched. He looked toward Mr. Ravel. "Come with me."

He rose up out of his seat and rushed toward the driver. Tank and I hurried after him.

"Excuse me, Mr...um..." Mr. Mantle paused. For a guy who was all brain and homework, he often forgot stuff. Like the driver's name.

"Mr. Ravel," I blurted out.

"Mr. Ravel, we seem to be off course." Mr. Mantle looked out the window. His tentacles stood straight. "Oh dear! Is that Coppe's Bridge? That means we're entering the Dark Depths."

We were now driving toward a crumbling bridge spanning a white landscape. No rocks jutted out from the whiteness below the bridge. No creatures moved along the ground. I realized it wasn't solid ground below the bridge at all. It was something else.

Mr. Mantle stared out the front window. His one eye was open wide. "Mr. Ravel, you are taking us into the Dark Depths. Turn the bus around this instant!"

The ogre shrugged. "Sorry, boss. That's not part of the plan."

The bus picked up speed. My brain picked up speed too.

"You have a plan?" I said. "You're not alone, are you?"

Mr. Ravel looked at me and growled before turning back to the road. "I knew you were a smart one, kid."

"What's the commotion up here?" It was Miss Blinx. She buzzed behind Tank's shoulder. Her wings skipped a beat when she looked out the window. "Where in the tar pits of Tanamoor are we?"

Mr. Ravel stared straight ahead. "We are right where we need to be. And we're on schedule."

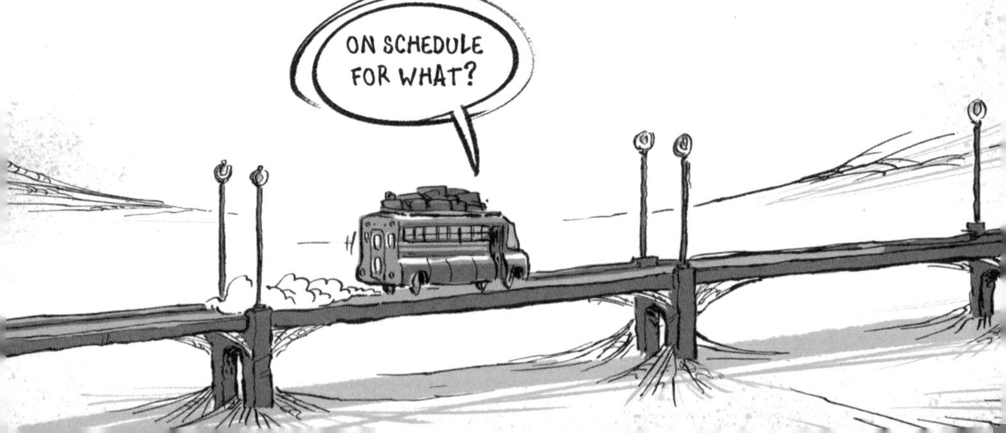
ON SCHEDULE FOR WHAT?

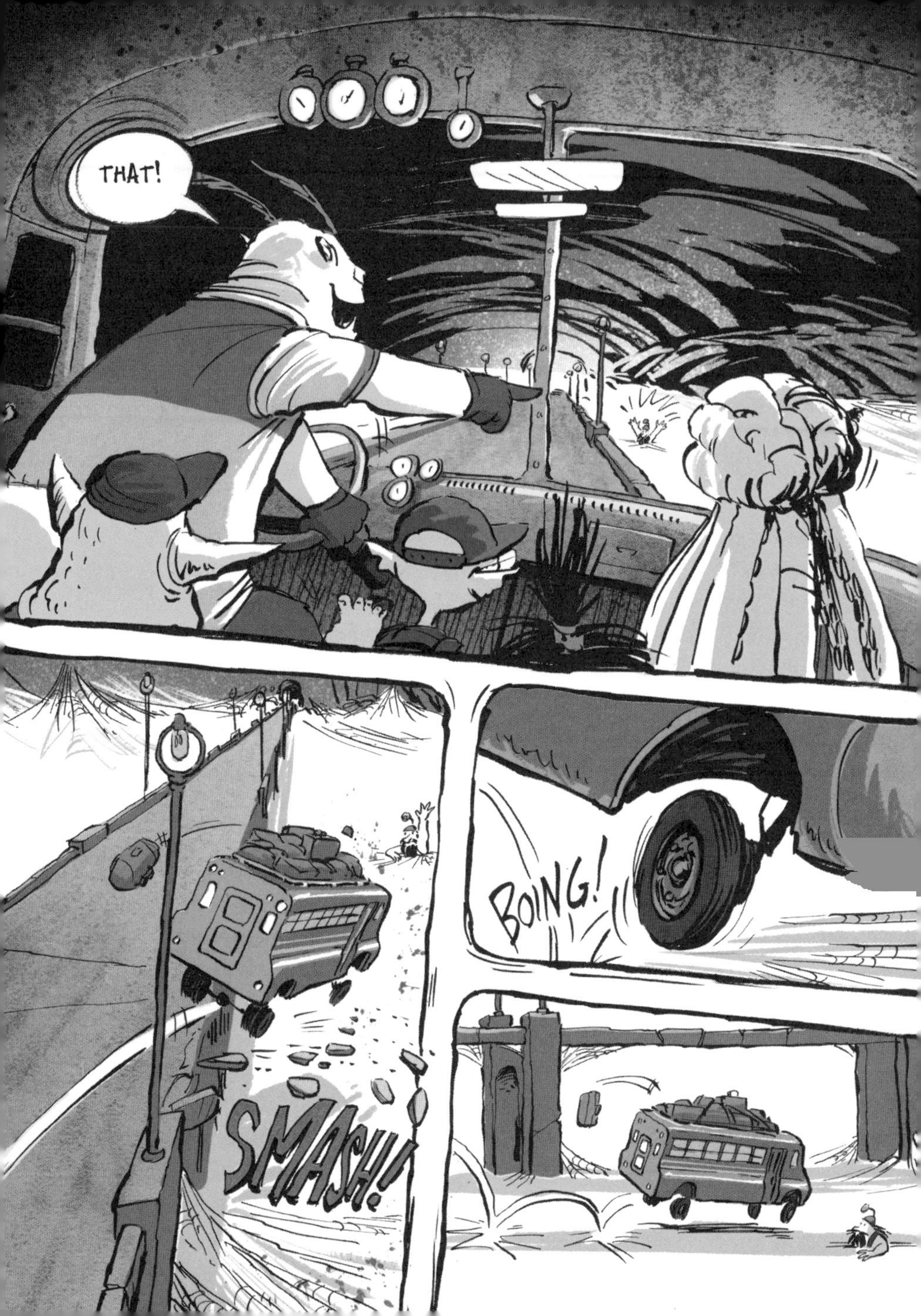
THAT!
SMASH!
BOING!

Inside the bus, everyone was thrown from their seats. I flew forward and crunched my snout against the dashboard before falling onto the sticky floor. Tank crash-landed beside me. Her phone tumbled from her hand and clattered to the floor. Mr. Ravel got up from the driver's seat. Without a word, the ogre stepped over Tank and me, pushed open the door of the bus and hurried outside.

Tank scrambled to her feet and picked up her phone. "Where's he going?"

"Let's find out."

I stumbled out the door. The white ground trembled as I stepped off the bus. It grabbed at my feet with every step.

"It feels like a spiderweb," I said.

The sticky white web stretched from one side of the valley to the other. Below us, a web mesh plunged deep into the valley. Strands of spidery silk crisscrossed the valley walls, creating a network of pathways. I didn't want to think about who, or what, used those webby walkways.

Tank arrived beside me, her troll feet covered in spiderweb silk.

"This is like visiting Principal Weaver's office,"

she grumbled. "Miss Blinx wants you back on the bus, Fizz. It's too dangerous out here."

"Tell that to Mr. Ravel," I said.

The ogre was on the roof of the bus, untying the straps that held our luggage in place. The bus was buried up to its wheels in the sticky web. I could hear Mr. Mantle inside the bus, telling the other students that everything was all right. I didn't have the heart to tell him that everything was all wrong.

Mr. Ravel pulled a long crate out from the pile of suitcases and tossed it over the side of the bus. It landed on the web not far away. The ground rippled like the surface of a lake. I stumbled backward. Tank caught my arm before I fell on my tail.

"Careful, Fizz," she said. "The ground is so sticky, one fall and you're not getting back up."

The crate burst open. The sides fell away to reveal a pile of twisted metal pipes. The metal hummed. Then it moved. Metal pipes unfolded and snapped into place one after the other, until it didn't look like a pile anymore.

"It's a self-assembling dual-drive rocket bike!" Tank's ears wiggled with tech-loving glee. "I've never seen one up close before."

Mr. Ravel jumped off the roof of the bus and landed beside the rocket bike, sending another tremor across the webby ground.

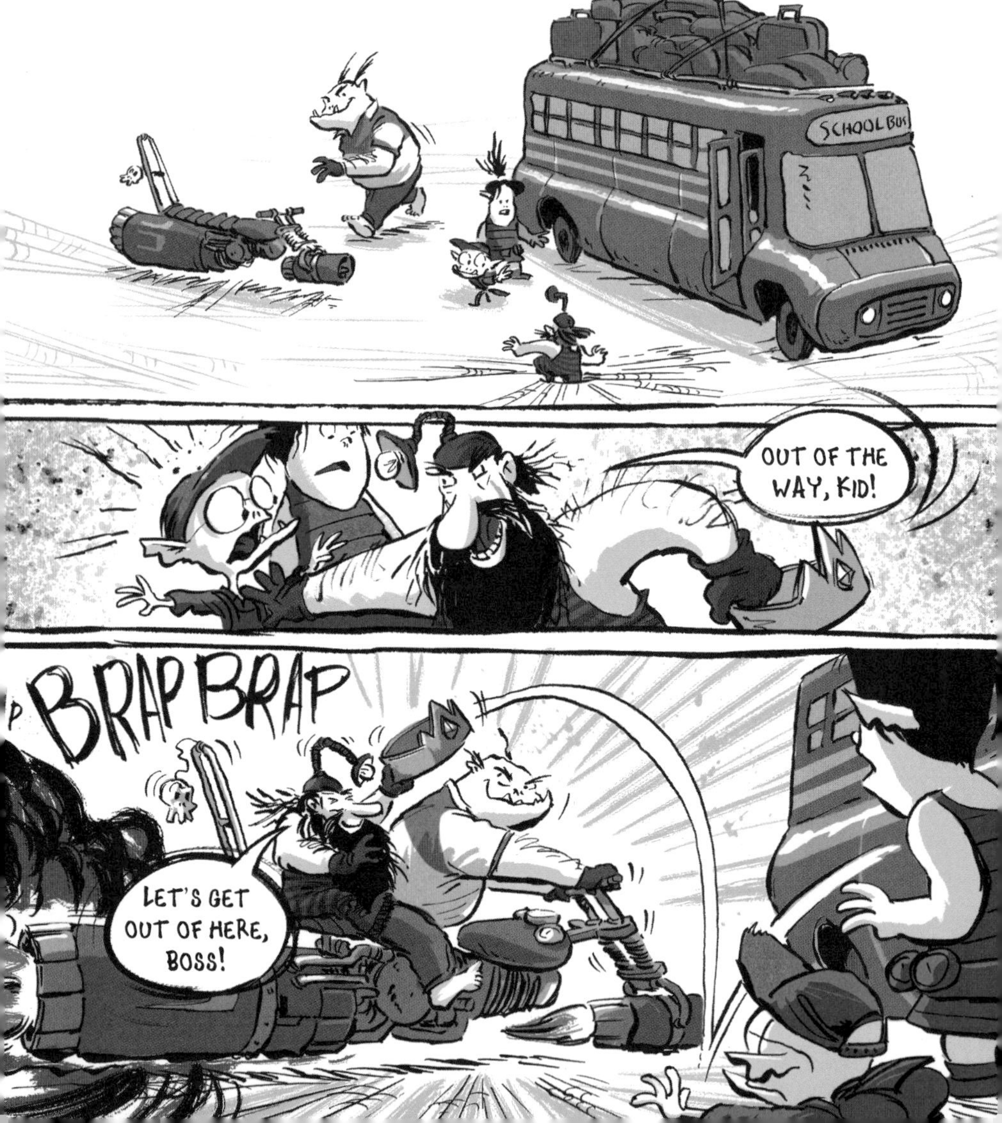
SCHOOL BUS
OUT OF THE WAY, KID!
BRAP BRAP
LET'S GET OUT OF HERE, BOSS!

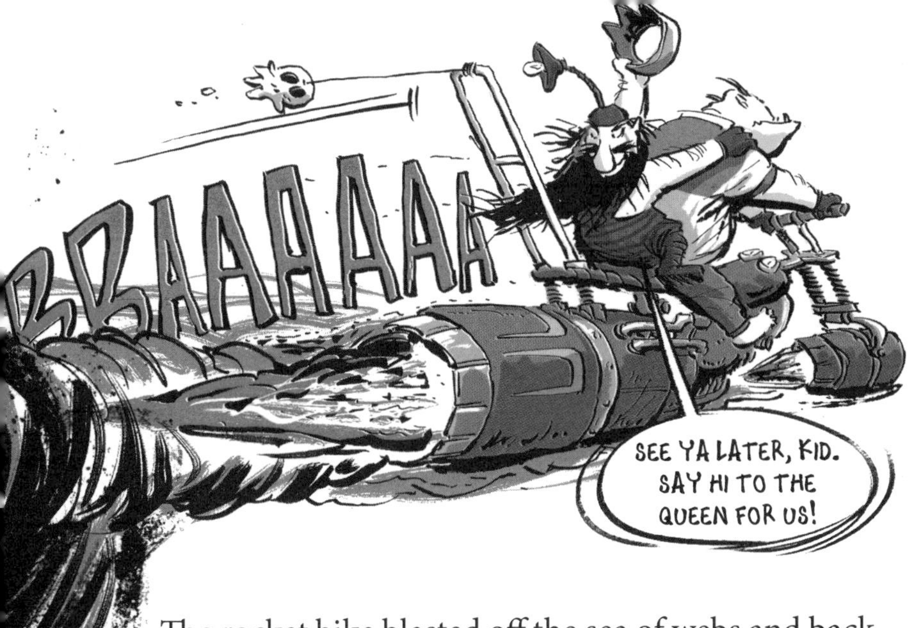
BRAAAAAAA
SEE YA LATER, KID. SAY HI TO THE QUEEN FOR US!

The rocket bike blasted off the sea of webs and back onto the bridge. It roared down the road before being swallowed by the shadows of the Dark Depths.

Tank's eyes were as big as a pair of glowshrooms as she watched the rocket bike disappear. "That was awesome!" My friend was in a total tech-trance. "Did you see those twin boosters auto-synch their blast capacity?"

"No," I snapped. "What I saw was our bus driver ditching our entire class in the Dark Depths!"

Tank's ears flopped. "Oh yeah, that part doesn't sound good."

"Fizz Marlow!" Miss Blinx zipped out of the bus and buzzed over to us. Her tiny wings carried her safely above the sticky web. "Get back on the bus this minute! I'm sure our driver is working on a way to get us out of this mess."

"Our driver got us into this mess!" I said.

"He just left with a dwarf that climbed out of that hole," Tank said.

"You must be mistaken." Miss Blinx dismissed us with a wave of her tiny hand. "I'm sure Mr. Ravel is around here somewhere."

I bit my tongue to stop from yelling. Why didn't adults ever believe kids?

A scream sounded far below us. The webby ground shook. More shrieks followed.

"What was that?" Miss Blinx asked.

Dark shapes moved quickly through the web walkways below.

"Something's coming," Tank said. She had her zoomers over her eyes and stared at the web beneath her feet. "Something big."

The ground around us exploded. Dark shapes crawled out of the white. The ogre's parting words ran through my terrified brain.

"I think we're about to meet the queen," I said.

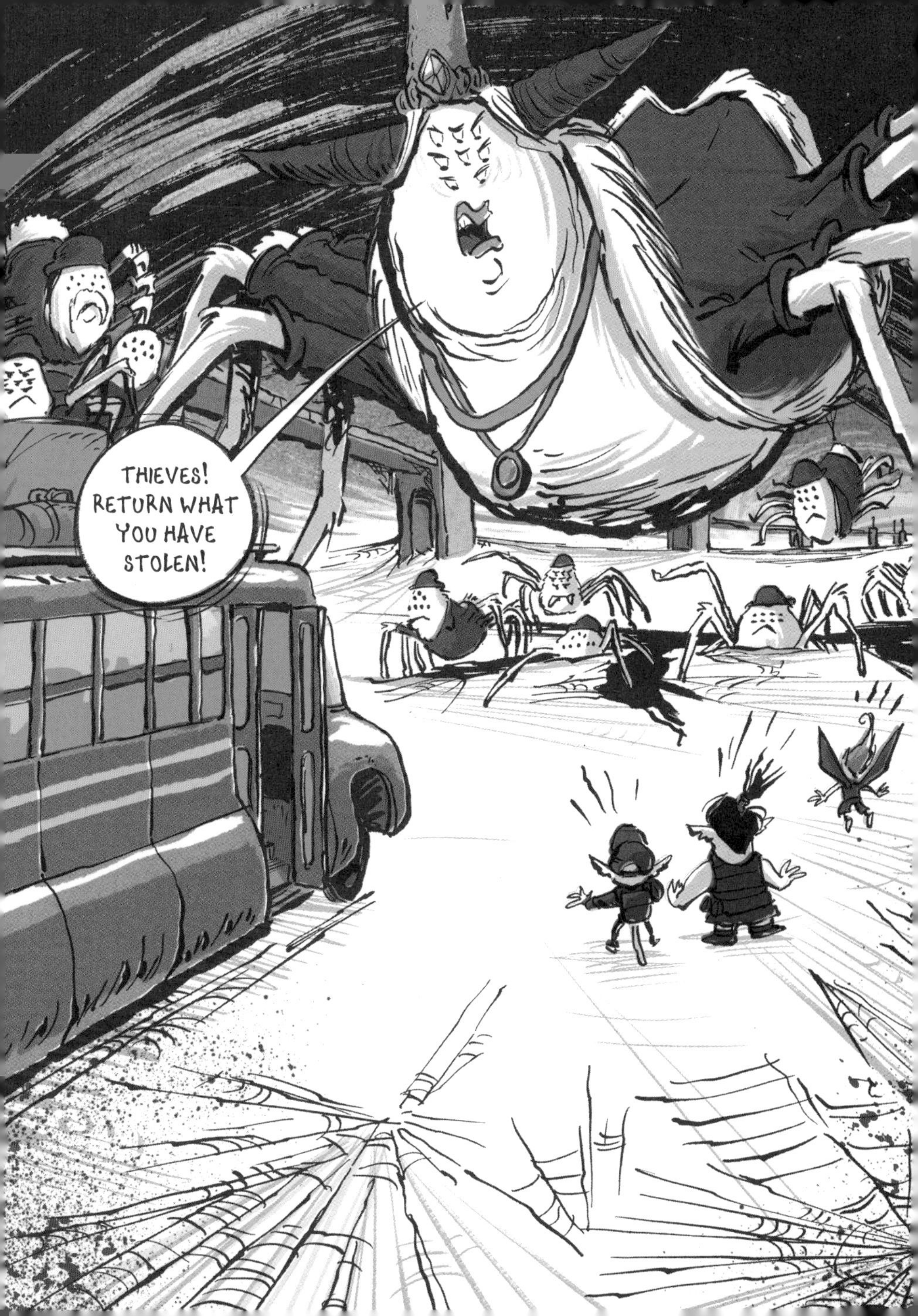
THIEVES! RETURN WHAT YOU HAVE STOLEN!

CHAPTER THREE
Caught in the Spider Queen's Web

The spider queen's lair smelled like an old lunchbox. Sticky webs hung from the rocky cliff walls and stretched overhead. Piled against the wall a stack of bones lay in the corner, the remains of the previous day's meal, waiting to be taken away. Today's meal dangled above the massive spiderweb at the end of the lair, ready to be eaten. Twenty-one little fourth-graders wrapped up like web-encased sausages ready to be the main course in a spider smorgasbord.

"This is the worst school trip ever," I grumbled.

Beside me, Tank squirmed in her own sticky cocoon. Next to her, Rizzo Rawlins dangled like a hairy sock on a washing line. He hadn't stopped moaning since we'd gotten here. For once I didn't blame him.

I'd never thought I'd see a spider scarier than Principal Weaver, but the spider queen definitely won that contest.

After she had burst through the web under Coppe's Bridge, the spider queen had ordered her eight-legged soldiers to wrap us up and carry us deep beneath the surface. With our whole class tied to the backs of spiders, we passed layers of woven walkways and sticky streets spanning the width of the deep canyon. Beneath the spot where our bus had crashed thrived a city of spiders. Along the walkways stood homes and shops, all crafted from spider's silk. Dark shapes crowded the streets, eager to see the queen's latest catch.

This was the Vale of Webs, home to the spiders of the Dark Depths. At the very bottom, the spider queen's royal chambers stretched across the canyon floor. And now, dangling high over the royal web, was a group of terrified fourth-graders.

The queen and her court of spider generals and advisors watched us hungrily with their countless eyes. She scurried to the center of her web and stopped only a fang away from two small figures stuck in place.

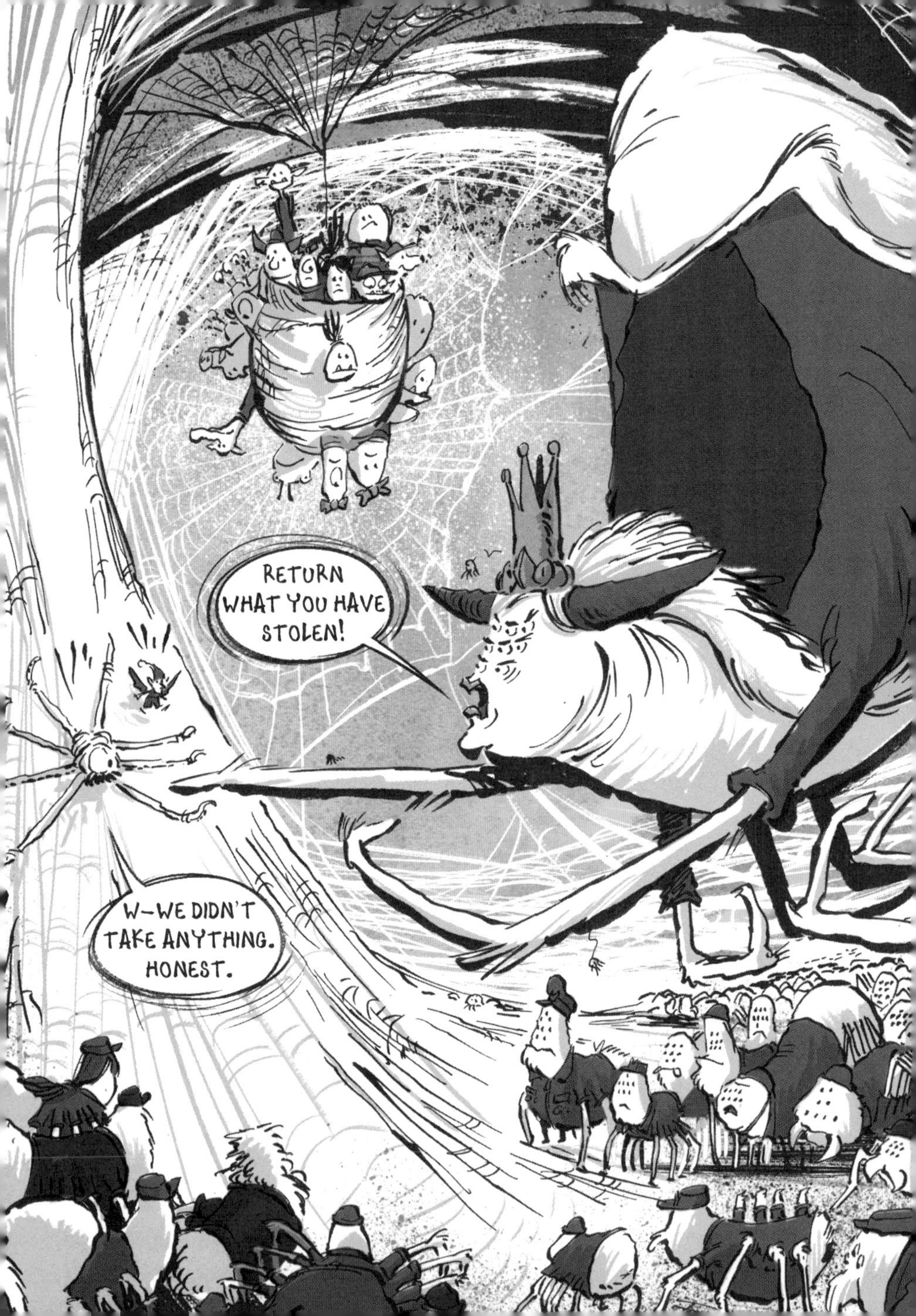
RETURN WHAT YOU HAVE STOLEN!
W-WE DIDN'T TAKE ANYTHING. HONEST.

Mr. Mantle's mustache trembled. "We are from Gravelmuck Elementary and—"

"Enough!" the queen snapped. "I will not hear that story again. I do not believe you are an innocent school group betrayed by your bus driver on a field trip to see some silly glowshrooms. You are thieves."

"We're not!" Miss Blinx whined. The blaze fairy pulled on the bonds holding her to the queen's web. Her fairy strength stretched the web a bit, but it soon snapped her arms back into place. "We were on our way to the Glowshroom Glades, and we took a wrong turn."

"Nonsense," the queen snapped. "I know you took the Crown of Peace! Where is it?"

Spiders had gathered around the edge of the queen's web. They chattered to each other as their queen interrogated the prisoners.

"*Crown of Peace*," Tank whispered. "Where have we heard that before?"

"Really, Tank," Henelle chuckled from her web cocoon beside me. "You need to listen in history class."

I hid my snout to stop from giggling. It was a rare day that Tank was told to pay attention in class. It was also a rare day to be captured by the spider queen.

"The Crown of Peace is an ancient artifact held by the lords of the Dark Depths," the octoclops continued. "It's priceless. Everyone knows that."

"Yeah, Tank, everyone knows that!" Rizzo Rawlins snickered from the other side of my detective partner.

Suddenly my tail tingled. "A crown! That dwarf had something like that. I saw it when he nearly knocked me over."

Below us, a large spider stood beside his queen. He was hairy and had many medals pinned to his chest.

"Queen Azelia, let us not bother ourselves with these fools," the new arrival said. "They do not have the crown. My soldiers have searched each of them and their bus."

"They must have it, Captain Scorn!" Queen Azelia snapped. "One of the little monsters snuck through my webs and into my royal chamber and stole it. We caught them just as they were making their escape."

"Perhaps, my queen," Captain Scorn agreed. "But the Crown of Peace is nowhere to be found. I can alert the dwarf and dragonkin territories. With all three ruling lands of the Dark Depths searching, we will find the crown."

"No!" Queen Azelia barked. "We cannot let the others know the crown is missing. That will make us look weak. We must keep the theft a secret until the crown is found."

"As you wish." Captain Scorn bowed his head. "But if you would allow me to search the Dark Depths, I can find the crown. I will search for this ogre bus driver the tentacle-face spoke about."

"The driver was with a dwarf," Miss Blinx said.

All spider eyes turned to her.

"Go on," said the queen. "How do you know this?"

Miss Blinx bit her lip, realizing she had said too much. Queen Azelia skittered closer and loomed over the terrified fairy.

"One of my students saw it," Miss Blinx said quickly.

The spider queen looked up to us, dangling above her. Her multiple eyes took in each of us, one at a time.

"Which student saw this dwarf?" she said.

"Um, I don't remember." Miss Blinx's voice trembled.

"Really? What a shame." Queen Azelia flashed her fangs. "Perhaps we should just eat a few of them to help jog your memory."

"Fizz Marlow!" Rizzo Rawlins yapped so loud, he nearly burst from his web wrapper. "He's the one."

I nearly jumped out of my cocoon at the sound of my name.

"Quiet, Rizzo!" Tank growled. "You'll get us all eaten."

The kobold turned his long snout toward me and kept yapping. "Fizz and his friend Tatanka Wrenchlin saw the whole thing! They just told me. They always see stuff. They're detectives. They can help you."

Queen Azelia's eight eyes locked onto me. Each one chilled me down to my tail. Her gaze pierced my web cocoon and bored right under my scales. It was like she could see everything I had ever done.

"Detectives? How interesting." She waved a leg to the spiders behind her. "Hugo, be a good spider and bring our detectives down to me. I want a closer look."

"Yes, my queen." A young spider scurried up the web-covered walls and over to us. With a snip of his fangs, he cut us free from the others.

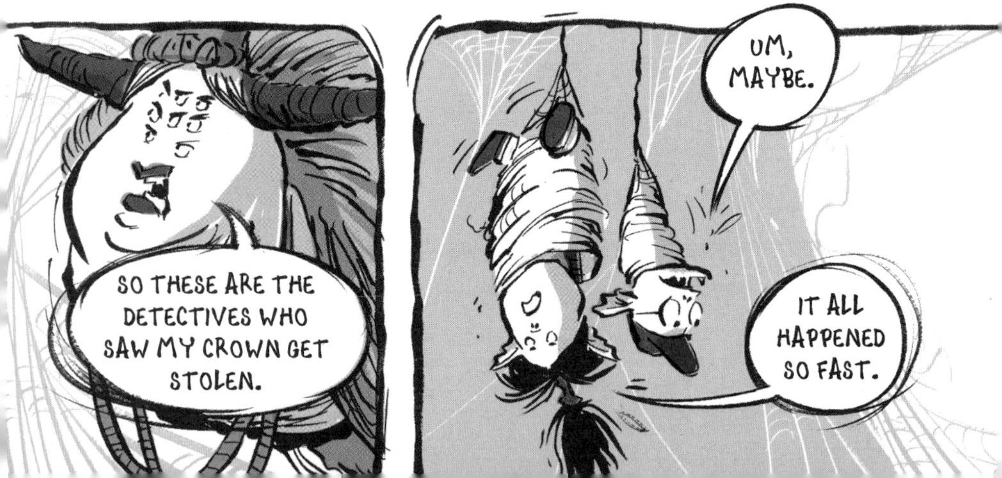
SO THESE ARE THE DETECTIVES WHO SAW MY CROWN GET STOLEN.
UM, MAYBE.
IT ALL HAPPENED SO FAST.

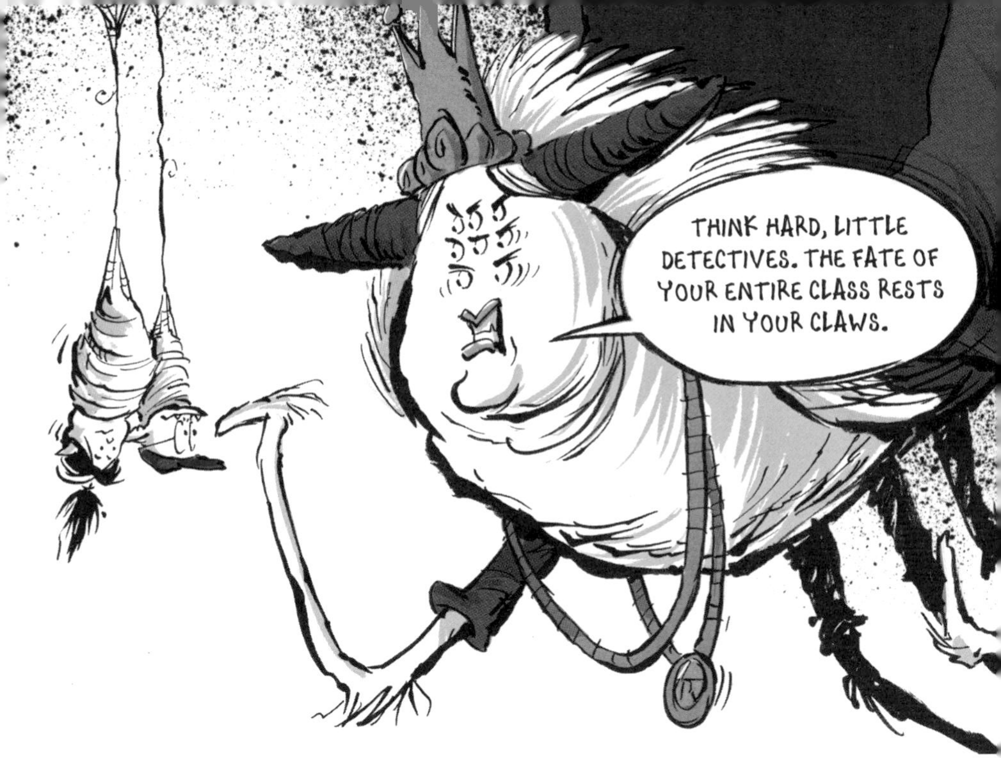
THINK HARD, LITTLE DETECTIVES. THE FATE OF YOUR ENTIRE CLASS RESTS IN YOUR CLAWS.

We told the queen everything.

Tank told them about Mr. Ravel and his "shortcut" that took us into the Depths. I told them about the dwarf with the scar on his face and the crown in his hands. When we had finished, the queen slammed her foreleg on the web, making the whole thing shake.

"Dwarves!" she growled. "I knew those bearded rockdiggers would be behind this."

"We do not know that for certain, my queen," a gray-furred spider said from the edge of the web.

"Stealing the Crown of Peace would break the agreement between our three kingdoms. It would be an act of war."

"Lord Dunhelm of the dwarves has never been a friend to the spiders, my queen," Captain Scorn said. "And I need not warn you of the danger Firebane Drakeclaw can bring. Both would gain much from taking the crown from you."

Tank's panicked eyes met mine at the mention of Firebane Drakeclaw. He was only the most feared creature in all of Rockfall Mountain. He was as old as the mountain itself and as tall as the Shadow Tower.

"Then it is settled, Captain Scorn," Queen Azelia said. "You will take your best soldiers and search for the thieves who stole my crown."

"As you wish." Captain Scorn bowed before his queen. "If they seek to sell the crown, then they will most likely head to the town of Lava Falls."

"Travel to Lava Falls, if you think it best." The spider queen's eyes returned to me. "And take our little detectives from Gravelmuck Elementary with you."

"My queen!" Captain Scorn scowled. "I do not need the help of a pair of children. Especially not a goblin and troll from the Shallows."

"I think you do, Captain," the spider queen said. "They are the only ones who saw the thief. Take them to Lava Falls. They will be able to point out this dwarf and ogre in the crowds that gather there."

"As you wish." Captain Scorn gave us a venomous glare.

"Well, Fizz Marlow and Tatanka Wrenchlin, detectives of Gravelmuck. You have a new mystery to solve." Queen Azelia's eight eyes flashed with satisfaction. "If you fail, your classmates will be my main course."

There are times I regret ever becoming a detective. Now was totally one of those times.

CHAPTER FOUR
Swampy Sabotage

The spider convoy was ready to roll.

Ten of Captain Scorn's best trackers and hunters waited on the edge of the spider queen's web. Ten spiders and two terrified monsters.

Tank and I were strapped to the backs of the sturdiest spiders, still wrapped up like lunchtime sandwiches.

"You could have untied us!" Tank grumbled to Captain Scorn as he skittered by.

Scorn turned and fixed his eight eyes on my friend.

"You will be untied when you find the dwarf and the ogre. And not a moment sooner." The spider captain hurried to the front of the line of soldiers, where Queen Azelia waited. "Our border scouts spotted the thieves and their strange machine heading to Lava Falls."

"It seems your suspicions were correct, Captain," the queen said. "Travel swiftly and bring back my crown."

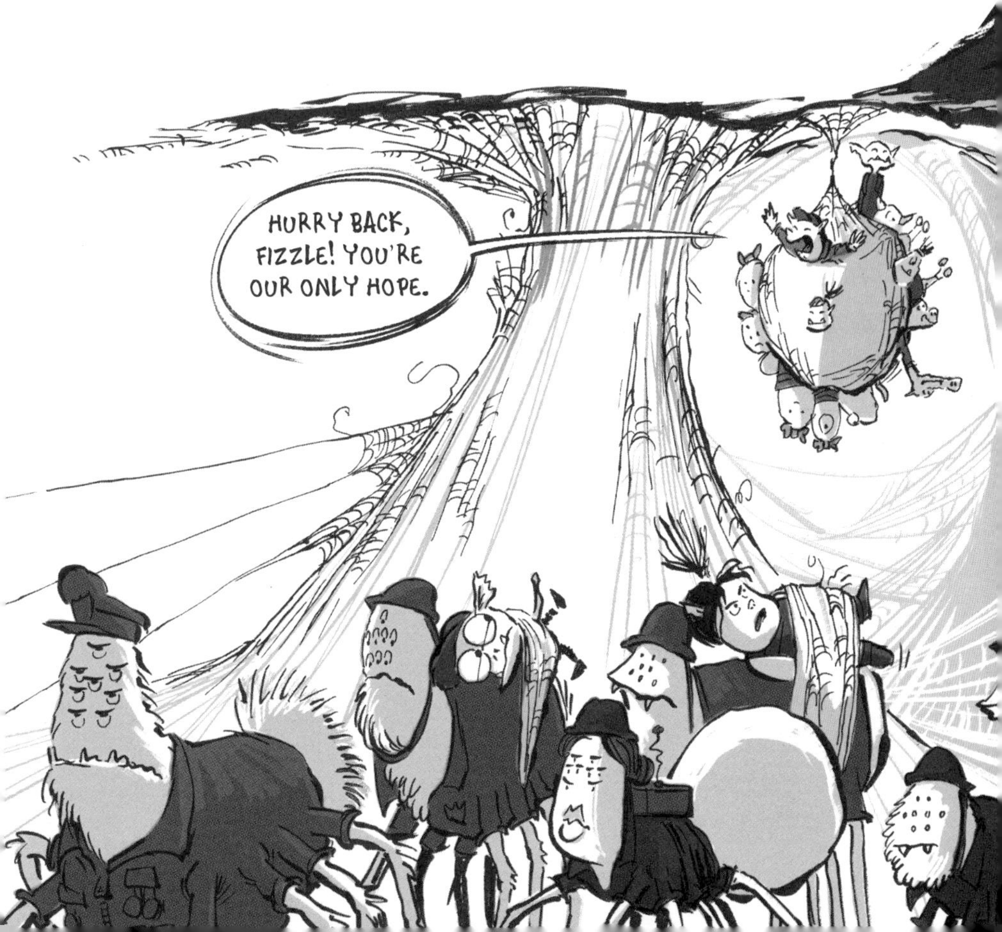
HURRY BACK, FIZZLE! YOU'RE OUR ONLY HOPE.

The spiders scurried up the web walkways, through the Vale of Webs and back to the web under the bridge. Our school bus was gone, and the hole made by the dwarf had already been repaired. All traces of our crash had been erased by the spider queen's web-weaving minions. If anyone from Slick City came looking for us, they wouldn't even know we had come this way.

Hopes of rescue got me thinking about my mom and all the parents of my classmates. Instead of admiring the wonders of glowshrooms, their children were hanging in a spider's pantry, ready to be served up as a feast. That is, unless Tank and I could travel across the most dangerous place in Rockfall Mountain, strapped to the backs of two goblin-eating spiders, and find a dwarf we had only seen once. Just thinking about it curled my tail.

Soundlessly Captain Scorn and his soldiers scurried across the sea of webs. Their spidery legs carried them across the surface like they were skating on ice. We raced along the length of the valley, running alongside the bridge and deeper into the Dark Depths. When the valley ended, the spiders climbed up the web-covered cliffs. They paused at the edge of a narrow road. The spider carrying Tank stopped beside me. She was wrapped tightly in her web cocoon but managed a smile.

"Fancy meeting you here," she said.

I was terrified from my tail to snout, but seeing my friend put a grin on my face.

"Wouldn't have missed it for all the choco-slug cookies in the mountain," I said.

"Silence!" Captain Scorn hissed. He spoke to his soldiers in a low voice. "That road leads to Lava Falls. I don't need to remind you—beyond these webs our queen's power is limited. Our fastest route takes us straight through the Swamp of Sorrows."

"Would it not be best to travel around the swamp, Captain?" one spider asked.

"We have no time," Scorn said. "If we are to find the thieves in Lava Falls, then we go through that stinking marsh."

"But Captain, the slimy ones will be waiting," another spider said quickly.

"Then we will move swiftly." Captain Scorn stood to his full height on all eight legs. He looked to Tank and me. "I have a surprise in store for the big-eyed water dwellers."

The spider captain hurried down the road. His soldiers exchanged worried looks before falling into step behind their leader. Wherever we were going, the spiders were even less thrilled about it than Tank and I were.

Soon the sticky web that had covered every surface disappeared. In its place glowing fungus bloomed on rocky outcrops, and the air grew heavy with moisture. The sound of dripping water echoed somewhere in the distance. The spiders slowed their pace as they moved farther away from their home.

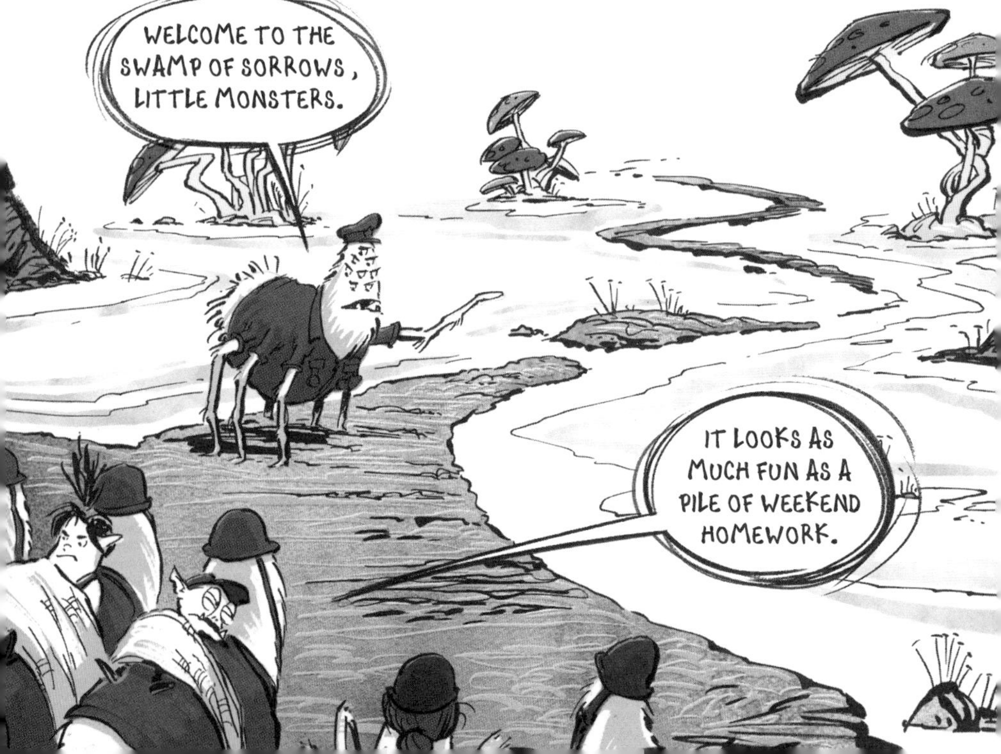
WELCOME TO THE SWAMP OF SORROWS, LITTLE MONSTERS.
IT LOOKS AS MUCH FUN AS A PILE OF WEEKEND HOMEWORK.

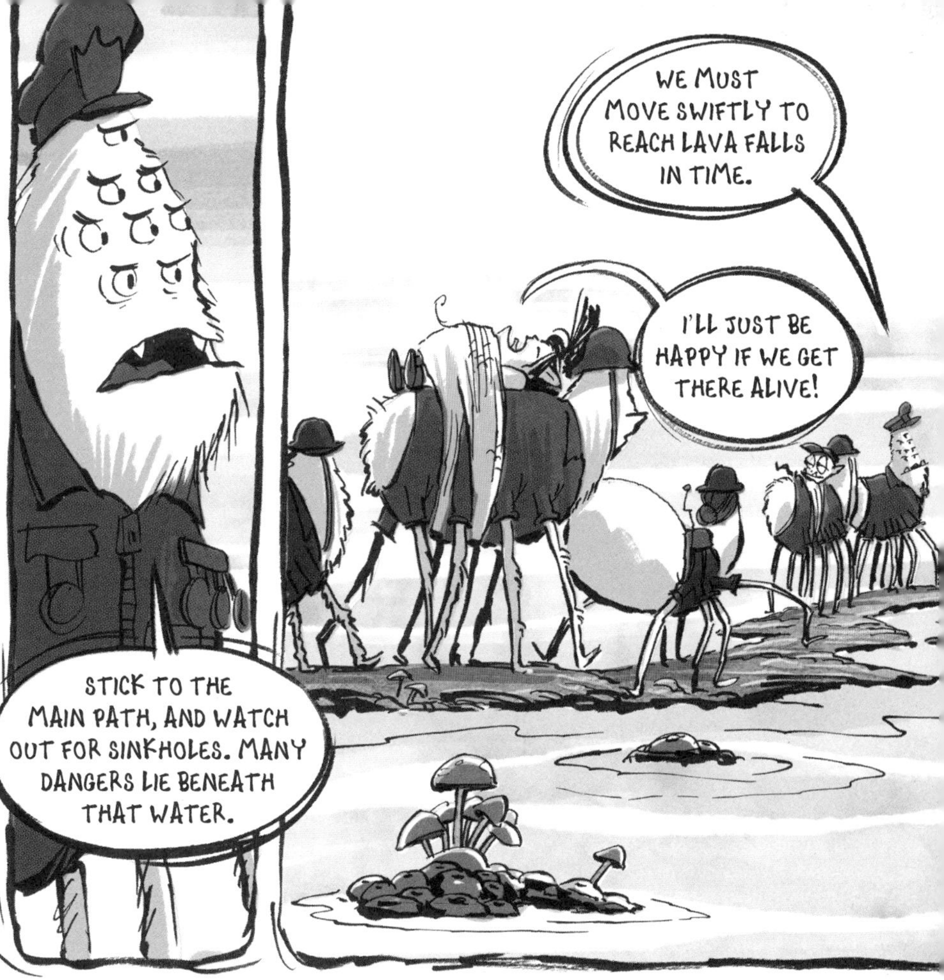
WE MUST MOVE SWIFTLY TO REACH LAVA FALLS IN TIME.
I'LL JUST BE HAPPY IF WE GET THERE ALIVE!
STICK TO THE MAIN PATH, AND WATCH OUT FOR SINKHOLES. MANY DANGERS LIE BENEATH THAT WATER.

The spiders threaded their way through the narrow path in the swamp. They really should have called it the Stinking Swamp. All that fungi and dirty water combined to create a stench worse than Rizzo Rawlins's gym shoes after a dodgeball tournament.

Encased in my sticky cocoon, I couldn't even cover my snout from the smell. The odor would have knocked me out if it wasn't for the bouncing of the fast-moving spider I was tied to.

Scorn's soldiers followed their captain's orders to the letter. They moved quickly along the path. They hopped from rock to rock and stepped around pools of murky water like they were in an eight-legged running race. That was probably why they didn't see the shapes moving through the water beside us until it was too late.

We were halfway across a long rock outcrop with large pools on either side of it. Suddenly the water exploded with a large splash. Dark shapes with large eyes and long arms leaped from the pools and landed on the rocks behind us.

"Lagalanders," one of the spiders whispered.

"The Fallen Ones have found us," said a second spider.

"Keep moving!" Captain Scorn growled.

The spiders doubled their speed and skittered to a larger patch of solid ground. But it was too late. The lagalanders had spotted us and were coming closer.

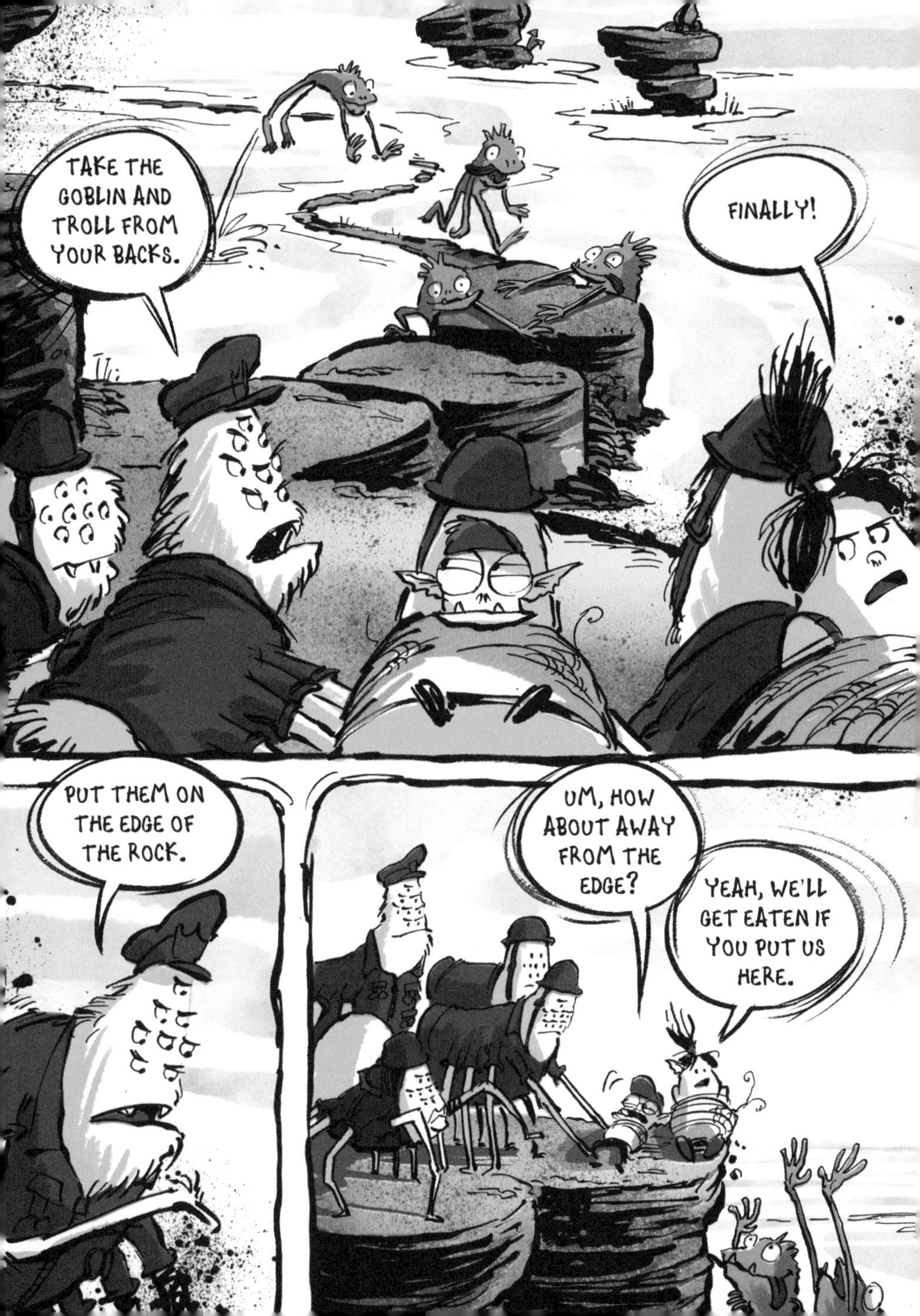
TAKE THE GOBLIN AND TROLL FROM YOUR BACKS.
FINALLY!
PUT THEM ON THE EDGE OF THE ROCK.
UM, HOW ABOUT AWAY FROM THE EDGE?
YEAH, WE'LL GET EATEN IF YOU PUT US HERE.

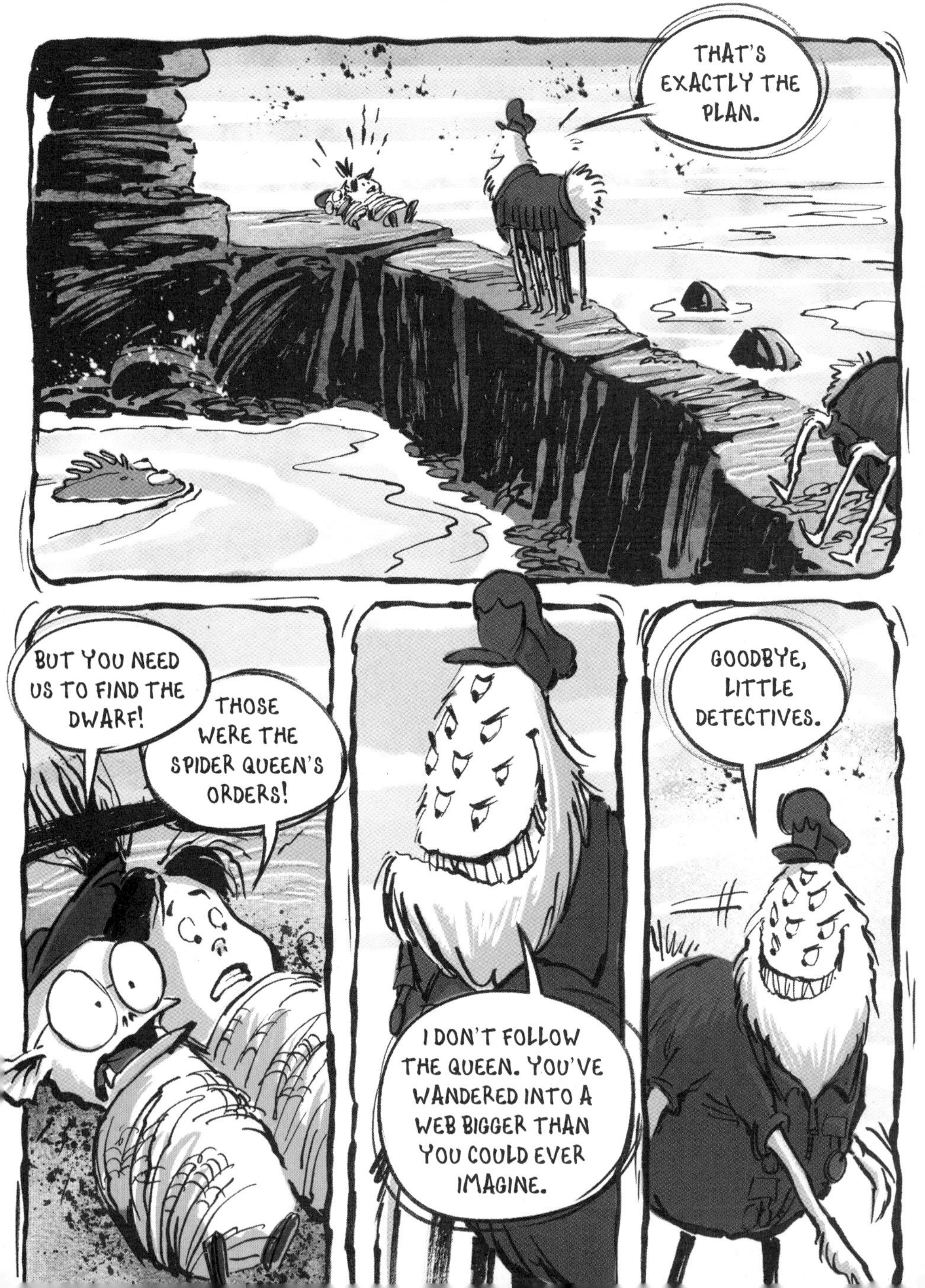
THAT'S EXACTLY THE PLAN.
BUT YOU NEED US TO FIND THE DWARF!
THOSE WERE THE SPIDER QUEEN'S ORDERS!
I DON'T FOLLOW THE QUEEN. YOU'VE WANDERED INTO A WEB BIGGER THAN YOU COULD EVER IMAGINE.
GOODBYE, LITTLE DETECTIVES.

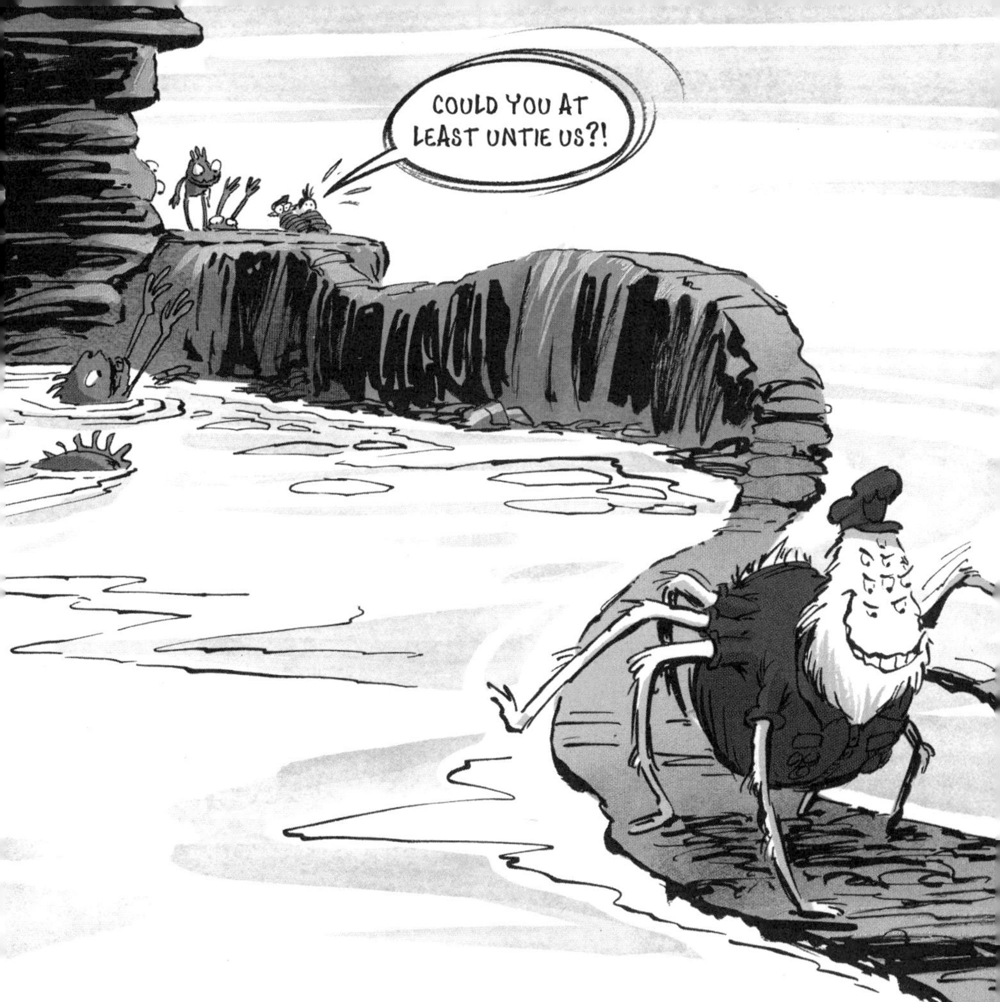
COULD YOU AT LEAST UNTIE US?!

The slimy ones lurched closer. My heart pounded under my scales. I wriggled, twisted and pulled but could not break free from the sticky web that bound me.

I was wrong—Swamp of Sorrows was a perfect name for this wretched place.

CHAPTER FIVE
Fish Heads and New Friends

"**S**o this is how it ends," Tank moaned. "Stuck on a rock and snapped up by a bunch of fish-headed freaks."

Tank and I thrashed against our web wrappings. But we were as stuck as grubnubs on a candy wrapper. Four lagalanders stepped off the path and onto the large rock where Captain Scorn had abandoned us. Their eyes glowed in the dim light as they circled around us. Their wide mouths hung open just enough for me to get a good look at the rows of razor-sharp teeth within.

"G-goblinsssss," said the largest.

"And a t-troll toooo," said another.

"We ain't had goblinssss for ages," said the third fish-head. A meaty, thick tongue slid around its fat mouth. "Tasty."

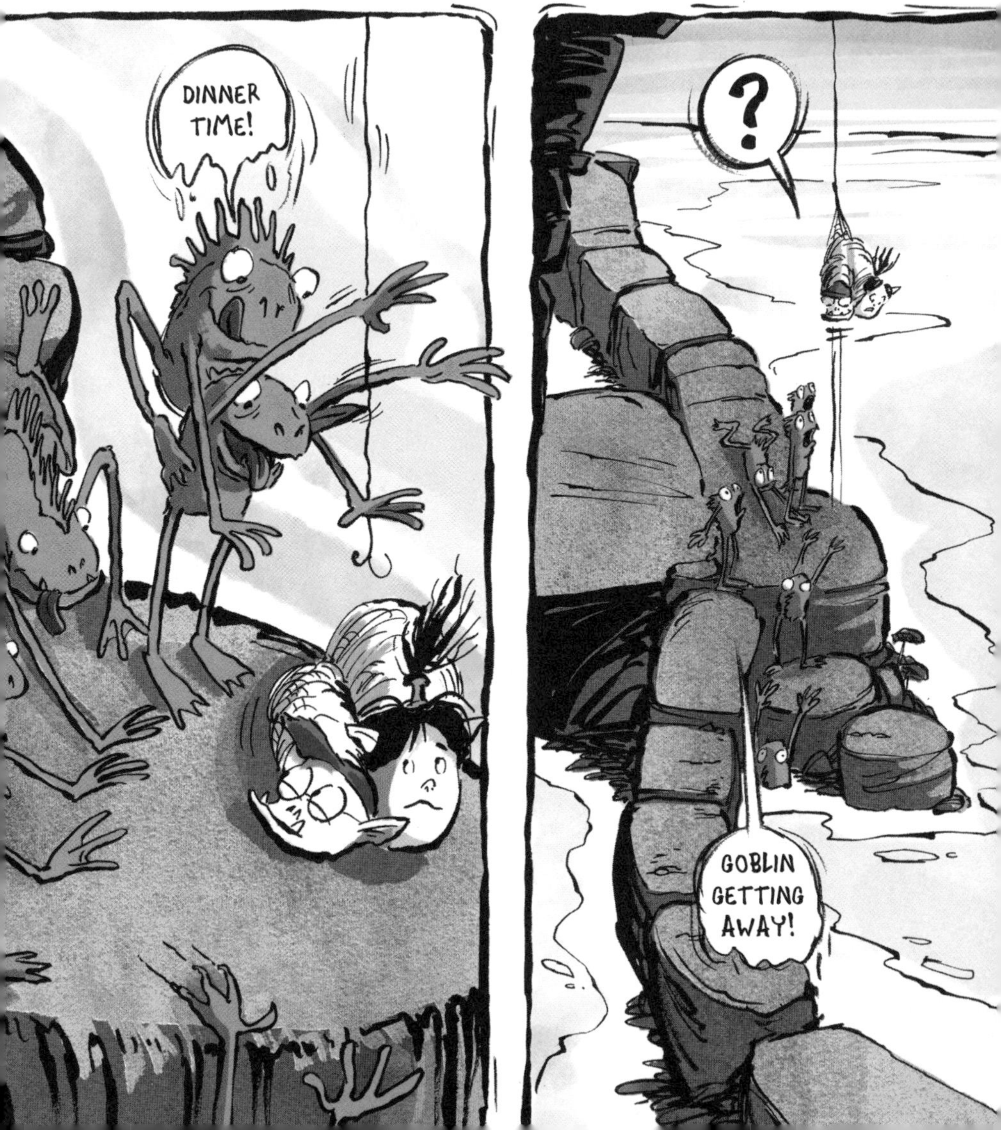
DINNER TIME!
?
GOBLIN GETTING AWAY!

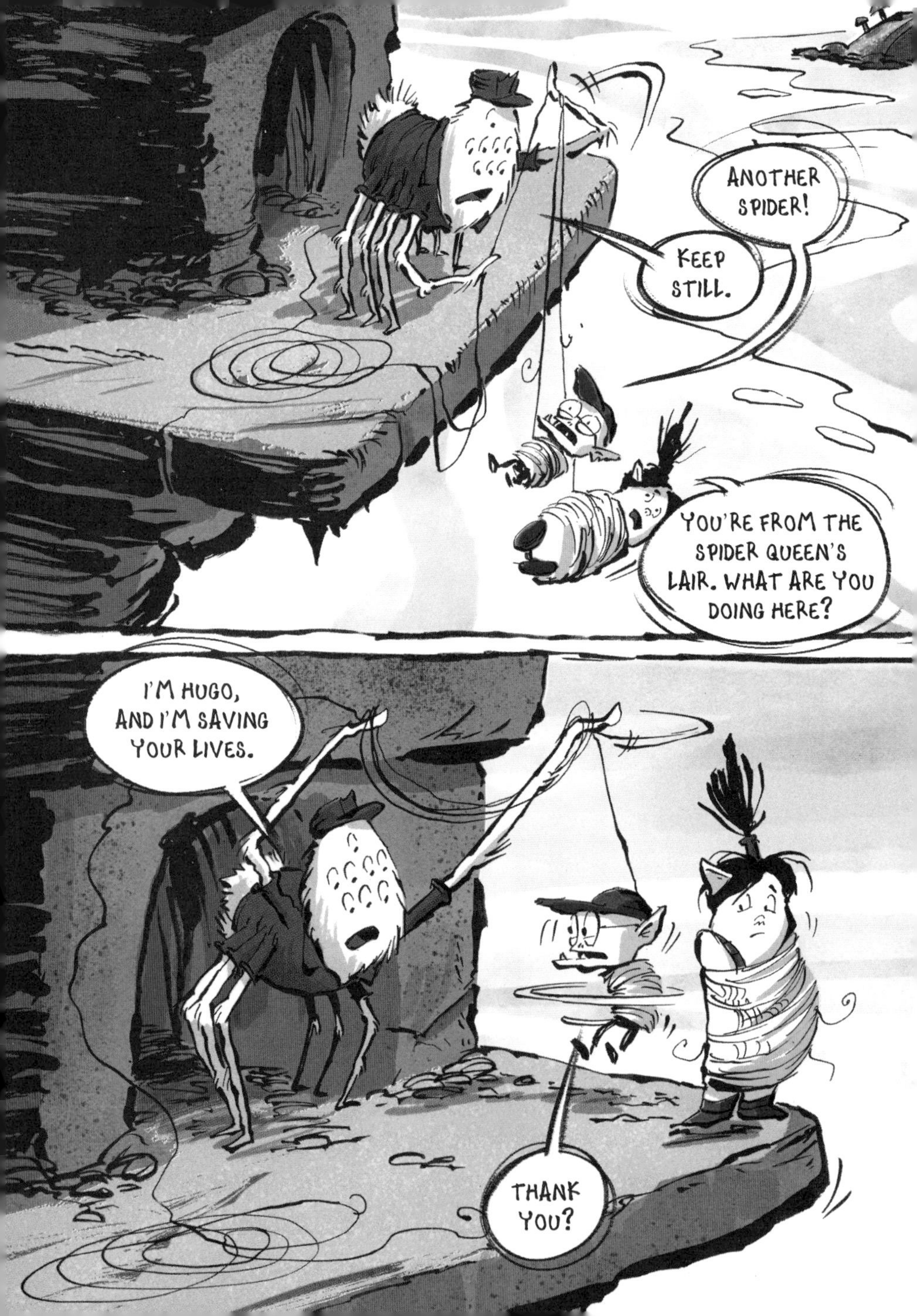
ANOTHER SPIDER!
KEEP STILL.
YOU'RE FROM THE SPIDER QUEEN'S LAIR. WHAT ARE YOU DOING HERE?
I'M HUGO, AND I'M SAVING YOUR LIVES.
THANK YOU?

My tail unfurled as the webby bonds fell to the ground. It felt good to finally scratch my snout. The good feeling didn't last long.

"Come back, tasty goblinsssss!"

The lagalanders snapped their fish jaws at us from the rocks below. Hugo skittered away from the edge and into a small cave just off the ledge.

"Be careful," he whispered. "Those lagalanders can jump surprisingly high."

A fishy hand slapped onto the ledge next to my foot. Sharp claws dug into the rock as one of the lagalanders pulled himself up.

"See?" Hugo hissed.

Tank moved quickly and stomped on the slimy hand. "Get back down!" she growled.

The creature yelped and let go. It landed with a splash.

"Ow!" it moaned. "Why you do that, troll? We just want to eat you."

The lagalanders splashed through the water below.

"They're going away," Tank said. "They're scared of my trollish stomp!"

"They'll be back," Hugo said from inside the small cave. It was just large enough for the three of us to huddle together. "We need to leave this swamp as quickly as possible."

"Hold on to your spinnerets, Hugo," I said. "We need some answers. One minute you're tying us up for your queen, the next you're setting us free. What in the name of the Depths is going on? Did Queen Azelia send you to follow us?"

Hugo shook his head quickly. "The queen does not know I'm here. If she did, I would lose my job as one of her royal attendants."

"Captain Scorn doesn't seem worried about upsetting the queen. What's with him ignoring her orders?" Tank said. "I thought she was the boss of all you eight-leggers."

Hugo rubbed his front legs together quickly and sighed. "She is our leader. But there are many in our webs who feel Captain Scorn should be our ruler."

"Including Captain Scorn?" I asked.

"He was not always like that," Hugo said. "Captain Scorn was once a kind spider, but something has changed him recently. Now he acts like a bully who dreams of ruling the entire Dark Depths. He would march his soldiers into this swamp and start a war with the lagalanders and other fallen beasts.

Queen Azelia is scary, but she doesn't pick fights with our neighbors, even if they are slimy fish-heads."

"Those lagalanders look a lot like the stream elves we've seen back home," Tank said.

Hugo nodded. "They are very similar, but lagalanders cannot use magic like their cousins the stream elves."

A pair of glowing eyes appeared in the darkness at the back of the cave. A lagalander had slipped through a hole there and flopped onto the ground.

"Yummy goblin and tasty troll!"

"Looks like your neighbor found the back door." I jumped to my feet and backed out of the cave.

Things weren't any better on the ledge. Below us, the other lagalanders had returned. They swam through the murky water, waiting for their supper to fall from the sky.

Tank hurried out of the cave and skidded to a stop beside me.

"Think you can troll-stomp your way past them?" I said.

"No, but maybe I've got something in here that will help." She searched through the pockets of her tool belt.

The little cave lit up with glowing eyes as more lagalanders slipped through the back entrance. Hugo raced out of the cave.

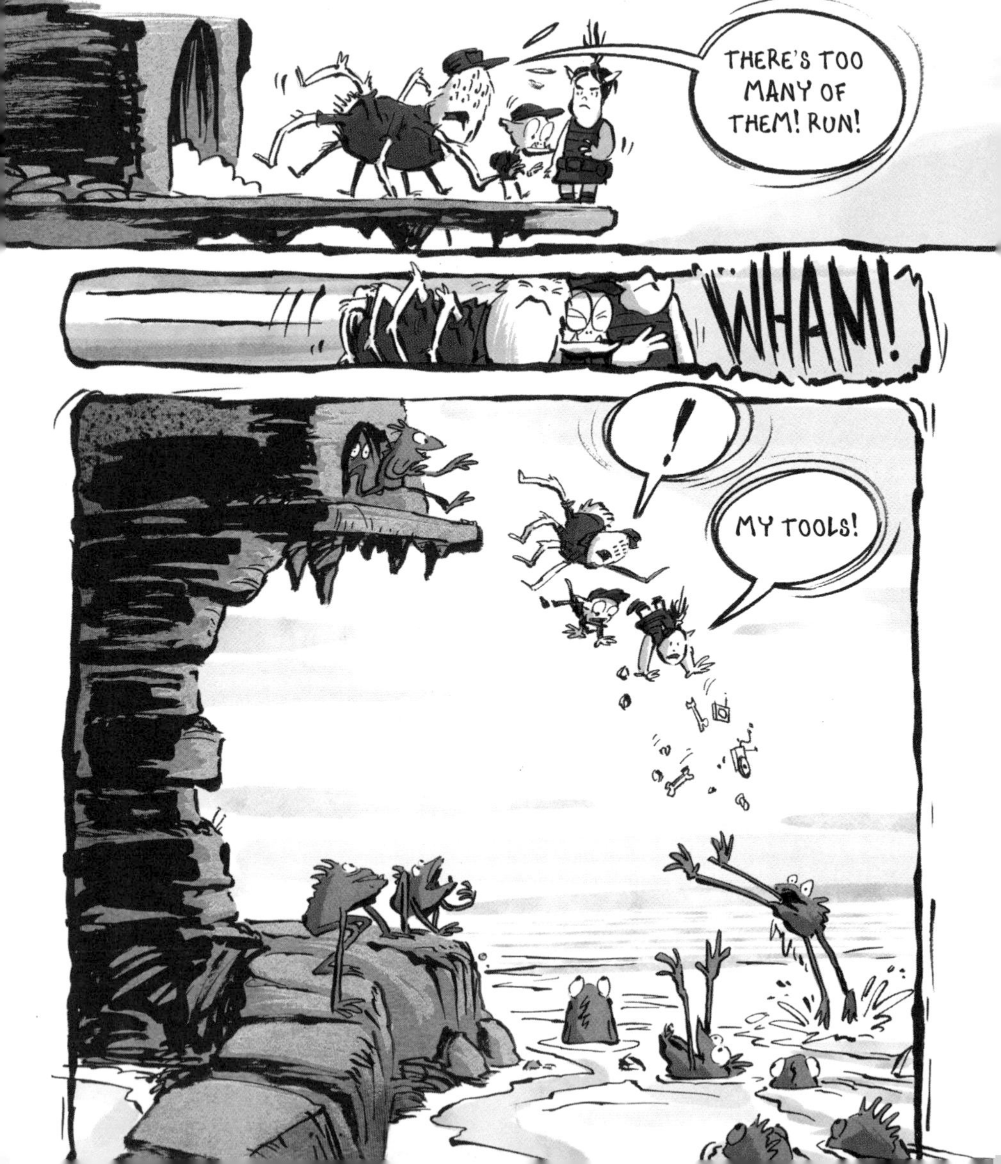
THERE'S TOO MANY OF THEM! RUN!
WHAM!
!
MY TOOLS!

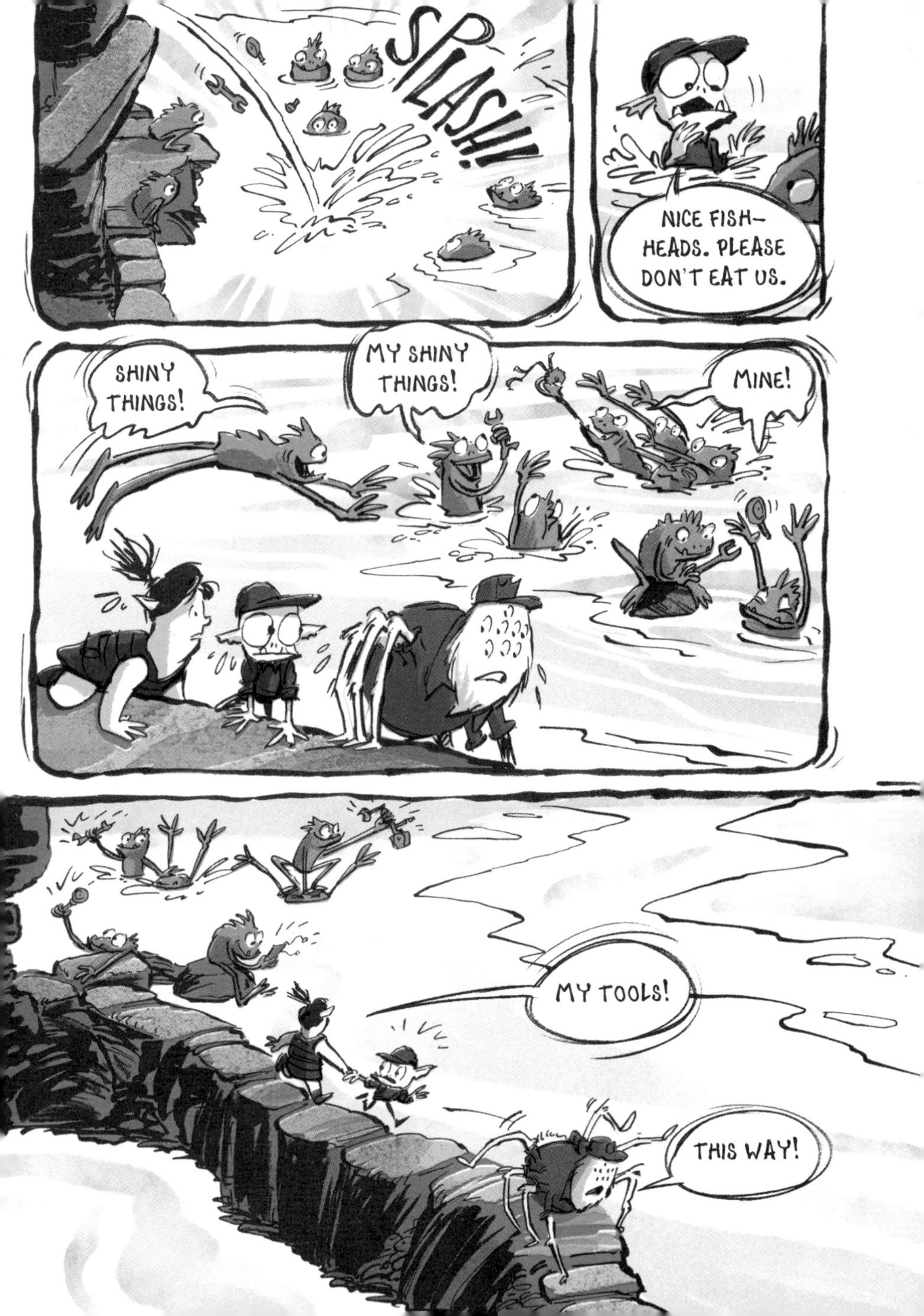
SPLASH!
NICE FISH-HEADS. PLEASE DON'T EAT US.
SHINY THINGS!
MY SHINY THINGS!
MINE!
MY TOOLS!
THIS WAY!

We scrambled away from the greedy lagalanders faster than a goblin detective fleeing math class.

Tank hesitated on the edge of the water. "They're taking my tools!" she cried.

I pulled my friend along the narrow path. "We'll get you more!"

"Hurry up, you two!" Hugo shouted from farther up ahead. "They won't be distracted for very long."

The spider led us along the winding path, around murky pools and past towering fungi. We didn't stop until the sounds of the lagalanders' bickering were far behind us. Hugo scurried to the top of a gloom-shroom growing out of the wet ground. He peered into the darkness.

"Are they following us?" Tank asked.

Hugo shook his head. "I don't think so. There's no sign of them."

"That's the first good news I've heard all day." I scratched my scales and stretched my tail. "We need to get back to the Vale of Webs and warn the queen."

"We cannot go back. Not yet," Hugo said. "The queen would never believe us. She will be furious that you disobeyed her orders. She would eat your class-mates and punish me for sneaking away."

"But it wasn't our fault!" Tank said. "Scorn dumped us here and left us to be lunch!"

"Queen Azelia doesn't listen to excuses." Hugo scrambled down from the gloomshroom. "She ordered you to go to Lava Falls and find the dwarf and ogre. If we are successful, there is a chance she won't eat you and your friends."

"What about Captain Scorn?" I said. "He's heading to Lava Falls too. If he sees us, we won't have to worry about the queen eating us. Scorn will take care of that."

"That is true," Hugo said. "But you're better off dealing with Scorn than with Queen Azelia. Trust me."

Tank looked to me with worried eyes. She tugged on her empty tool belt. One look at my friend and I knew she had the same questions running through her mind. *Can we trust Hugo? Is it better to face an angry queen or a lying spider captain?*

I stood beside my friend and faced Hugo.

"Why did you follow us?" I asked. "You said yourself that the queen won't be pleased to know you disobeyed her orders. Why risk all that for a goblin and troll you don't even know?"

Hugo's eyes dropped to the dark water around us. He spoke quietly.

"Because I believed you," he said. "I believed you saw the thieves, but I did not trust that Captain Scorn would keep you safe."

"You were right on that," Tank said. "But why not just tell your queen?"

Hugo smirked. "She would never believe a young spider like me. I don't know what it is like in your home, but down here adults rarely believe young monsters about serious matters like this."

Tank rolled her eyes. "We know all about that."

"Yeah, no one ever believes us until it's too late," I said.

Hugo smiled. "Then we have something in common."

"I guess we do." Tank grinned.

My scales relaxed. Hugo might have six more legs than I did, but he was right. We weren't so different after all.

"That settles it," I said. "Which way to Lava Falls?"

"That's a very good question." The spider's voice went quiet. "I've never been through the Swamp of Sorrows before. We usually follow the road around it."

Puddles of murky water surrounded us. Slippery rocks poked out of the puddles, but there was no clear path that my goblin eyes could spot.

I sighed. "So we lost the lagalanders and got ourselves lost along the way."

"I'm sorry." Hugo hung his head, all eight eyes staring at the ground.

Under my scales, my heart felt for the spider. He'd risked the wrath of the spider queen to find us and save us from those fish heads. We were lost in the Dark Depths, far from our friends and family. We had no food and no idea where we were going. This field trip had turned from disastrous to deadly. But we had made a new friend.

That was good, wasn't it?

CHAPTER SIX
Strangers in the Swamp

My scales were soaked with swamp water.

We had slipped, slopped and splooshed our way through muddy pools, over slick rocks and through fetid fungi. I ached all over and longed for a comfy chair and a pile of cookies. But right now all I had was a set of waterlogged claws and a drooping tail.

"We are totally lost," Tank said. "I knew we should have gone right at that last patch of sparkle spores!"

"You said we should go left!" I snapped. "And that's exactly what we did."

Tank's ears crumpled. "Yeah, well, you shouldn't have listened to me."

"I'll remember that for next time."

Hugo called to us from farther ahead. "Dry land!"

The spider stood on top of another tall gloom-shroom. From his perch he could see over the low mounds of rock and dirt that dotted the swamp and blocked our path.

Tank walked faster. "That means we're nearly out."

"We just have to cross a big pool to get to it," Hugo said.

"What are we waiting for?" I said.

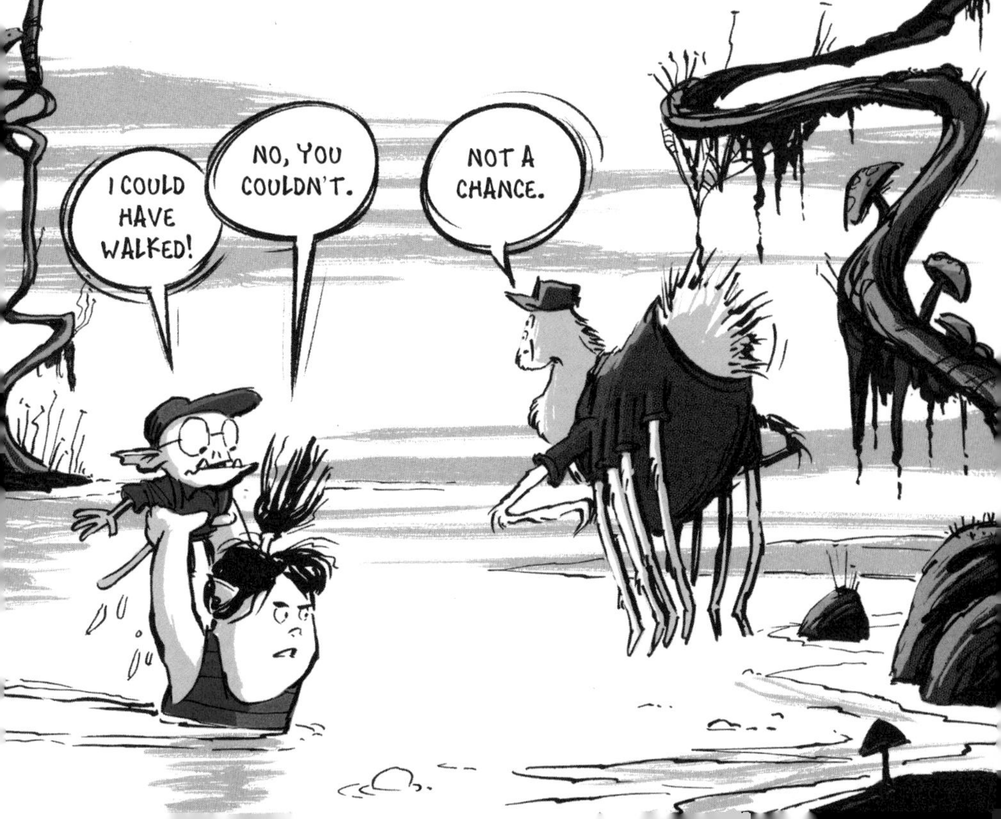
I COULD HAVE WALKED!
NO, YOU COULDN'T.
NOT A CHANCE.

Tank dropped me like a sack of old hammers on the other side of the pool.

"Ouch!" I grumbled. "You're going to crack my scales."

"At least you're not soaking wet," she snarled.

"I am wet, and now I'm sore too!"

"Quit bickering, you two!" Hugo whispered. "Someone's coming."

We were on another rocky outcrop, surrounded on three sides by murky water. A path of uneven stones led into the darkness. The soft glow of a light appeared in the distance. The light floated in the air, bobbing up and down as it came closer.

"What is it?" Tank said.

"Whatever it is, I don't want to meet it!" I hissed. "We need to hide."

"Where?" Hugo hopped on his eight legs. "There's nothing but rocks, and none are big enough to hide us."

I dropped to the ground and wrapped my tail around me. "Get small and hope it goes away!"

Tank flopped onto the ground. "Trolls don't do small!"

Hugo tucked his legs under him and huddled in close. The light drifted closer. A shape next to the light emerged from the shadows. Two large eyes, shuffling feet and the head of a fish.

"It's a lagalander!" Tank grabbed her tool belt. "I'm not giving away any more gadgets."

The lagalander took another step and stopped suddenly. He was stooped over and leaning on a gnarled stick made of petrified fungi. The little glowing light hung from the tip of the staff. The stranger tilted his head and sniffed the air.

"What's this?" he said in a slow voice. "A spider, a troll and a goblin traveling together?"

"He sees us!" Tank whimpered.

"I smell you more than I see you, young troll." The lagalander shuffled closer. "Have no fear, I won't harm you. There's too much misery in this swamp for me to add more." He stopped next to where we were huddled. "You can stop pretending to be rocks now. You're not very convincing. Besides, it's getting late, and I would prefer to camp with company."

I uncurled my tail and got to my feet. "Camp? With you?"

"Why not?" The lagalander chuckled. "Have you got a better offer?"

"No. It's just…" Tank's words trailed off.

"It's just the last lagalanders we met tried to eat us," I said.

"I think you will find I am a different sort of fish," the stranger said. "I am Gilthil. I look after the rocks in this swamp."

"Look after the rocks?" I said. "Why?"

"Someone has to." Gilthil shrugged. "Why not me?"

The old fish had me there. Hugo stepped forward and bowed his head.

"I am Hugo from the Vale of Webs," he said. "This is Tank and Fizz. We were hoping to make it to Lava Falls."

"You're certainly taking the scenic route. Lava Falls is that way." The stranger waved his staff to the right of our little island. "I advise you not to travel the swamp when the gloomshrooms have faded."

"It *is* getting darker," Tank said. "I thought it was my imagination."

The lagalander chuckled again. "You are an observant young troll. The gloomshrooms will recharge in darkness and light up again in the morning."

Tank nodded. "Like the glowshrooms back home."

"Indeed, Slick City has many glowshrooms to light its roads. Down here in the Depths, it is their cousin the gloomshroom that lights our way."

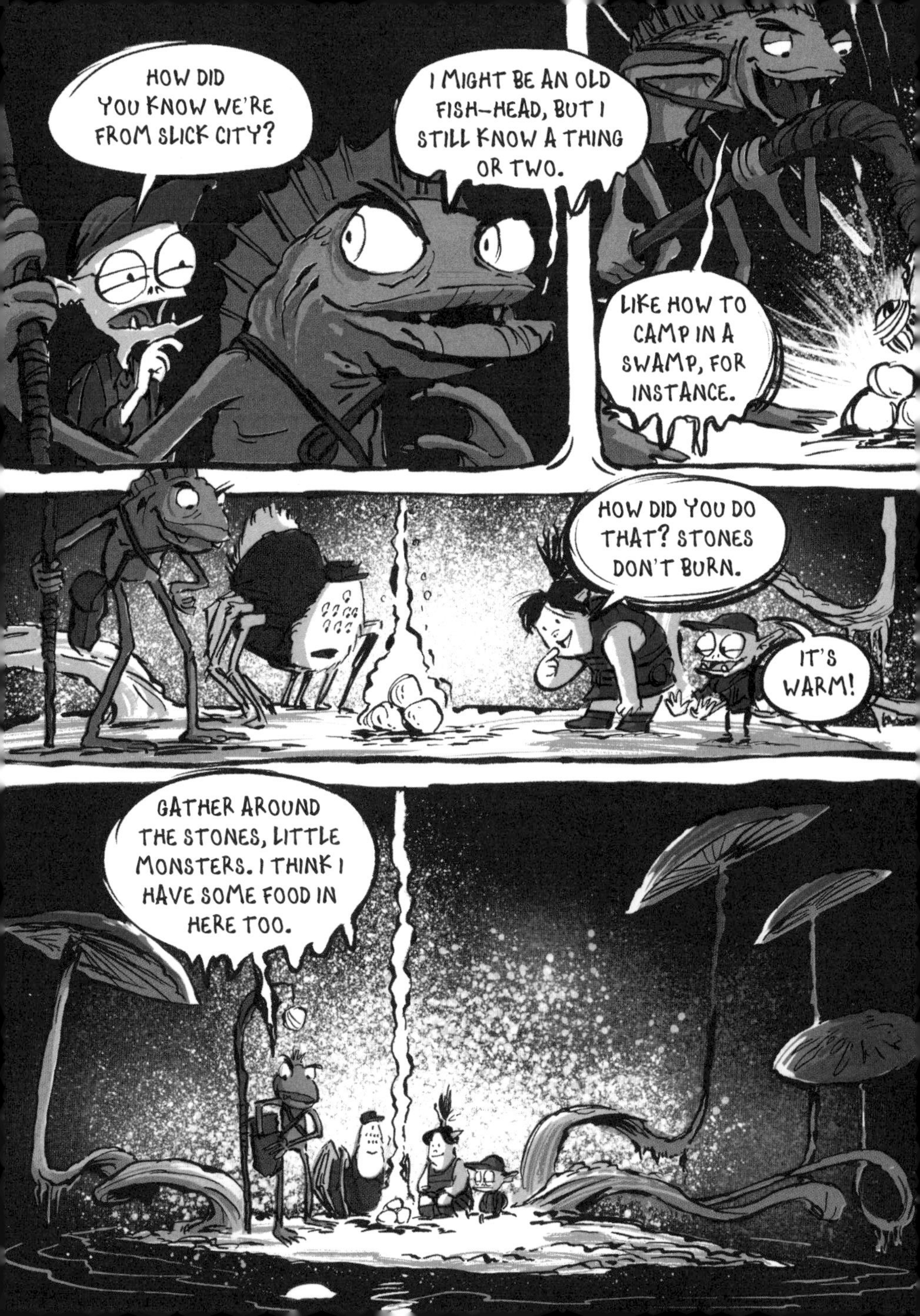
HOW DID YOU KNOW WE'RE FROM SLICK CITY?
I MIGHT BE AN OLD FISH-HEAD, BUT I STILL KNOW A THING OR TWO.
LIKE HOW TO CAMP IN A SWAMP, FOR INSTANCE.
HOW DID YOU DO THAT? STONES DON'T BURN.
IT'S WARM!
GATHER AROUND THE STONES, LITTLE MONSTERS. I THINK I HAVE SOME FOOD IN HERE TOO.

With Gilthil and his toasty rocks, the swamp didn't seem so scary or sad. The glow from the pile of stones pushed the shadows away, while their warmth dried the damp from my scales. The strange lagalander gave us each a crunchy biscuit from his satchel. For a few minutes we sat on our tiny island, quietly chewing. When the final biscuit had been eaten, Gilthil spoke.

"You search for the missing crown. Am I right?"

I nearly spat out my last bite at the question.

"H-how do you know that?" I asked.

"Has word of the robbery already spread across the Depths?" Hugo moaned. "If the dwarves and dragonkin hear the crown is missing, there will surely be trouble."

"Calm down, Hugo." Gilthil waved a webbed hand reassuringly. "Only those who listen have heard of the theft. And very few listen these days. Your quest is still a secret."

Tank glanced quickly to me and then to Gilthil.

"Then how do you know about it?" Her eyes narrowed as she spoke.

"As I said, I listen." The lagalander shrugged. He looked to me with his big round eyes. "What I don't know is how a troll and a goblin from the Shallows got involved in the whole mess."

Maybe it was the warm stones or tasty biscuits or that we were totally lost and far from home, but we told Gilthil everything. I told him about our field trip and our bus driver crashing us into the spider queen's web. Tank added the bits about the crown-stealing dwarf. Finally, Hugo told the lagalander about Captain Scorn's deception.

When he had heard it all, Gilthil shook his head sadly. "It sounds like your Captain Scorn wants the Crown of Peace for himself, so he can rule the Vale of Webs."

"Do you think he is behind the theft?" Tank asked.

"Almost certainly," Gilthil said. "With the resetting of the braces happening very soon, his timing is most perfect."

"Resetting of the braces?" I said. "My cousin had braces on his fangs. They looked painful."

"They are not that kind of braces." Gilthil smiled.

"The Braces of Balance are below the Dark Depths," Hugo said.

"There's something below the Dark Depths?" I said. "I thought we were at the very bottom of Rockfall Mountain."

"We are," Gilthil said. "But below the mountain is the Abyss, a chaotic, swirling storm of energy constantly pulling on the mountain. Every day, the power of the Abyss threatens to drag Rockfall Mountain into its heart. If that happened, the mountain would be crushed into nothing more than fine sand."

"*That* sounds painful," I said.

"More than painful, Fizz," Gilthil said. "It would be the end of Rockfall Mountain and all who live inside it. From the Dark Depths to the Shadow Tower in Slick City, every monster, wizard and slime would be destroyed."

"The Abyss formed under the mountain many generations ago," Hugo said. "We learned about it in school. The Braces of Balance are pillars that support the mountain. They hold it in place above the Abyss. They were created by the three lords of the Dark Depths: the dwarf king, the spider queen and the lord of the dragonkin. They each control one of the three lands that make up the Dark Depths."

"But what does all this have to do with the crown being stolen?" Tank said.

"The crown keeps the braces balanced," Gilthil said. "The constant pull by the Abyss takes its toll on the braces, making them unstable. Every year, the braces need to be reset to their original position.

This can only be done with the Crown of Peace. It fits into the braces like a key and allows them to be readjusted."

"Sounds like an engineer's tool to give a machine a tune-up," Tank said.

"That's exactly what it is, Tank." Gilthil nodded. "But not just anyone can use the crown to adjust the braces. It must be done by one of the three lords of the Dark Depths. To ensure power is shared fairly between lands, the crown is passed between the leaders each year. This way the three rulers agree to share the Dark Depths and not try to take over all the lands down here."

"What about the lagalanders?" I asked. "Don't they get a turn with the crown?"

Gilthil's large eyes narrowed before his wide mouth split into a grin.

"A very astute observation, Fizz. I can see why you are a great detective." The lagalander sighed. "Alas, my people are not as civilized as the dwarves, spiders and dragonkin. You have already met some of them, so I think you will agree on that. The lagalanders are lower beasts. They live in the Dark Depths, but they do not rule."

"That doesn't sound fair," Tank said. "You seem civilized enough."

"I am an exception," Gilthil said. "This is the way it has always been. Last year, Lord Dunhelm, the dwarf king, had the crown."

"And this year it was my queen's turn," Hugo said. "Queen Azelia is the only one who can reset the braces this year."

"Very true," Gilthil said. "And that is why the crown must be found. The resetting will happen in a few short days. If you are headed to Lava Falls, I can warn your queen of Captain Scorn's treachery and suggest she send more spiders this way. Find the dwarf, and when the queen's soldiers arrive, you can report to them."

"How will you speak to the spider queen?" I asked. "I didn't think lagalanders and spiders spoke to each other."

Gilthil smiled again. "As I'm sure you've already deduced, young detective, there is more to me than meets the eye."

A splash echoed in the waters somewhere in the distance. My friends turned toward the noise. I did not. Gilthil's round eyes held me fast.

The smooth, fishy skin of the lagalander vanished. In its place rows of dark scales covered Gilthil's body. I blinked. The scales vanished. The bulbous eyes and fish mouth returned.

I scrambled backward. My foot hit the glowing stones. Gilthil reached out and caught me before I fell.

"Be careful, little goblin. You could get hurt." The lagalander looked over my shoulder to where Tank and Hugo still watched the waters. "Relax, young monsters. As long as these rocks glow, no creatures will step on this island. We are perfectly safe. Perhaps we should turn in for the night?"

"I don't think I'll be able to sleep out here," Tank muttered. But a second later she was yawning and stretching out on a dry patch of rock.

"I'd much prefer a web, but there is something soothing about those rocks." Hugo tucked his eight legs under himself and closed his eyes.

I had to agree. I stretched out on the ground and watched the glowing rocks. Even with unknown monsters swimming through the waters around us, my eyelids grew heavy. As I drifted off to sleep, Gilthil's words ran circles in my tired brain.

Be careful, little goblin. You could get hurt.

CHAPTER SEVEN
Showdown in Lava Falls

Chaos swirled beneath me.

I stood on an iron bridge above a churning mass of dark energy. The Abyss. There was no mistaking the heavy pull of that rumbling pit of doom under my feet. A series of pillars ringed the Abyss, each one planted firmly in bedrock and rising to meet the massive rock slab hanging over my head. Rockfall Mountain. My home. How did I know that? The question drifted away as quickly as it came. I also knew those pillars were the Braces of Balance. They were the only thing stopping the mountain from falling into the gaping maw of the Abyss. I was far underground, even deeper than the Dark Depths. And I wasn't alone.

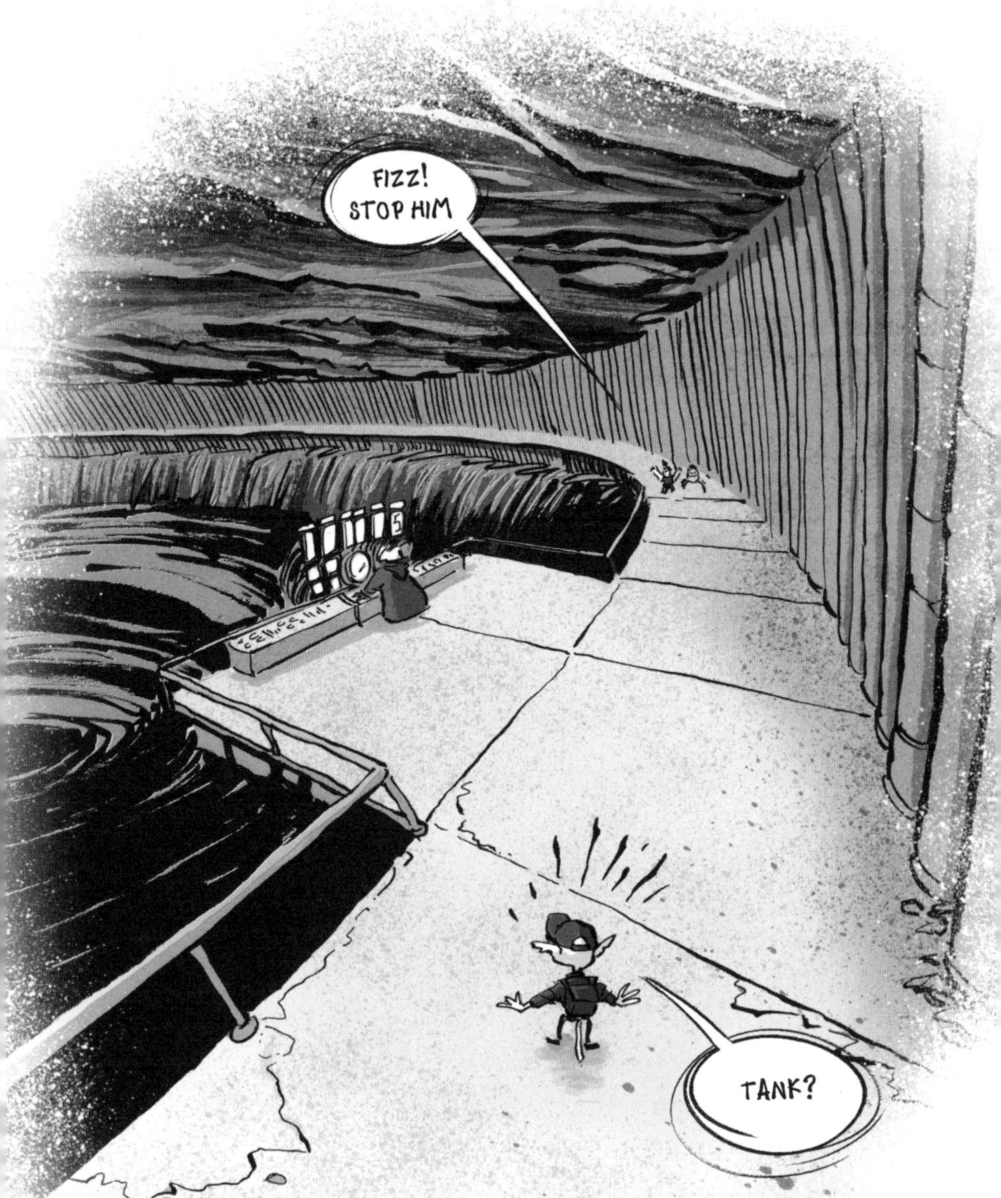
FIZZ! STOP HIM
TANK?

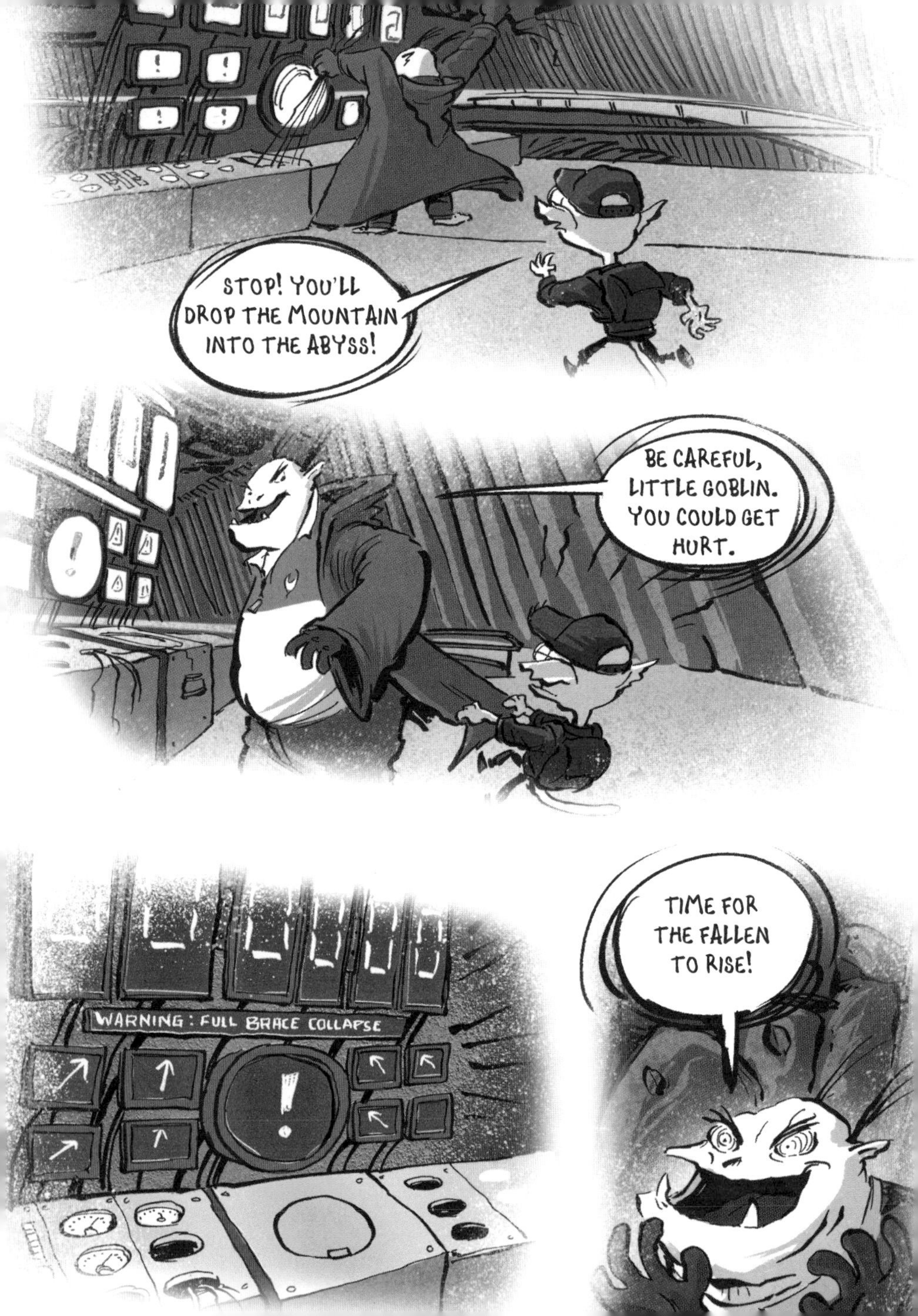
STOP! YOU'LL DROP THE MOUNTAIN INTO THE ABYSS!
BE CAREFUL, LITTLE GOBLIN. YOU COULD GET HURT.
WARNING: FULL BRACE COLLAPSE
TIME FOR THE FALLEN TO RISE!

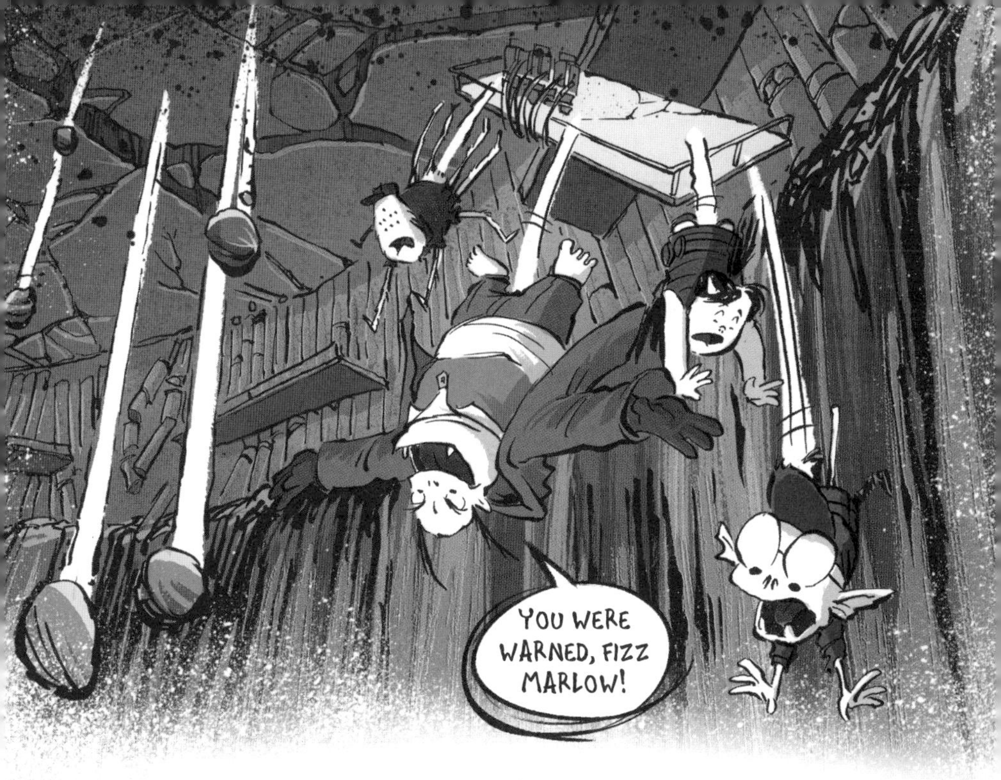
YOU WERE WARNED, FIZZ MARLOW!

I bolted awake.

Tank stood beside me. "He's alive! Finally. For a small goblin, you sure can snore."

I scrambled to my feet. "Mr. Ravel!" I gasped. "He destroyed the mountain."

"Relax, Fizz. It was just a dream," Tank said.

"But I saw it." The threads of my dream were already slipping from my mind. "He was in front of a machine, wearing a wizard's cloak or something."

"A wizard messing with technology? That sounds like a nightmare." Tank put out a hand to steady me. "Forget about it."

"You're probably right." I shook the sleep from my head.

"Besides," Tank said, sighing, "we have bigger problems to deal with."

The Swamp of Sorrows stretched into the distance behind me. Ahead, the marshy path climbed a low hill of solid and very dry rock. We were not on our little island anymore. Our island was gone. And so was Gilthil.

"Where are we?" I said. "Where is Gilthil? This isn't where we camped last night."

"Gilthil is gone," Hugo said. The spider picked his way back down the rocky path to us. "And somehow we have reached the edge of the Swamp of Sorrows."

"That doesn't make sense," I said. "Gilthil himself said we had a long way to go."

"What can I say? There's no sign of the old fish-face. All he left us was this." Tank handed me a folded piece of paper.

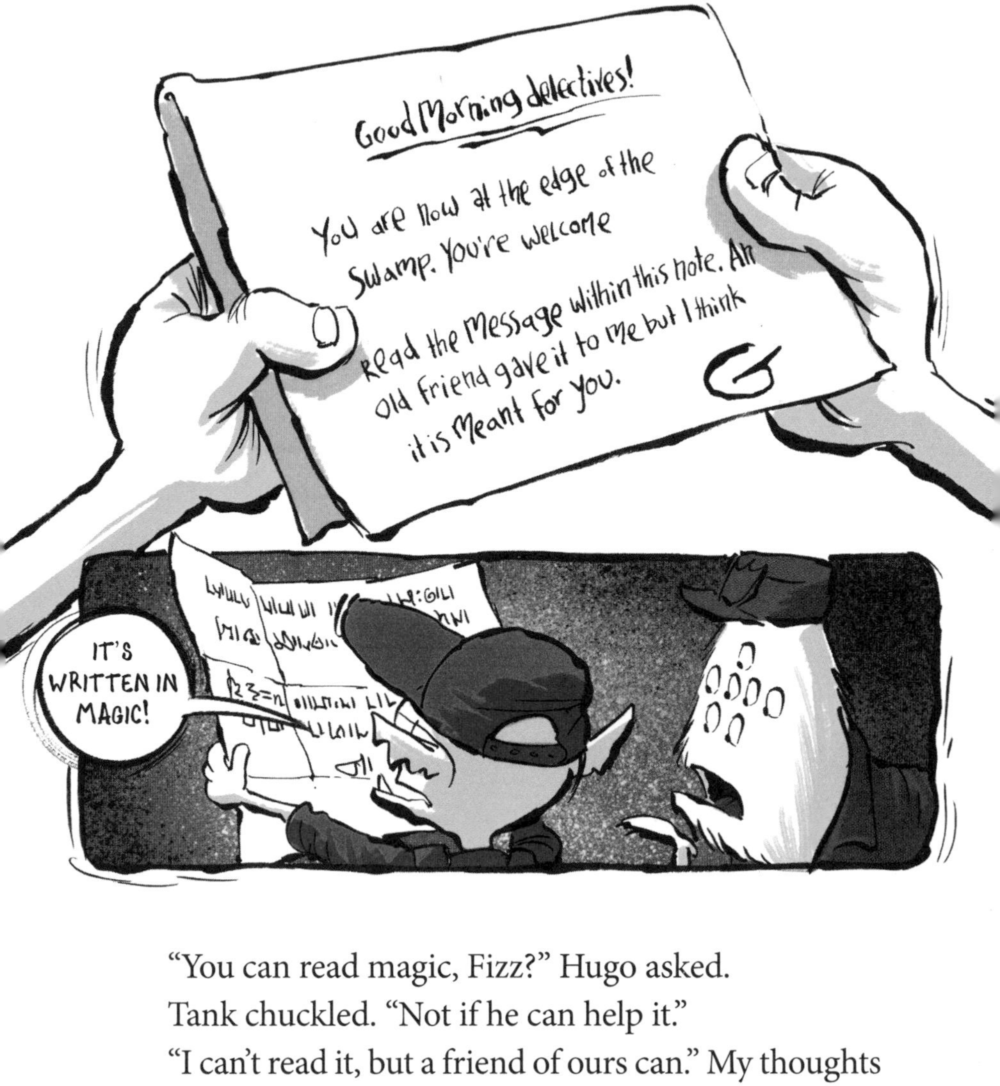
Good Morning detectives!
You are now at the edge of the Swamp. You're welcome
Read the message within this note. An old friend gave it to me but I think it is meant for you.
G
IT'S WRITTEN IN MAGIC!

"You can read magic, Fizz?" Hugo asked.

Tank chuckled. "Not if he can help it."

"I can't read it, but a friend of ours can." My thoughts sailed up through the Dark Depths to my home far away. "Aleetha. She's training to be a wizard in the Shadow Tower."

"She probably has her nose buried in a thick book right now." Tank scratched her ears. "She could read that in a wink."

"Then we must speak to her!" Hugo danced on all eight legs.

"How?"

"There is a wizards' outpost in Lava Falls," he said. "They will know how to reach her. Even if the wizards can't contact your friend, they should be able to read the magic note."

"Can we trust the wizards in the outpost?" Tank asked. "They could just take the note and ditch us in Lava Falls somewhere, just like Captain Scorn left us in the swamp."

My snout twitched. Wizards in the Dark Depths sounded like trouble. I'd had enough of their magic to last me until graduation. Now they were haunting my dreams and sending me notes.

"Tank has a point," I said. "We show the note only to Aleetha."

Tank studied the note over my shoulder. "Why would that old fish-head give us a message written in magic?"

"I have no idea." I handed it back to my friend. "Keep it safe for now. There's more to that old lagalander than we know."

"You've got that right!" Hugo said. The spider skittered back up the rocky path. "Look where we are!"

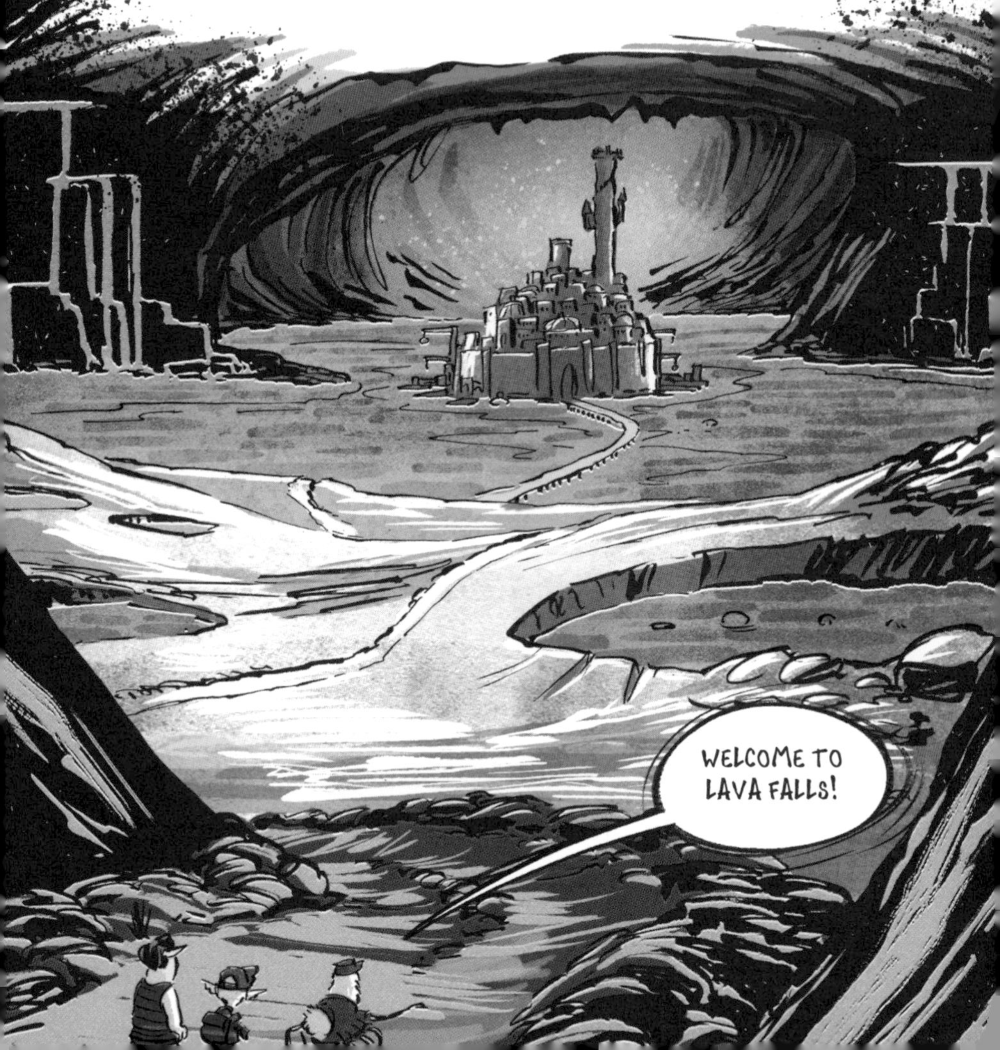
WELCOME TO
LAVA FALLS!

The murky, moist air of the Swamp of Sorrows was replaced by the sweltering heat of bubbling lava. Around us, small pools of fiery liquid bubbled and boiled. Squat, tough-looking fungi grew along the edges of the pools. A narrow road cut a winding path through the swamp of fire, leading to the gates of Lava Falls.

"These are the Fire Fields." Hugo moved around a puddle of bubbling lava and onto the winding road. "Stick to the road, and be careful where you step."

Tank stood on the edge of the path with her zoomers over her eyes. They were one of the few tools that hadn't spilled from her belt. She pointed off to the far side of the Fire Fields.

"Who are they?"

Many shapes lumbered across the field. They looked about as tall as an ogre and just as wide. The creatures walked through lava puddles as if they weren't there. It took me only a second to see why.

"They're made of fire," I said.

"Those are fire folk," Hugo said. "They live in the lava and don't like strangers. Avoiding them is wise."

"Good advice." Tank pulled the zoomers from her eyes and followed Hugo onto the road.

The journey across the Fire Fields was hot and twisting but, thankfully, uneventful. As the walls of Lava Falls drew closer, my tail curled tighter.

From dragonkin to dwarves, creatures never seen in Slick City lived in Lava Falls. Other monsters, like goblins and trolls, also lived here. They came from all over Rockfall Mountain to seek their fortunes working in the dwarf mines and the shops of the city. And if the stories were true, the ancient dragon Firebane Drakeclaw called this place home. Very soon I would see these sights with my own eyes. I couldn't tell if I was curious or terrified.

The guards at the main gates barely gave us a second glance as we passed by. They were too busy dealing with the morning rush of merchants arriving with wagonloads of goods to sell.

"Lava Falls is a hub for all monsters in the Dark Depths," Hugo explained as we slipped through the gates. "They come here to stock up on supplies and trade their goods. It's always busy."

"At least we can blend in with the crowd," Tank said. "With any luck, we'll find the dwarf without being spotted by Captain Scorn."

"He won't be happy to hear we survived the swamp," I said.

"First we find the wizards' outpost," Hugo said. "They will know how to contact your friend."

Together we moved down the bustling street. Monsters of all sizes packed the road, going about their daily business. Wide-shouldered rockstompers pulled wagons loaded with heavy-looking crates. Goblin traders skipped alongside the four-legged beasts, calculating the price of the goods inside each crate. Down one side street, a group of tool-carrying trolls worked on broken machines piled in a repair yard.

We soon arrived at a wide plaza that was filled with even more monsters. Rows of stalls filled with fruit, fungi and other goods lined the flat open space. Vendors stood by their stalls, haggling with customers and shouting for others to come see the deals they had on offer.

"This is the town square," Hugo said. The spider pointed to a large building on the edge of the square. Wide steps carved from rock led up to a set of brightly painted doors. Guards stood in front of the doors. "That is the town hall. Far below that building lie the Braces of Balance. The only way to the braces is through that door."

"That explains the guards out front," Tank said.

"It does." Hugo nodded. "But it is not the building we are looking for."

It turned out the building we were looking for was kind of hard to miss.

Not far from the town square we spotted a spire of black rock rising up from the ground.

"Is that the Shadow Tower?" Tank gulped.

"More like a Shadow Tower Junior," I said.

The spire was a replica of the wizards' school in Slick City, but much smaller. It didn't come close to matching the height of the original tower back home. But it was one of the tallest buildings in Lava Falls and loomed menacingly over the city, just like the tower in my hometown.

"Are you sure about this?" I said when we got near the tower. "Couldn't we just use your phone, Tank?"

Tank shook her head. "I'm not getting a signal this far under the mountain."

"The wizards will have a way," Hugo said. "They always do."

The spider hurried up the steps to the wizards' outpost. He opened the ornate door at the base of the tower and slipped through without a second's thought.

Tank followed, then stopped when she saw I hadn't moved.

"It'll be all right, Fizz," she said. "Wizards love us. We saved the Shadow Tower from destruction, remember?"

"And we nearly got smushed a quadrillion times." I glared at the tower. "I don't want to go in there. Magic still freaks me out. And you know that magic messes with your technology."

"All true," Tank said. "I'll do the talking. It'll be fine. You'll see."

Hugo popped back out. "We're in!" The spider crawled to the top of the doorway. "Les the Magnificent will see us."

Tank looked to me, ears alert. "Les the *what*?"

A creature made of rock stepped through the door. "The Magnificent!" he said. "It's a nickname the other wizards gave me."

"You're a rock elf!" I said.

Les reached out a rocky hand. "I'm Les. Pleased to meet you."

It turned out Les was a boulder mage and just a little older than Aleetha. He led us into the tower and explained that this was his first posting after graduating from the Shadow Tower. He didn't know Aleetha, but he knew how we could contact her. We followed Les down a narrow hallway and into a small curved room. A table and a wide screen hovered near the wall.

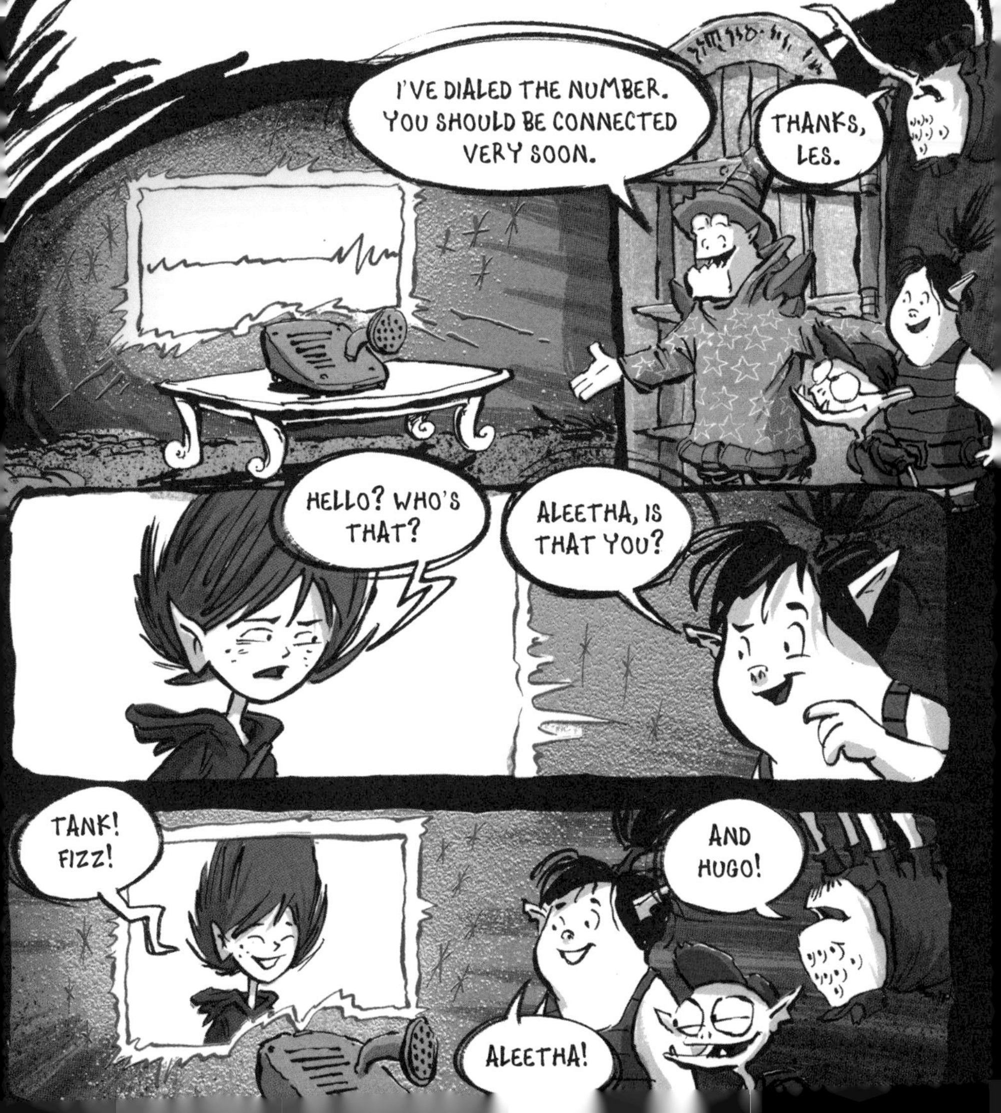
I'VE DIALED THE NUMBER. YOU SHOULD BE CONNECTED VERY SOON.
THANKS, LES.
HELLO? WHO'S THAT?
ALEETHA, IS THAT YOU?
TANK! FIZZ!
AND HUGO!
ALEETHA!

The room filled with laughter. My tail danced. Aleetha's ebony hair bounced. And Tank, well, Tank was practically in tears. Aleetha had been in our class until she was accepted to train to be a wizard in the Shadow Tower. Now she was too busy studying to hang out with us, like she used to.

"Aleetha! It's so good to see you. We need your help. Everything has gone wrong." Tank took a breath and then filled our wizard pal in on the whole situation. I chipped in here and there, and soon Aleetha was up to speed like a snagbat on a gubberslug. Tank showed her the note from Gilthil.

"Magic?" Aleetha's eyebrows arched. "Old magic. I don't recognize these symbols. I'll need time to work it out."

"Time?" I said. "We don't have this connection for long."

"No problem. I'll just borrow it." Aleetha leaned forward and reached out of the screen. Her hand darted to the note and snatched it from Tank's hand. The hand and the note slipped back through the screen. Aleetha opened the note and read it closely.

A red light flashed on the screen.

"We're out of time," Hugo said.

"Thanks for the new mystery, you two!" Aleetha waved. "I'll be in touch soon."

The screen went dark, and she was gone. The room suddenly felt empty.

The door opened and Les the Magnificent stuck his rocky head into the room. "Sorry your call ended so quickly," he said. "That's all the connection time we can offer you. I hope it was enough."

We followed the rock elf out of the tower.

"Come again, friends." Les waved a stony hand and shut the door to the wizards' outpost.

Around us, the street buzzed with traffic. We headed back to the town square. Tank stopped in mid-step with her jaw hanging open.

"Rocket bike," she gasped. "Twin-boosters. Auto-synch blast capacity."

I yanked her arm. "No time for geeking out."

But she wouldn't stop. She was like a kobold with a bone. Not letting it go.

"Just like Mr. Ravel's bike," she said.

I spun to where she was pointing. There it was. Mr. Ravel's rocket bike. Parked there in front of the Molten Burger Diner.

"What's the matter?" Hugo asked.

"That's the thief's rocket bike," I said. A dwarf pushed through the restaurant's front door. He had a scar that ran down his face. "And that's the thief."

Tank grinned. "That was easy."

The dwarf climbed on the rocket bike. The twin-boosters roared to life, sending a jet of flame out the back of the bike.

"Maybe not *that* easy," I said. "He's getting away!"

The bike swerved into the traffic and raced down the street. As quickly as he had appeared, the crown thief had disappeared.

And along with him went any chance we had of finding the crown.

But as soon as things got bad, things got worse. Someone else stepped out of the diner.

Captain Scorn.

CHAPTER EIGHT
Snatched by the Scales

We hid.

What did you expect us to do?

Tank jumped behind a barrel of fish on ice. Hugo zipped into the air like spiders do. And me? I stood there frozen like a gremlin in a rainstorm.

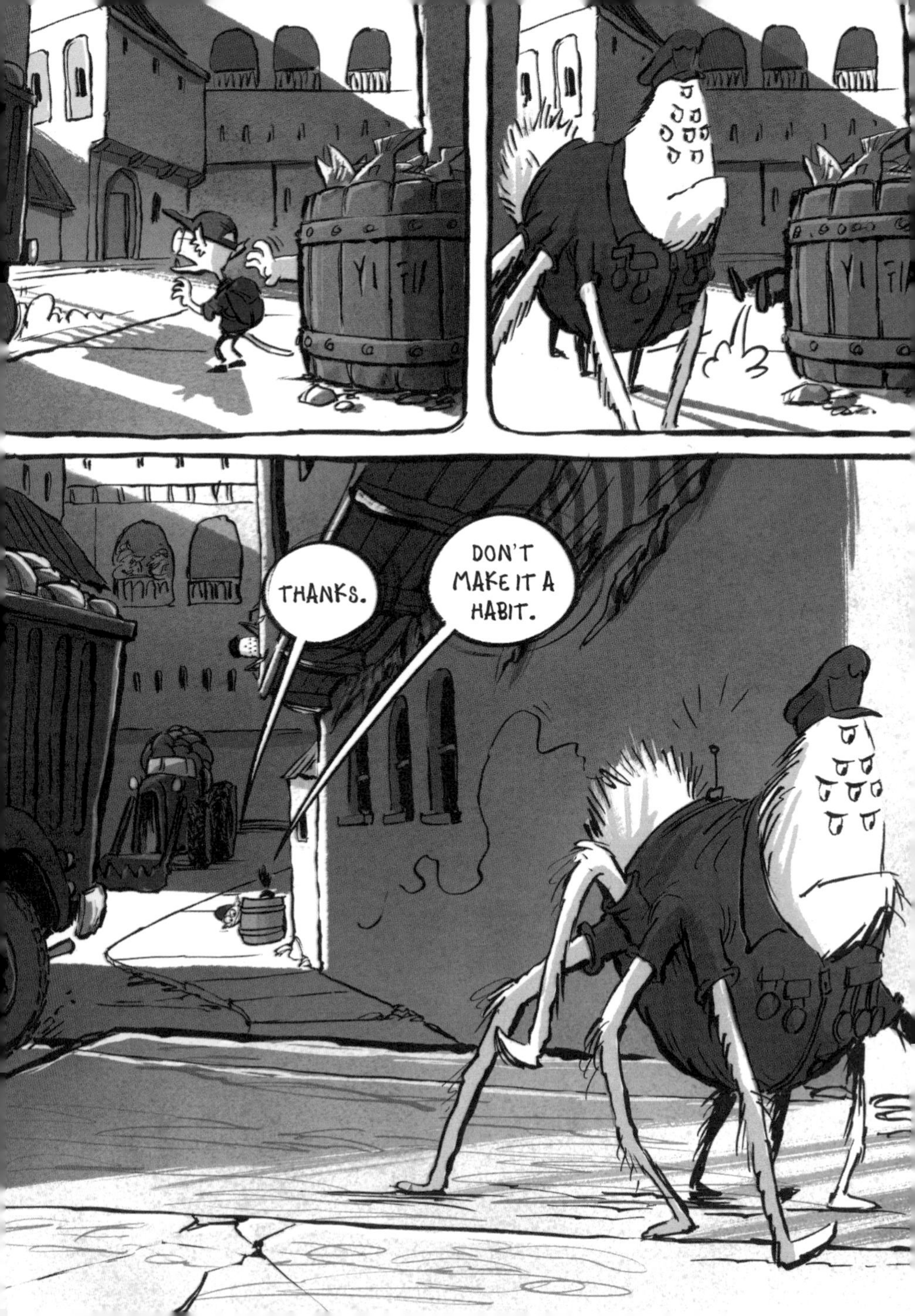
THANKS.
DON'T MAKE IT A HABIT.

Hugo dropped down on a thread. "Whoa." The spider's eyes were wider than a surprised lagalander's. "That was close."

Tank stepped out from behind the barrel. I followed with my tail between my legs. Literally.

"I'm sorry," I mumbled.

"It's all good," Tank said. "He didn't see us."

"Yeah, but now he's gone," I said.

"No, he's not." Tank held up her phone. "I tagged him with a tracker as he passed."

"And grabbed me at the same time?"

"What can I say?" Tank winked. "I'm that good."

"Wait a minute," I said. "I thought you lost all your gadgets in the swamp."

"A smart troll always carries a few spare parts in her pockets." Tank wiggled her ears. "But we have to be quick. The signal is cutting in and out. Hurry!"

Tank took off down the street in the direction Scorn had gone. Hugo swung his way deftly over the busy street. I followed them both and hoped no one would step on my tail.

We caught up with Tank in a back alley. It was a narrow, empty laneway. There were no vendors. There was nobody, actually.

She shook her phone and growled. "I lost the signal here."

I spun around. There were no doors or hiding spots.

"Where did he go?" I said. "He didn't just vanish. Did he? Can spiders do that, Hugo?"

Before Hugo could answer, something scraped along the ground. My snout twitched. I know the sound of claws when I hear them. I spun around. Two dragonkin marched into the alley. They walked straight toward us. More of the scaly creatures followed. The largest of the dragonkin waved a long-clawed hand in our direction.

"Seize them," he said.

The dragonkin moved quickly and grabbed us. Their cold hands held my arms tightly. I didn't even try to fight back. And my mind was too busy with questions to think about escape. Where had Scorn gone? Who were these dragonkin, and how did they know we were here? Were they working with Scorn?

The dragonkin's claws tightened around my arm until it felt like he was crushing my scales. Beside me, Tank yelped in pain and suddenly collapsed in a heap.

Her captor picked her up and carried her away. My vision blurred. The alley swirled like it was getting sucked down a drain. Then everything went dark.

When I woke, everything was on fire.

A wall of flames surrounded me. The fire reached as high as I could see. I sat on a stone floor, warmed by the heat of the flames. Beside me, Tank and Hugo shook themselves awake.

"My head feels like it was stomped by a battle bot." Tank rubbed her ponytail. She pulled herself to her feet. "What happened?"

"Those dragonkin. That's what happened." My arms ached where the lizards had held me. Two small marks dotted my elbow scales. "They did something when they grabbed us."

"Poison," Hugo said. The spider rubbed all eight of his eyes. "Their claws ooze a powerful poison. One scratch can paralyze an ogre. They gave us just a little dose. We got lucky."

"I don't want to know what unlucky feels like," I said. "But I do want to know where we are."

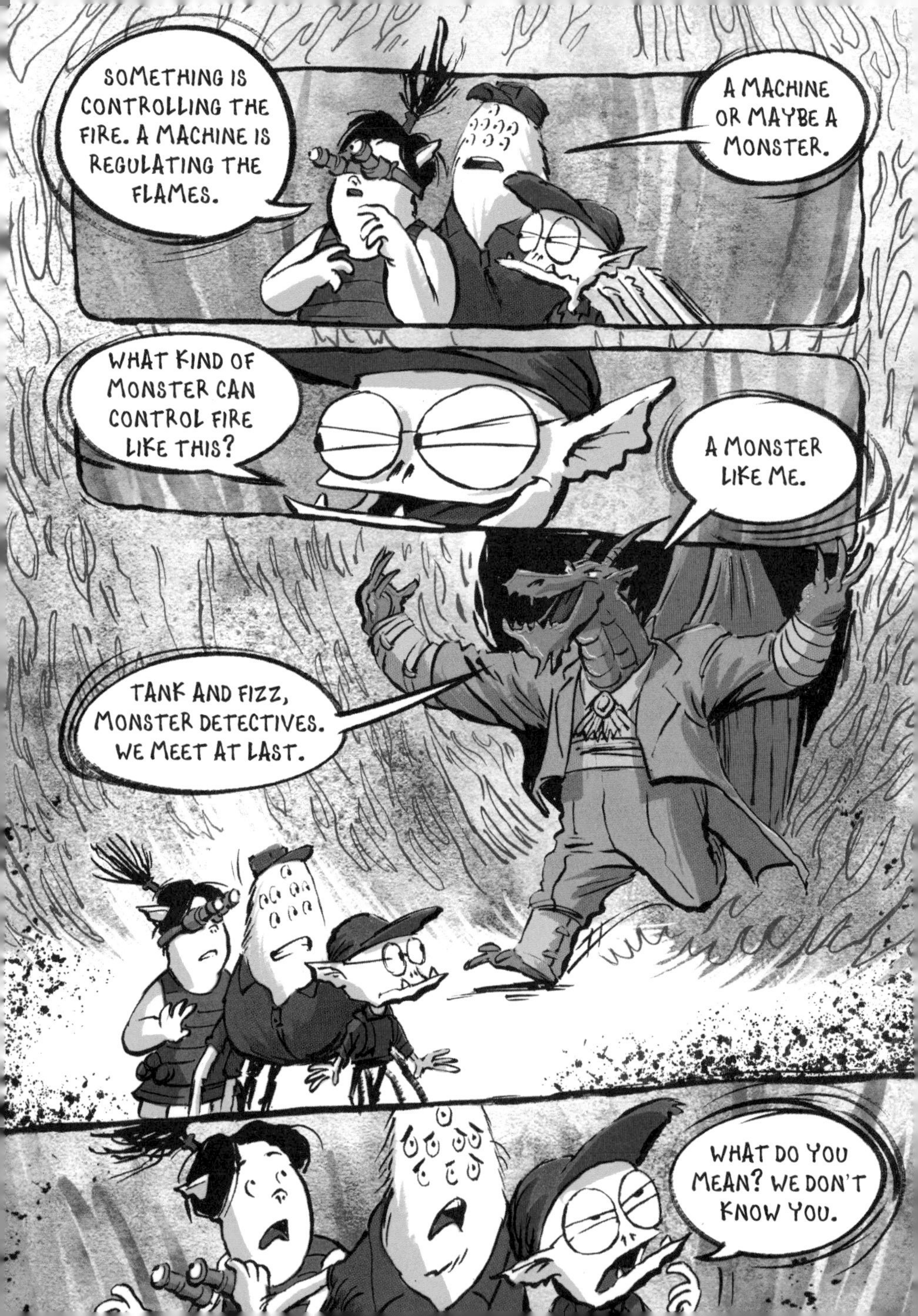
SOMETHING IS CONTROLLING THE FIRE. A MACHINE IS REGULATING THE FLAMES.
A MACHINE OR MAYBE A MONSTER.
WHAT KIND OF MONSTER CAN CONTROL FIRE LIKE THIS?
A MONSTER LIKE ME.
TANK AND FIZZ, MONSTER DETECTIVES. WE MEET AT LAST.
WHAT DO YOU MEAN? WE DON'T KNOW YOU.

"But I know you." The dragonkin grinned.

His voice sounded as old as Rockfall Mountain. His scales were as black as scorched obsidian. I tried to speak, but my jaw just hung open. How did he know our names? Who was this stranger? One thing I did know. He was no ordinary dragonkin.

"You have wings." Hugo scurried backward, stopping only when he got too close to the wall of fire behind him.

"Indeed, I do." Two massive wings unfurled from the stranger's shoulders. Each wing stretched almost to the flaming walls around them.

My jaw stayed open as my brain played catch-up. I had never heard of a dragonkin with wings. From the way Hugo was jumping on the spot, he clearly had.

"If you have wings, that means you're an actual dragon," he said.

The stranger's eyes danced. "Correct!"

Tank's eyes narrowed as she looked at the stranger from scaly head to sharp-clawed toe.

"But there's only one dragon in Rockfall Mountain," she said.

"Correct again." The stranger's eyes blazed. His wings doubled in size and spread out wide around us. We watched, stunned, as the creature transformed from dragonkin to dragon.

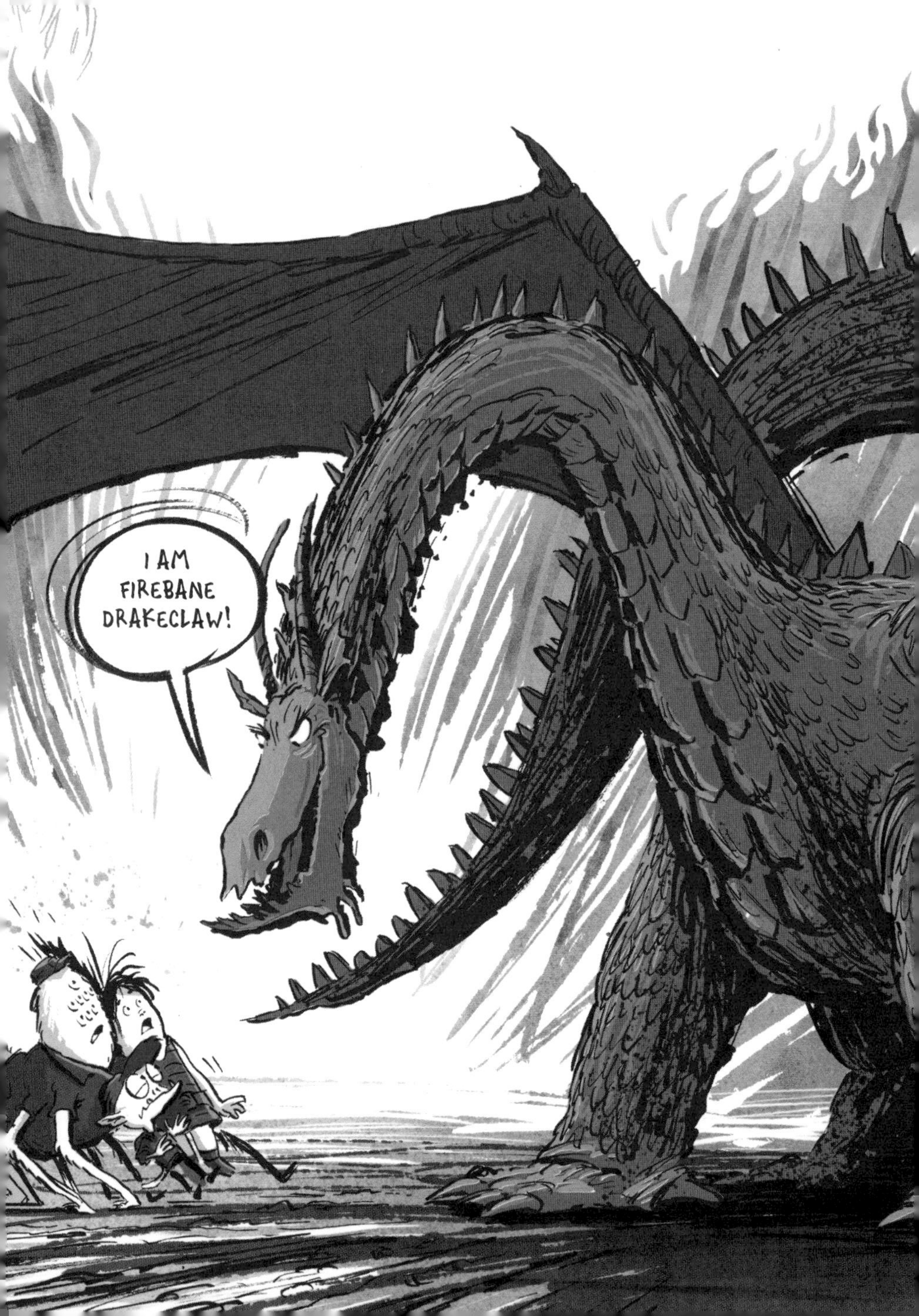
I AM FIREBANE DRAKECLAW!

CHAPTER NINE
A Dragon's Deal

Firebane Drakeclaw loomed over us like a month of detentions.

"Greetings, young monsters." A smile ran the length of the dragon's snout, exposing rows of sharp teeth.

My scales trembled and my tail quivered. Beside me, Tank tugged on her tool belt while her mouth moved up and down. No words came out. Hugo hopped on the spot, all eight of his eyes fixed on the giant monster suddenly in front of us.

Firebane Drakeclaw, the deadliest monster in Rockfall Mountain, stood within biting distance of me and my friends. Stories of the dragon's rage and destruction were legendary. Goblin mothers merely had to mention Firebane's name to quiet their noisy children. Principals would threaten to invite the beast to their schools to deal with unruly students. And here he was, standing in front of us, grinning like we were on an after-school playdate.

Firebane stretched his massive wings to their full width.

"Ahhh," he sighed. "It feels so good to return to my natural form."

"Dragons can change their shape?" I said.

"Oh yes," Firebane said. "Being able to shape-shift often comes in handy, but it plays havoc on my old bones. And it is very good to finally meet Tank and Fizz, Gravelmuck Elementary's finest detectives."

That snapped me out of my fear. "How do you know we go to Gravelmuck?"

"We've never met you before," Tank added. "I would remember meeting a dragon."

"Very true, Tank." Firebane laughed. It sounded like an army of slag giants marching to war. "We have not met, but your detective skills are well known. You saved me from losing a large portion of my treasure to the Gremlin Gang. Remember?"

Memories of our first big case flooded back to me. Tank and I had stopped a gang of thieves stealing a roomful of treasure. Firebane Drakeclaw's treasure.

"You heard about that?" Tank asked.

"Of course! It was my treasure you saved," Firebane said. "I tell all my friends about the fourth-grade detectives who saved my loot. I've wanted to meet you ever since. And here we are. Isn't it wonderful?"

Tank and I both agreed it was wonderful. It's never good to argue with a dragon who thinks you're a supersleuth.

"Let's get down to business, shall we?"

Firebane waved a claw, and the wall of fire vanished.

We were in a library of dragon-size proportions. Bookshelves taller than my school and packed with books ran along the walls. A table as wide as three ogres dominated the middle of the room. Spread across the table were papers, books and a pile of colorful gems. Against the far wall stood a massive set of glass doors that opened onto a wide balcony. Gloomshrooms sprouted along the edge of the balcony. They had dimmed for the evening, so I couldn't see much beyond their soft glow.

"Where are we?" Tank asked.

"My home." Firebane paced past a set of glass doors large enough to accommodate his massive size.

"How long were we out?" I rubbed my arm where the dragonkin had grabbed me. "It was early morning when your goons jumped us. Judging by those gloom-shrooms, it's evening already."

Firebane looked toward the dim lights on the balcony and frowned.

"Sorry about that," he said. "My soldiers were a bit too enthusiastic with their sedatives. You slept for much of the day. But you are awake now, and I'm sure you're wondering why I brought you here."

"It had crossed my mind," I said.

"It has to do with that stolen crown." Firebane's forked tongue flicked out between his massive fangs.

"You know it's missing too?" Hugo said. "First Gilthil, and now you. Does everyone know?"

"Not at all, Hugo," Firebane said. "Gilthil is a wise lagalander who often sees more than others. I happen to share that same trait. I doubt anyone else other than your spider queen and the thieves know the crown is missing. And I'd like to keep it that way. The resetting of the braces happens tomorrow. Queen Azelia and Lord Dunhelm of the dwarves will arrive in Lava Falls first thing in the morning. If word got out that the crown is missing, there would be widespread panic across the Depths. We can't have that."

"Can the resetting be delayed until we find the crown?" I said.

"I'm afraid not," Firebane said. "The pressure on the braces builds up over time. For them to remain intact, all that pressure must be absorbed by the Crown of Peace each year. To wait any longer would overload the braces and cause them to collapse. Unfortunately, that is the only way I could design them to work properly."

"You designed the braces?" Tank asked.

"The braces are ancient," Hugo said. "They've been around as long as the mountain has been here."

"And so have I." Firebane grinned. "When the Abyss first formed long ago, the dwarves and spiders could not find a way to close it, and neither could I. The leaders of each land agreed that the first monsters to find a way to close the Abyss would be crowned rulers of the Dark Depths. I created the braces, which stopped the mountain from falling into the Abyss."

"You solved the problem," I said.

"So I thought," Firebane said. "I expected them to name me their ruler, but instead they mocked my device.

They claimed I had failed because I did not close the Abyss. It remained open and dangerous. The spiders said my braces would not work for long. They called my machine Firebane's Folly."

"But they were wrong," Tank said. "The braces do still work. They just need a tune-up every year like any other machine."

"That's what I tried to explain," Firebane said. "I had even designed a ring that acted like a key to reset the braces. The dwarf king at the time was a stubborn but wise fellow. He took the ring I created down to his forge deep under the mountain. He reshaped the metal into the Crown of Peace and added a panzantium stone at its base."

"That's the big purple gem in the crown," Hugo said. "Some believe panzantium has magical powers."

"That's what the dwarf king believed," Firebane said. "It was his idea that we pass the crown and share control of the Dark Depths. He said the panzantium had powers that would ensure the crown was handed over each year."

"What happens if a ruler doesn't share the crown?" Tank asked.

"We don't know," Firebane said. "No one has ever tested it. The crown has always been passed around and the braces reset."

"Until now," I said.

"Precisely." Firebane turned to the glass doors leading to the balcony. "That is why we are going on a trip. Follow me."

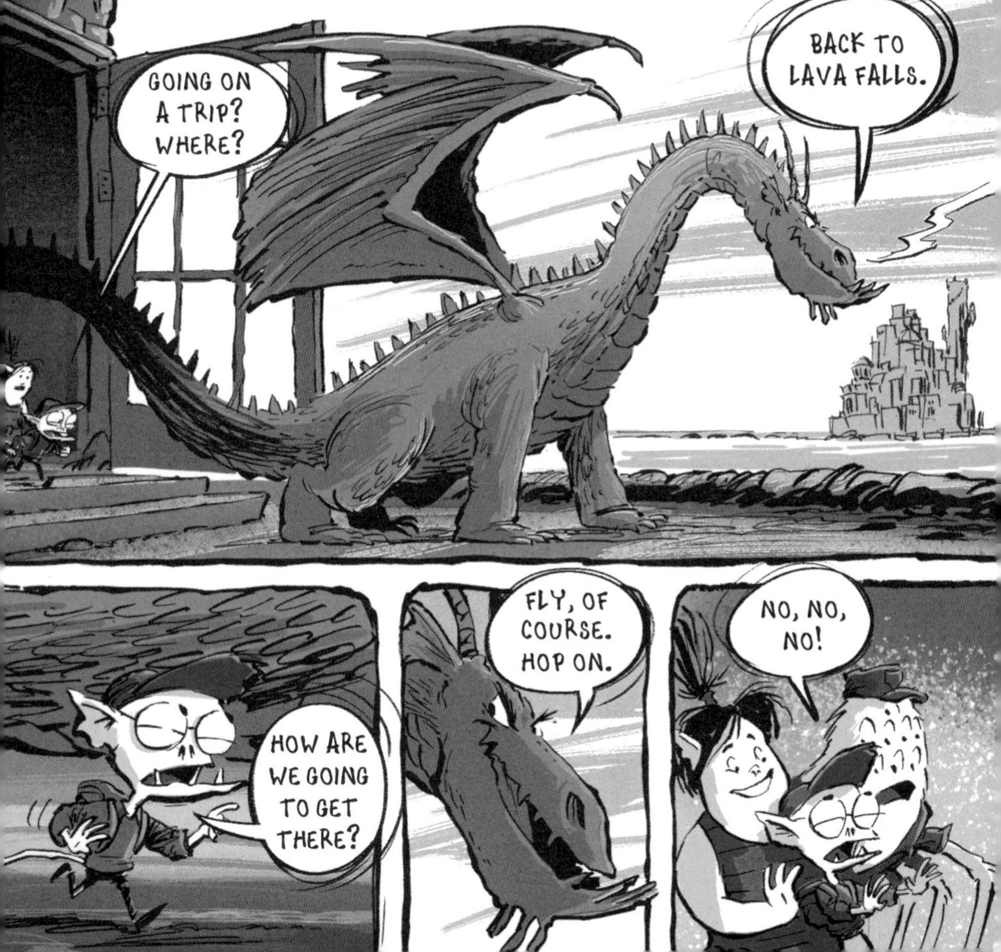
GOING ON A TRIP? WHERE?
BACK TO LAVA FALLS.
HOW ARE WE GOING TO GET THERE?
FLY, OF COURSE. HOP ON.
NO, NO, NO!

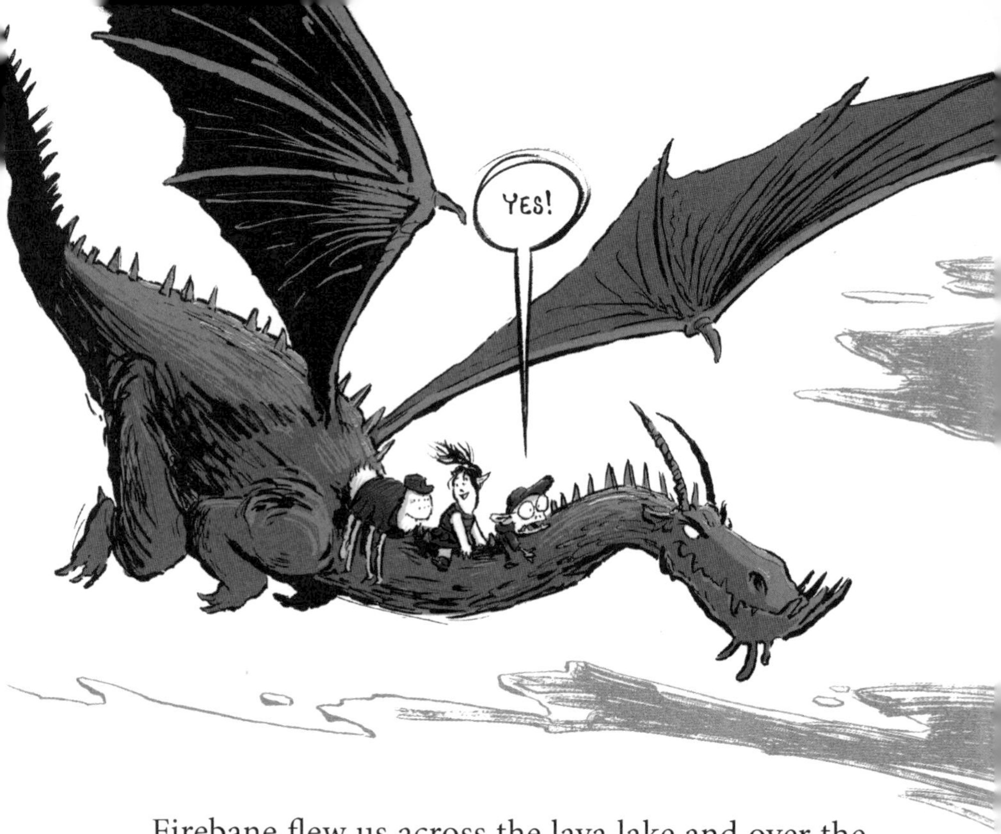
YES!

Firebane flew us across the lava lake and over the roofs of the buildings and homes of Lava Falls. Tank and Hugo both grinned through the whole journey. The beating of Firebane's wings calmed my racing brain. It feels good to have someone on your side. Especially if it's an ancient dragon the size of a department store.

After another lap around the lake because Hugo practically begged, we landed on the roof of the town hall. We climbed off Firebane, and he shifted back into dragonkin form. He led us to a trapdoor set into the roof.

"We'll slip in through here," Firebane said. "Too many curious monsters in the town square. No need to announce our visit to all of Lava Falls." We followed him through the trapdoor, down a ladder and into a dusty corridor. At the end of the hall stood doors to an elevator. He pushed the button next to the doors. "It's mostly storage up here. Old files. And stuff."

The elevator doors opened, and we went down. And down. And down.

"Where are we going?" I asked. My gut felt like it had already reached the ground floor.

Firebane smiled.

"You'll see."

Beside me, Tank wiggled her ears. "This is going to be so cool."

After much more dropping, we stopped with a thud.

"We're here," Firebane said.

The doors slid open. Firebane stepped through and we followed. A sea of chaos boiled beneath me. Firebane marched forward, smiling like a barker at a kobold carnival.

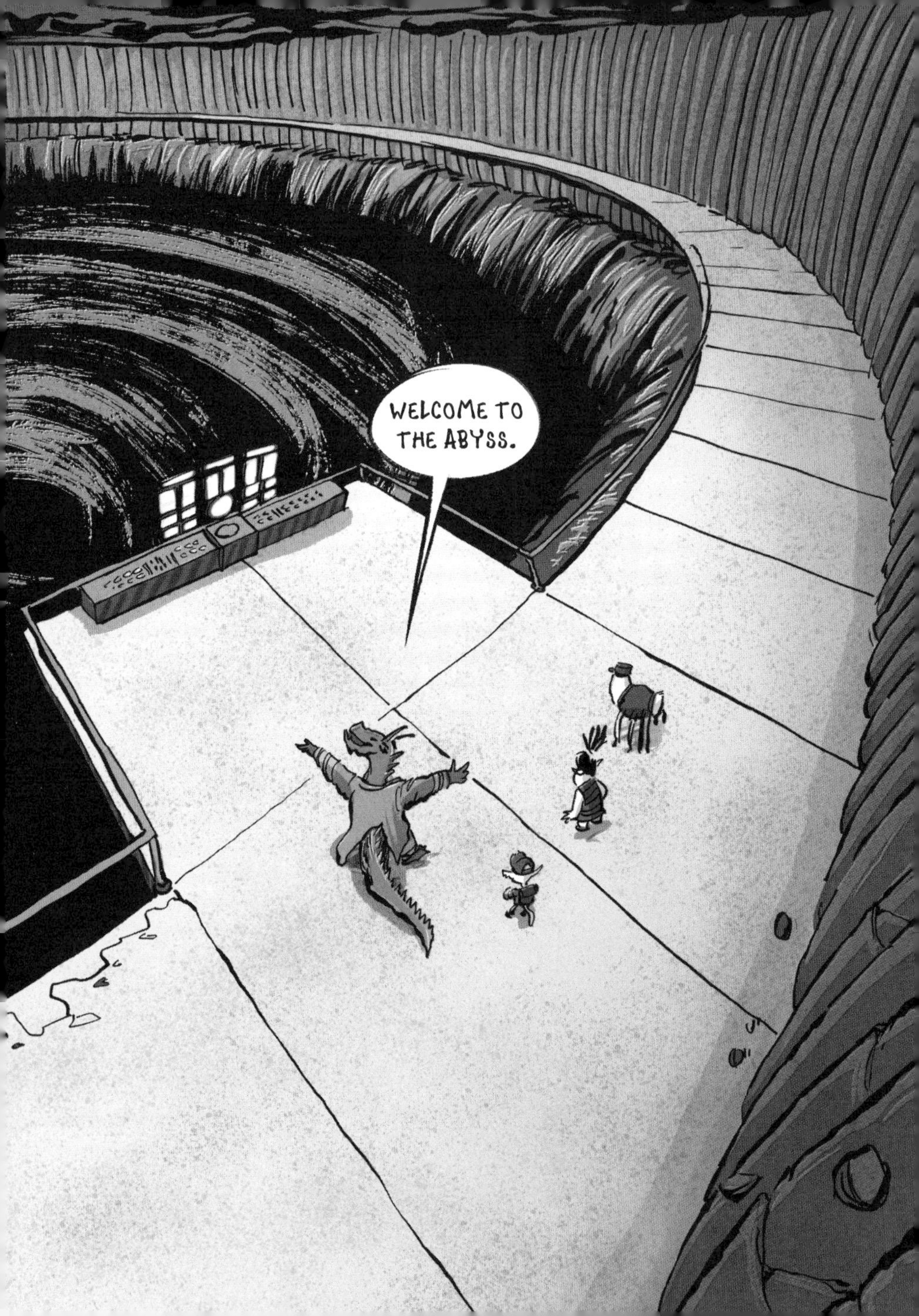
WELCOME TO THE ABYSS.

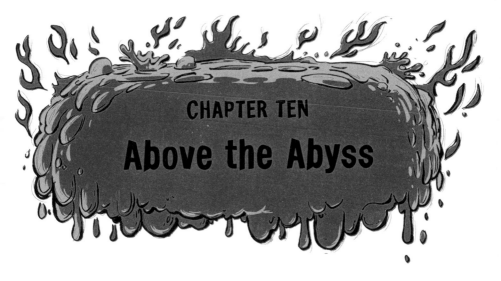

CHAPTER TEN
Above the Abyss

There wasn't much between me and a belly flop into oblivion.

My feet were rooted to the metal walkway ringing the Abyss. Tank threw herself at the railing and froze, wide-eyed and still. Hugo had four legs on opposite railings, holding on like a furry kite. This first sight of the Abyss was too much for them. Unlike the others, I had seen it before.

The Abyss was exactly as it had been in my nightmare the night before. The same swirling sea of chaos that had rumbled through my dream now churned under our feet. Firebane grinned at our confused stares.

"Questions?"

"Um, yeah." Tank cleared her throat. She had managed to stand up and now had her zoomers on. She watched the chaos spin around us. "If we're standing over the Abyss, why are we not dead?"

"The spirit of curiosity is alive and well with our tinkering troll," the dragon said. "We are alive because of my genius."

Tank spun the zoomers onto the dragon. "Are these the braces of balance?"

"All 346 of them!" Firebane beamed. "They run the entire circumference of the Abyss."

"That means all the way around," Tank said to me.

"I knew that!" I snapped.

Firebane continued. "The gravitational pull of the Abyss is so strong, it will swallow anything that gets within its grasp. Above us you will see rock. A lot of rock."

A ceiling of dark, jagged rock ran into the darkness in all directions. Above the Abyss, it crumbled and cascaded downward. Pieces bigger than a family of ogres snapped off the ceiling and tumbled into the gaping maw of the Abyss.

"That is the bottom of Rockfall Mountain," Firebane said. "We're inside a pocket of rock deep below the deepest tunnels. That elevator is the only way in or out of here."

"You built the town hall on top of the Abyss?" Tank said. "Was that a good idea?"

Firebane smirked. "It has allowed us to watch it and ensure it doesn't grow. But I can see why you might be nervous. Believe it or not, some believe that the Abyss gives as much as it takes."

"I have heard that," Hugo said. "There is a group of the queen's advisors who say the Abyss is responsible for much of the life in the mountain."

"Well, monsters are allowed to believe what they like." Firebane sighed. "No matter how silly."

"I kind of like the idea," Hugo said. "It helped me not be scared of it growing up. But now that I'm standing over it, I'm not so sure."

"Indeed." Firebane turned to the control panel behind him. "The braces are the only thing ensuring the Abyss doesn't devour the mountain."

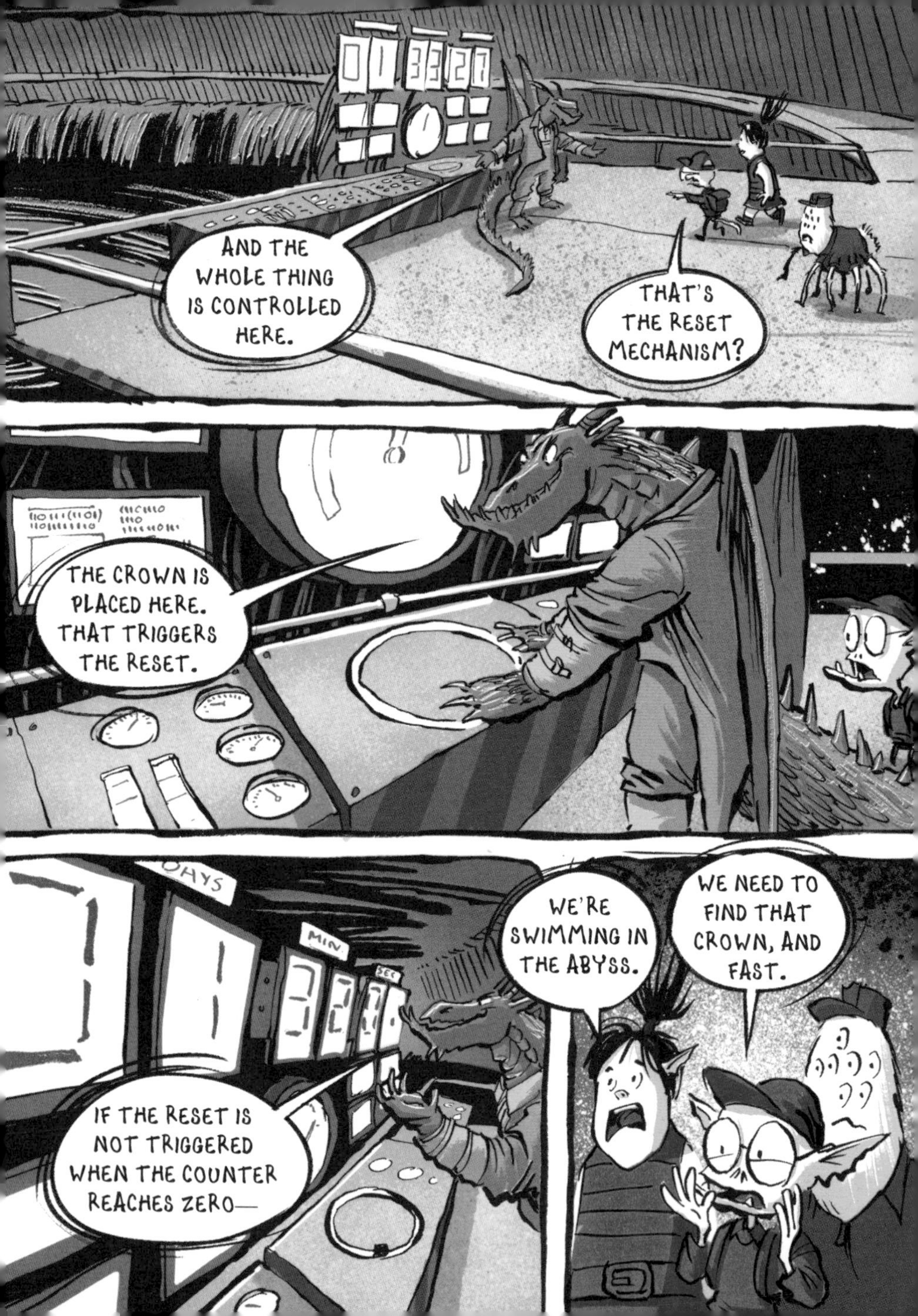
AND THE WHOLE THING IS CONTROLLED HERE.
THAT'S THE RESET MECHANISM?
THE CROWN IS PLACED HERE. THAT TRIGGERS THE RESET.
DAYS
MIN.
SEC
IF THE RESET IS NOT TRIGGERED WHEN THE COUNTER REACHES ZERO—
WE'RE SWIMMING IN THE ABYSS.
WE NEED TO FIND THAT CROWN, AND FAST.

"How are we going to do that?" Hugo asked. "By the order of my queen, we can't tell anyone it's missing."

"Your queen is correct to keep the theft a secret, Hugo," Firebane said. "If word got out that the crown is missing, there would be panic from the Depths to the top of Shadow Tower."

"Yeah, but the monsters of the mountain deserve to know that their home might be plunged into the Abyss," I said.

"That still might not happen." Firebane's eyes twinkled. "We can't tell anyone the crown is missing, but we know who took it."

"Yeah, a nameless dwarf and an ogre who could barely drive a school bus," I said. "That's not going to help us."

"Perhaps I can fill in some details." Firebane stepped away from the reset mechanism. Two faces now appeared on the machine's display screen.

Mr. Ravel stared out from the screen. His hatchet eyes sent a shiver down to my tail. Next to the ogre, the dwarf with the scar glared at us.

"That's them!" Tank gasped. "That's Mr. Ravel and the dwarf who knocked over Fizz."

"*Nearly* knocked me over," I corrected. "How did you track them down?"

"I have eyes and ears throughout Lava Falls," Firebane said. "These two were spotted coming into the city late last night. They are both well known to the Lava Falls authorities." Firebane pointed a claw to the image of the dwarf. "That is Bramgrum Rocksplitter. He is a renegade engineer wanted across the Dark Depths for many other crimes. He's the mastermind behind the operation to steal the crown."

Bramgrum had a face like a bad report card. His beard looked like it was home to a family of gremlins. His eyes burned with anger. Just looking at him made my scales shake.

"Bramgrum recruited Scorn," Firebane said. "The spider captain helped the dwarf sneak into the queen's chambers to steal the crown."

"And what about Mr. Ravel?" Tank asked. "I'm guessing he's not really a school-bus driver."

"The only buses he drives are the ones he steals." Firebane chuckled. "That is Hagnar Grushnik. A petty criminal on the run from Slick City police. He's hiding out down here in the Depths."

"And keeping busy by helping steal priceless artifacts," I said.

"Exactly," Firebane said.

Hugo scanned the photos with his eight eyes. "If we know who they are, why don't you just grab them like you did us?"

"If only it were that easy, Hugo." Firebane sighed. "We tracked them to the harbor in Lava Falls but lost them shortly after that."

"So you don't know where they are?" I said.

"Correct." Firebane reached into his coat pocket and pulled out a small box with a short antenna and a small light. "But this will help us find them and, hopefully, the Crown of Peace."

Tank's ears perked up. "That looks like a tectonic-frequency tracker."

The light on the box flashed and pinged like a bell.

"Very good, Tank." Firebane handed the device to my friend. "That's exactly what it is. Its frequency rate has been modified to focus on tracking the Crown of Peace."

"That makes sense." Tank took the tracker and studied it closely.

"It does?" I said.

"It does, Fizz." Tank rolled her eyes. "The faster the light flashes, the closer it is to the crown."

"It's wonderful we have a machine that goes ping,"
I said. "But what are we going to do with it?"

Firebane's grin doubled in size.

"You are going to steal back the crown."

CHAPTER ELEVEN
Diving Deep in a Leaky Bucket

Firebane rolled through the streets of Lava Falls.

Even this late in the evening, the town was busy. The dragon cut a path through the crowded streets as we traveled from the town hall. Firebane was in his dragonkin shape, with his wings hidden under a large cape. If you didn't know better, you'd think he was a regular old dragonkin.

But I knew better. I also didn't like what I was hearing. Why did a dragon who ruled much of the Dark Depths need help from a pair of fourth-grade detectives and their spider friend?

Firebane had explained it all as we rode the elevator back up to the surface. This time he led us through the town hall's main doors and into the town square. From there we followed him through the crowded market, past groups of dwarves, trolls and other monsters. I quickened my steps and walked alongside Firebane.

"Let me see if I understand this," I said. "You want us to follow that pinging machine into a wanted criminal's hideout and steal back the Crown of Peace."

"Exactly!" Firebane said. "You are a sharp goblin."

My scales bristled at the compliment. "I'm sharp enough to know your guards last saw Bramgrum the dwarf get into a submarine at the lava-lake harbor. Goblins don't like swimming in lava."

"Neither do trolls!" Tank called from a step behind us.

"Nonsense. You'll be perfectly safe." Firebane dismissed our concern with a wave of his hand. "We believe Bramgrum is hiding in a cavern under the lake. The tracker has pinpointed the crown's location to an abandoned dwarven mining station down there. With any luck, you'll surprise the thieves and be able to grab the crown."

"That still sounds like a tall order for a bunch of kids," I said. "Why don't you get help from the spider queen?"

"She is already aware of your mission," Firebane said. "She agrees that we should keep news of the theft secret to avoid panic. And the queen is keen to not have any more treachery from her soldiers. Captain Scorn's defection is enough. We are among the few who know life in the mountain will most likely end tomorrow unless that crown is found. Imagine what would happen if the monsters around here knew what we know."

"They'd freak out," I said.

"Exactly. It would be chaos down here and all the way up to Slick City," Firebane said. "The resetting is tomorrow. Queen Azelia and Lord Dunhelm of the dwarves are due to arrive at the gloomshroom's first light. Our only hope is a small group sneaking in quietly to reclaim the crown."

"What about your dragonkin soldiers?" I said. "I bet they could steal the crown quietly and avoid causing panic."

"I would prefer that," Firebane said. "But Bramgrum the dwarf and his ogre partner have been quite good at avoiding my guards. Every time we find them, they vanish before we can catch them. I suspect I might have a defector in my army too. That is why I was so thrilled to find you here in the Dark Depths. I haven't told any of my soldiers about your mission. Bramgrum most likely thinks you were eaten by Queen Azelia when she found you in her webs. You are the perfect monsters for the job."

I nearly tripped at the memory of how close we'd come to being Queen Azelia's lunchtime snack. The rest of my class still faced that fate, if they hadn't been eaten already. I was having trouble wrapping my detective brain around this case. I wasn't sure whom I feared most, the dwarf I was tracking or the spider queen I was working for.

We arrived at the top of a long set of stairs leading down to the harbor. A lake of lava stretched in front of us. Boats of all sizes floated on the fiery liquid. How they didn't burst into flames I did not know. Dockworkers moved up and down the piers, loading and unloading cargo from boats.

"Looks a bit like Fang Harbor back home," Tank said. "Except with more fire."

"The cave is at the bottom of this lava lake," I said. "You still haven't told us how we're getting down to the bottom of the lake without turning into charred monsters."

The grin returned to the dragon's snout. "That's where the dwarves come in."

Tank nearly fell off the stairs. "What is *that*?"

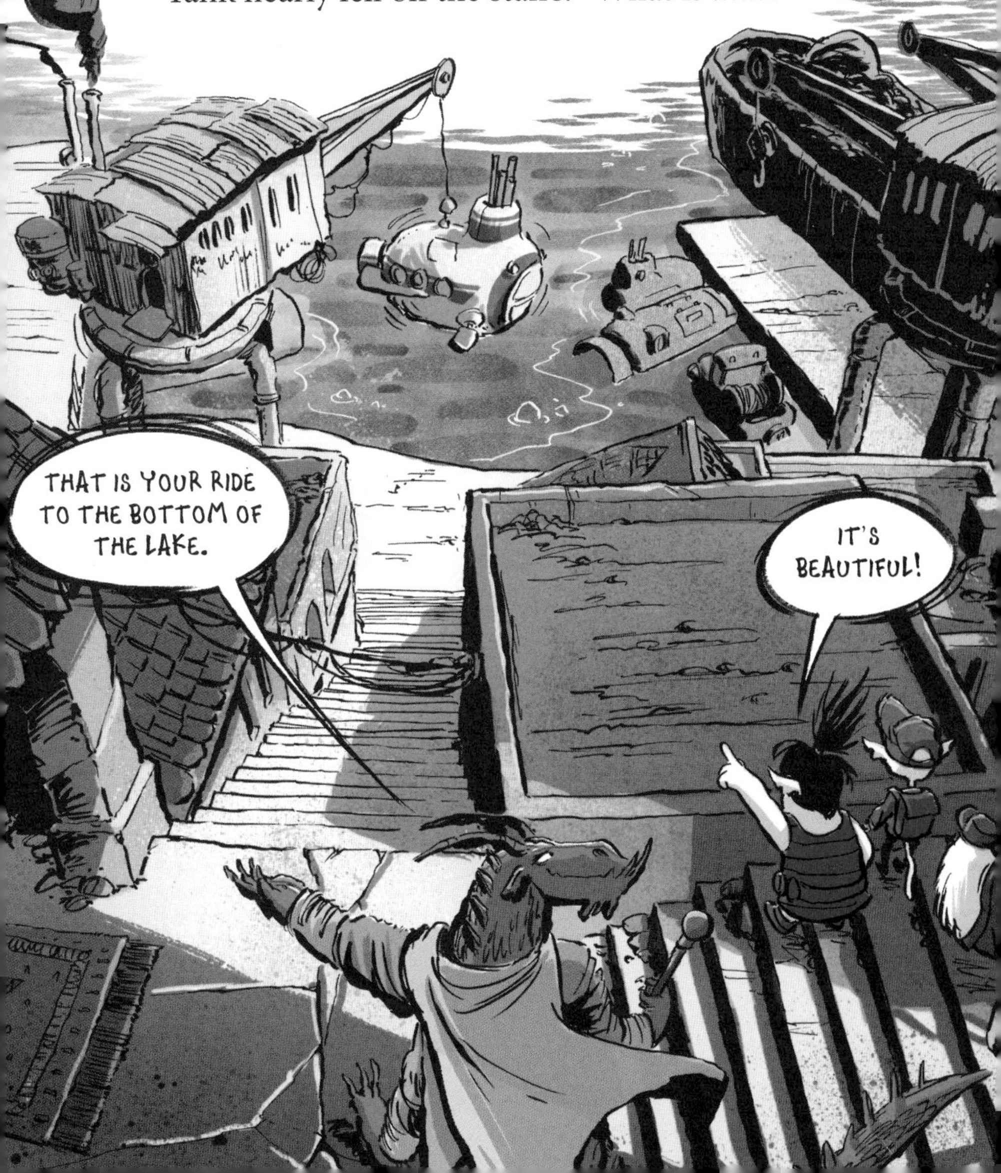
THAT IS YOUR RIDE TO THE BOTTOM OF THE LAKE.
IT'S BEAUTIFUL!

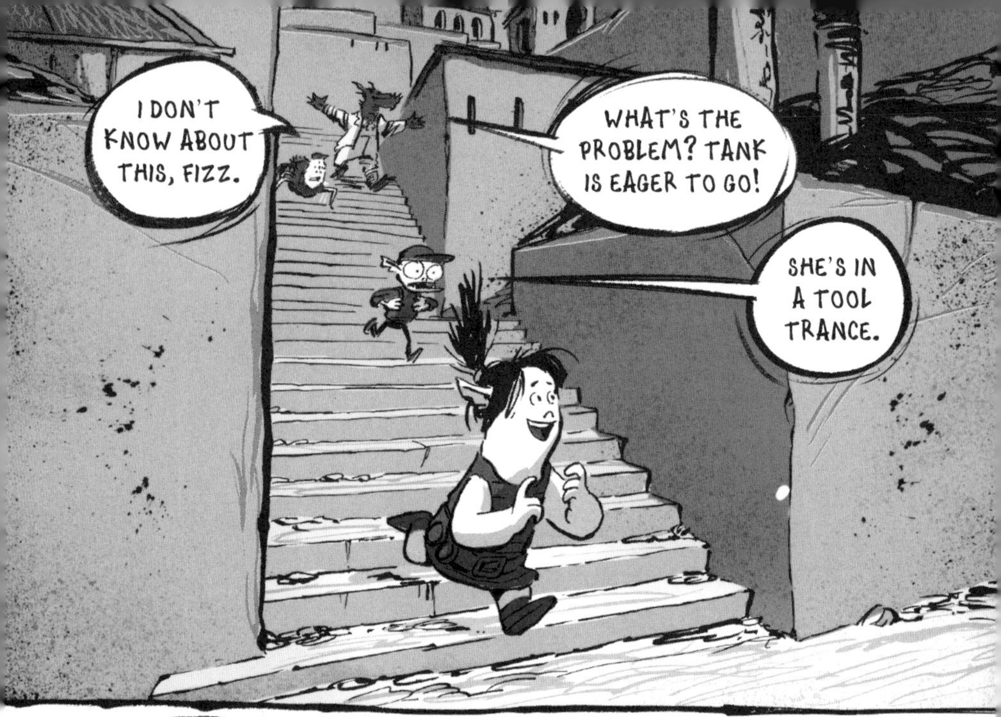
I DON'T KNOW ABOUT THIS, FIZZ.
WHAT'S THE PROBLEM? TANK IS EAGER TO GO!
SHE'S IN A TOOL TRANCE.

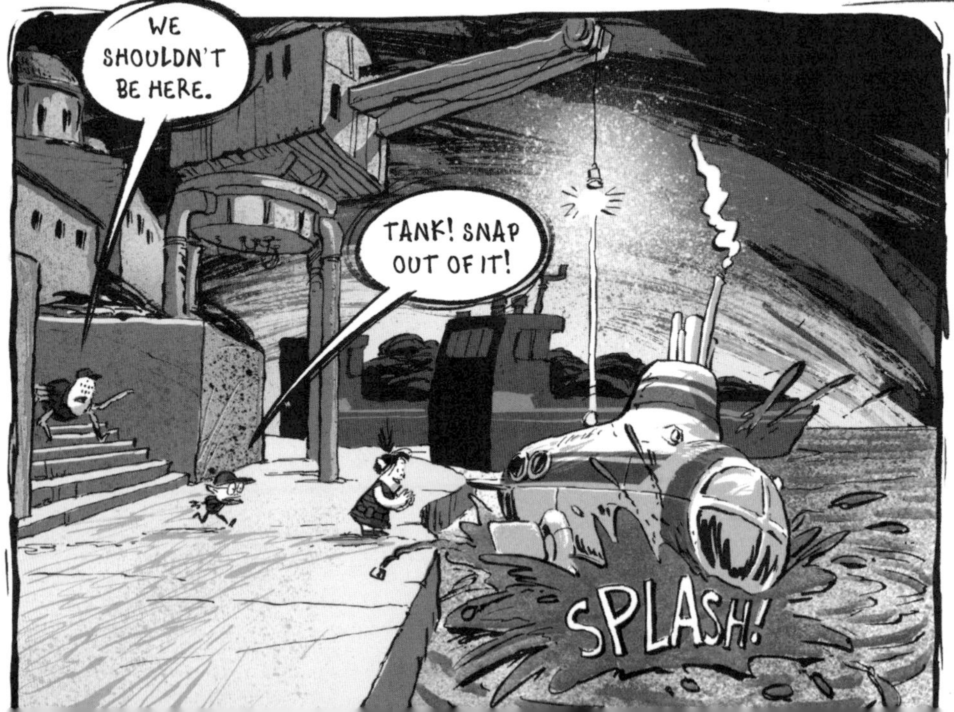
WE SHOULDN'T BE HERE.
TANK! SNAP OUT OF IT!
SPLASH!

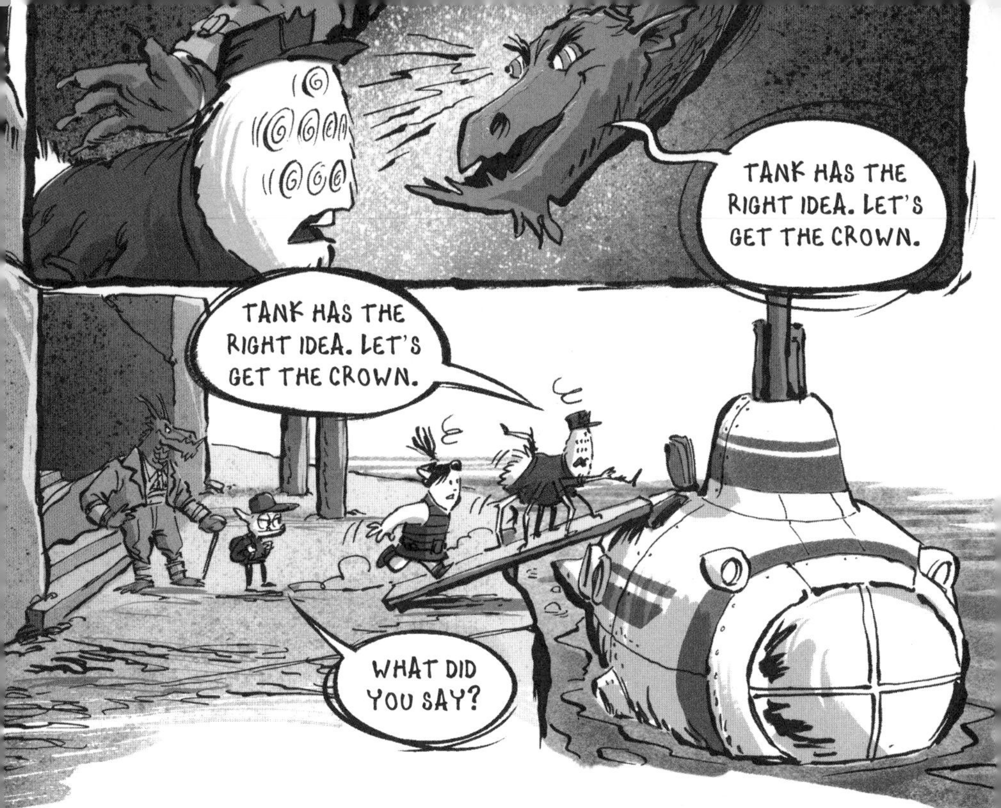
TANK HAS THE RIGHT IDEA. LET'S GET THE CROWN.
TANK HAS THE RIGHT IDEA. LET'S GET THE CROWN.
WHAT DID YOU SAY?

Hugo scuttled over to the sub and was on top in a hop. Tank raced along the plank and onto the sub. They both disappeared down the hatch. Swallowed into the blackness of that mechanical contraption.

Firebane appeared at my side.

"It seems your friends know what they want." The dragon grinned. Teeth sharp and ready. "The only question is, do you?"

The fires of the lake danced on the magma waves. The rhythm of the flames soothed the rushing in my head.

“Go on, Mr. Detective!” Firebane’s words soothed. “Find the Crown of Peace and you will be the greatest detective in Rockfall Mountain.”

“The greatest detective in Rockfall Mountain.” Firebane’s words spilled out of me. Saying them made me realize the dragon was right. If I retrieved the crown, I would be a hero. My name would go down in history. The smartest sleuth in Rockfall Mountain. My worries vanished. Firebane’s words danced in my mind. I stepped into the sub.

The hatch closed with a slam, and everything went dark. The ringing in my head returned. Followed by a big burst of light.

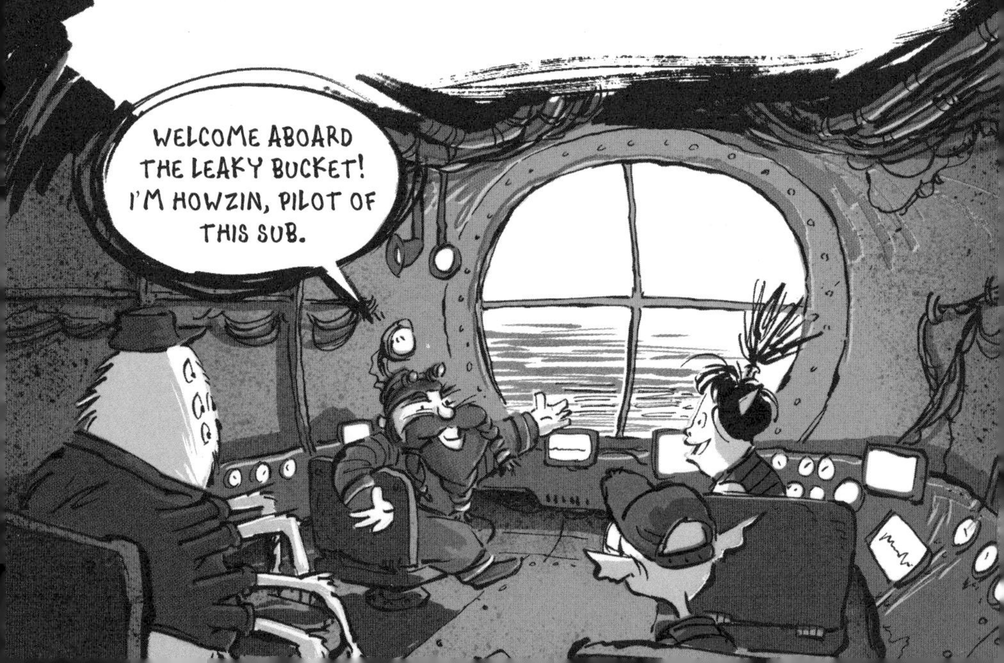
WELCOME ABOARD THE LEAKY BUCKET! I'M HOWZIN, PILOT OF THIS SUB.

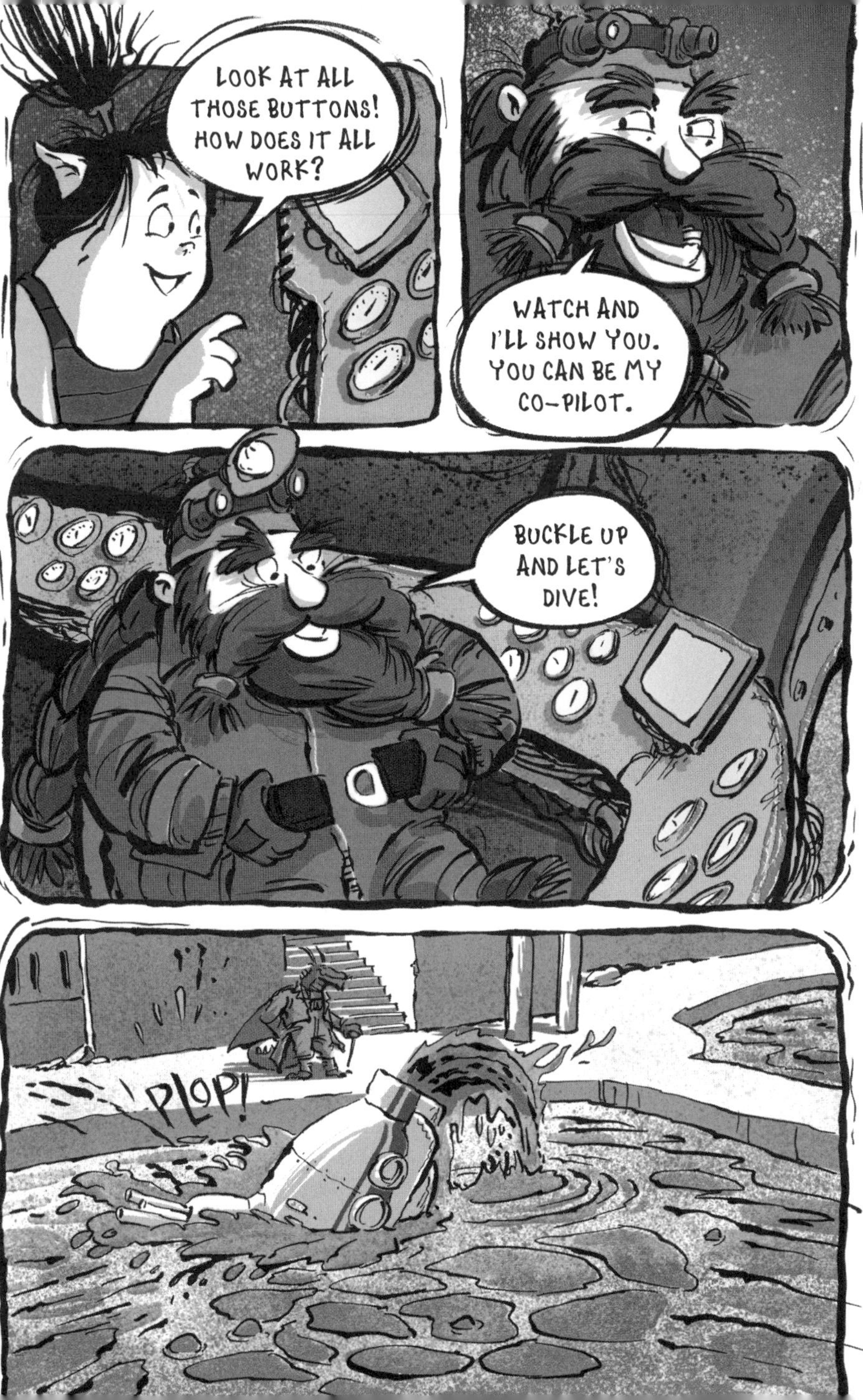
LOOK AT ALL THOSE BUTTONS! HOW DOES IT ALL WORK?
WATCH AND I'LL SHOW YOU. YOU CAN BE MY CO-PILOT.
BUCKLE UP AND LET'S DIVE!
PLOP!

The *Leaky Bucket* creaked as it dropped under the surface of the lava lake. Liquid fire washed over the submarine, but we didn't burst into flames or melt away. Through the front window we saw currents of glowing red lava swirling around the tiny craft.

"Don't you worry, my friends. We're perfectly safe in here." Howzin's wide face lit up with a wide smile. "The *Leaky Bucket* is the safest sub in all of Lava Falls. No lava has ever breached her hull."

"Then why is she called the *Leaky Bucket*?" I asked.

"For good luck, silly goblin!" The dwarf burst into laughter. He chuckled as he pointed to a row of controls in front of Tank. "All right, co-pilot, activate those switches one at a time, please. We need to speed up our descent."

Tank eagerly flipped the switches. The *Leaky Bucket* groaned again, and my stomach did a backflip. The lava outside the window swirled by us a little faster. The engine banged like it was trying to escape.

"Don't worry about those noises," Howzin said. "The sub is just adjusting to all the heat. That lava sure is hot."

"I'll take your word for it," I said.

"Are you sure we're safe in here?" Hugo hugged his chair with his long legs.

"Perfectly safe!" Howzin said. "These subs travel through the lake every day, carrying supplies to the dwarf mines. The best gems are always under lava lakes. Relax and enjoy the view."

That's kind of hard, when your view is filled with scale-scorching lava. Outside the windows a fiery world filled with life drifted by. Tiny shapes floated in the lava. They darted away as we got closer.

"Are those fish?" Tank asked.

"They sure are," Howzin said. "The lava lakes are bursting with life. Flaming flounders, cinder eels, searing pike and more. Each lava pool is a world of living creatures."

Howzin steered the sub through the lava, past schools of mysterious fish and deeper into the mountain we all called home. Firebane's words ran through my mind. If I could find the Crown of Peace, I would be saving all those lives from destruction. That was worth risking a ride through fire in a sinking metal ship, wasn't it?

Suddenly a dark shape, larger than the others, moved across the sub's front window.

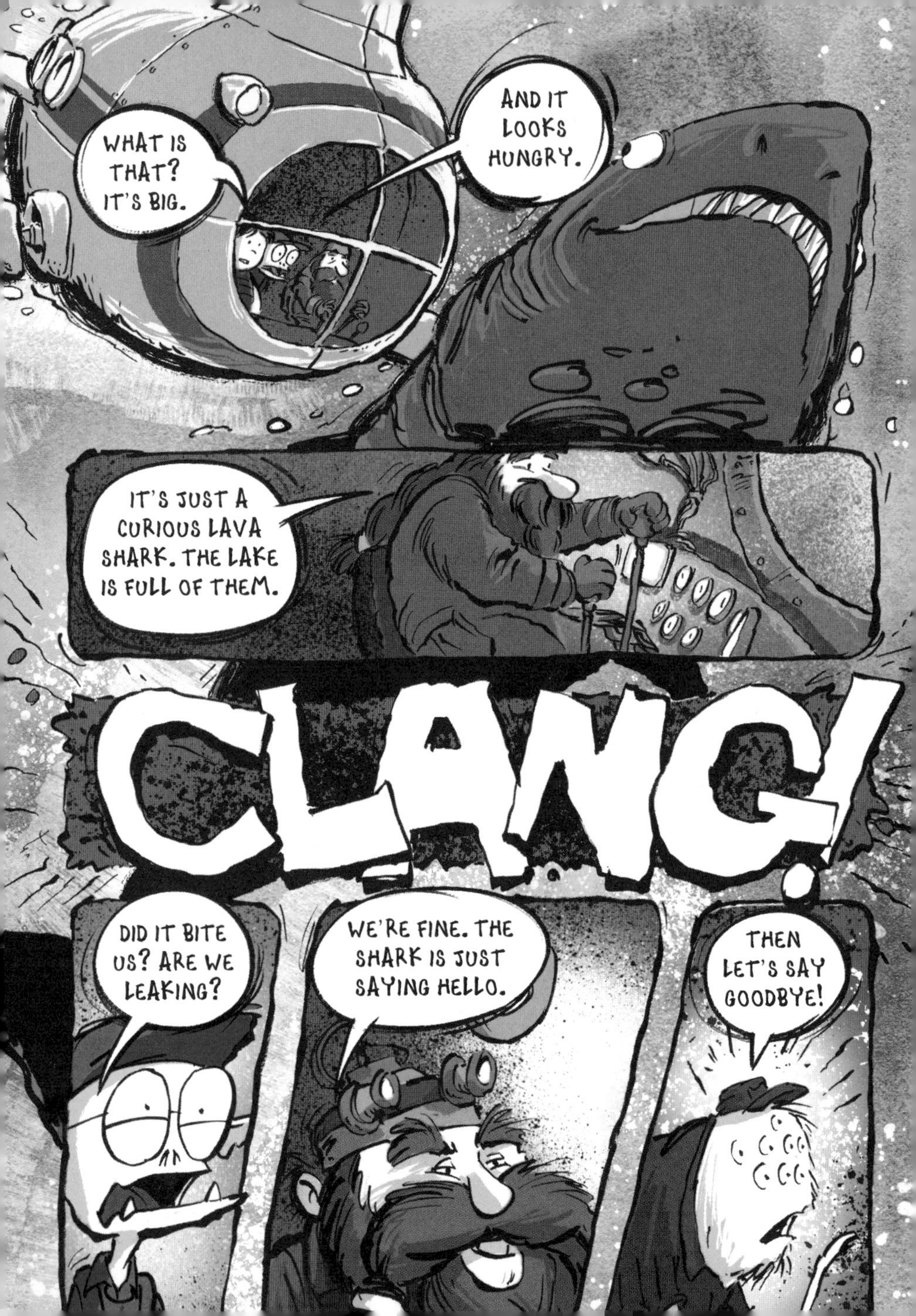
WHAT IS THAT? IT'S BIG.
AND IT LOOKS HUNGRY.
IT'S JUST A CURIOUS LAVA SHARK. THE LAKE IS FULL OF THEM.
CLANG!
DID IT BITE US? ARE WE LEAKING?
WE'RE FINE. THE SHARK IS JUST SAYING HELLO.
THEN LET'S SAY GOODBYE!

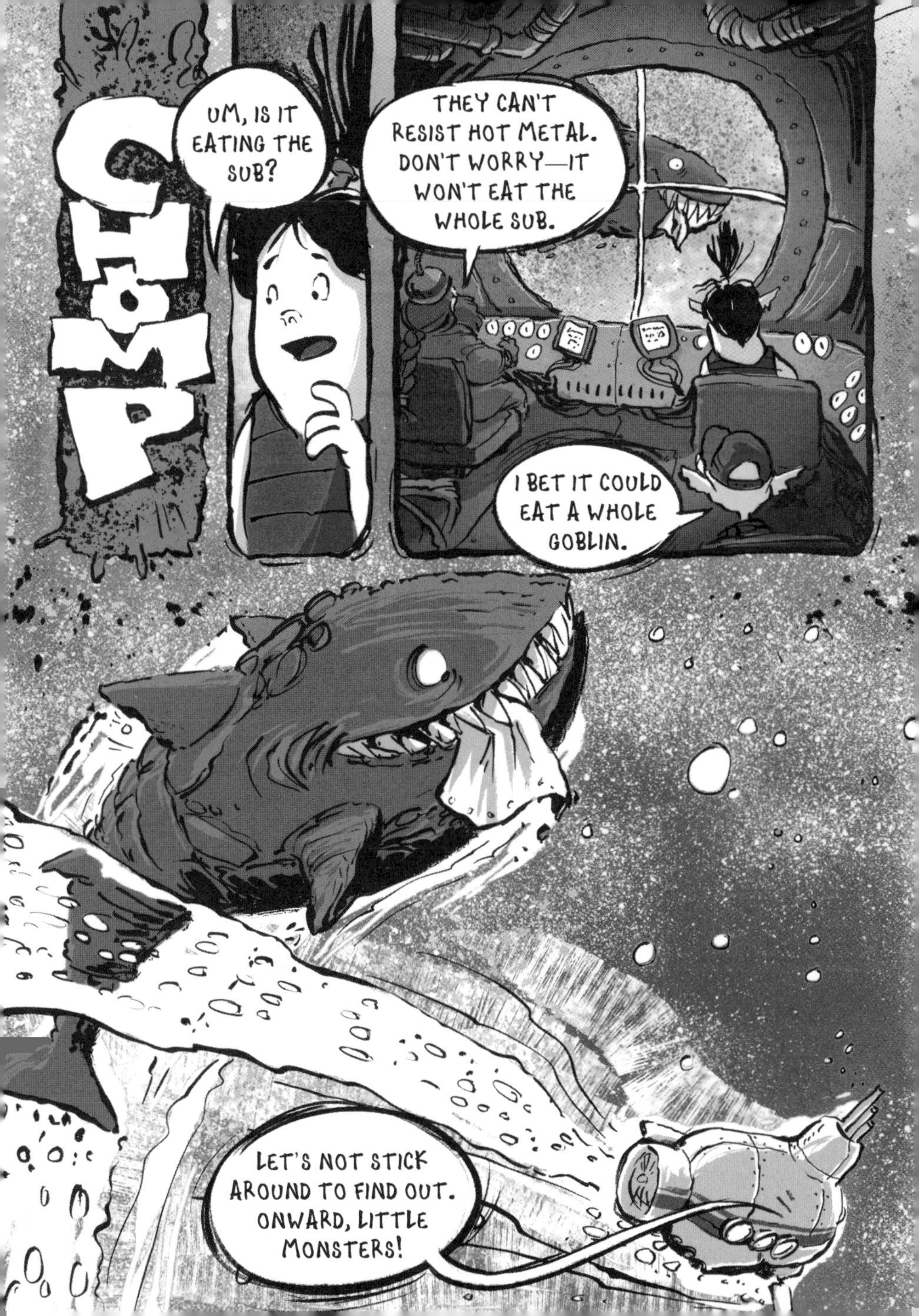
CHOMP
UM, IS IT EATING THE SUB?
THEY CAN'T RESIST HOT METAL. DON'T WORRY—IT WON'T EAT THE WHOLE SUB.
I BET IT COULD EAT A WHOLE GOBLIN.
LET'S NOT STICK AROUND TO FIND OUT. ONWARD, LITTLE MONSTERS!

Howzin steered the sub away from the hungry lava shark. I shuddered as its long body disappeared in the red gloom of lava. If the burning magma didn't get you, the lake's hungry creatures surely would.

I pushed thoughts of sub-eating sharks from my mind and tried to focus on what lay ahead. All we had to do was sneak into Bramgrum's hideout, find the most powerful artifact in all of Rockfall Mountain and sneak back out with it. What could be easier? The craziness of the plan rushed in around me like the sub had sprung a leak. There was no way three kids could sneak past a pair of seasoned criminals like Bramgrum and Hagnar. My scales stood on edge. This was all a big mistake. We had to turn back. I opened my mouth to demand we stop the sub, but nothing came out. Firebane's words swam into my head like a passing lava shark. *Greatest detective in Rockfall Mountain.* Everyone would call me that. That's what I wanted. Wasn't it?

The sub pushed through the surface of the lava. Thick magma dripped off it like cleaning slimes chasing a tasty piece of garbage. Dim light spilled through the sub's window.

We were in a cavern deep under the lake. The low ceiling was spiked with hanging rocks ready to fall into the small lava lake below. Our sub bobbed across the surface toward the docks on the rocky shore.

"There it is!" Howzin called. "Get ready to dock, little monsters."

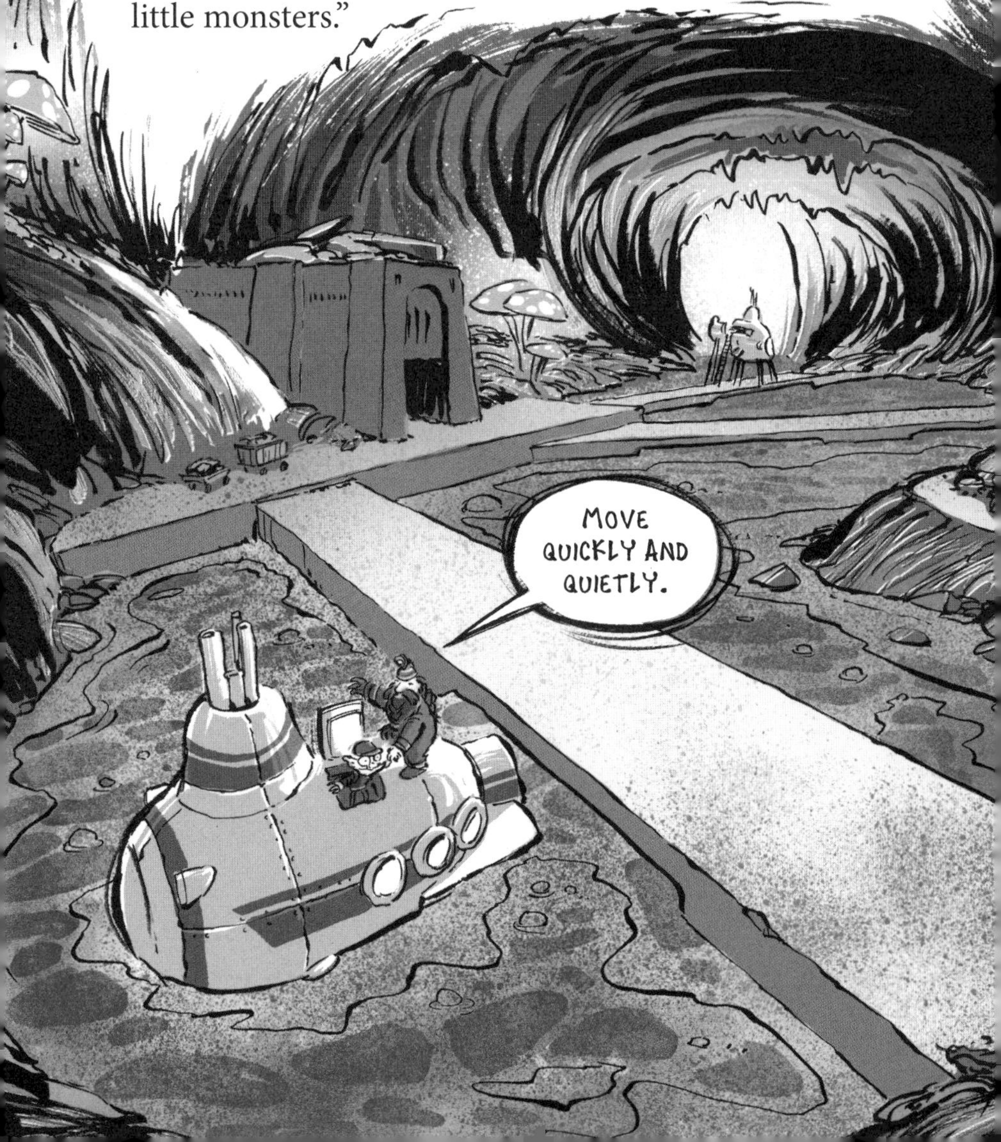
MOVE QUICKLY AND QUIETLY.

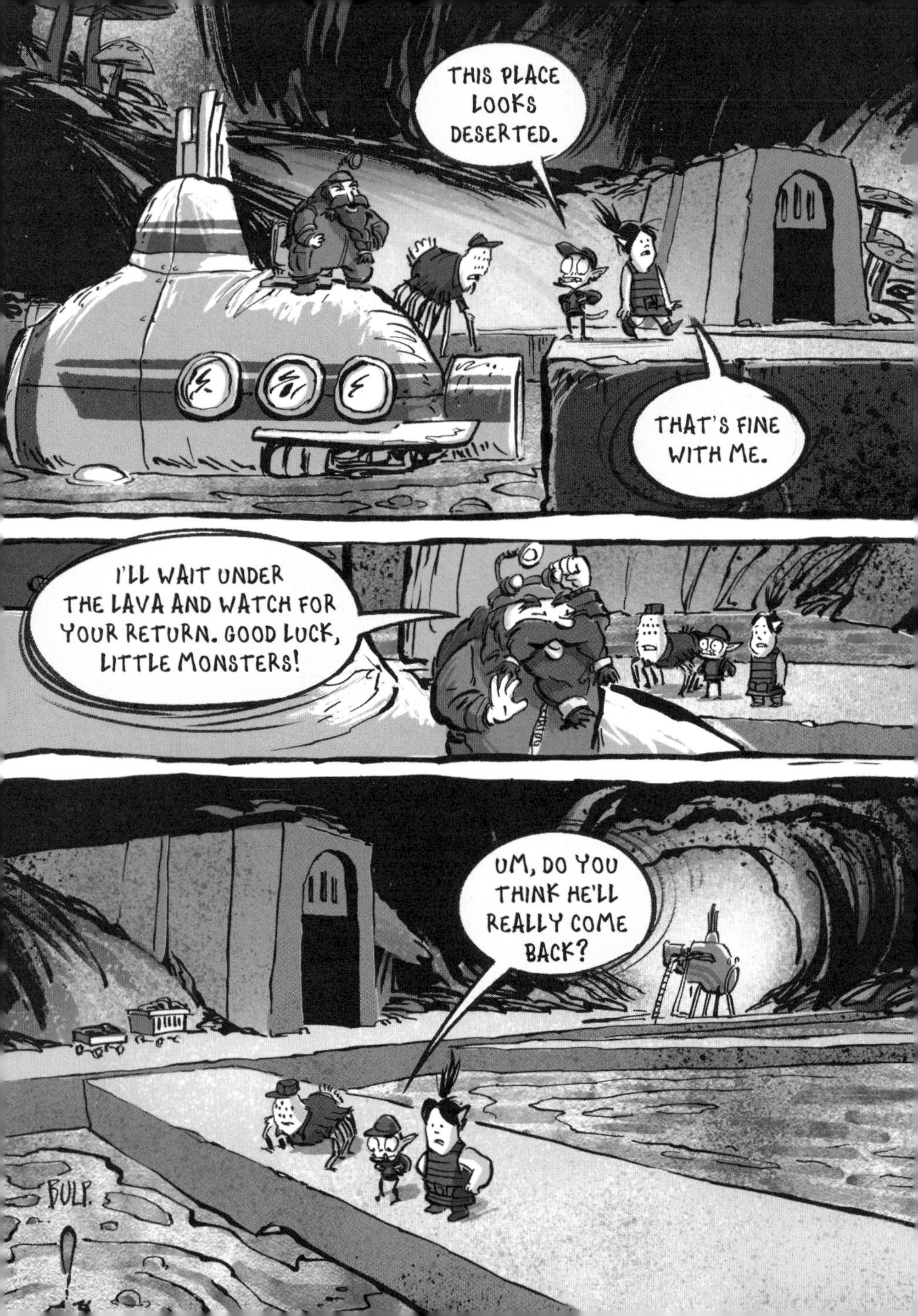
THIS PLACE LOOKS DESERTED.
THAT'S FINE WITH ME.
I'LL WAIT UNDER THE LAVA AND WATCH FOR YOUR RETURN. GOOD LUCK, LITTLE MONSTERS!
UM, DO YOU THINK HE'LL REALLY COME BACK?
BULP.

CHAPTER TWELVE
Beneath the Flames

Bramgrum's hideout was as empty as my folder of finished homework.

After Howzin disappeared under the lava, we hurried from the deserted docks. Hugo led us toward a large tunnel in the wall of rock that surrounded the cavern. The sandy ground leading into the opening had been trampled smooth by many passing feet. Now, however, the tunnel loomed dark and silent in front of us. Behind us, the small lava lake bubbled and boiled like it was ready to erupt. I guess lava is always like that. There was no sign of Howzin or the *Leaky Bucket* in the fiery liquid. Hugo scurried up the wall of the tunnel.

"Wait here. I'll scout ahead." He looked back down at us from the roof of the tunnel. "Spiders are good in the dark."

He vanished in the shadows. Beside me, Tank studied the tectonic-frequency tracker. The machine's light flashed more quickly down here under the lava lake.

"The docks might be empty," she said, "but the crown is definitely close. I'm picking up a strong signal down that tunnel."

"I don't get it," I said. "Why steal the crown and then hide it down here? You would think Bramgrum would be demanding a mountain of gems for its return before the resetting in a few hours. Hiding it down here guarantees the mountain is going to be destroyed."

Tank shrugged. "Maybe Bramgrum isn't as smart as everyone says."

"Do you really believe that?"

"I don't know what to believe anymore," Tank said. "All I know is, we need to get the crown back to the braces very soon, and this machine is telling me it's down that tunnel somewhere."

"Hopefully, that's all that's down the tunnel."

Hugo appeared from the shadows. He crawled along on the roof, then zipped down to the ground on a thread of thin web.

"It's really quiet in there—too quiet," he said. "I went as far as the end of the tunnel and didn't see anyone. It's strange."

"It's very strange," I said.

"Let's just get in, find that crown and get out of here." Tank stepped into the tunnel. Her eyes stayed glued to the tracker as she went.

Hugo zipped back up his thread and scuttled along the tunnel after the troll. I gave the deserted dock one last glance and followed them both into the darkness.

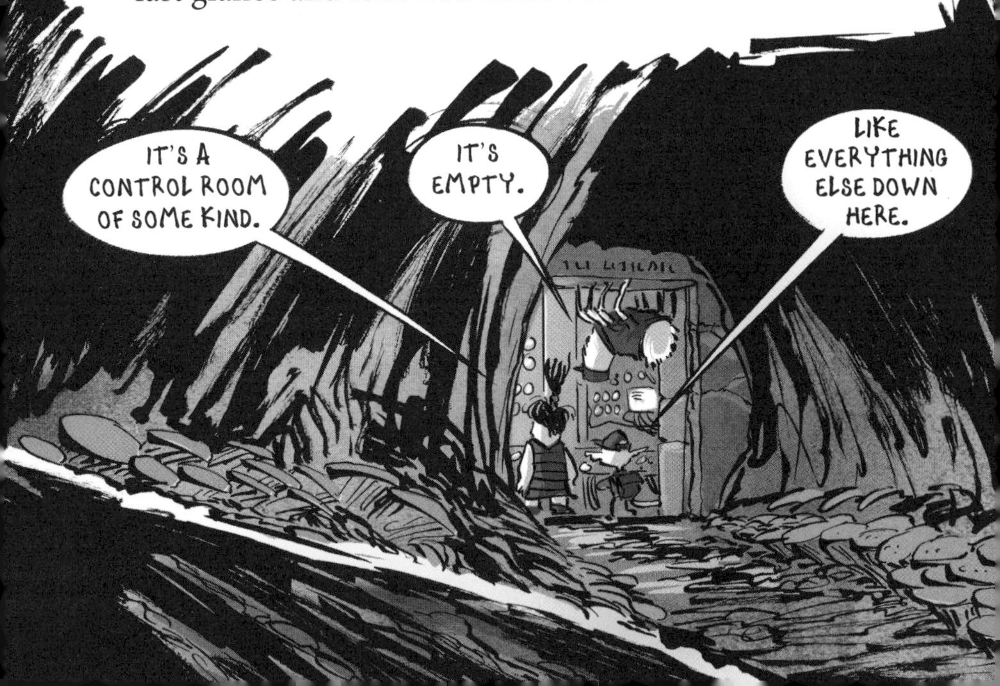
IT'S A CONTROL ROOM OF SOME KIND.
IT'S EMPTY.
LIKE EVERYTHING ELSE DOWN HERE.

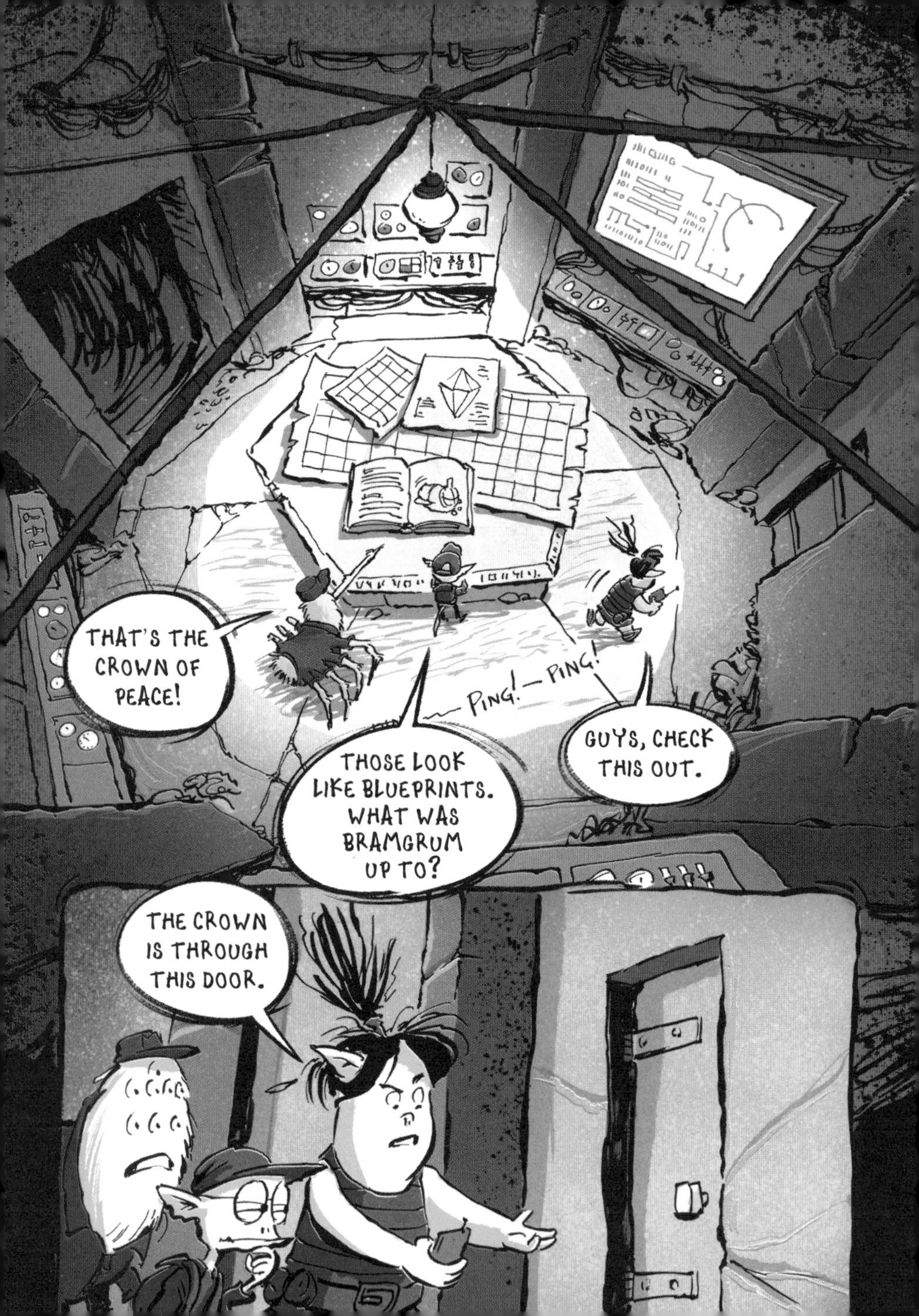
THAT'S THE CROWN OF PEACE!
THOSE LOOK LIKE BLUEPRINTS. WHAT WAS BRAMGRUM UP TO?
PING!—PING!
GUYS, CHECK THIS OUT.
THE CROWN IS THROUGH THIS DOOR.

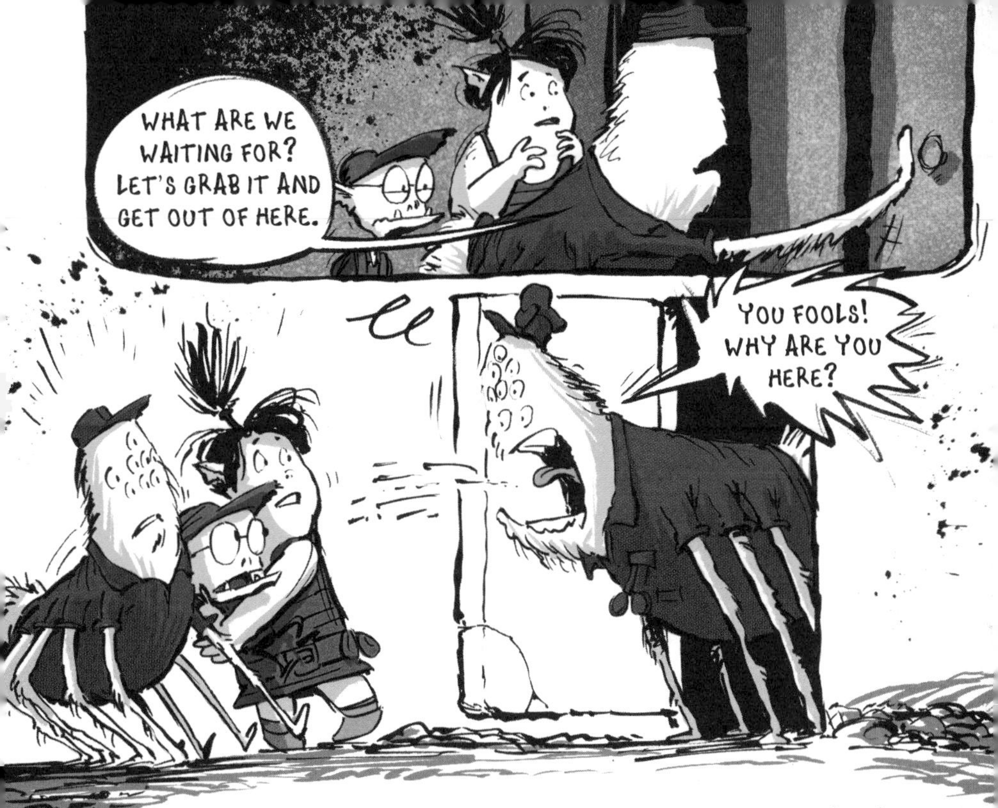
WHAT ARE WE WAITING FOR? LET'S GRAB IT AND GET OUT OF HERE.
YOU FOOLS! WHY ARE YOU HERE?

The spider captain rose up on his legs. He rushed from the room. He pushed past Tank and jumped onto the big table, sending the maps scattering to the ground. His eyes darted around the room.

"You shouldn't have come here!" Scorn shrieked.

You'd think I'd run away from Scorn as fast as my green feet could take me. But I didn't. There was something about the way the spider captain was acting that made me stay. He hopped around nervously on the table with a wild look in his eyes.

"Captain Scorn? Are you all right?" Hugo approached the spider slowly. "It's me, Hugo. It's your son."

My scales nearly fell off.

"Y-your son?" I stammered. "Hugo, what are you talking about?"

The young spider raised a leg to silence me.

"Father, it's me. Hugo. Something has come over you." Hugo took another step closer to Scorn. "You are ill—that's why you betrayed the queen. But I'm here to help."

Scorn's eyes locked onto Hugo. Confusion flashed across the captain's face. He wasn't the only one at a loss. All this time, Hugo had kept his connection to Scorn a secret. No wonder the spider was willing to sneak away from his home. He didn't go into that swamp to rescue us. He was searching for his father.

Tank's voice came from the other room.

"Fizz! Get in here!"

I left Hugo with his father and joined Tank in the smaller room. It was some sort of storage closet. There was barely enough room for both of us.

"You won't believe what just happened!" I said.

It was Tank's turn to silence me with a raised hand. The tracker in her hand was pinging like it was going to pop.

"It says the crown should be right here." Tank's ears flopped down the side of her head. "But I can't see it anywhere."

A small grate sat in the floor at her feet.

"You think it's in there?" I said.

"Why would the crown be stuck in a drainage grate?" she said. "It makes no sense."

"There is very little that makes any sense right now, Tank."

I pried open the grate. Something glittered at the bottom of the hole. I reached in and picked up something small and heavy. When I pulled my arm out of the hole, I held a purple rock the size of a choco-slug cookie. Tank's phone went into pinging overload.

"That's not the crown." My friend's ears perked up and then sagged again. "Something's not right."

Tank's tracker continued to ping like it was sitting right on top of the crown. But all I had was a purple rock, a growing headache and no idea what was going on. And then I did.

"Do you think this rock is actually made of pan-whatever-you-call-it?"

"Panzantium? That's it!" Tank's ears returned to wiggling. "The tracker wasn't looking for the crown. It was looking for the jewel in the crown, panzantium."

"But Firebane said panzantium is really rare," I said. "What are the chances of a piece just sitting in a drain for us to find?"

"Pretty slim." Tank turned off the tracker, and the pinging stopped. "Who would put an incredibly rare gem in a hole down here?"

"Someone who knew you'd be looking for it," I said.

"Scorn will know," Tank said.

I stopped her at the door. "Yeah, there's something you need to know about Scorn."

I filled my friend in on the family reunion happening in the other room. Tank peered through the door and frowned.

"Um, what is Scorn doing now?" I asked.

The spider captain had climbed to the highest corner of the room and covered it with sticky web. He zipped from one side of the web to the other, adding more threads of webbing to his creation. Hugo watched from the ground, shaking his head sadly.

"He is not well," the young spider said. "He doesn't recognize me."

"But he's your dad, right?" Tank said.

"He is," Hugo said quickly. "And I'm sorry I didn't tell you before. I didn't think you would trust me if you knew I was related to the spider who left you in the swamp."

"No need to apologize," I said.

"Don't worry about it." Tank put her arm around Hugo. "Families are complicated."

"Thanks." Hugo wiped a tear from one of his eyes. "He is under some kind of spell."

Scorn continued to dart around in the corner, weaving his web.

"Hopefully, he can still answer some questions." I held up the panzantium. "Captain Scorn, who hid this in the other room?"

Scorn turned at the sound of his name. His eyes doubled in size when he saw the stone in my hand.

"You found it!" He zipped from one side of his web to the other and back again. "We're doomed. Why did you take it?"

My gut tightened like I had just eaten a pile of stale fungi fries. Questions poured through my mind, each one stickier than Scorn's web.

"Who put the stone in the grate, Scorn?" I said.

"They did!" Scorn moaned. "They said you would come, and no one must touch the stone. But you did. And now we're doomed!"

"Who are *they*?" Tank said. "Who knew we were coming? Bramgrum the dwarf and Hagnar the ogre?"

"Ogre? Silly troll, there's no ogre." Scorn scurried around his web, adding more sticky thread as he went.

"No ogre?" I said. "Maybe Hagnar didn't come down here. But where's the crown?"

"The crown is gone!" Scorn shouted. Then he whispered, "And it's never coming back."

"But it was here before?" I stepped closer to the spider.

Scorn nodded quickly. "They did experiments on it. Improved it, they said."

"Improved the crown?" Tank said. "How?"

If Scorn knew, he wasn't telling us.

"Now only the shiny stone is here," the spider said. "They wanted you to find it. And you did!"

"Who wanted us to find it?" Hugo asked.

"The dwarf and his boss. Who else?"

"The dwarf's *boss*?" Tank tugged her ponytail. "Firebane said Bramgrum was in charge."

Hugo nodded. "He called him the ringleader. Maybe Scorn, er, I mean Dad, is mistaken." My brain felt like it was swimming in lava. Scorn was either talking nonsense or the complete truth. How would Bramgrum know we would be down here? The only other monster who knew we were coming was Firebane. This whole thing smelled like a setup. Had Bramgrum spied on Firebane to learn his secrets?

The screen on the wall above the control panel crackled to life. The static cleared to reveal a scarred face we knew all too well.

"Bramgrum!" Tank said.

"Greetings!" The dwarf waved into the camera. "It's so good to finally meet Tank and Fizz, the famous detectives."

Tank turned to me. "Why does everyone know us down here?"

"We're onto you, Bramgrum!" I shouted at the screen. "We know you have the crown. Return it before Rockfall Mountain gets sucked into the Abyss."

"That's a funny one, Fizz Marlow!" Bramgrum laughed so hard his beard nearly fell off his face. "For a detective, you're clueless. You're not living up to the stories I've been forced to listen to. But you did find the panzantium, right? Fresh from the scaly one's vault, that is."

Tank held up the stone. "We found it in your little hidey-hole."

"Well done!" Bramgrum cheered. "That hidey-hole should be filling up nicely right about now."

"*Filling up*? What are you talking about, Bramgrum?" I snapped.

Before I got my answer, the screen went blank and Bramgrum was gone. What did he mean he had been *forced* to listen to stories about us? Who would make a known criminal sit through tales of a fourth-grader like me? And what was this talk about the panzantium coming from the scaly one's vault? My tail froze in midswing.

"Firebane!"

"What about him?" Hugo asked.

"He set us up," I said. "Bramgrum isn't the ringleader. Firebane is. There's only one scaly monster rich enough to have a vault filled with rare gems like panzantium."

"Firebane told Bramgrum all about us." Tank's ears wiggled. "The old dragon bragged that he tells all his friends about the detectives who saved his loot. Remember?"

I nodded. "And Firebane sent us all down here with that pinging machine. He knew it would lead us right to the hidden panzantium stone."

"And that's how Bramgrum knew we would be here," Tank said.

Hugo scratched his head with three of his legs. "But why would Firebane send us to an empty room in the bottom of a lava lake? I don't get it."

My tail started swinging again. "I'm still working on that."

Captain Scorn's head popped out from his webby nest.

"Here it comes!" he shouted. "You sprung Bramgrum's trap."

I turned to the spider captain. "What trap?"

Scorn pointed a leg toward the room where we had found the panzantium. Lava bubbled up from the grate in the floor and spilled through the doorway. As I watched, the trickle of lava turned into a gushing fountain of fire.

"Oh, *that* trap," I said.

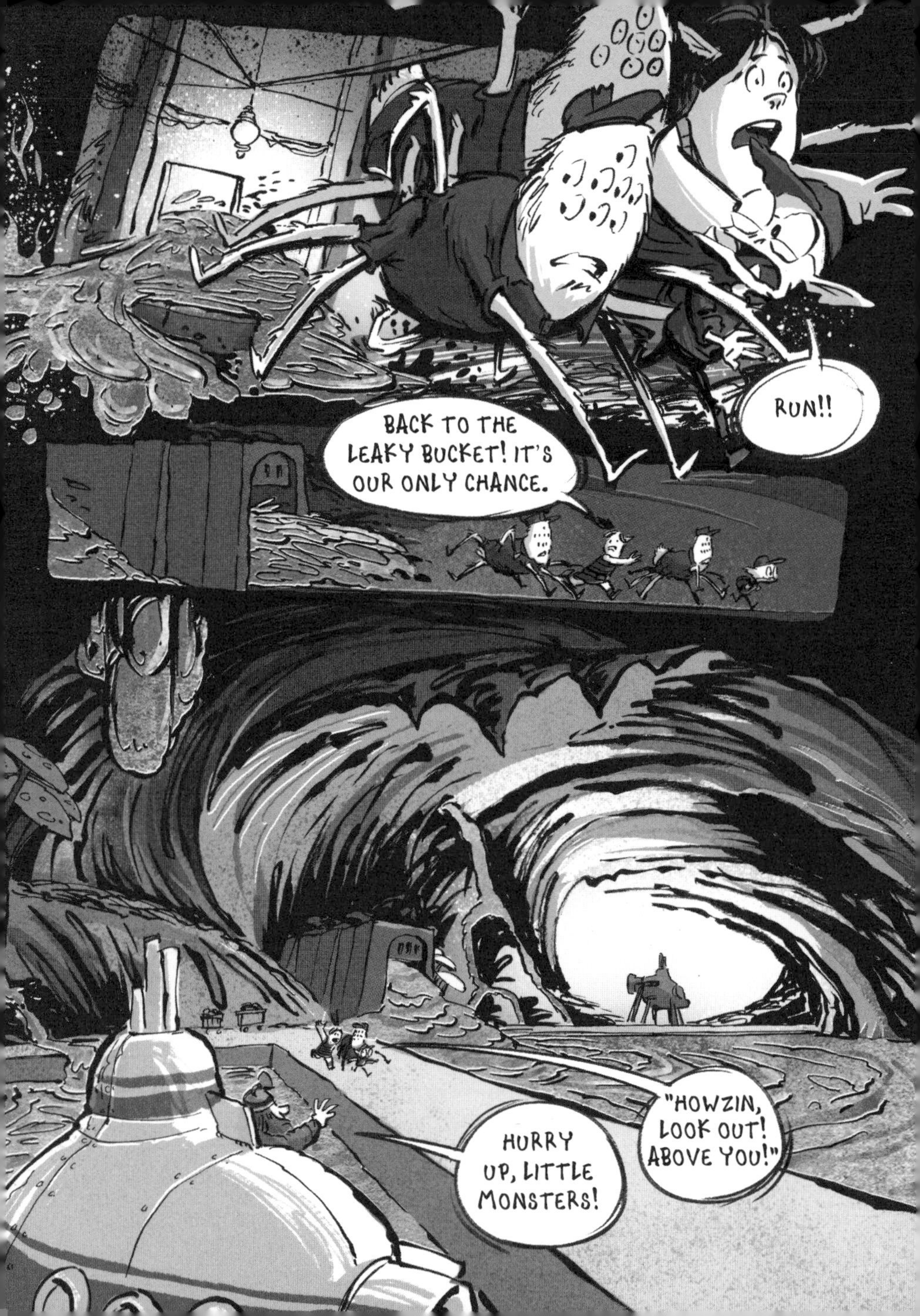
RUN!!
BACK TO THE LEAKY BUCKET! IT'S OUR ONLY CHANCE.
"HOWZIN, LOOK OUT! ABOVE YOU!"
HURRY UP, LITTLE MONSTERS!

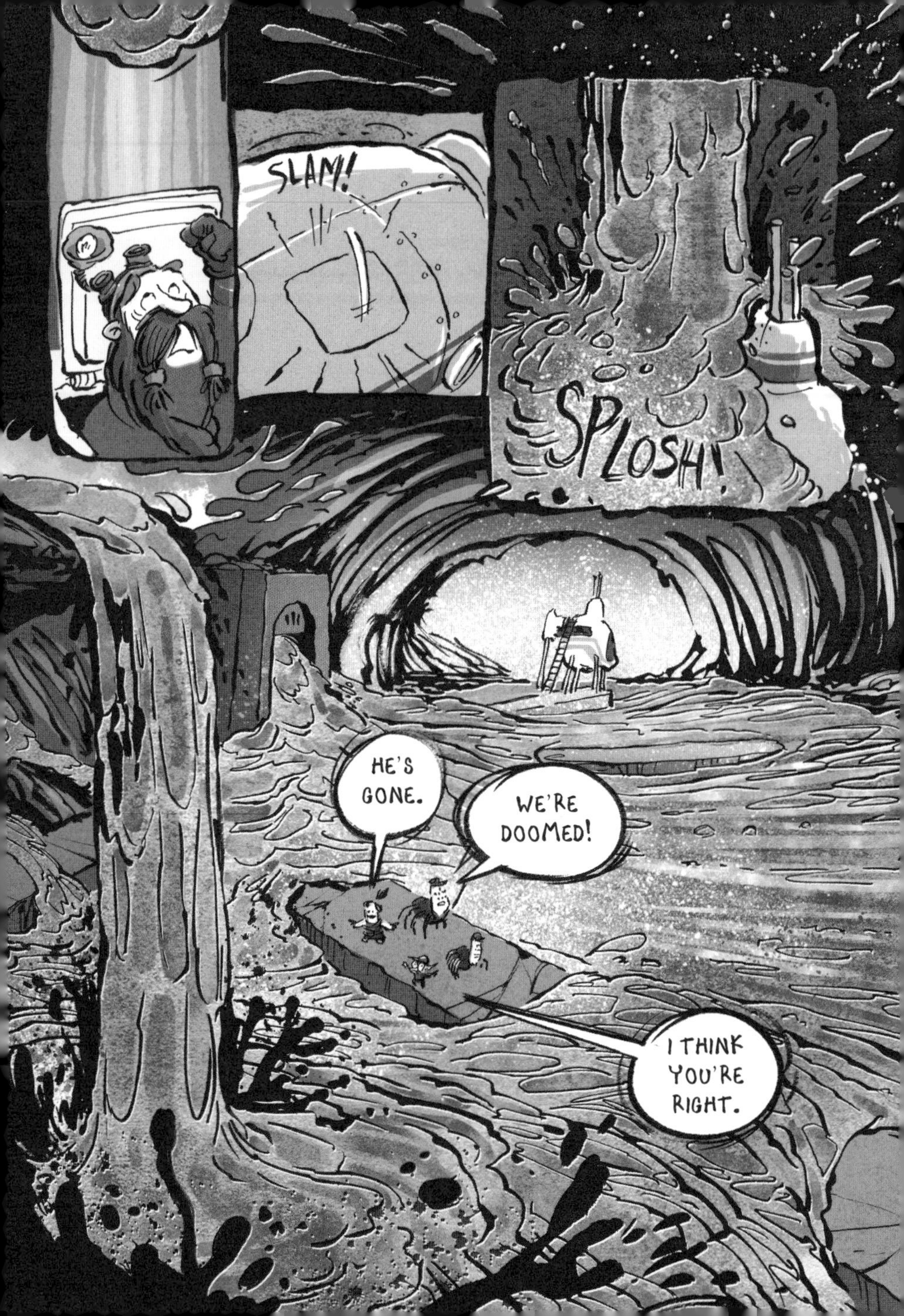
SLAM!
SPLOSH!
HE'S GONE.
WE'RE DOOMED!
I THINK YOU'RE RIGHT.

CHAPTER THIRTEEN
Fiery Escape

Lava roared around us.

Molten rock gushed, splashed and poured into the cavern. The *Leaky Bucket* had vanished under the waves of magma. Bramgrum and Firebane had booby-trapped the whole cavern. And we were the boobies. Pulling the stone from the grate had released a floodgate of lava.

My scales burned, and it wasn't because of the burning liquid surrounding me. I had been duped. We all had. Firebane had played us for fools. He had filled my head with dreams of being a hero when he knew he was leading us to our doom. We were right where he wanted us, trapped and far away, with the resetting of the braces happening very soon.

"There's no way out!" Tank moaned.

"Maybe there is." Hugo shot a web into the ceiling above us. "Dad, follow me. Tank and Fizz, hang on!"

Hugo zipped up the web and into the air high above me. Something sticky smacked into my back, and I was pulled into the air.

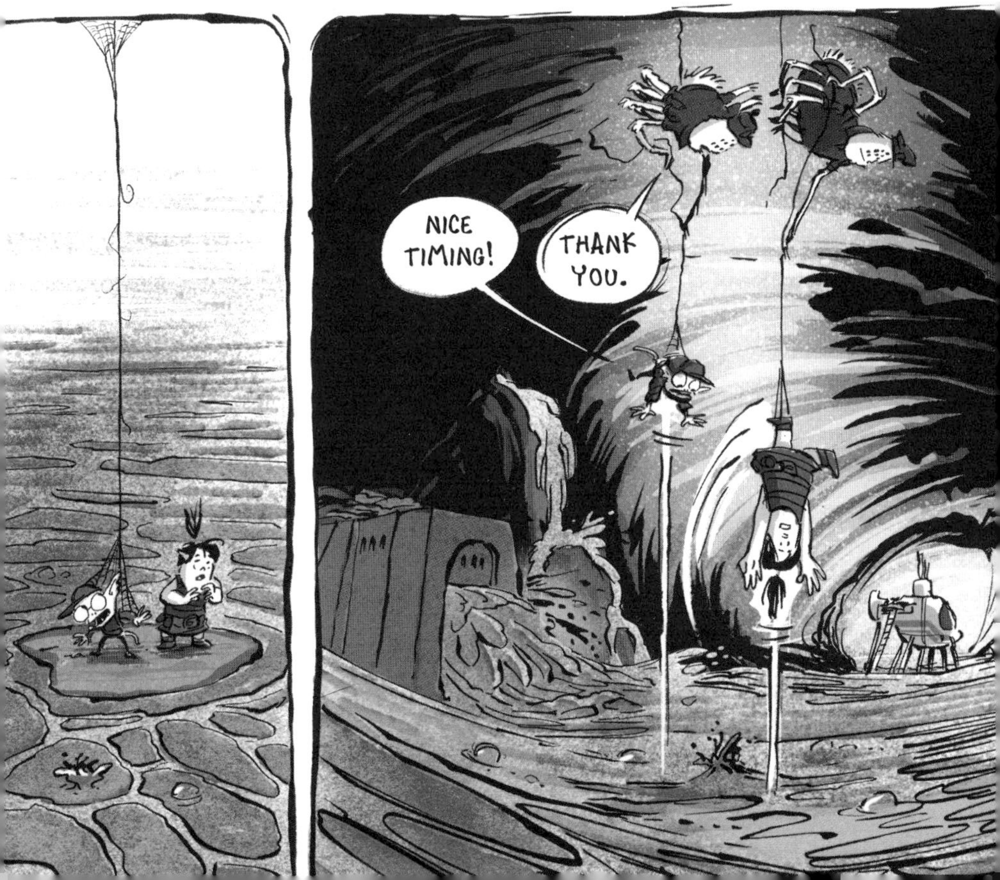
NICE TIMING!
THANK YOU.

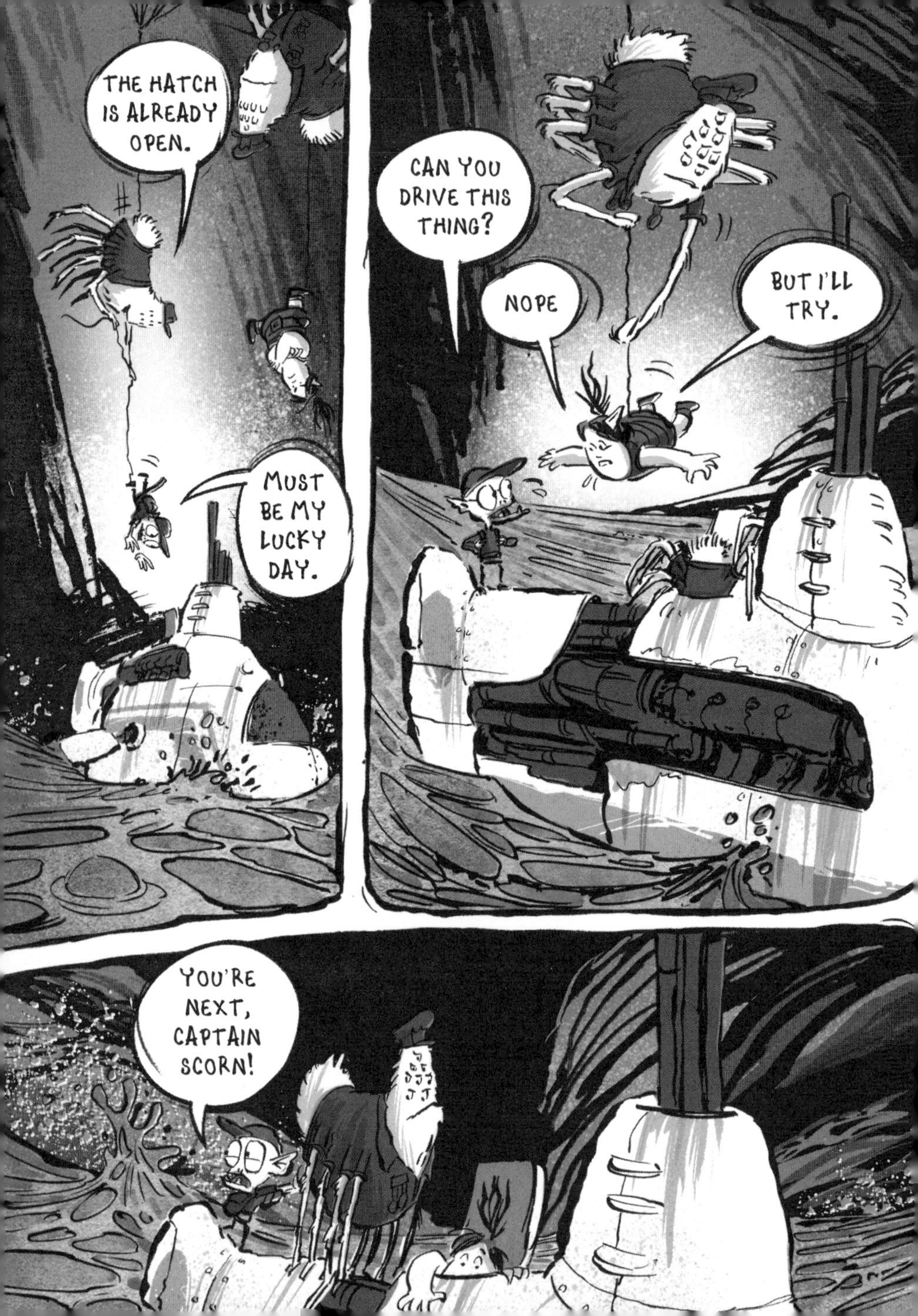
THE HATCH IS ALREADY OPEN.
MUST BE MY LUCKY DAY.
CAN YOU DRIVE THIS THING?
NOPE
BUT I'LL TRY.
YOU'RE NEXT, CAPTAIN SCORN!

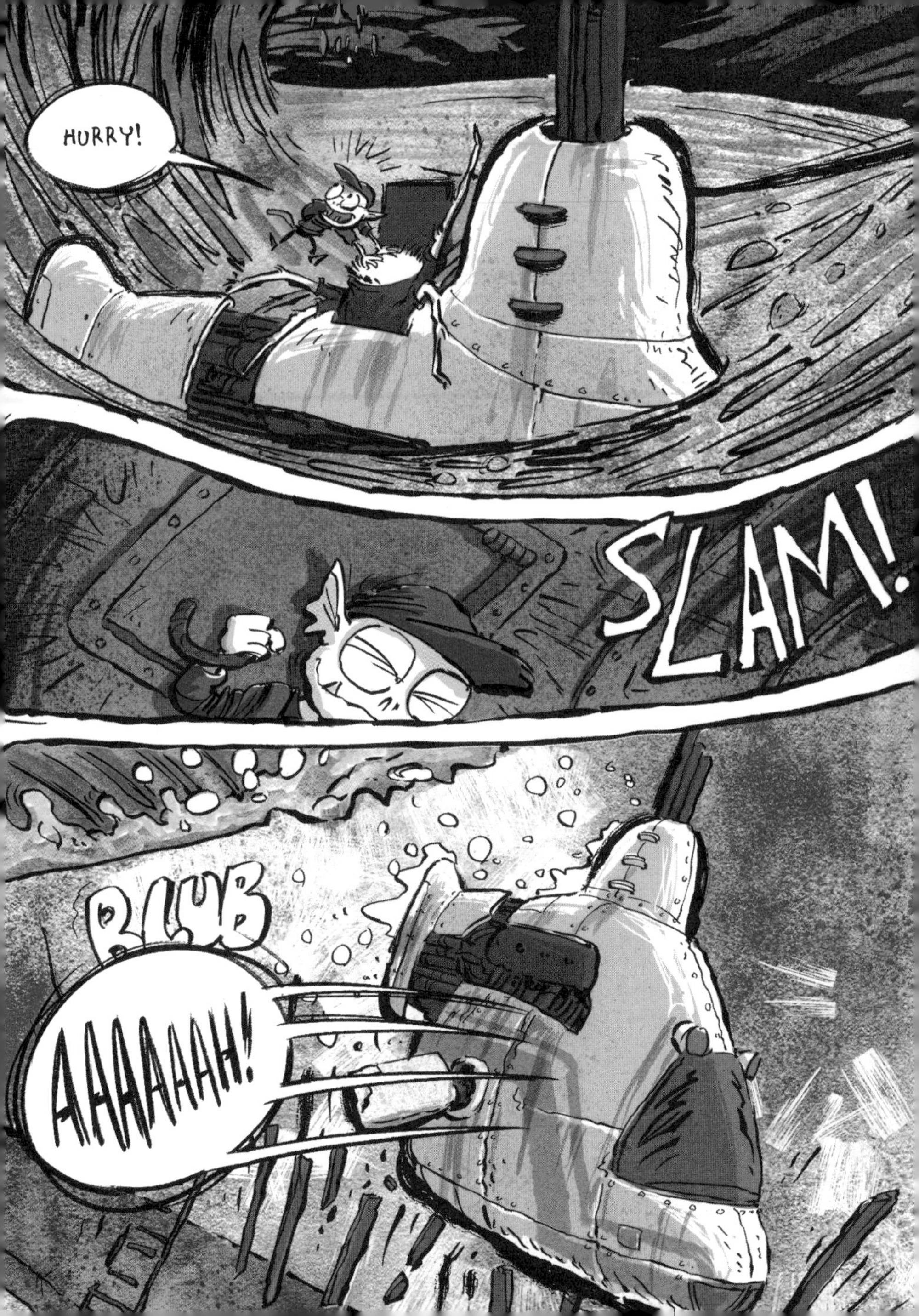
HURRY!
SLAM!
BLUB
AAAAAAH!

The sub was a mess, but it was better than swimming in lava.

The seats were missing. The flashing lights and switches were gone. Wires sprouted from large holes in the command deck where the controls had been. Tank stood in front of the controls. She pressed an important-looking red button several times. Nothing happened.

"There's no power," she said. "I can't pilot this thing anywhere."

"That's not what I wanted to hear," I said.

Another wave of lava crashed against the rusting hull. The sub rolled with the wave, sending us all to the floor.

"We need to get to the surface," Hugo said.

"That's going to be hard if I can't get the engine to work." Tank was on her knees in front of the command deck. She grinned suddenly. "Hello there. Be right back."

She squeezed into a gap under the control deck and vanished.

"Where'd she go?" Scorn snapped.

Outside the front window, a churning soup of molten rock burned and raged. All that separated us from extreme crispiness was a wall of welded metal a little thicker than my tail. The sub lurched again, but this time we stayed standing. We were being tossed around like a dodgeball in gym class.

Tank crawled out from under the control deck. Grime covered her face.

"The engine looks like it's in good shape," she said. "But the slick tanks are empty. We have no fuel. That's why nothing works."

"We can't get back to Lava Falls without fuel," Hugo said.

"And we can't stay down here for much longer," Tank said. "The rear wall panels are cracked. They'll be letting in lava pretty soon."

"We're at the bottom of a lake of lava, trapped in a submarine that's falling apart and has no fuel," Scorn said. "I liked it better when I was stuck in that room."

Something solid slammed into the sub.

"That didn't sound like a lava wave," Tank said.

Hugo skittered up the wall of the sub. "Did we hit a rock?"

A dark shape drifted past the window. A second shadow followed behind it.

"I think we hit a shark," I muttered. "There's a swarm of lava sharks out there."

"I knew coming in here was a bad idea!" Scorn climbed to the ceiling of the sub and frantically started spinning a web. "They won't stop hitting us until the sub breaks apart."

Another lava shark slammed into the sub, sending us to the floor again.

"You see?" Scorn wailed.

Tank got to her feet and stared out the window. More sharks gathered around the sub with every passing second.

Tank's shoulders slumped. "I'm out of ideas."

"It's okay. You tried." I stood by my friend. A wisp of dark smoke traced a path between us. "Tank, why is your tool belt smoking?"

Tank's hand went to the pocket on her belt. She pulled out a glowing stone. "The panzantium!" She tossed the stone from hand to hand. "It's hot."

"It burned a hole in your belt," I said. "How did it get so hot?"

Hugo zipped along the control panel and peered at the glowing stone with all eight eyes.

"It's the lava," he said. "Panzantium can get hot from just being near fire."

I looked at the swirling sea of lava beyond the window. "There's no shortage of that."

"The dwarves say if panzantium gets hot enough, it can power a whole city," Hugo said.

"Did you say *power*?" Tank's eyes lit up. She turned to me and pointed to the red button on the command deck. "When I shout, push that. Be right back."

She dove under the command deck and disappeared from sight. Seconds later banging sounds came from deep inside the sub.

"What is she doing?" Hugo asked.

"Hopefully, saving our scales," I said.

Outside, more lava sharks had arrived. They swam in wide arcs around the sub before charging straight at the window. Each smash shook the sub and sent us sprawling to the floor.

From somewhere under the floor, Tank shouted, "Now, Fizz!"

I jumped at the panel and pushed the red button. Nothing happened.

"It didn't work, Tank!" I shouted.

Another shark smashed into the sub.

"Fizz, look!" Hugo gasped.

A crack had formed in the window where the shark had struck. Another blow and we'd be swimming in lava.

"Another shark is coming!" Scorn shrieked from his webby hiding spot.

I leaned into the hole below the command deck. "Hurry up, Tank!"

"Try now!" she called back.

I slammed my hand on the red button.

Nothing.

The shark crashed into the window. A shudder ran through the sub. The crack splintered in all directions, but the window didn't break. Yet.

"We're running out of time, Tank!" I called.

Laughter came from under the control deck. My tail curled. My friend had finally lost it. The pressure was too much. I wasn't too far behind.

Another shark rounded on the sub and charged.

"I'm such a noob!" Tank shouted from below. "I forgot to connect the polarity diameter controller!"

"Technical details later, Tank!" I shouted. The lava shark swam straight toward the window. "Can I press the button?"

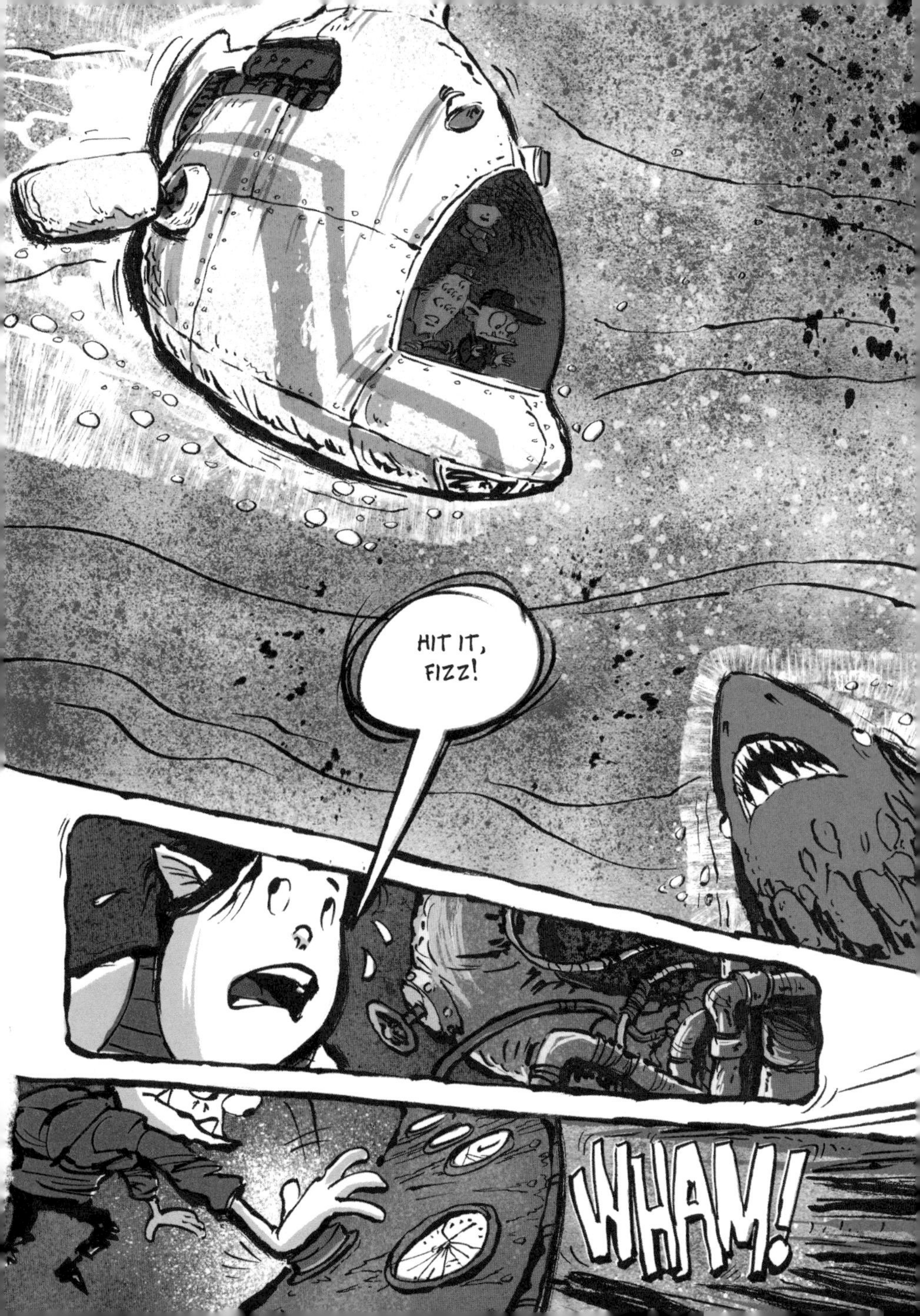
HIT IT, FIZZ!
WHAM!

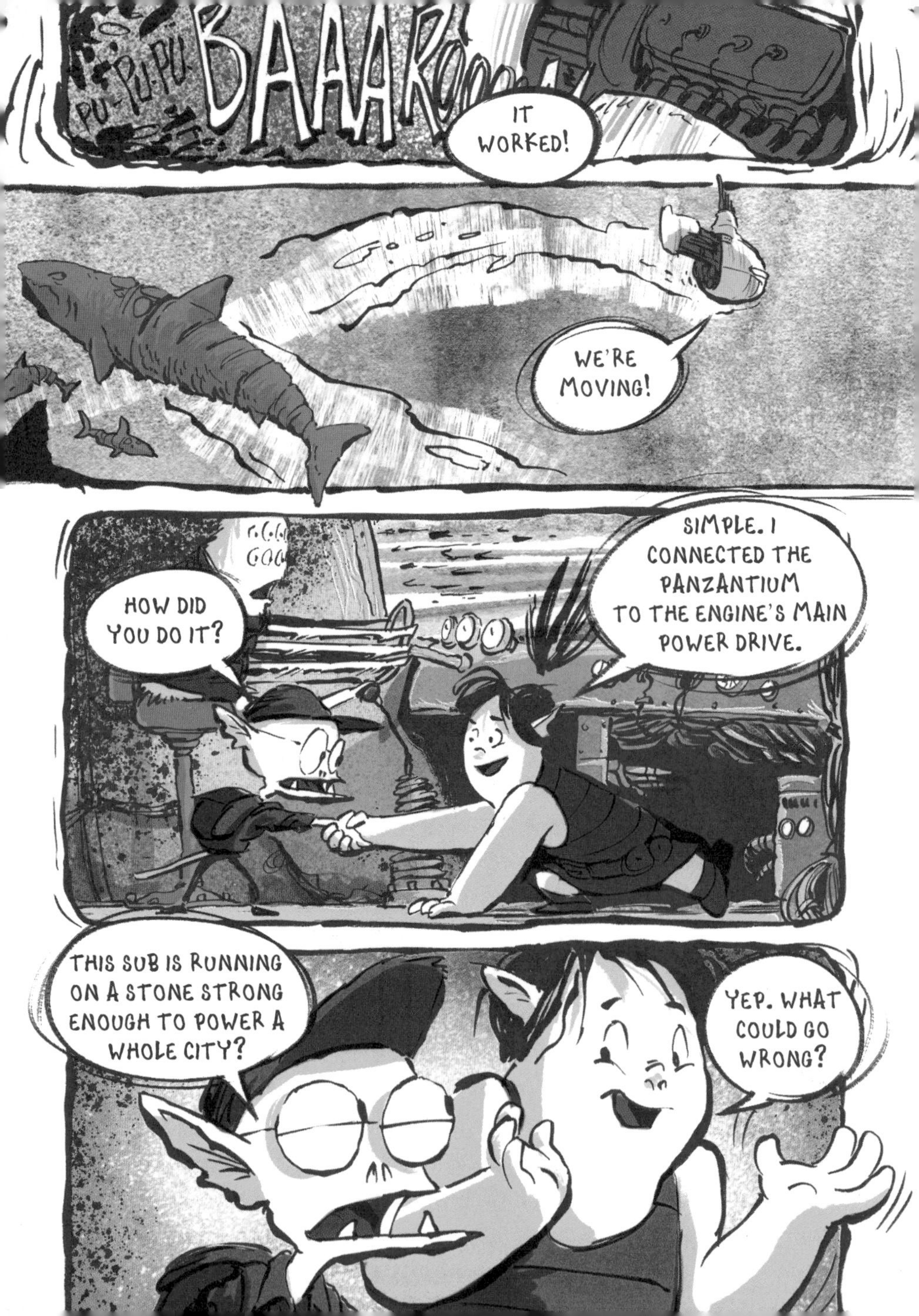
PU-PU-PU-PU-
BAAAROOO...
IT WORKED!
WE'RE MOVING!
HOW DID YOU DO IT?
SIMPLE. I CONNECTED THE PANZANTIUM TO THE ENGINE'S MAIN POWER DRIVE.
THIS SUB IS RUNNING ON A STONE STRONG ENOUGH TO POWER A WHOLE CITY?
YEP. WHAT COULD GO WRONG?

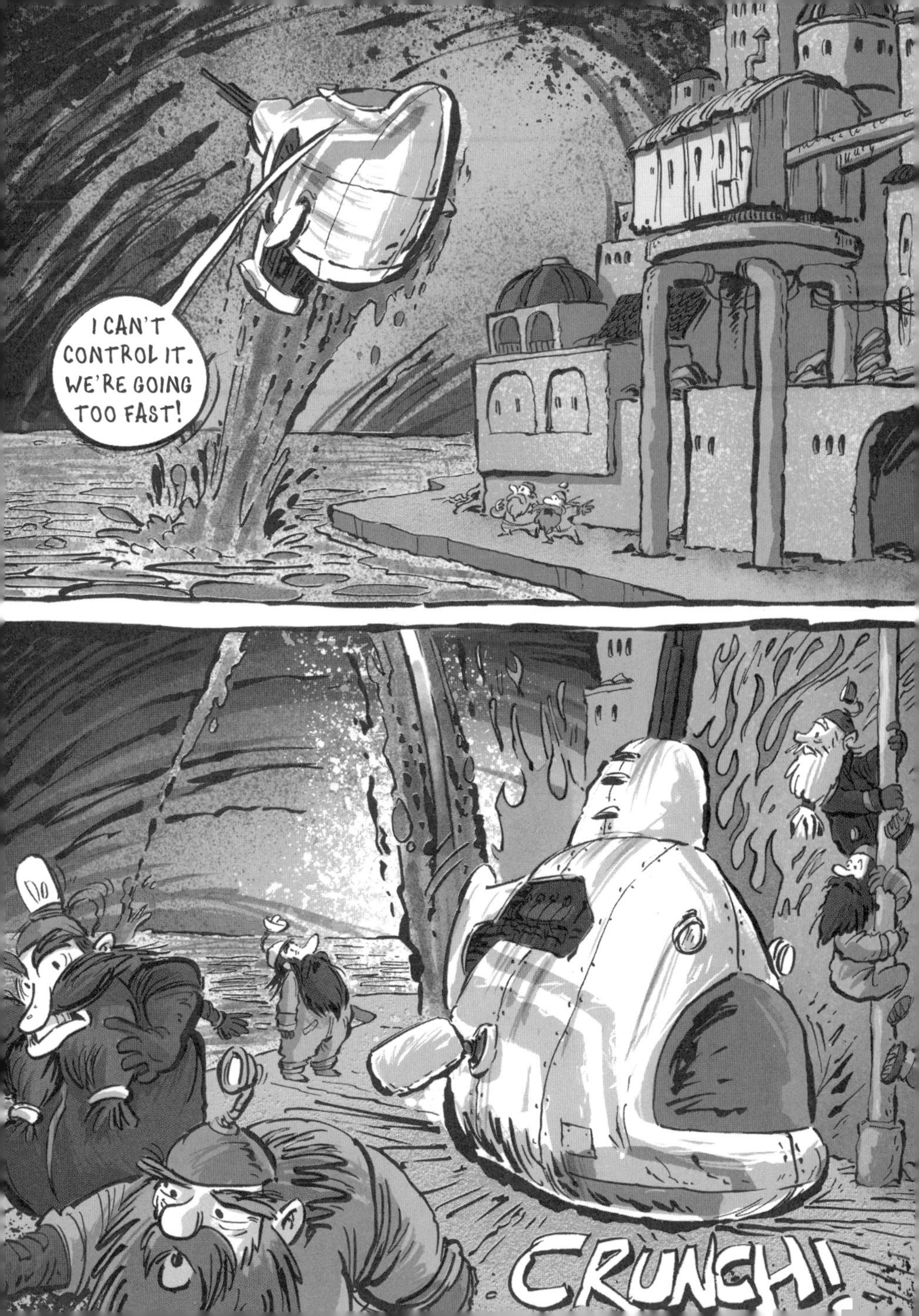
I CAN'T CONTROL IT. WE'RE GOING TOO FAST!
CRUNCH!

I felt like I'd been body-slammed by a lava shark.

We were sprawled across the floor of the sub. Through the splintered window glass we saw a crowd of annoyed dwarves gathered on the docks. I guessed they weren't crazy about nearly being squashed by heavy machinery. Relief washed through my scales. I'd take angry dwarves over charging lava sharks any day.

"Nice driving, Hugo," I said. "But you might want to work on your parking."

"I'll take it under consideration." The spider crawled to the sub's ceiling and opened the hatch.

Tank dove back under the command deck.

"What are you doing?" I hissed. "We have to get to the braces to warn the others!"

"I just have to grab something," Tank shouted from under command deck. A second later she reemerged, grinning like she'd just won the Tinkering Troll of the Year Award. In her hand she held the panzantium. The stone wasn't glowing anymore. She put the stone in her belt. "Just in case."

We climbed out of the sub. We didn't get much further.

"What do you think you're doing, crashing into our docks!" shouted a dwarf with one eye and a lava-shark tattoo on his arm.

"You nearly killed us!" barked another. "Get down here so we can deal with you."

Clearly, getting down from the sub was not a good idea.

"Great." Tank sighed. "We've gone from an angry swarm of sharks to a mob of mad dwarves!"

Captain Scorn climbed out of the hatch. "I'll deal with this."

He stepped past us. The panic had left his eyes. The cold, calculating stare had returned. He straightened his uniform and looked down on the gathered dwarves. "Step aside, citizens! We are on official business. Slow us down and risk the wrath of Lord Dunhelm, the dwarf king."

Anger vanished from the dwarves. They fell silent. A few muttered their apologies and stepped away from the crashed sub. Scorn held them with his piercing eyes until a clear path had formed on the dock.

"Move quickly," he whispered to us. "And don't stop until we're off these docks."

Hugo scurried off the sub like his webs were on fire. Tank and I followed. Scorn caught up to us at the top of the steps leading down to the harbor. He froze when he saw his son.

"Hugo? Is that you?"

"Father!"

Scorn wrapped Hugo in an eight-legged hug.

"So you recognize me now?" Hugo stepped back from his dad.

"I do," Captain Scorn said. "My head is clear now that we're back on solid ground and away from all that lava. Firebane's cursed words are gone from my mind."

"So it *was* Firebane!" I said.

"That dragon told me I would rule the webs if I let his dwarf into the queen's chamber." Scorn looked to the ground. "He charmed me with visions of heroism and power. I was a fool."

"We were all deceived, Father." Hugo hugged Scorn again. "Firebane's words led us all into that trap."

"But it was your web slinging that got us out," Tank said.

Scorn and Hugo both smiled.

"We make a good team," Scorn said. "Don't we, son?"

"We sure do, Dad."

"Gloomshrooms!" I shouted. Everyone looked at me like I was under Firebane's spell again. I pointed to the gloomshrooms shining over the street. "The gloomshrooms are glowing. It's morning."

Around us the streets of Lava Falls filled with monsters beginning their day. They hurried to work and chatted happily to each other, every creature oblivious to the doom they faced if Firebane wasn't stopped.

"We have to warn Queen Azelia," Hugo said. "She must know Firebane is the thief!"

"They will be gathering at the braces," Scorn said. "Follow me."

We rushed through the crowd, Tank and I following the pair of spiders. With every step my questions grew. Why had Firebane stolen the crown? Was he going to let my home fall into the Abyss? One thing I did know for certain. I had a lot more questions for Firebane Drakeclaw.

And this time, I was getting answers.

CHAPTER FOURTEEN
Return of the Queen

The guards outside the town hall saluted as we passed. Captain Scorn returned the salute, and we hurried into the building in the center of Lava Falls. Inside, Tank's phone beeped. She snatched the phone from her belt and started dancing.

"I've got a signal!" she said. "Ooh, and I have messages."

"Focus, Tank." I rolled my eyes. "We can read how much your mom misses you after we save all of Rockfall Mountain from falling into the Abyss."

Tank scowled. "There's a message from Aleetha."

I skidded to a stop and went to my friend's side. "That one we *can* read. What does she say?"

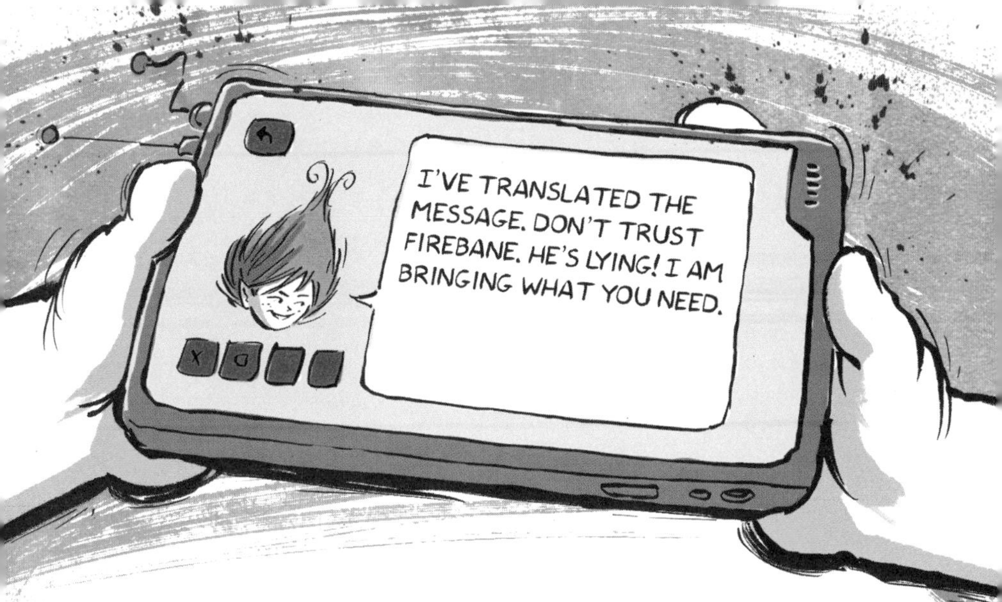
I'VE TRANSLATED THE MESSAGE. DON'T TRUST FIREBANE. HE'S LYING! I AM BRINGING WHAT YOU NEED.

"*Don't trust Firebane*?" I said. "Thanks, Aleetha. We figured that one out on our own. What does she mean she's bringing what we need?"

"No idea," Tank said. "She also sent a copy of the message translated from old magic."

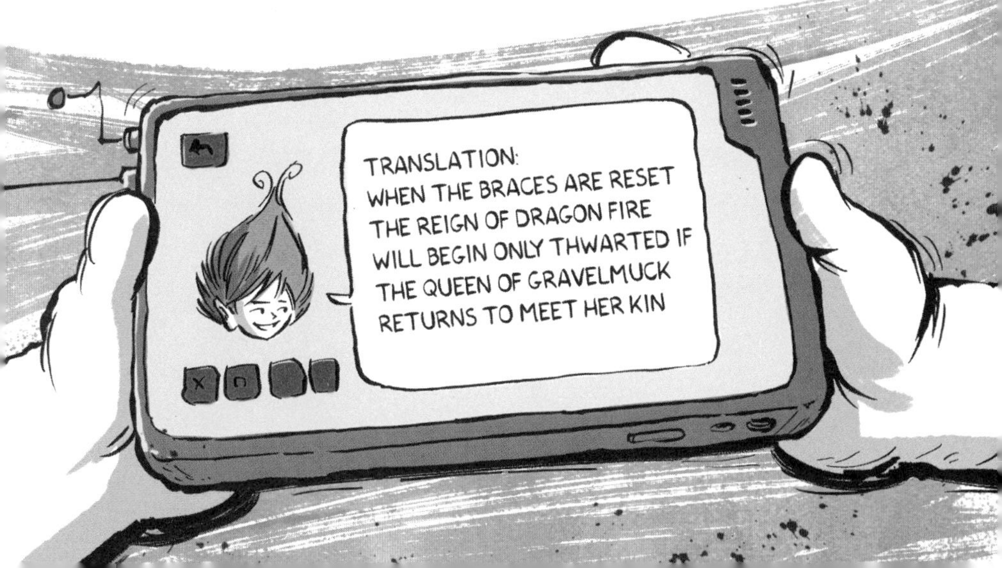
TRANSLATION:
WHEN THE BRACES ARE RESET
THE REIGN OF DRAGON FIRE
WILL BEGIN ONLY THWARTED IF
THE QUEEN OF GRAVELMUCK
RETURNS TO MEET HER KIN

"It's just a warning about what will happen if the braces don't get reset," I said. "*Dragon fire* is just a fancy way of saying 'tossed into the Abyss.'"

"Why does it mention Gravelmuck?" Tank said. "That's the name of our school."

"Hurry up, you two." Hugo stood inside an elevator on the other side of the room. "We don't have time to chat."

"Hugo is right," Tank said.

I looked at the message on her phone. "If we had gotten this earlier, we wouldn't have been tricked by Firebane," I said. "Now it's just too little, too late."

"Then let's get going while there's still time to warn the others about Firebane." Tank ran to catch up with Hugo.

Scorn closed the elevator doors the moment my tail was inside. Immediately we began to drop.

"This will take us all the way to the bottom of the mountain and to the braces," he said. "Hopefully, we won't be too late."

Long seconds later the elevator's floor retracted, and the walls zipped back up to the top. The Abyss roared below us. And we weren't alone.

The walkway surrounding the Abyss was crowded with dwarves, spiders and dragonkin leaders from the Depths. They joked and laughed with each other as they got ready to watch the annual resetting. It was like they were at a school play and not about to witness the end of the world.

At the front of the crowd, Queen Azelia and Lord Dunhelm stood next to the reset mechanism. Beside them stood Firebane in his dragonkin form, grinning like a politician.

Hundreds of braces stood around the Abyss, holding up Rockfall Mountain and protecting it from certain doom. The reset mechanism next to Firebane flashed an angry red warning. On the screen, the countdown had begun. There was less than a minute to go. The pressure needle was tipped to one side, well into the *Imminent Danger* range. The pressure on the braces increased with every second. We didn't have any time to spare.

I raced out of the elevator.

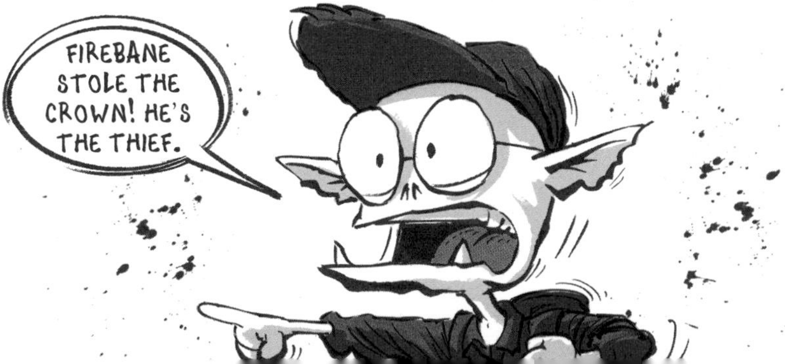
FIREBANE STOLE THE CROWN! HE'S THE THIEF.

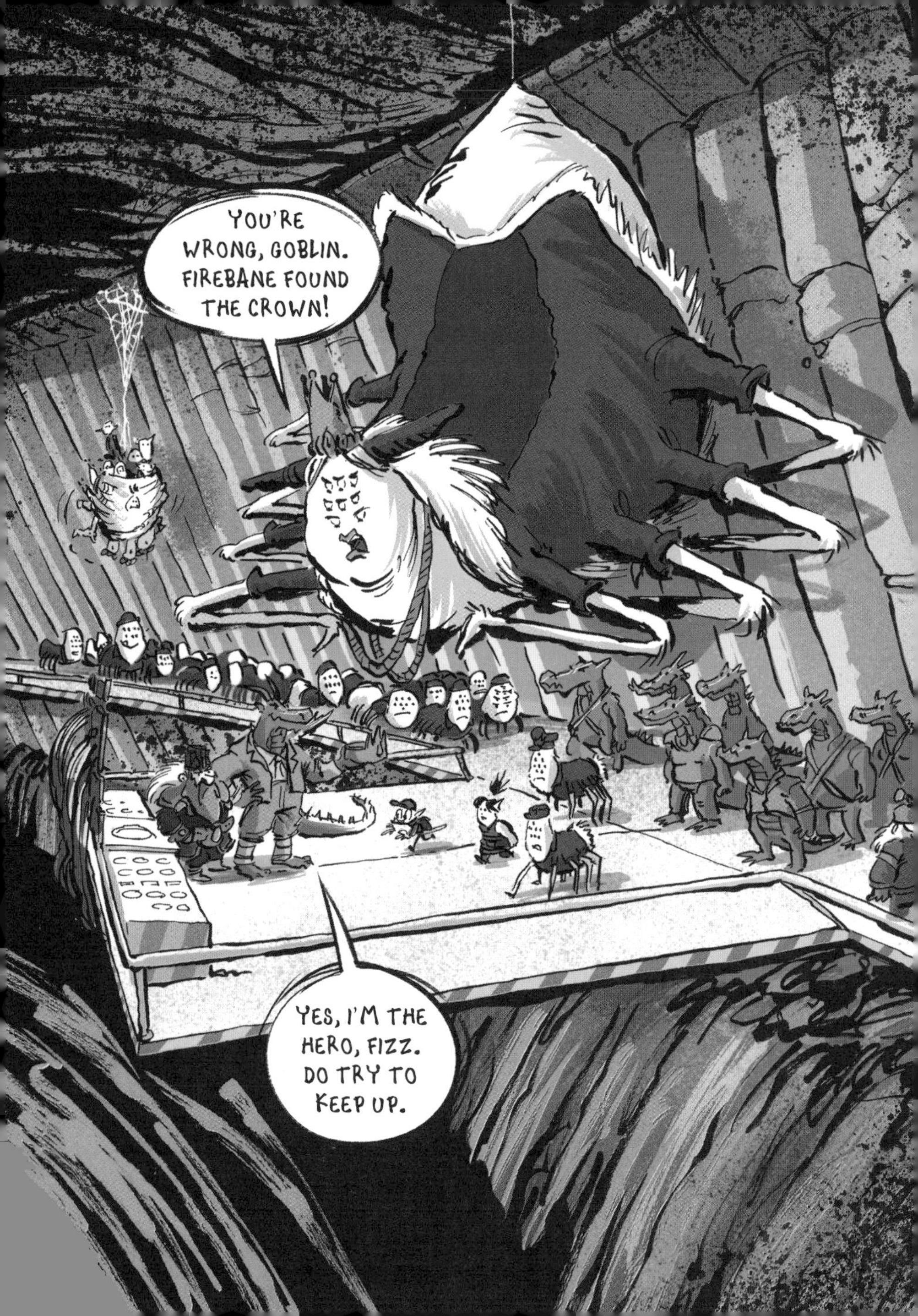
YOU'RE WRONG, GOBLIN. FIREBANE FOUND THE CROWN!
YES, I'M THE HERO, FIZZ. DO TRY TO KEEP UP.

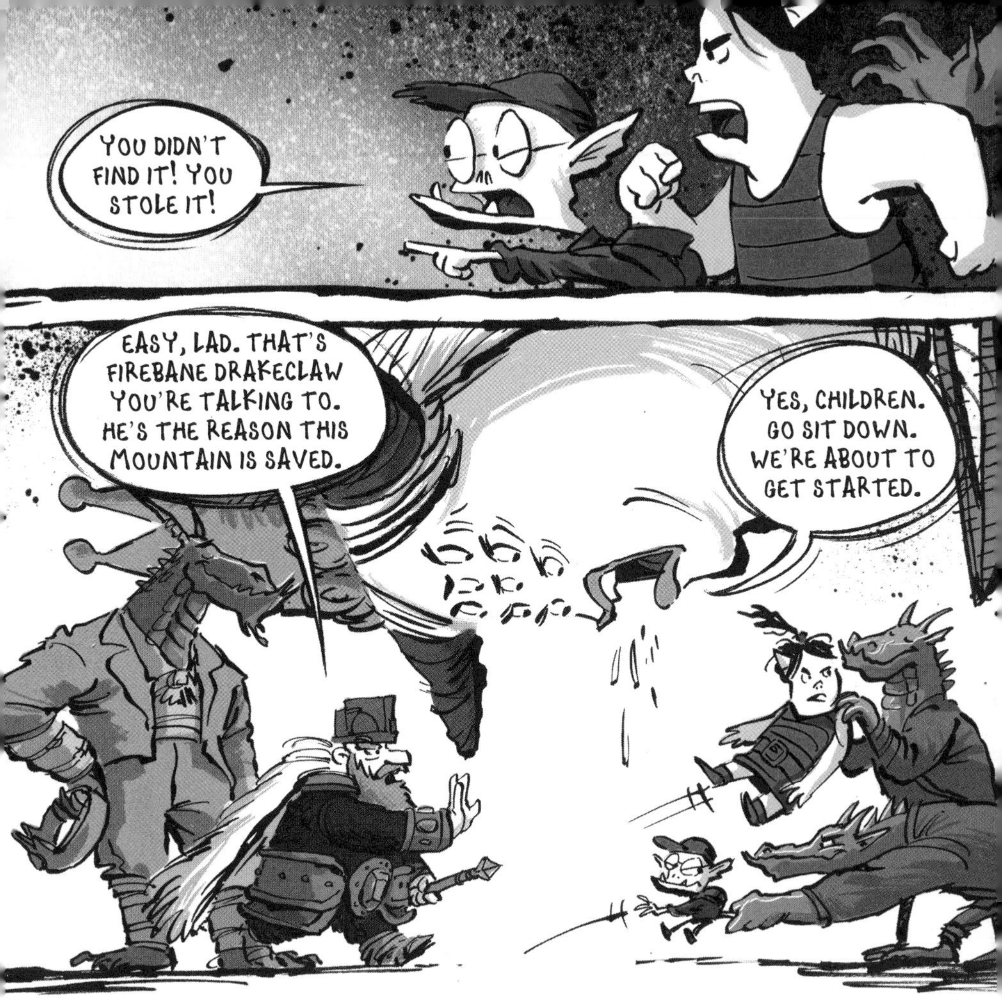
YOU DIDN'T FIND IT! YOU STOLE IT!
EASY, LAD. THAT'S FIREBANE DRAKECLAW YOU'RE TALKING TO. HE'S THE REASON THIS MOUNTAIN IS SAVED.
YES, CHILDREN. GO SIT DOWN. WE'RE ABOUT TO GET STARTED.

"He's lying!" I shouted. "He stole the crown, and he's done something to it."

"You don't know what you are talking about," Queen Azelia said.

"We do!" Tank stomped her foot. "We found blueprints in an abandoned mining station."

"Blueprints? In a mining station?" the queen snapped. "I sent you to find a dwarf. Instead, you vanished. Your classmates were very worried. Don't worry—I haven't eaten them. *Yet.* I'm saving them for our celebratory dinner once the braces are reset."

The queen waved one of her legs absently toward the long table behind her. My classmates dangled above the table, still wrapped in web cocoons. My scales burned. After all we'd been through, my classmates were still trapped and in danger. With everyone thinking Firebane was Dragon of the Month, saving them seemed impossible.

The spider queen turned to Scorn. "And you, Captain! I send you away, and you vanish. No reports. Nothing."

Captain Scorn bowed his head. "My queen, I can explain everything."

"Silence!" the queen ordered. "We have no time. The braces must be reset. I will deal with you later. Firebane, hand me the crown so we can get started."

"Of course, Queen Azelia." Firebane gave the Crown of Peace to the spider queen.

A hush fell over the crowd as the queen took the crown. She held it high for all to see and approached the reset mechanism. It continued to flash red with the needle tipped all the way to the side, pointing at *Imminent Danger*.

"Mark this day, fellow Depths dwellers," the queen said in a loud voice. "We come together, put aside our differences and share power between our lands to keep our home safe from the ever-present Abyss."

A murmur ran through the crowd at the mention of the Abyss. Queen Azelia held the crown over the reset mechanism. She slowly lowered it into the round slot designed just for this purpose. The crown clicked into place. The crowd of spiders, dwarves and dragonkin all watched intently. Every eye was on the crown.

Immediately the flashing stopped. The needle slowly drifted away from *Imminent Danger* to rest on *All Safe*.

The monsters cheered. The Dark Depths and all of Rockfall Mountain had been saved for another year. Everyone breathed a sigh of relief.

Except me.

I was happy not to be hurled into the Abyss, but something wasn't right. Could we have gotten it so wrong? Was Firebane telling the truth? What was I missing?

Queen Azelia moved to join the celebrations, then stopped. Two of her legs still held the crown in place. She pulled on the crown and frowned.

"I'm stuck." She tugged on the crown again. Still her legs stayed with the crown. She spun to face Firebane. "There's something wrong."

The monsters in the crowd were too busy congratulating each other to hear the queen's complaints.

"Wrong, Queen Azelia." A knowing smile spread across Firebane's snout. Sharp teeth flashed. "Everything is just right."

The panzantium in the center of the crown began to glow brightly. My gut churned like it was being dumped into the Abyss. Something was definitely wrong, and it started with the grinning dragon standing in front of me.

"Firebane, stop!" I stepped closer to help Queen Azelia. A dragonkin grabbed me by the shoulders and held me in place.

"That's far enough, Fizz Marlow," Firebane said. "You've done your job already."

"My job?"

"What are you talking about?" Tank started to rush to my side, but a dragonkin stopped her after two steps.

"Just stay where you are," Firebane said. Amusement danced in his eyes. "Everything will become clear very soon."

Dragonkin soldiers took hold of Hugo and Scorn. The celebrating monsters fell silent.

The glow around the crown grew brighter. Tendrils of wispy light reached into the air. The spider queen's eyes doubled in size as the strands of energy reached over her head.

"What's happening?" she wailed.

The tendrils grew longer and stretched in all directions. They flailed around like the arms of an octoclops.

THE GOBLIN WAS RIGHT. YOU ARE UP TO SOMETHING, FIREBANE!

INDEED, I AM.

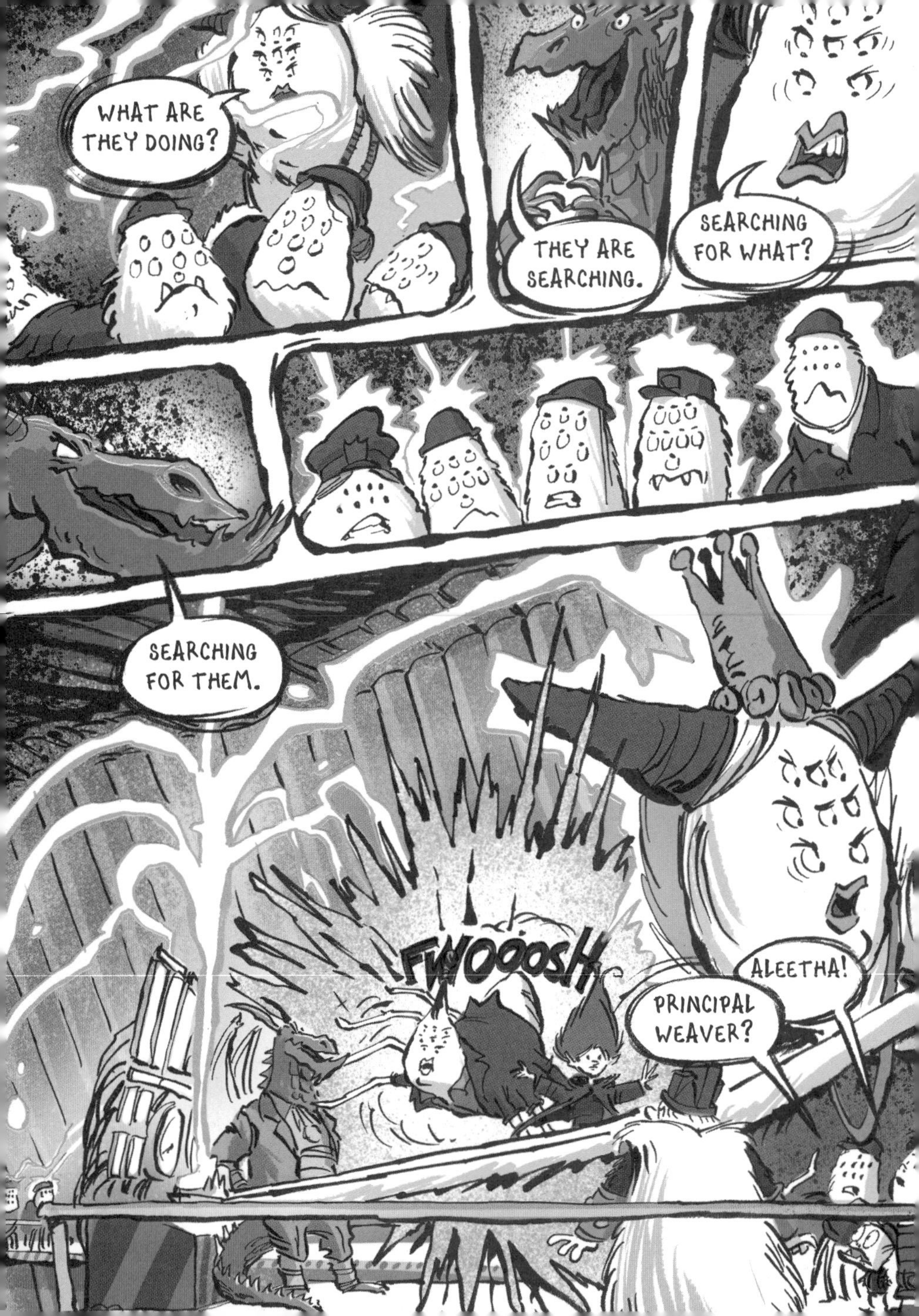

WHAT ARE THEY DOING?
THEY ARE SEARCHING.
SEARCHING FOR WHAT?
SEARCHING FOR THEM.
FWOOOSH
ALEETHA!
PRINCIPAL WEAVER?

CHAPTER FIFTEEN
Reunions and Revenge

My tail almost fell off.

"Aleetha!"

Tank rushed to the lava elf and wrapped her in a big hug. "How did you get here?"

"With this." Aleetha held up her hand. A ring flashed on her finger. "It's a teleport ring. I borrowed it from the school library. When you put it on, the magic in the ring locates anyone you share a strong bond with and brings you to them."

"Like two good friends in trouble in the Dark Depths?" Tank said.

"Exactly." Aleetha smiled.

"Finally!" I cheered. "A kind of magic that even I can like."

"But what are you doing here?" Tank asked.

"Bringing what you need." She grinned, then frowned. "Didn't you get my message?"

"We did," I said. "But we didn't really understand it."

Tank looked to the spider standing next to Aleetha.

"Yeah, um…" She tugged on her tool belt and lowered her voice. "Why did you bring Principal Weaver?"

"I don't understand it either, Tatanka." Principal Weaver never used Tank's real name. The spider scanned the platform warily. "Where are we, Aleetha? You said I was needed in my ancestral home. This is not the Vale of Webs."

All around us the confusion continued. The strange tentacles of energy streamed out of the Crown of Peace. They writhed chaotically, grabbing terrified spiders one by one before letting go and moving on to the next monster. Firebane sauntered closer to us.

"Welcome, Aleetha Cinderwisp." The dragon's wings unfolded from his shoulders. His fangs flashed and his eyes danced. "You have arrived just in time."

Aleetha's jaw dropped. Even in his dragonkin form, there was no mistaking who or what the creature coming toward us was.

"Is…is that…?" she stammered.

"Yes, it is," I said.

"You were right, Fizz Marlow," Firebane crooned. "I am up to something. You have all been very helpful."

"Helpful?" Tank asked.

"Why yes," Firebane said. "You and the little goblin very kindly passed along my message to your wizard friend."

"Message?"

For a second the dragon's face changed. Suddenly, Gilthil the strange lagalander stared back at us. The fish-head vanished as quickly as it appeared. Firebane's scaly snarl returned.

"You were Gilthil?" I said.

"Give the goblin a gold star!" Firebane chuckled. "And that's not all."

"Mr. Ravel!" I said. "When I fell into you, I saw you."

"You are always seeing too much, Detective," Firebane snarled. "Except that night in the swamp. You were tired and hungry and ready to listen to an old fish with camprocks. I saved you from the Swamp of Sorrow. I gave you the note, written in old magic. And you very kindly passed it along to your little wizard friend in Slick City, who brought the very thing I needed."

"Principal Weaver," Tank said. "She's the Queen of Gravelmuck, just like the note said."

"The queen is meant to stop the reign of fire, not help it," Aleetha said. "That's what the note said."

"I'm sorry. I wasn't very truthful with that part," Firebane said. "Your principal isn't here to stop anything. She is here to start the chaotic destruction!"

"I'm not going to destroy anything!" Principal Weaver snapped.

"I'm afraid you are, Principal Weaver." Firebane swept a claw toward the reset mechanism. "Especially when you see who is waiting for you."

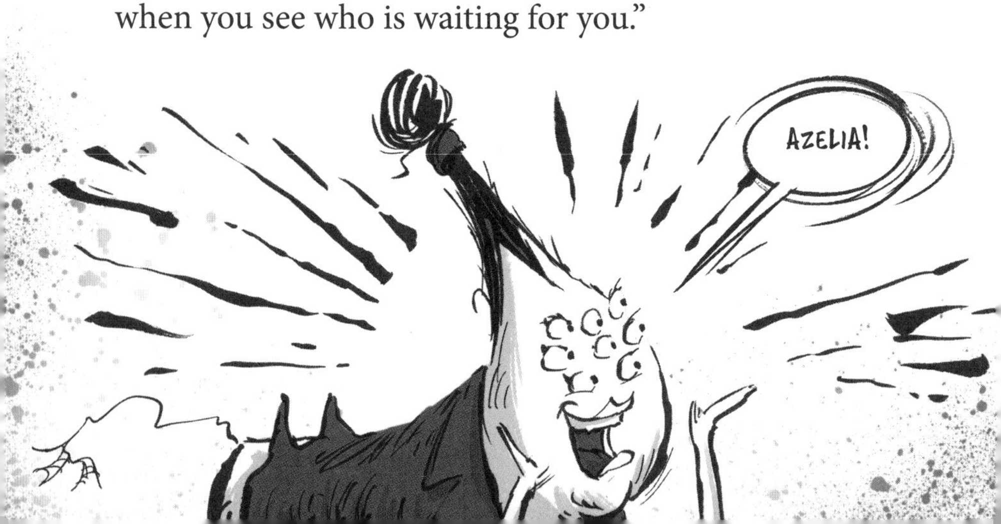
AZELIA!

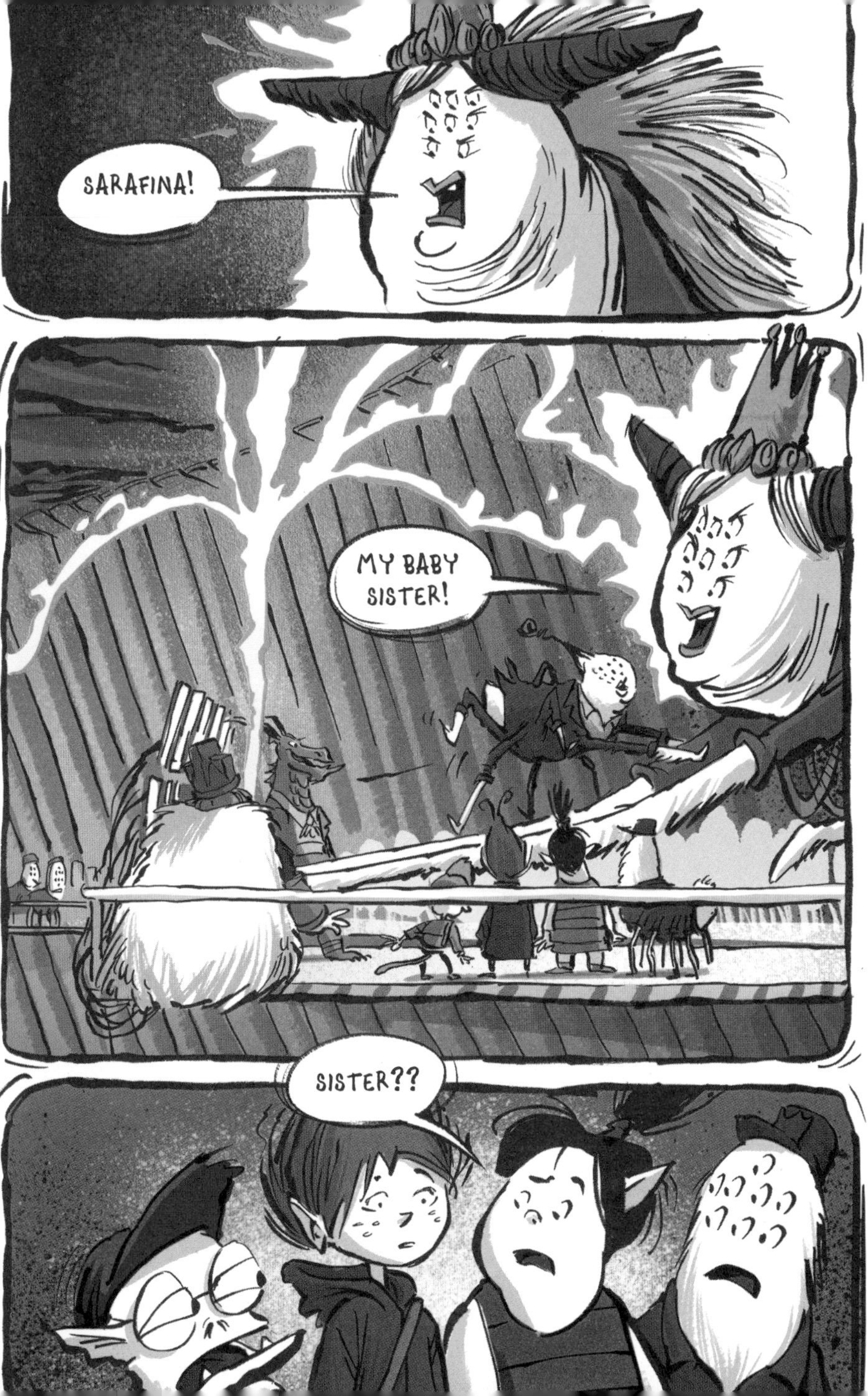
SARAFINA!
MY BABY SISTER!
SISTER??

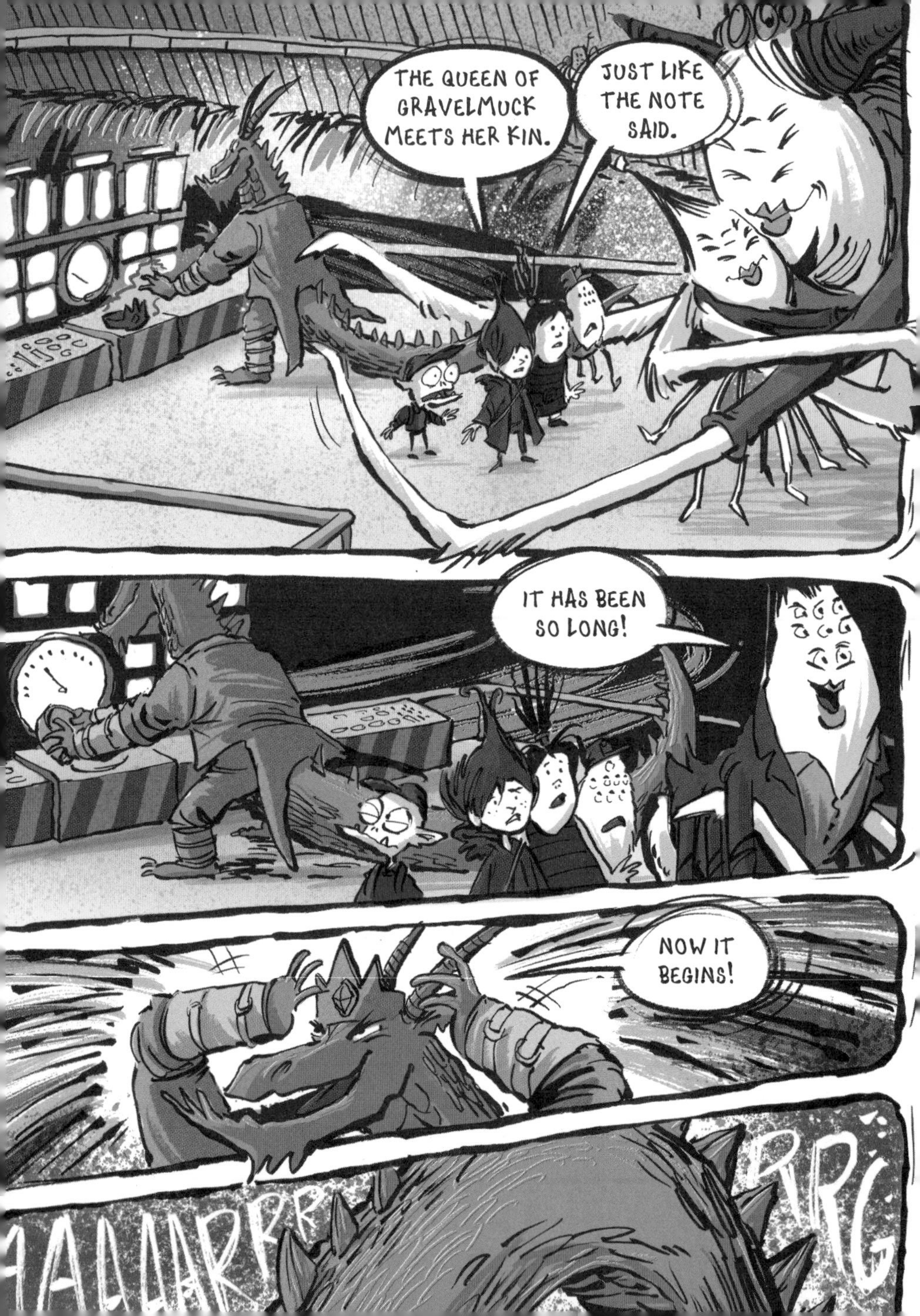
THE QUEEN OF GRAVELMUCK MEETS HER KIN.
JUST LIKE THE NOTE SAID.
IT HAS BEEN SO LONG!
NOW IT BEGINS!
AALLAARRR
RRG

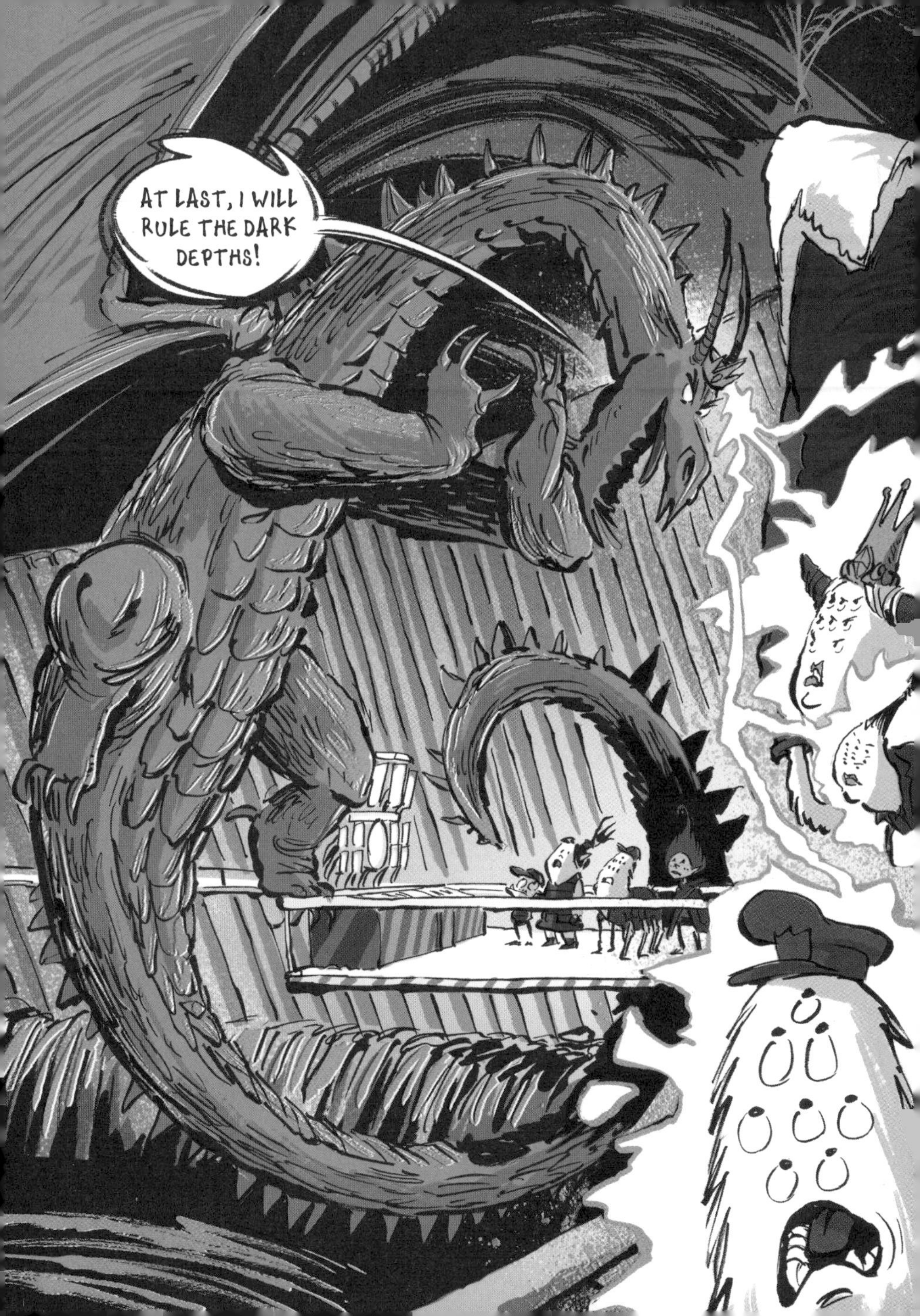
AT LAST, I WILL RULE THE DARK DEPTHS!

Firebane towered over the confused monsters. He transformed into full-on dragon mode right in front of us with the Crown of Peace on his head.

"The Dark Depths are mine," he roared. "No longer will I be forced to share power with the dwarves or spiders. Now you will all bow down before me!"

"Have you lost your mind, Firebane?" Lord Dunhelm shouted. His guards readied for a fight. "The dwarves denied you ultimate power long ago, dragon. You will be denied again today. My soldiers are not afraid of your scaly face."

"They should be." Firebane grinned. "Because I can do *this* now."

On the dragon's head, the gem at the heart of the crown grew brighter. A ray of light blasted from the crown, engulfing the dwarves. Just watching it hurt my brain. I turned my eyes from the bright light. When I looked back, the light was gone—and so were the dwarves. All that remained was an empty patch of ground.

Tank rubbed her eyes. "Did he just make those dwarves disappear?"

"Not quite." Firebane turned to face us. He tapped the crown on his head with a sharp talon. "I simply relocated them."

The gem in the center of the crown pulsed with the rhythm of a heartbeat. The bearded face of Lord Dunhelm appeared in stone for a brief moment and then vanished.

"The dwarves are inside the crown!" I said.

"Isn't it wonderful?" The dragon beamed. "All the strength and wisdom of the dwarves belongs to me now."

The gem continued to pulse. Below us, the Abyss raged. The threat it once held paled in comparison to the one looming over us now.

"What is the meaning of all this, Firebane?" Queen Azelia shouted. "We have an agreement. We share power in the Dark Depths. What you're doing is a disgrace!"

Firebane rose to his full height to tower over the spider queen.

"Wrong. This is revenge!" Firebane laughed while his dragonkin soldiers surrounded us. "Your forefathers mocked my design for the braces many years ago. They called it Firebane's Folly and refused to make me king of the Dark Depths. But could they create a better way to save our mountain from falling into the Abyss? No, they could not!"

Firebane stamped his foot. The walkway shook, and the braces trembled but remained standing.

"I waited patiently, sharing the crown with the spiders and dwarves. I let you rule this land when I should have been its master. But while you ruled, I learned all there is know about the crown. In my search, I uncovered the secret to unlocking its true power."

"Family," Aleetha gasped. "When two members of the same family hold the crown, its true power is released. That's why you wanted Principal Weaver to meet Queen Azelia down here. They're sisters."

"A gold star for the little wizard." Firebane's eyes danced with delight. "And now that power belongs to me. I am claiming my right as ruler of the Dark Depths and soon all of Rockfall Mountain. With every passing moment, my army grows. Monsters once shunned by the spiders and dwarves are answering the call of the crown. The Fallen Ones are drawing near. Soon I will lead them across the Dark Depths, past the Vale of Webs and all the way to the Shallows." Firebane spun to me. "Where a crowded metropolis awaits."

"You wouldn't."

"I would." Firebane flashed a fang. "When this day is finished, Slick City will be mine, and all in Rockfall Mountain will bow before Firebane Drakeclaw!"

"Never!" Queen Azelia shouted. "My spiders will fight you down to our last webs, Firebane!"

"Not a wise choice, Spider Queen." The stone in the Crown of Peace glowed more brightly. "Join the dwarves in my crown!"

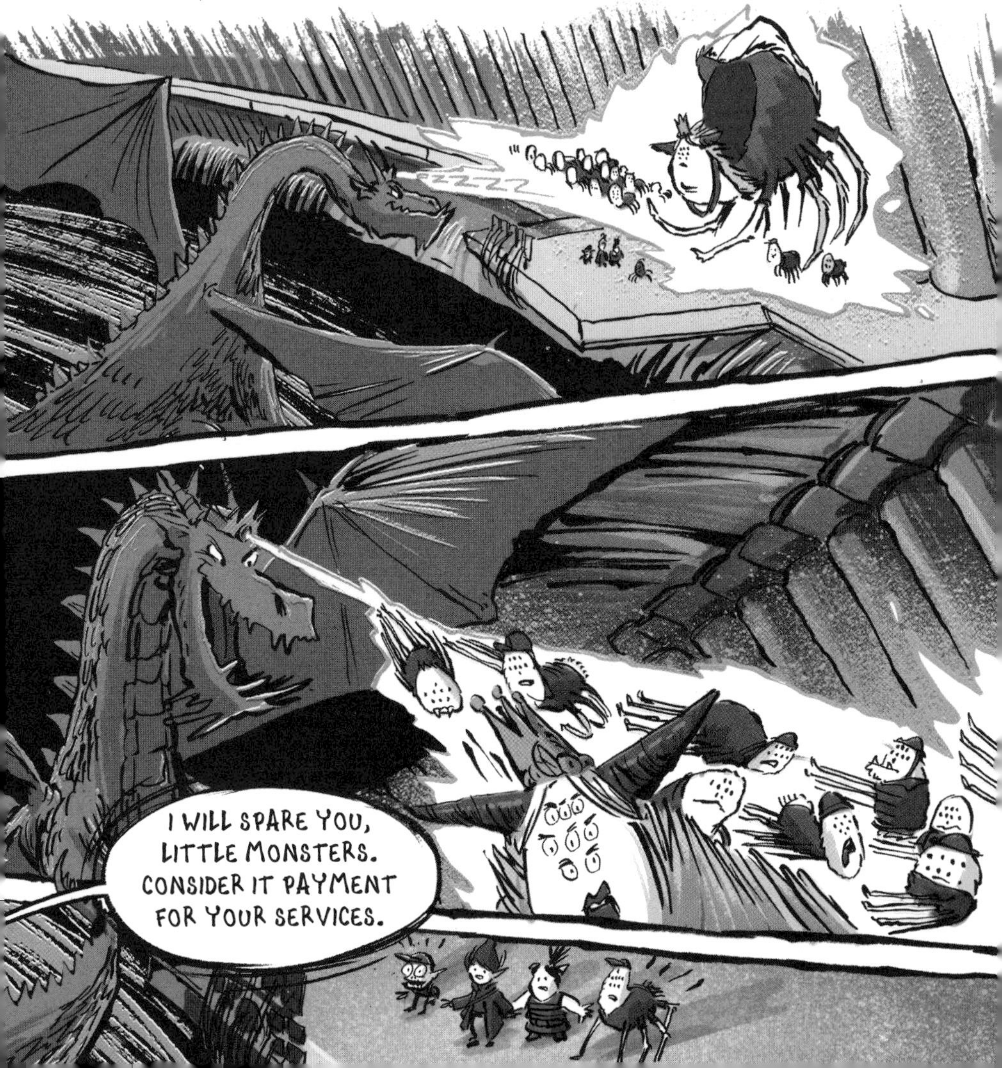
I WILL SPARE YOU, LITTLE MONSTERS. CONSIDER IT PAYMENT FOR YOUR SERVICES.

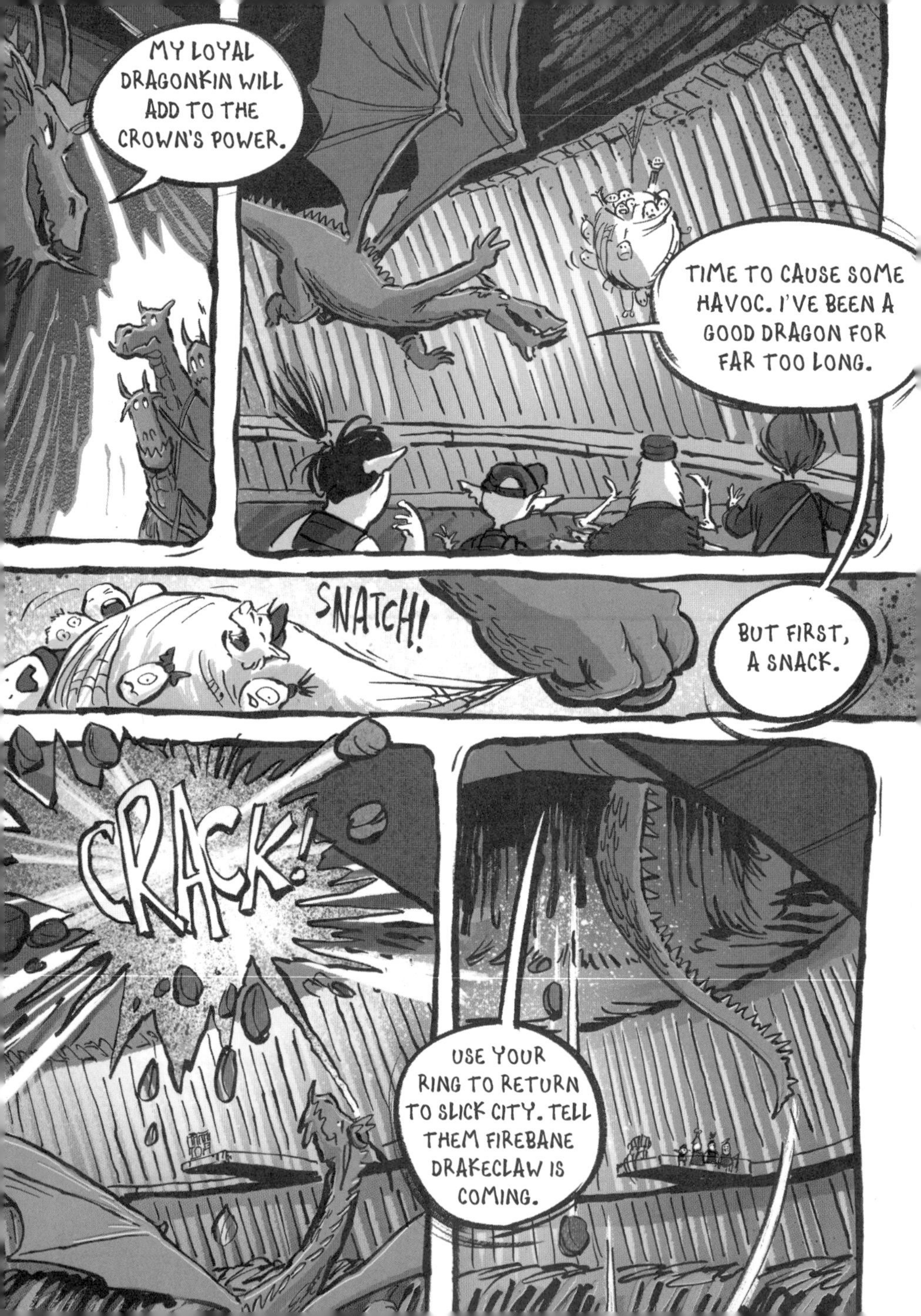
MY LOYAL DRAGONKIN WILL ADD TO THE CROWN'S POWER.
TIME TO CAUSE SOME HAVOC. I'VE BEEN A GOOD DRAGON FOR FAR TOO LONG.
SNATCH!
BUT FIRST, A SNACK.
CRACK!
USE YOUR RING TO RETURN TO SLICK CITY. TELL THEM FIREBANE DRAKECLAW IS COMING.

My heart felt like it had been chucked into the Abyss. Suddenly that gaping void of destruction swirling around us seemed to be the least of our worries.

Firebane Drakeclaw was on the rampage, with my entire class packed along as a mid-havoc snack. We had worked so hard to save Rockfall Mountain, but all we had really done was guarantee its doom.

It was times like these that really put that pile of unfinished homework back home in perspective.

CHAPTER SIXTEEN

Secrets in the Stone

The Abyss roared.

Around us, the walkway was now suddenly very empty. Every single spider and dwarf, from queen to servant, was now trapped inside the Crown of Peace. Screams from the streets of Lava Falls echoed down the shaft Firebane had blasted into the bottom of the mountain.

"Sounds like the havoc wreaking has begun up there," I said.

"We need to get up there and stop Firebane," Hugo said. The spider scurried along the metal walkway. He shot several strands of web at the edges of the shaft running up to the surface. Each shot was swallowed by the Abyss before it could even stick. "My webs won't stick and we'll get sucked into oblivion if we try climbing up that thing."

"We need to get the elevator back," Tank said.

Aleetha stood by the reset mechanism. "Maybe this thing controls it."

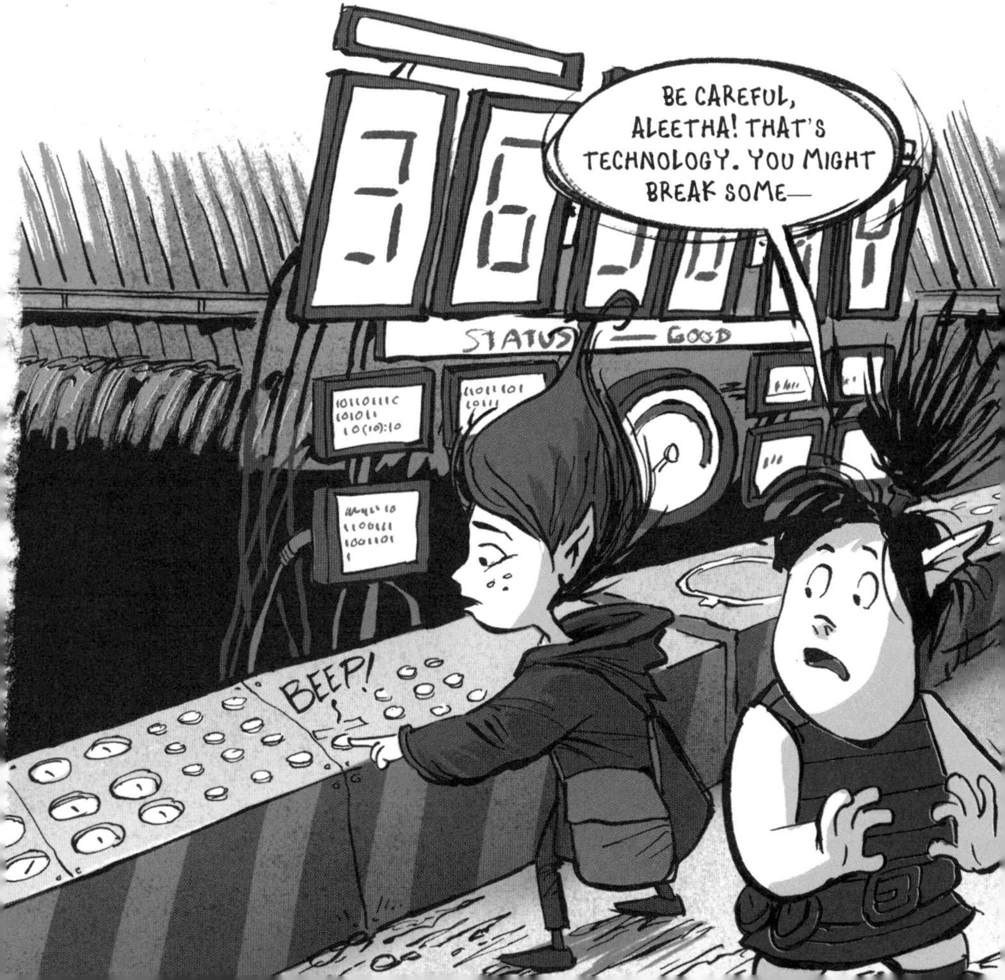
BE CAREFUL, ALEETHA! THAT'S TECHNOLOGY. YOU MIGHT BREAK SOME—
STATUS — GOOD
BEEP!

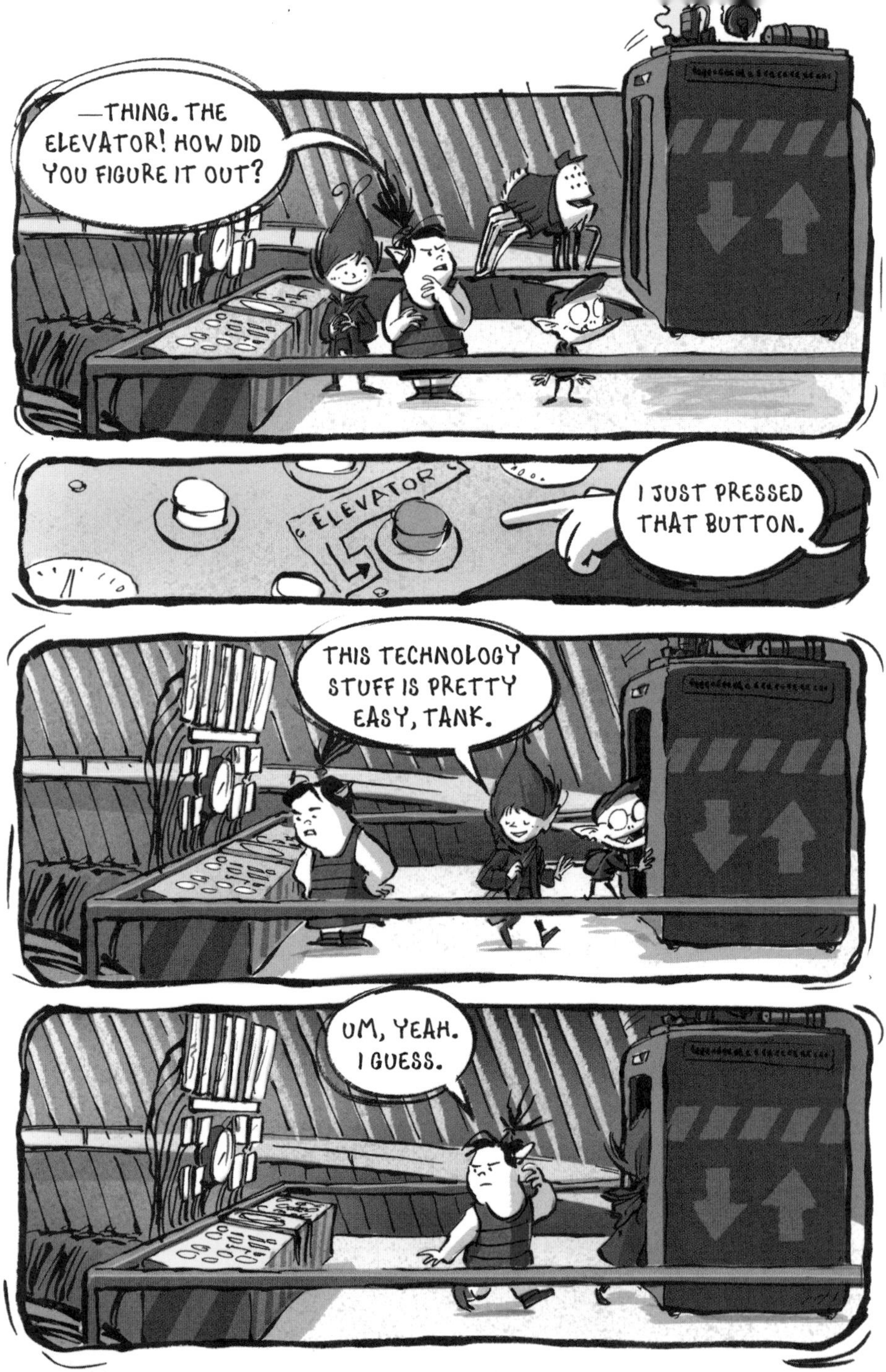
—THING. THE ELEVATOR! HOW DID YOU FIGURE IT OUT?
ELEVATOR
I JUST PRESSED THAT BUTTON.
THIS TECHNOLOGY STUFF IS PRETTY EASY, TANK.
UM, YEAH. I GUESS.

Up top, Lava Falls was falling apart.

Dragonkin swarmed the streets, rounding up spiders, dwarves and every other monster unlucky enough to get in their way. High above it all, Firebane soared. The dragon flew a wide circle around the city. The Crown of Peace rested on his scaly head, and the gem at its heart continued to pulse as he sailed over the chaos. In his claws, my class dangled in their cocoons. Their cries for help echoed across the lake and under my scales.

We stood in the doorway of the town hall and watched. I felt as helpless as a booger in a tissue.

"We have to do something!" Tank moaned.

"There's no point." Hugo slumped against the doorframe. "The battle here is over. You should listen to Firebane and return home. There is still time to warn them he is coming."

"Even if we wanted to, we can't return," Aleetha said. "The teleport ring needs a full day to recharge before it can be used again." The lava elf looked at Tank and me. Her eyes twinkled. "Besides, I came here to stop Firebane. We aren't giving up until we knock some sense into that scale-brain."

"I was afraid you were going to say that." I sighed. "How are we going to fight a laser-shooting dragon carrying a grudge the size of this mountain?"

"With knowledge." Aleetha turned to Hugo. "Where's the wizards' outpost in town?"

Getting across a town surrounded by lava and crawling with lizards was slow going. We moved as a group, picking our way carefully through the streets of Lava Falls. Dragonkin were everywhere, herding innocent monsters into the town square. Firebane was up to something with these poor creatures, but we didn't have time to find out. Apparently, we had a date with a library. I didn't get it, but I'd learned to trust Aleetha and her wizardy brain.

Many long minutes later and after much dragonkin dodging, we stood in front of the Lava Falls wizards' outpost. Les the Magnificent answered the door.

WHO'S THERE?

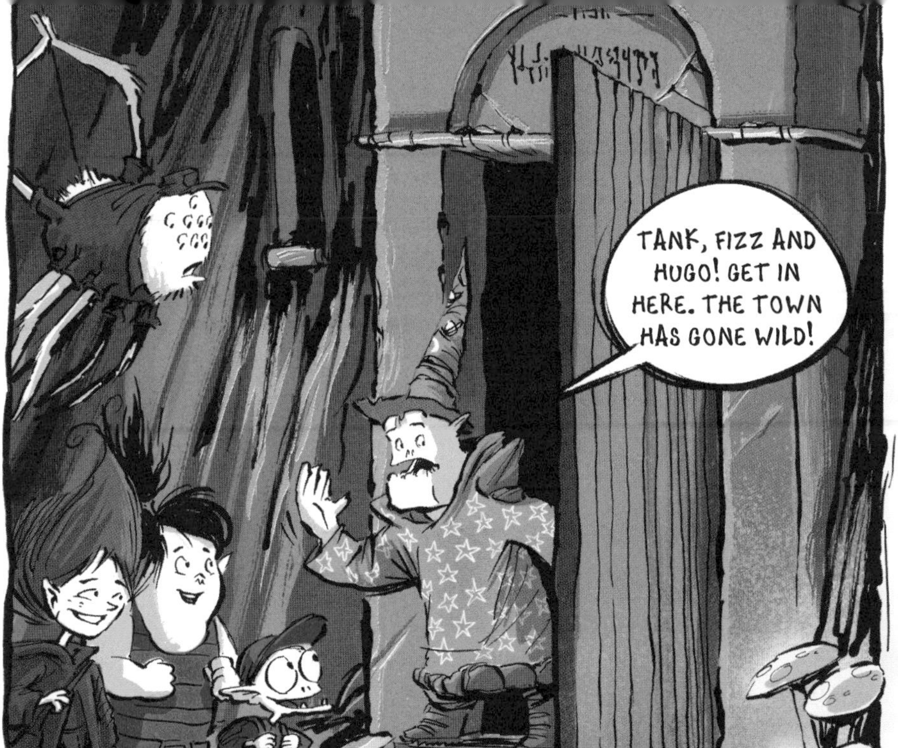
TANK, FIZZ AND HUGO! GET IN HERE. THE TOWN HAS GONE WILD!

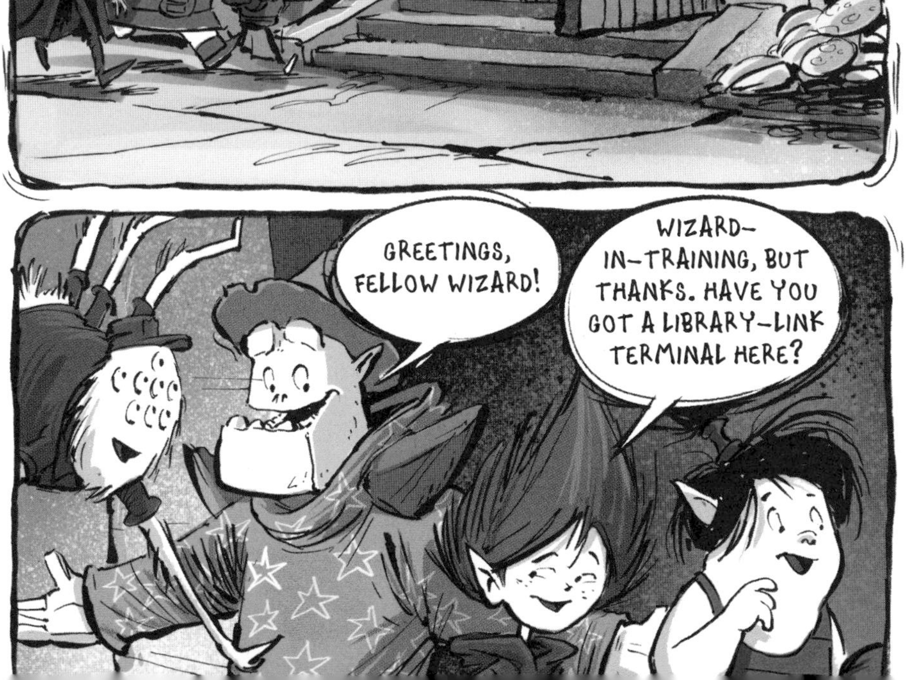
GREETINGS, FELLOW WIZARD!
WIZARD-IN-TRAINING, BUT THANKS. HAVE YOU GOT A LIBRARY-LINK TERMINAL HERE?

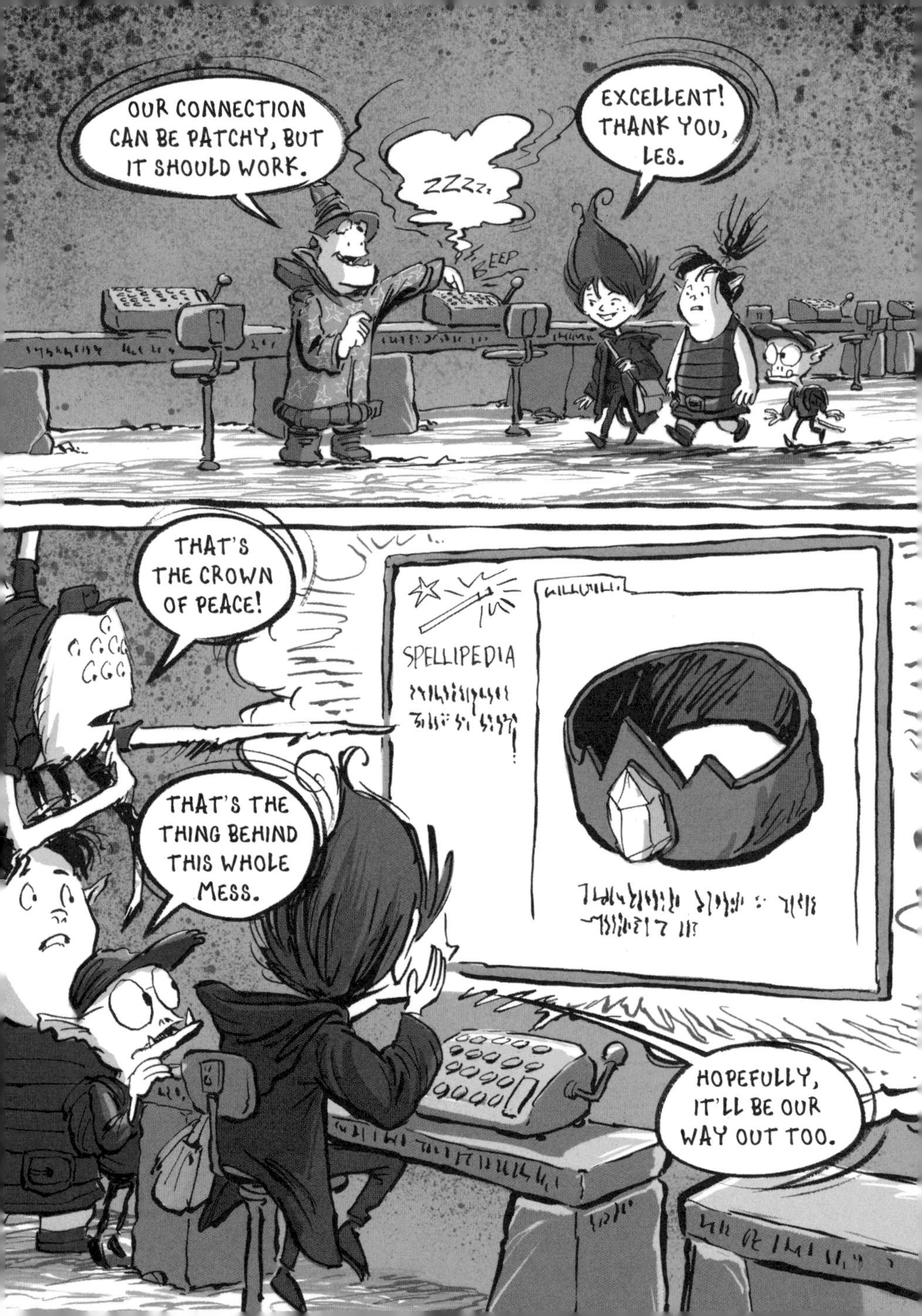
OUR CONNECTION CAN BE PATCHY, BUT IT SHOULD WORK.
ZZZzz
BEEP
EXCELLENT! THANK YOU, LES.
THAT'S THE CROWN OF PEACE!
SPELLIPEDIA
THAT'S THE THING BEHIND THIS WHOLE MESS.
HOPEFULLY, IT'LL BE OUR WAY OUT TOO.

Aleetha zipped through the pages on the screen with expert speed. From book reports to group projects, the lava elf was always a school star. Just standing next to her made me feel smarter. Now that she was studying to be a wizard at the Shadow Tower, her academic skills were supercharged.

"Ever since I got your message I've been thinking about this crown." Her eyes stayed glued to the screen as she read page after page of text. "I did some research, and I thought I understood how it worked."

"Firebane said it had to do with dwarves who forged the crown long ago," Tank said.

Aleetha shrugged. "Yeah, they had wizards enchant the metal as they made the crown. But gold is a pretty dumb metal."

"Aren't all rocks and minerals dumb?" I said.

"Don't say that to Les the rock elf." Aleetha smiled and kept reading the screen. "What I mean is that you can't really put powerful spells into gold. Not the kind of spells that swallow monsters and shoot lasers."

A deep roar sounded outside, followed by the sound of buildings crashing. My tail curled. Firebane's army was destroying the town, and we were in here using our library privileges.

"Who cares how Firebane is zapping monsters!" I snapped. "What matters is that he's doing it, and he'll destroy the whole mountain if we don't stop him."

Aleetha spun in her chair and faced me. All laughter was gone from her face.

"The *how* of something is always important, Fizz," she said. "It's not the crown that is letting Firebane do all this stuff."

"Then what is it?" Tank asked.

Aleetha pointed to the screen. "It's that."

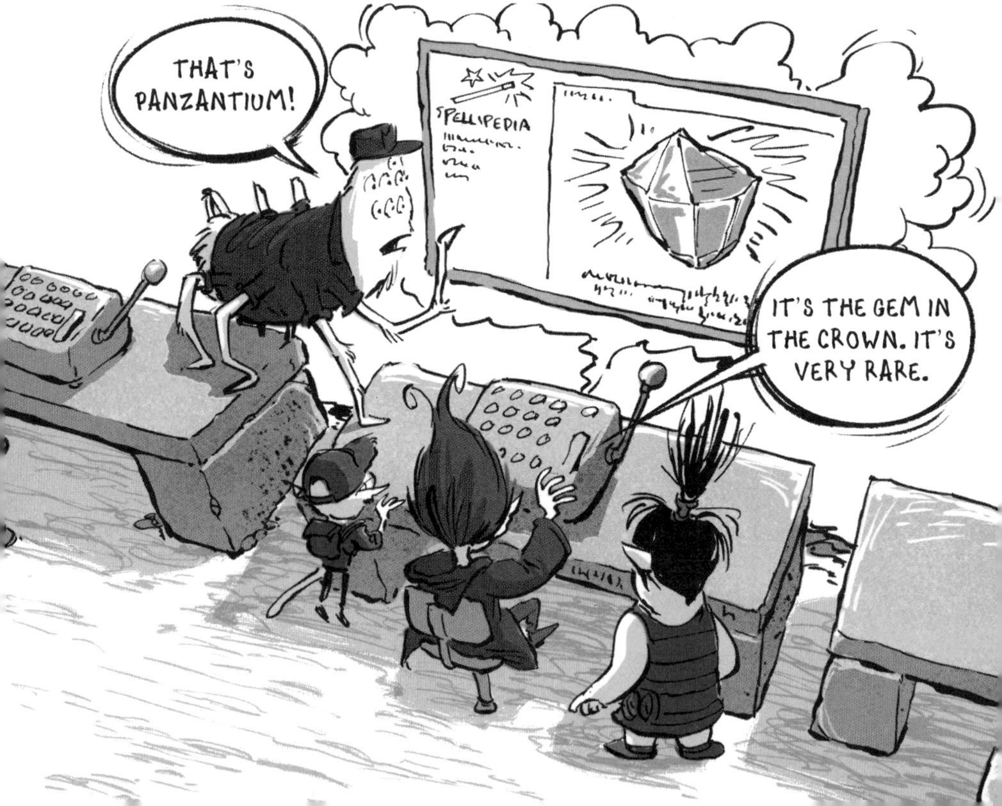
THAT'S PANZANTIUM!
SPELLIPEDIA
IT'S THE GEM IN THE CROWN. IT'S VERY RARE.

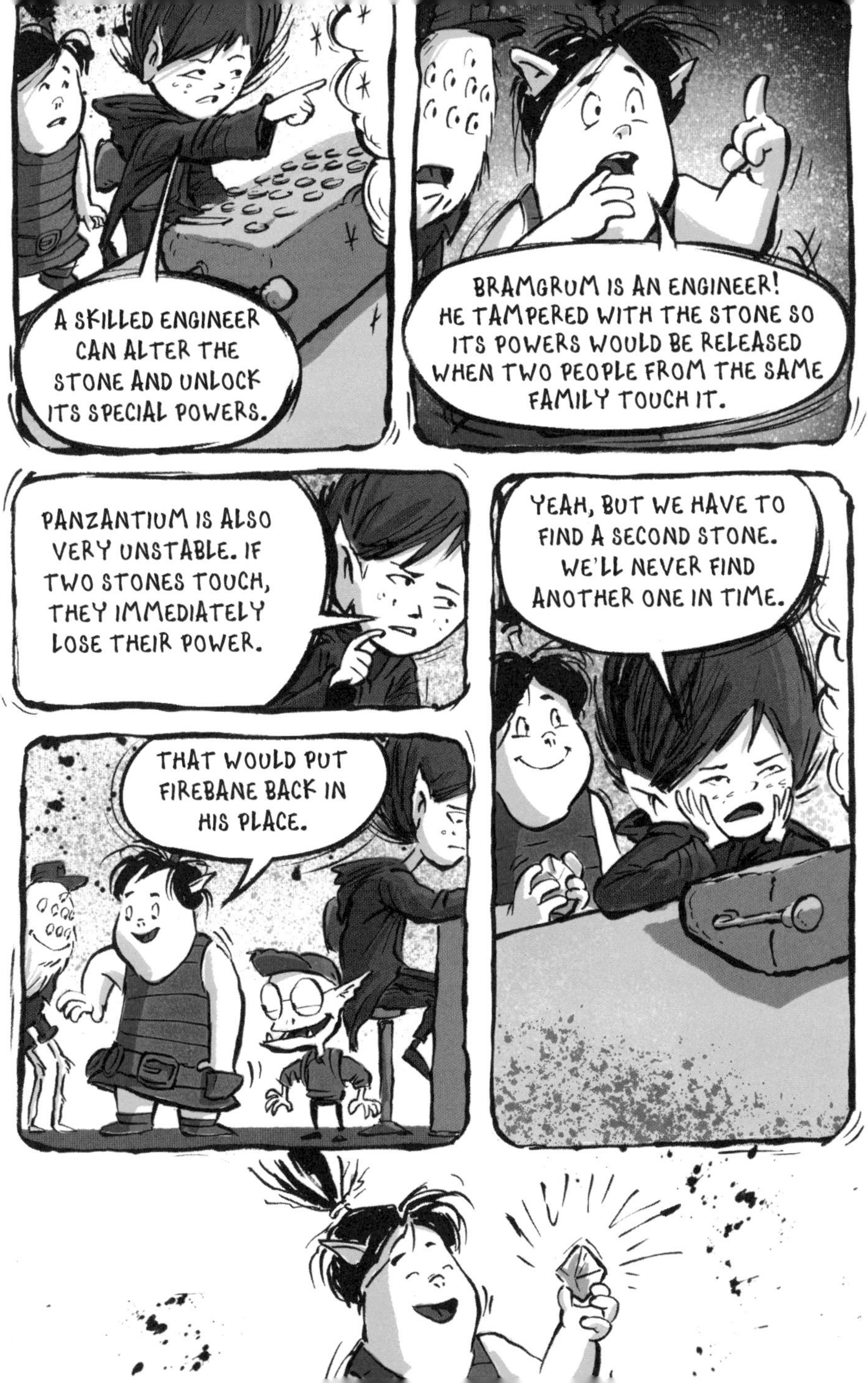
A SKILLED ENGINEER CAN ALTER THE STONE AND UNLOCK ITS SPECIAL POWERS.
BRAMGRUM IS AN ENGINEER! HE TAMPERED WITH THE STONE SO ITS POWERS WOULD BE RELEASED WHEN TWO PEOPLE FROM THE SAME FAMILY TOUCH IT.
PANZANTIUM IS ALSO VERY UNSTABLE. IF TWO STONES TOUCH, THEY IMMEDIATELY LOSE THEIR POWER.
YEAH, BUT WE HAVE TO FIND A SECOND STONE. WE'LL NEVER FIND ANOTHER ONE IN TIME.
THAT WOULD PUT FIREBANE BACK IN HIS PLACE.

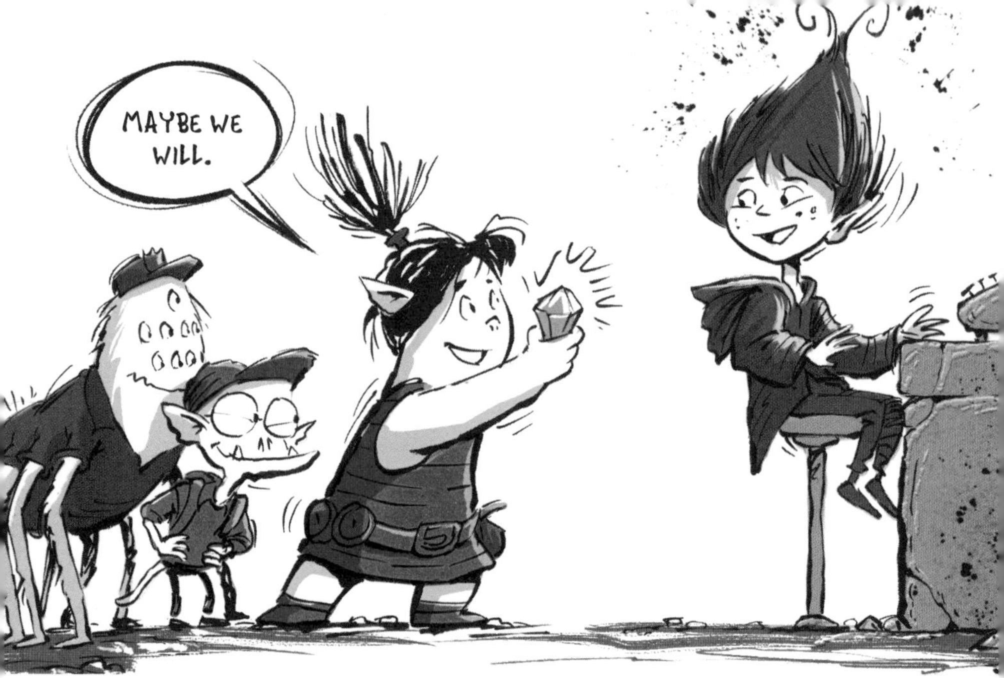
MAYBE WE WILL.

I wished I had a camera to capture the look on Aleetha's face. Her eyes popped out like a pair of loomerbugs. She jumped out of her chair.

"Where did you get that?"

Tank's ears wiggled. "It's a long story."

"But it's really panzantium," I said. "Trust us."

Aleetha carefully took the gem from Tank. "It looks different than the one in the crown," she said.

"The one in the crown has been cut to look pretty," Hugo said. "That one is how it looks when it's pulled from the ground."

"It's from Firebane's vault," I said. "He used it to trick us."

"Then it's only fair we repay the favor." Aleetha studied the stone like she was reading her spell book.

Outside, Firebane howled again. We had to act quickly. The dragon would soon be bored with tormenting the monsters of Lava Falls. Whatever the dragon was up to, there was no doubt he'd soon fly off to wreak havoc in the rest of the Dark Depths.

"We need to get this stone to touch the one in the Crown of Peace," Aleetha said. "That will drain them both of their powers. I hope."

"That crown is on his head. How are we going to get the panzantium to hit the crown?"

Hugo danced on the spot. "Perhaps I can help with that problem."

CHAPTER SEVENTEEN
Rise of the Fallen

Firebane's plan became clear from the top of the wizards' outpost.

As Les led us up a narrow staircase to the roof, Tank and Hugo discussed their plan to hit Firebane's panzantium. Once we got to the top of the tower, we could see across the Dark Depths, and it didn't look good. The planning stopped and the panic began.

"I've never seen so many monsters in one place," I said.

In the distance, the Swamp of Sorrows crawled with lagalanders. Hundreds of the big-eyed fish-heads were gathering on the edge of their swamp. More arrived every second.

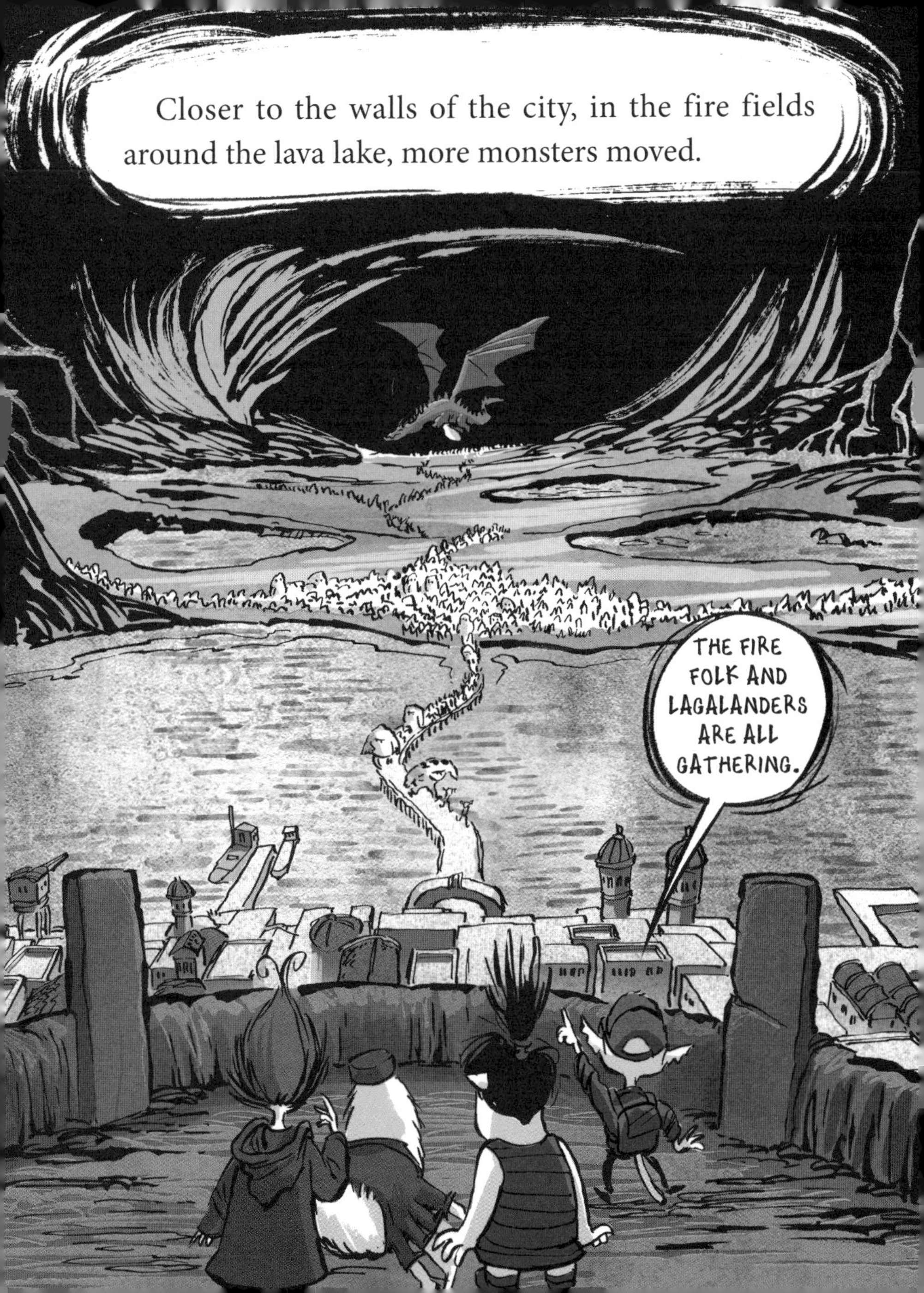
Closer to the walls of the city, in the fire fields around the lava lake, more monsters moved.
THE FIRE FOLK AND LAGALANDERS ARE ALL GATHERING.

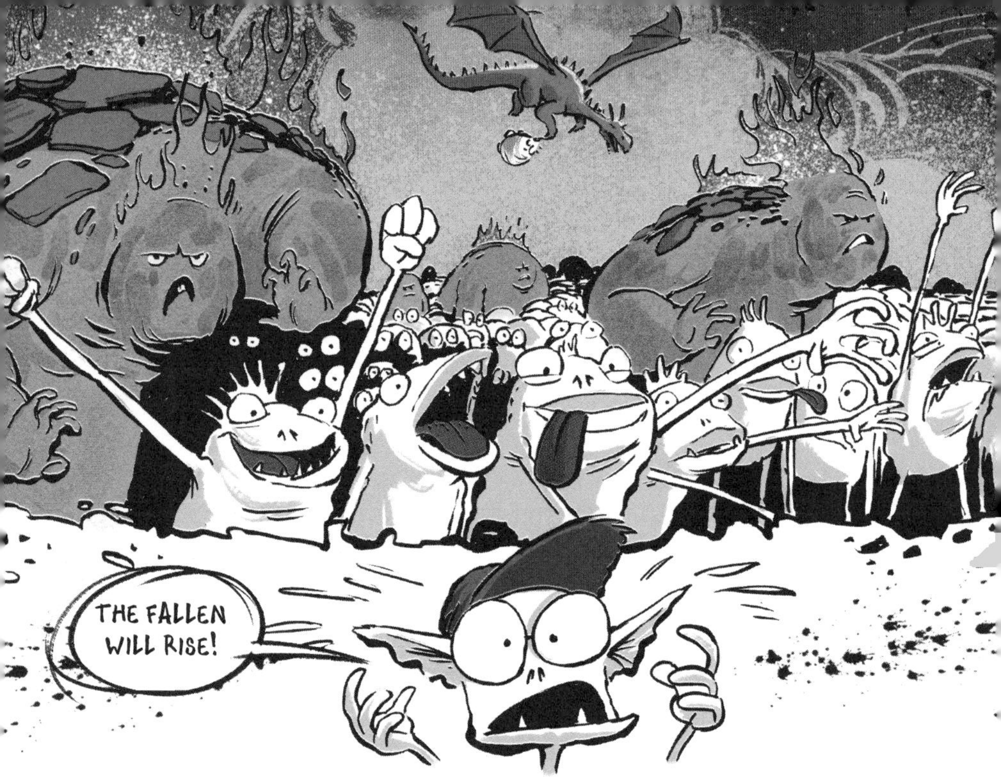
THE FALLEN WILL RISE!

The others turned to me.

"That's what Mr. Ravel said in my dream," I said. "The signal from the panzantium is calling to all the fallen monsters in the Depths."

Aleetha jumped on my thought. "And the more spiders and dwarves he zaps with the stone, the stronger the signal grows."

"And the more beasts join his army," Hugo finished. "The lagalanders and fire folk have been treated badly for many years. With Firebane leading them, they probably see a chance to get revenge on the spiders and dwarves."

"And then he'll take this army to Slick City and the rest of the mountain," I said. "We need to warn everyone."

"Les is sending a message back to the Shadow Tower," Aleetha said. "Hopefully, the wizards will get Mayor Grimlock to listen and be prepared."

"Grimlock is a stubborn old ogre," Tank snorted. "He won't believe the wizards until Firebane is breathing fire on the Slick City town hall."

Aleetha grinned. "That's why we have to stop Firebane here in Lava Falls."

"Then we better get to work, Tank." Hugo moved to the far side of the tower. The spider spun a thick thread of web and worked it into shape with his front legs. "We should set up right about here."

Tank peered over the edge of the tower. "That'll do."

She took one end of Hugo's web and tied it to the tower's ledge. Hugo raced along the ledge and stuck more bits of web along the tower's wall until their web contraption was complete.

Thick strands of web stuck to the walls like pieces of rope. Each piece ran back to a larger patch of web shaped like a bucket.

"It looks like a hammock for spiders," I said. "Are we napping our way to victory?"

"Very funny, Fizz." Tank rolled her eyes.

"It's a catapult!" Hugo said. "It will launch the panzantium at Firebane."

I pointed to the bucket of the catapult. "That scoop is way too big to hold the stone. It'll just fall out."

"That's exactly what we thought," Tank said. "Our original plan was to shoot the stone at Firebane."

Hugo tied another thick strand of his web to the catapult. "But now that we've seen how fast that dragon can fly, we knew we'd never hit the stone in the crown. On the way up here Tank had a brilliant idea."

The troll's ears wiggled, and a grin spread across her face.

"What if someone carries the stone to Firebane?" she said. "Then they climb along the dragon's body to the crown and touch the two stones."

"So we adjusted the size of the catapult to make it bigger." Hugo stood by the web bucket proudly.

"Bigger for whom?" I said.

Tank rolled her eyes. "For the monster that's getting shot onto Firebane's back, silly."

My gut tightened as my friend's plan became more clear. "And who exactly is that going to be?"

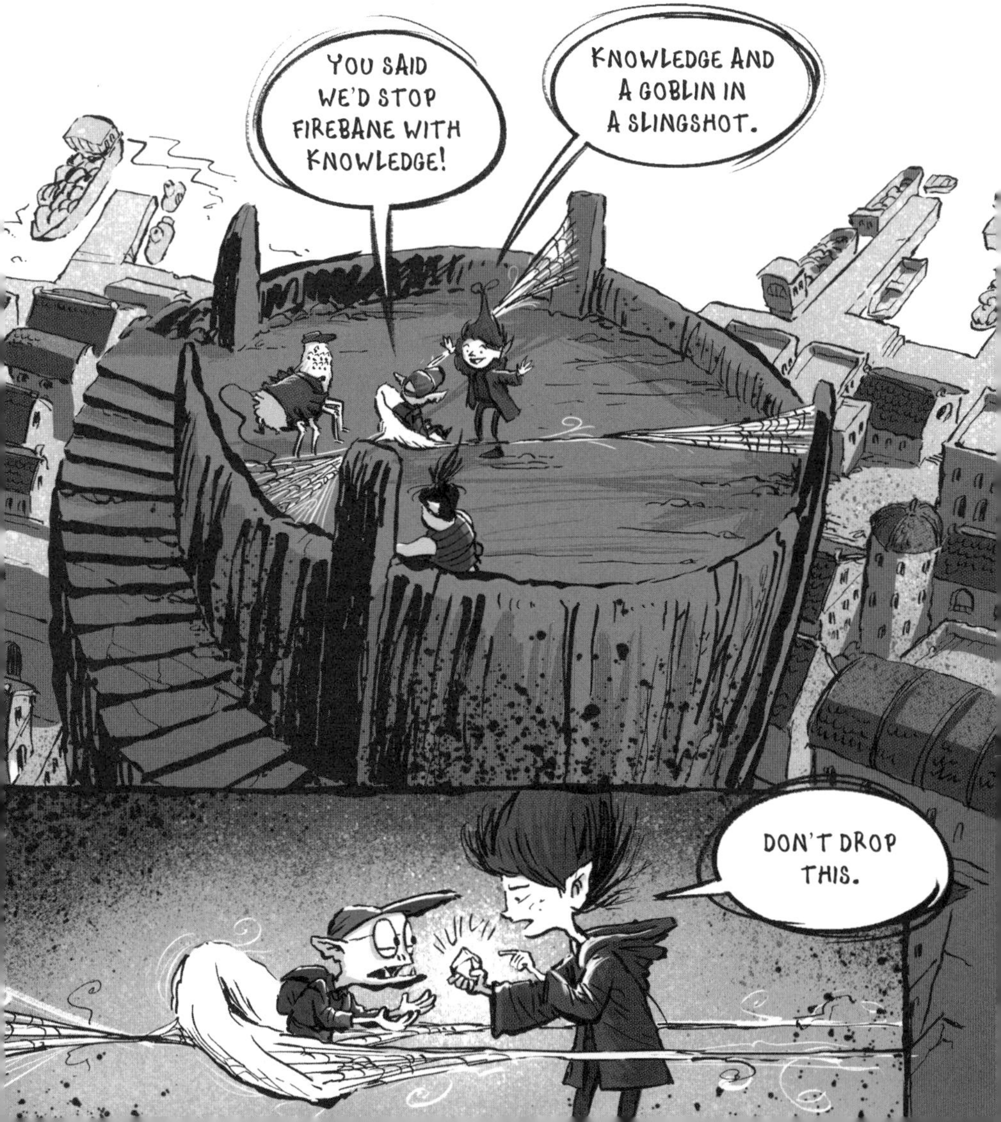
YOU SAID WE'D STOP FIREBANE WITH KNOWLEDGE!
KNOWLEDGE AND A GOBLIN IN A SLINGSHOT.
DON'T DROP THIS.

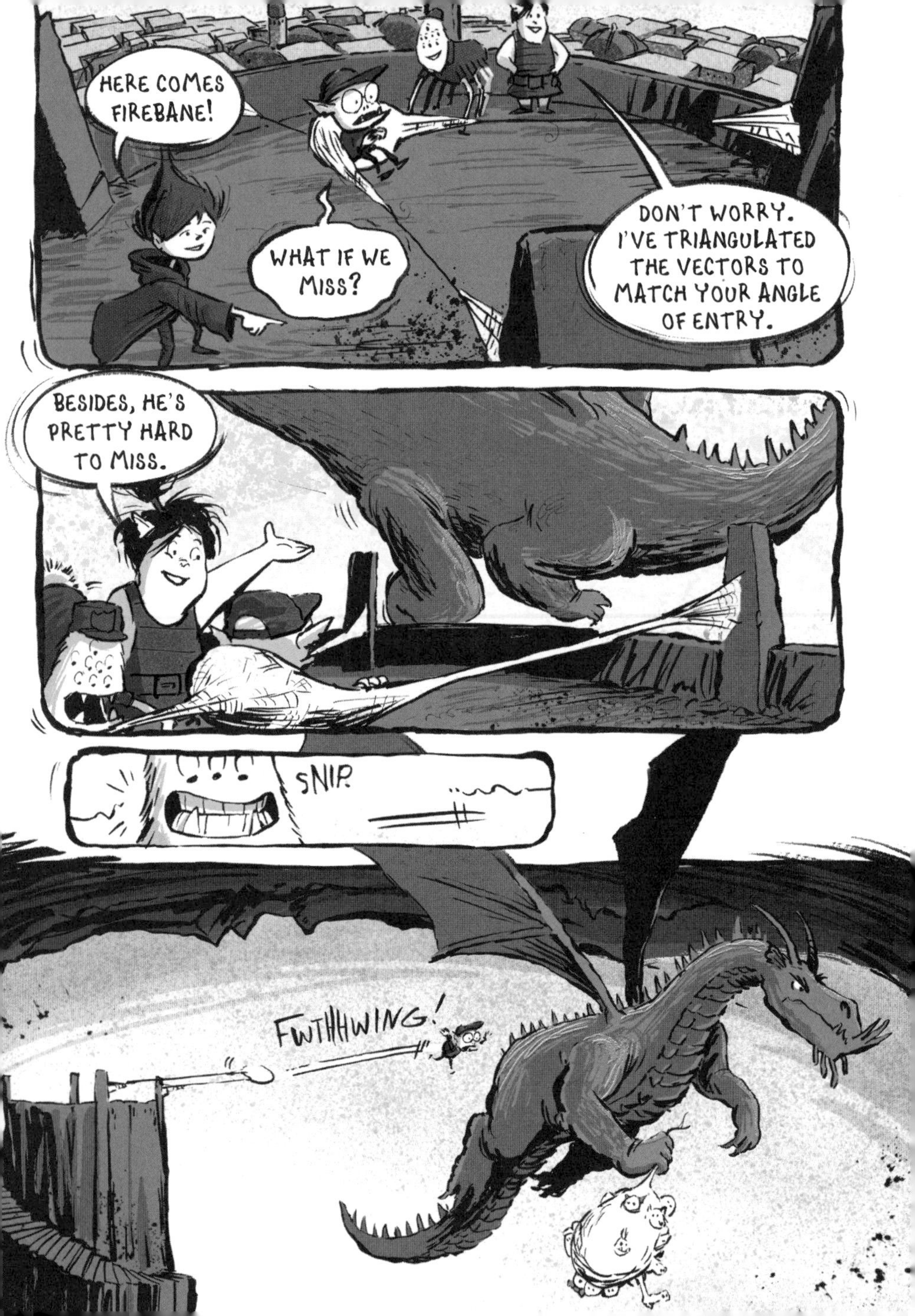
HERE COMES FIREBANE!
WHAT IF WE MISS?
DON'T WORRY. I'VE TRIANGULATED THE VECTORS TO MATCH YOUR ANGLE OF ENTRY.
BESIDES, HE'S PRETTY HARD TO MISS.
SNIP.
FWTHHWING!

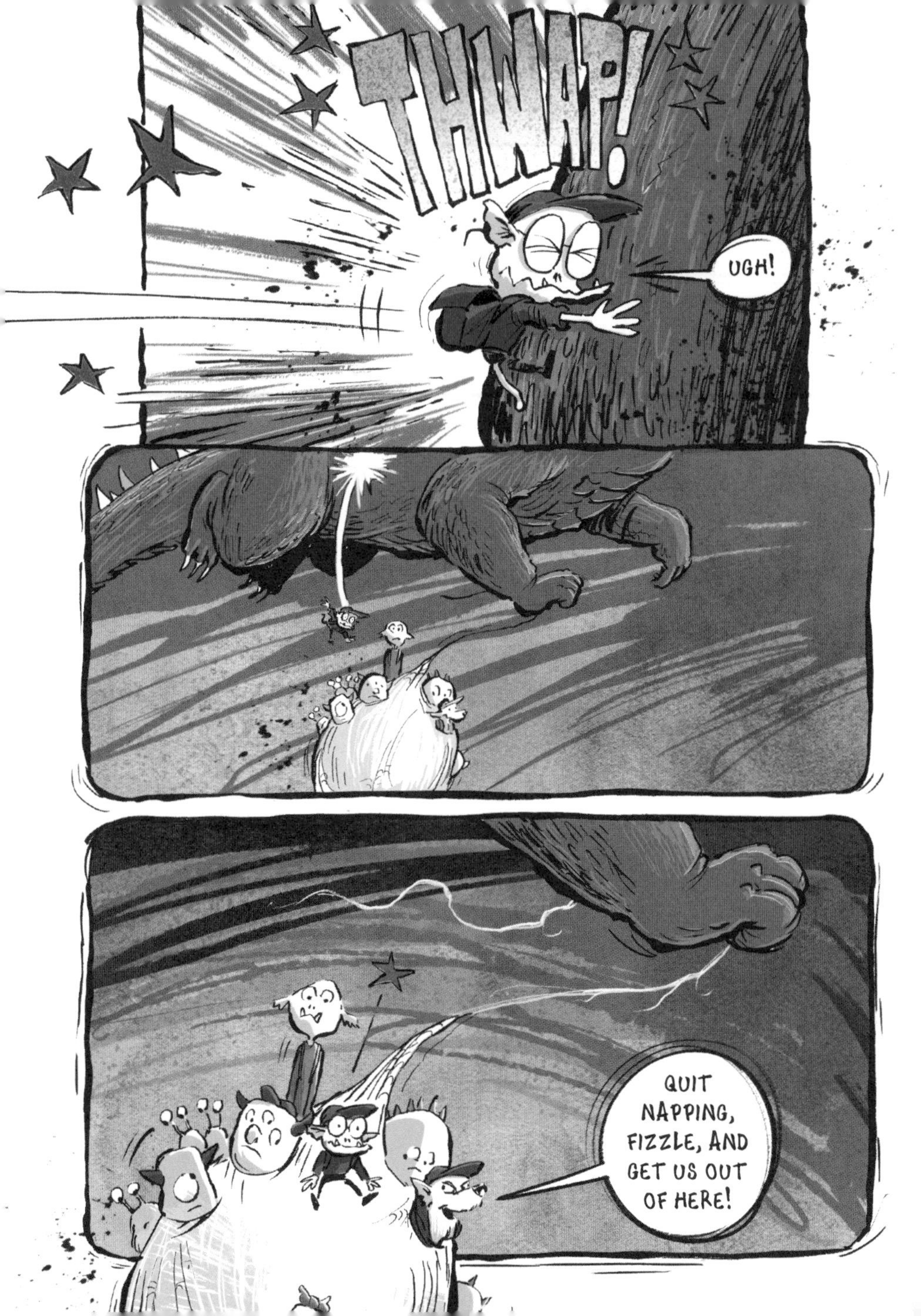
THWAP!
UGH!
QUIT NAPPING, FIZZLE, AND GET US OUT OF HERE!

CHAPTER EIGHTEEN

How NOT to Ride a Dragon

I didn't know which was worse, dangling below a flying dragon or being so close to Rizzo Rawlins and his stinky breath.

"Wake up, Fizzle!" Rizzo growled. "You're the one that got us into this mess. Now get us out!"

The smell of kibble sandwich snapped me to my senses. I made a mental note to thank the kobold and his terrible dental habits for that. But first I had a dragon to climb.

I tightened my grip on the strand of web hanging from Firebane's claw and let my head clear. Far below me, Lava Falls roared by. Above me, Firebane's wings beat with a steady rhythm. The big dragon hadn't noticed a little goblin smacking into his side, but my luck wouldn't last long. Each second I hesitated, the closer the dragon came to ordering his army of fallen beasts to march across the Depths.

My free hand went to my pocket and touched the panzantium tucked safely away. The stone was small and didn't weigh much, but with the fate of the mountain on my scales, it felt like I was carrying a boulder. At my feet, my classmates wriggled in their wrappings. I hung on to the web tendril just below Firebane's claws. A hole appeared in the web at my toes. Henelle, the octoclops with attitude, glared at me through the gap with her one eye.

"This is all your fault, Fizz Marlow!" she shouted.

"Henelle," I snapped, "give it a rest. I'm trying my best."

"I'm still reporting you to Principal Weaver when we get back!"

"The principal is in Firebane's crown!"

Above me thunder rumbled, but it wasn't from the sky.

"What have we got here?" The dragon turned his long neck in our direction. "Fizz Marlow. Here to save the day, are we? You are a determined detective, little goblin."

"So they tell me," I croaked.

Henelle had vanished. Probably reporting Firebane for bad behavior.

The dragon flew toward the town hall. The building's roof had been destroyed when Firebane blasted his way up from the Abyss. Now, all that remained was a gaping hole leading down to the Abyss. I could see the glow of the deadly opening from up here.

"But the question is, Fizz Marlow, can you fly?"

Firebane opened his claws, releasing the web strands in his grip.

We fell. Obviously.

The last thing I saw as my class fell into the Abyss was Rizzo Rawlins's orange snout poking through the hole in the web.

"I'll get you for this, Fizz Marlow!" he shrieked.

Considering how many times I had wished for this to happen to the kobold, I wasn't enjoying it. But I had no time to worry about my classmates. I was too busy jumping from the falling web.

The moment Firebane let go, I leaped. My hand snagged a claw, and I climbed. As much as I hate gym, climbing is the one thing I'm good at. I pulled up again from the dragon's claw and grabbed a leg.

From there it was as easy as climbing to the top of stinkhorn stalks back home. I got halfway up the leg when I felt Firebane's gaze on me.

"Really Fizz," the dragon said. "This is getting boring."

"Too bad." I scrambled onto his back and locked in with my claws. "I'm just getting started."

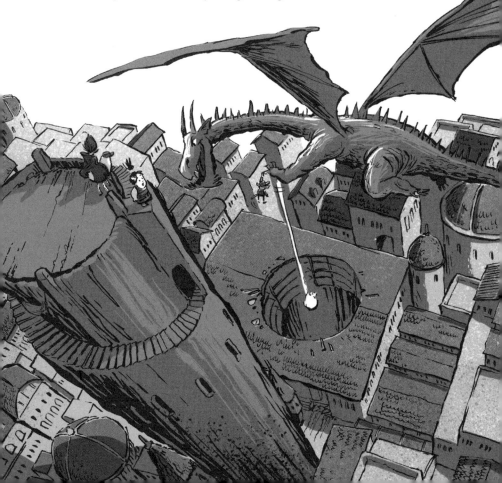

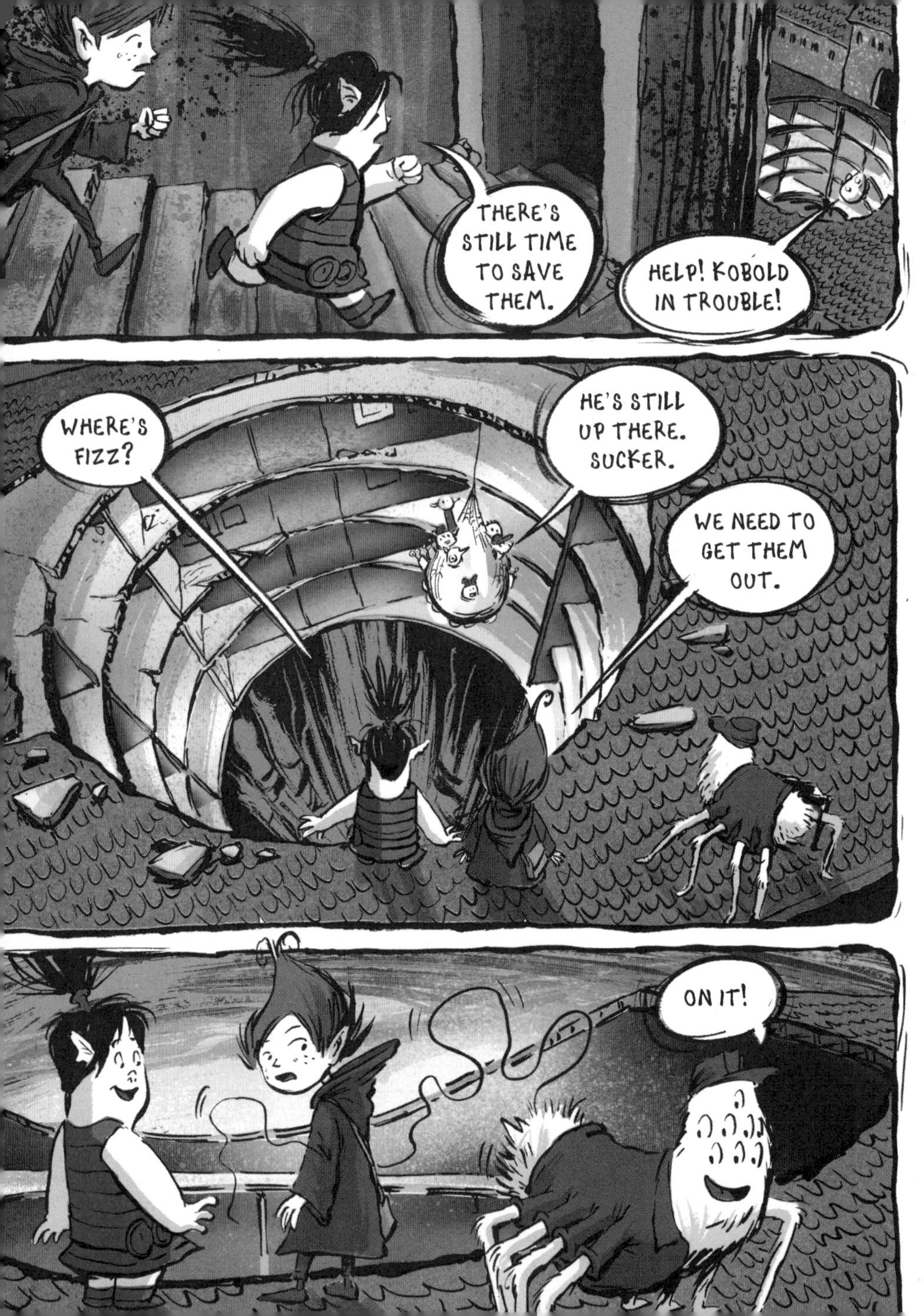
THERE'S STILL TIME TO SAVE THEM.
HELP! KOBOLD IN TROUBLE!
WHERE'S FIZZ?
HE'S STILL UP THERE. SUCKER.
WE NEED TO GET THEM OUT.
ON IT!

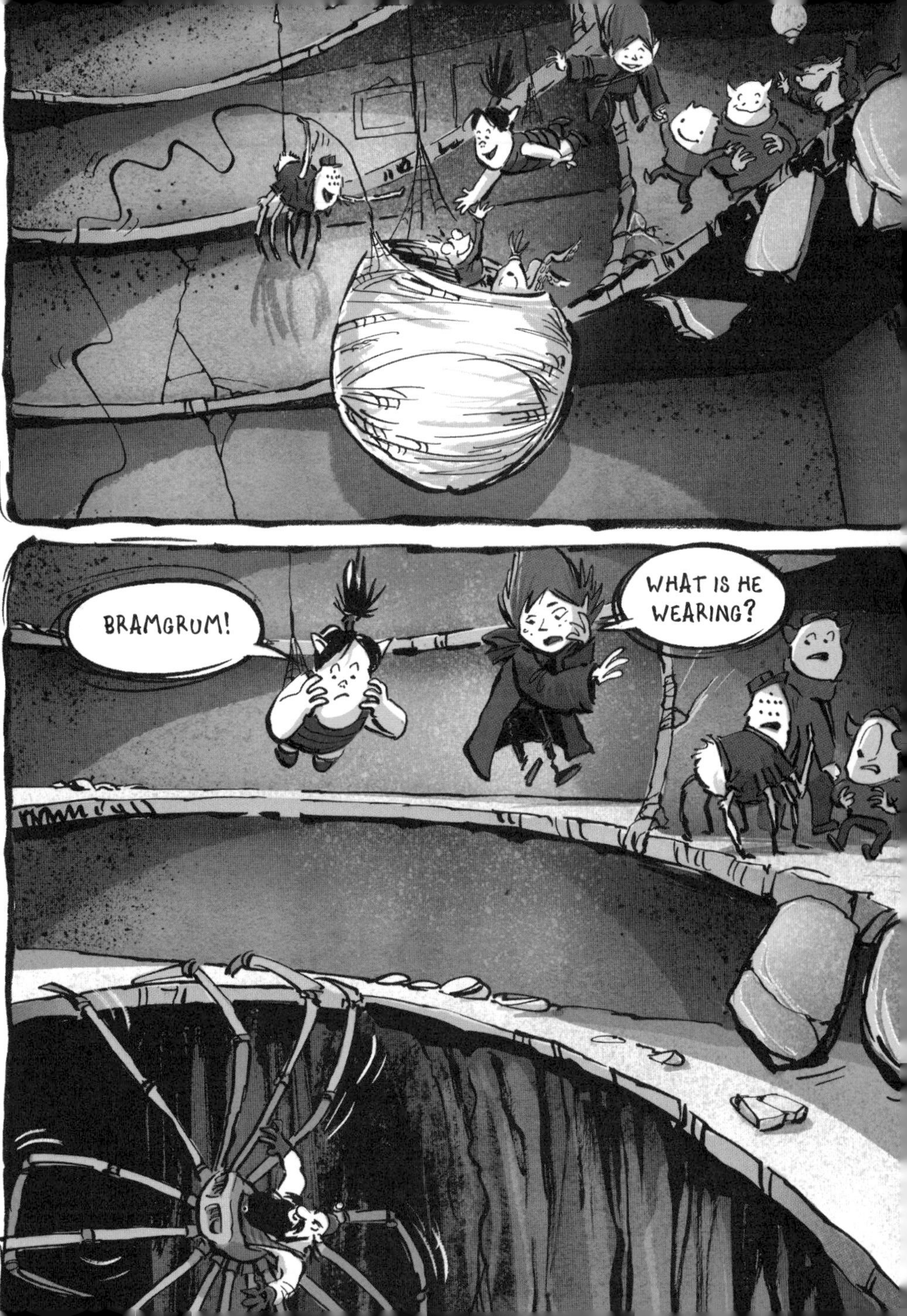
BRAMGRUM!
WHAT IS HE WEARING?

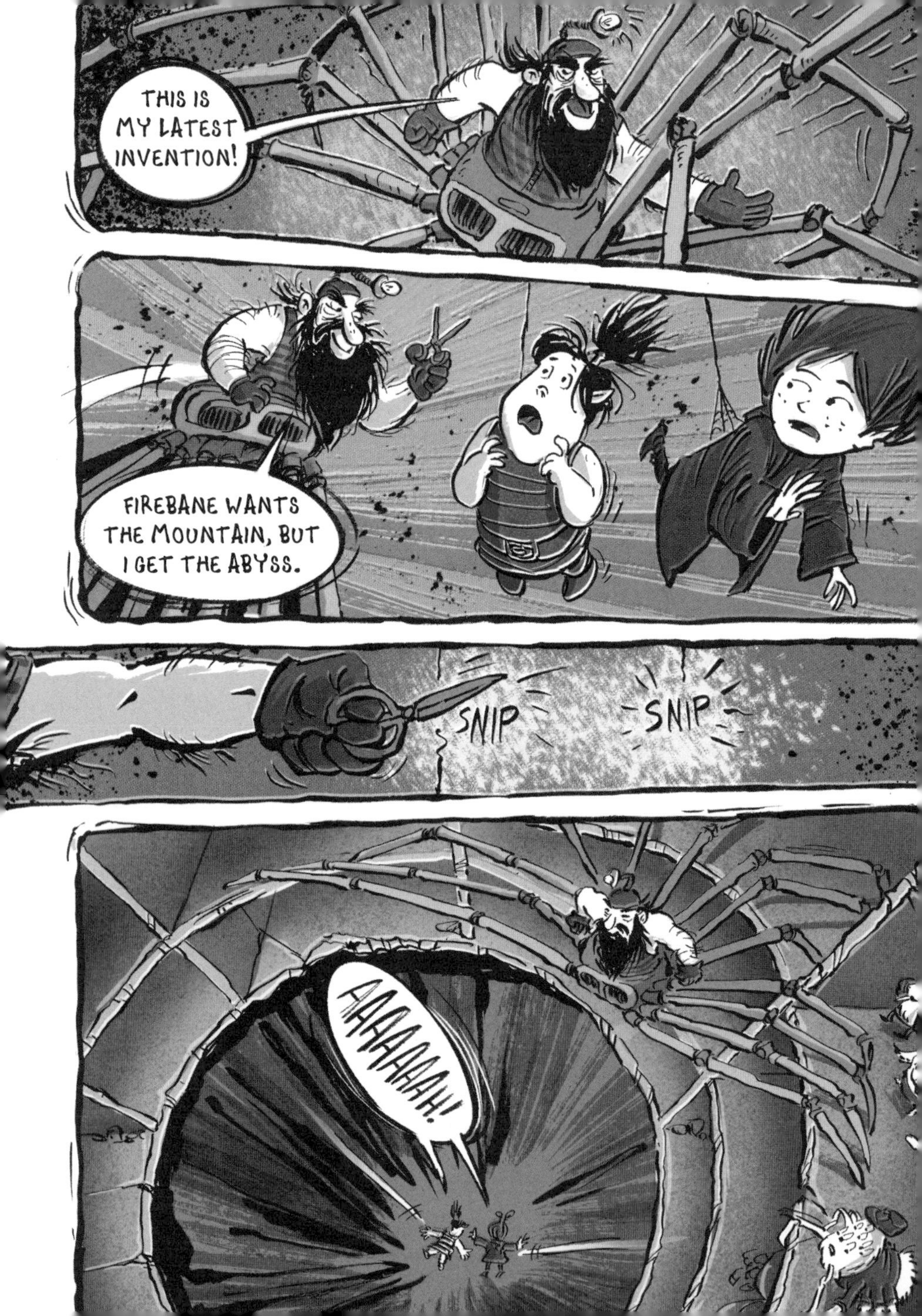
THIS IS MY LATEST INVENTION!
FIREBANE WANTS THE MOUNTAIN, BUT I GET THE ABYSS.
SNIP
SNIP
AAAAAAAH!

I had figured something out.

I knew what Firebane was going to do next. In the time it took me to get to his back, I had guessed the dragon's every twist and turn. He climbed, and I was ready. He barrel-rolled, and I hung on. I knew his next move just like I had seen through his disguise as Mr. Ravel and Gilthil. It was like we were connected. Firebane had known it all along, of course. The trouble with fighting the smartest monster in the mountain is, well, he's smart.

"I see you're figuring it out, Fizz. We have a bond, you and I. There is no use denying it."

The dragon's words chilled my claws.

"I don't want to bond with you," I shouted. "I want to stop you!"

I also wanted to get as far away from him as possible. But first I had a stone to bash. I scurried along Firebane's spine until I could see the crown resting on his big, fat, scaly head. Even with our newfound "bond," getting close enough to put the two panzantium stones together wasn't going to be easy.

We soared out over the fire fields. The fire folk were gathering on the edges of the fields bordering the dwarf lands. They were an army of fire and destruction, ready to march when the order came from their dragon master. The creatures of flame cheered as Firebane flew by.

"Soon, my soldiers," the dragon roared. "Soon we march!"

Firebane turned back toward Lava Falls. I raced up to his massive shoulders. I pulled the panzantium stone from my pocket. *Soon* was right. Soon Firebane would pay for his chaos. Soon the power of the panzantium in the dragon's crown would be finished.

I jumped to my feet as we soared back over the Abyss. I held the stone in my hand, ready to jump onto the dragon's neck.

The dragon's shoulder suddenly jerked. Instead of jumping forward, I fell backward. I tumbled down Firebane's back with his laughter ringing in my ears.

"You can't read my *every* move, Fizz Marlow," he called. "And you cannot win this battle."

I rolled down the dragon's tail and made the mistake of looking down.

Far below me, in the hole that was the town hall, I saw the purple stone falling toward the Abyss.

Firebane swooped low. He whipped his tail, sending me falling to the ground. I landed with a crunch. Pain spiked through my scales.

"I do not wish to harm you, Fizz Marlow," he said. "Go home. Rana is worried."

"Rana?"

"Home is where you belong, Fizz."

He was in the air by the time my brain got back online. *Did he just say Rana? As in, my mom?* My scales went cold. I didn't have time to think about that. I had bigger problems.

I had dropped the panzantium into the Abyss.

It was official. We were totally doomed.

CHAPTER NINETEEN

Into the Abyss

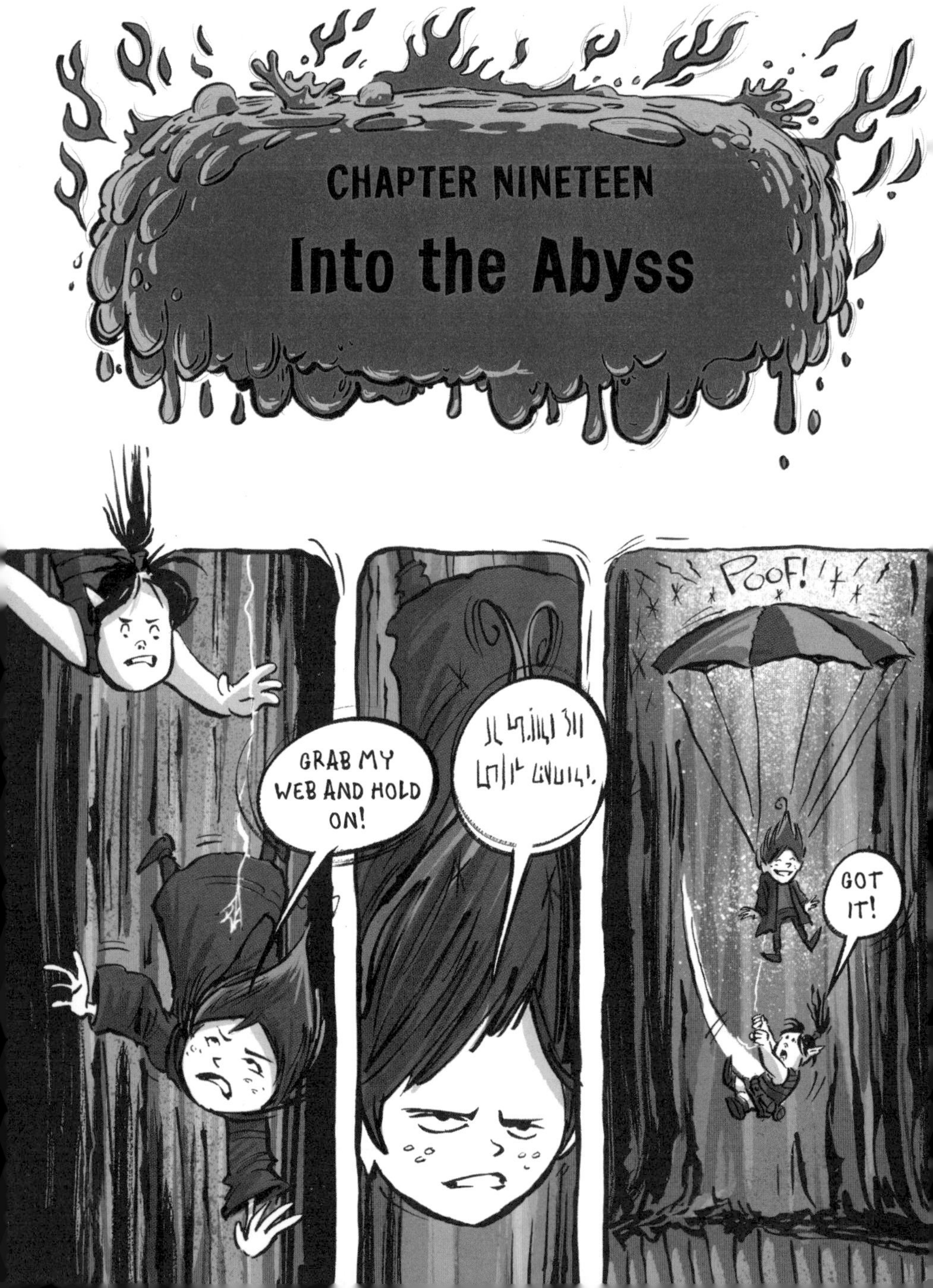
GRAB MY WEB AND HOLD ON!
POOF!
GOT IT!

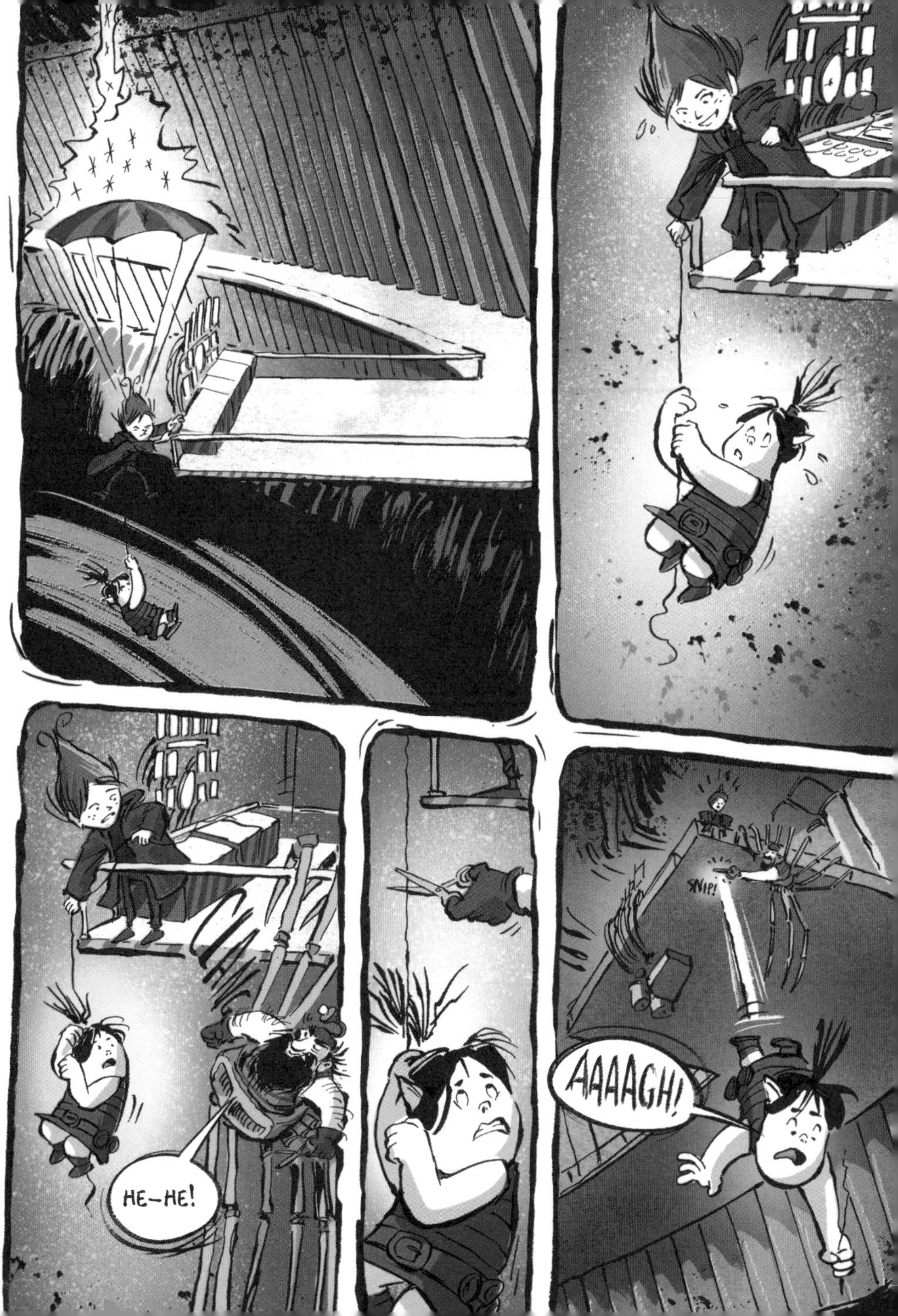
HE-HE!
SNIP!
AAAAGH!

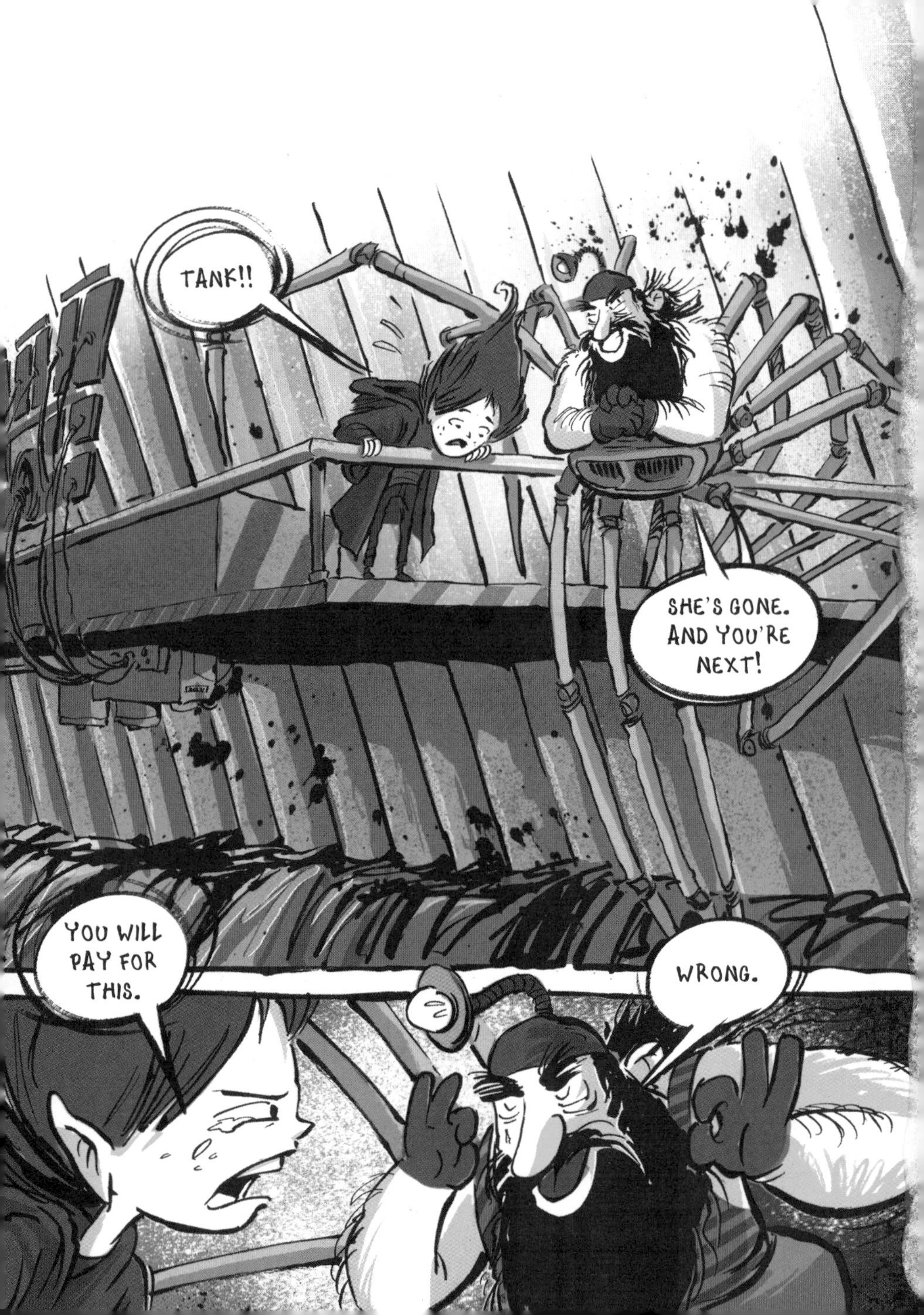
TANK!!
SHE'S GONE. AND YOU'RE NEXT!
YOU WILL PAY FOR THIS.
WRONG.

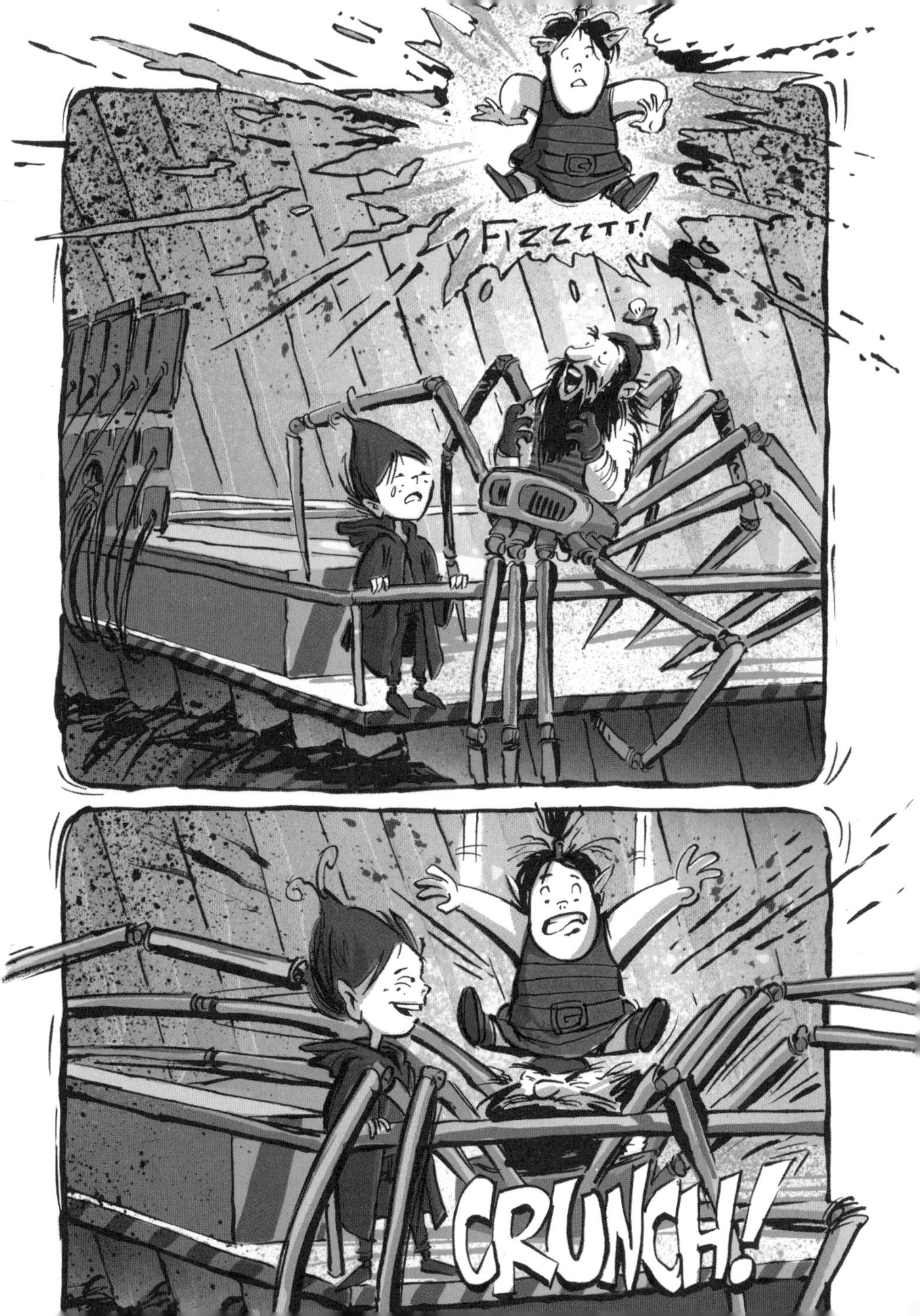
FIZZZTT!
CRUNCH!

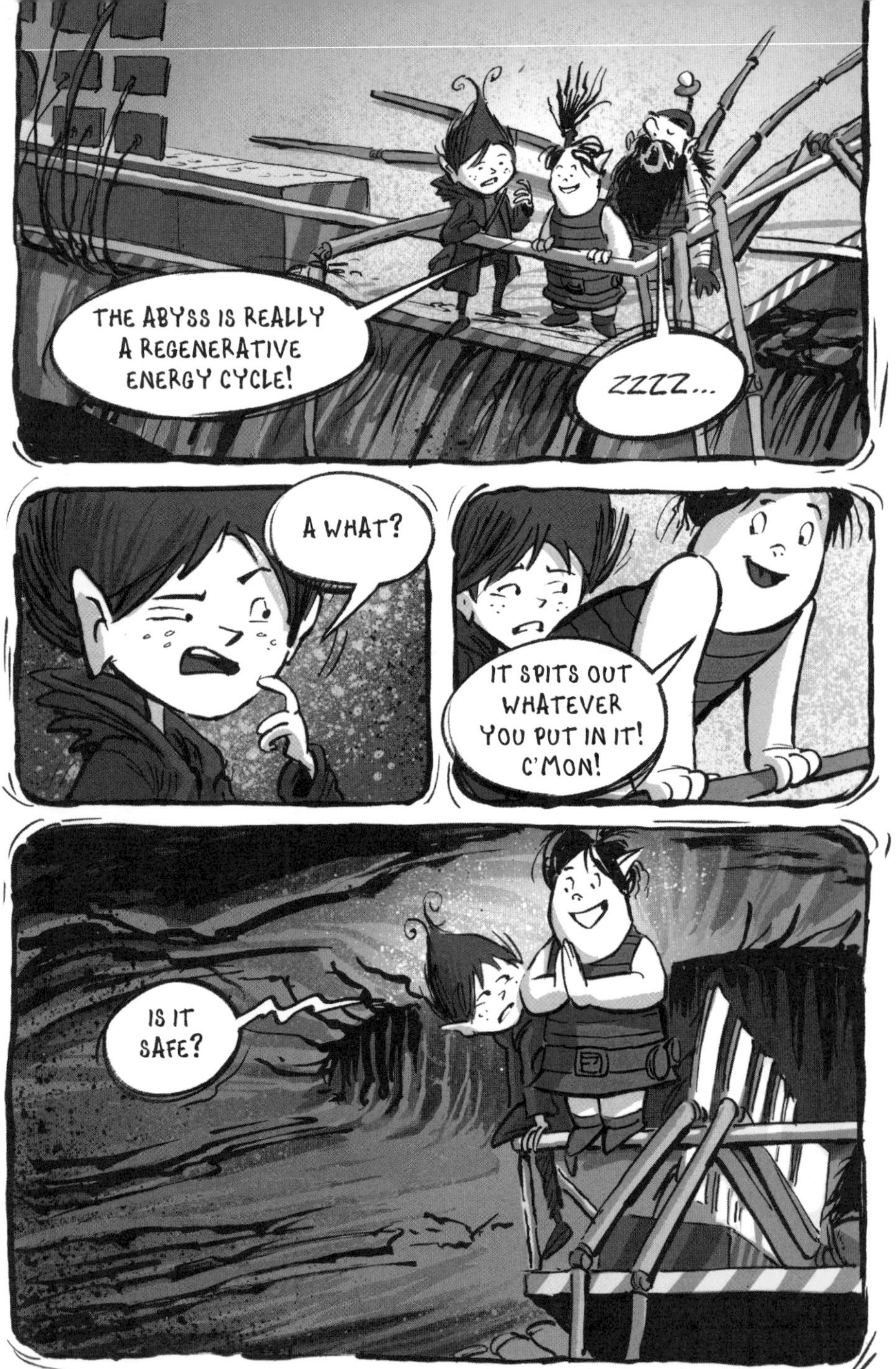
THE ABYSS IS REALLY A REGENERATIVE ENERGY CYCLE!
ZZZZ...
A WHAT?
IT SPITS OUT WHATEVER YOU PUT IN IT! C'MON!
IS IT SAFE?

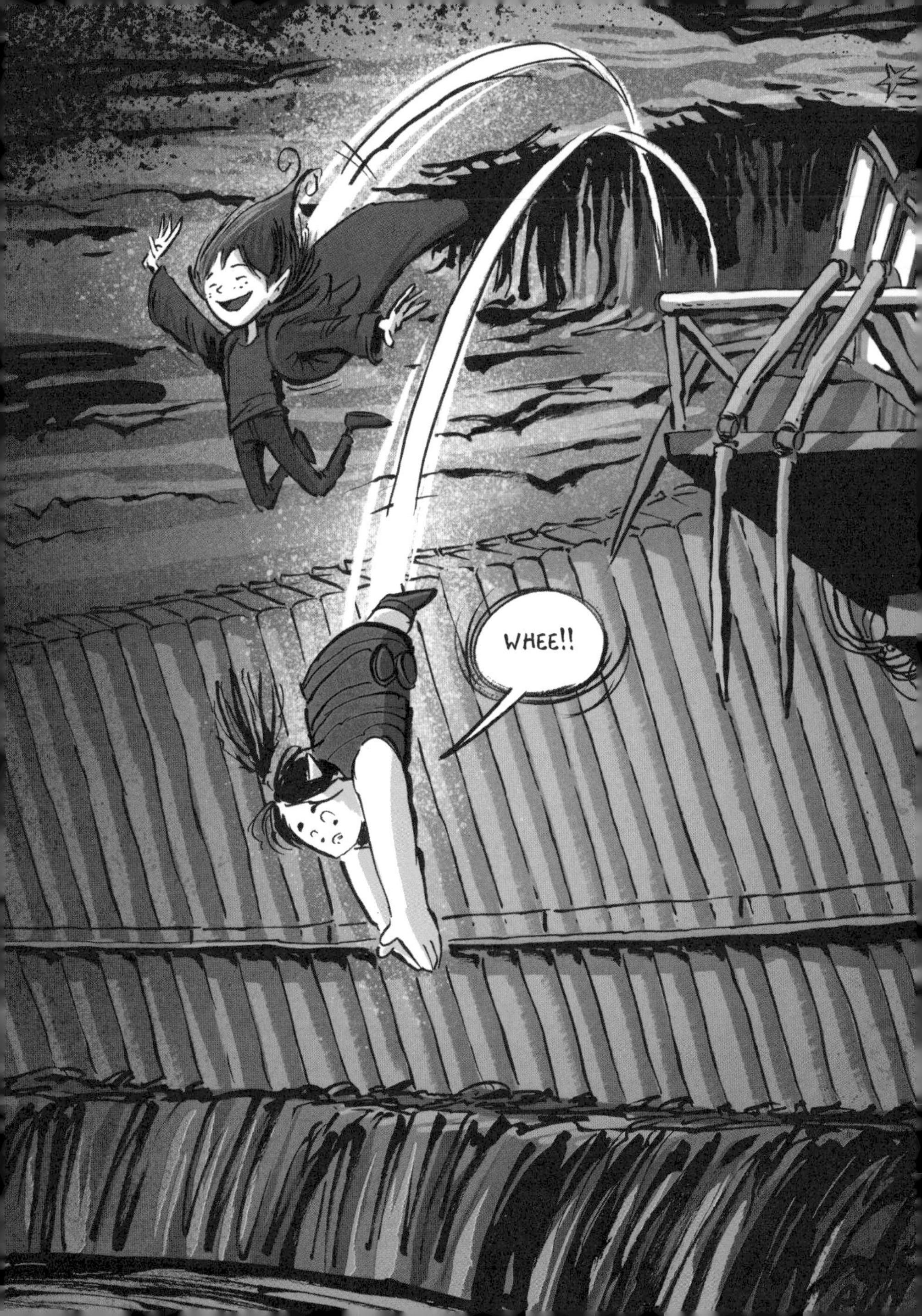
WHEE!!

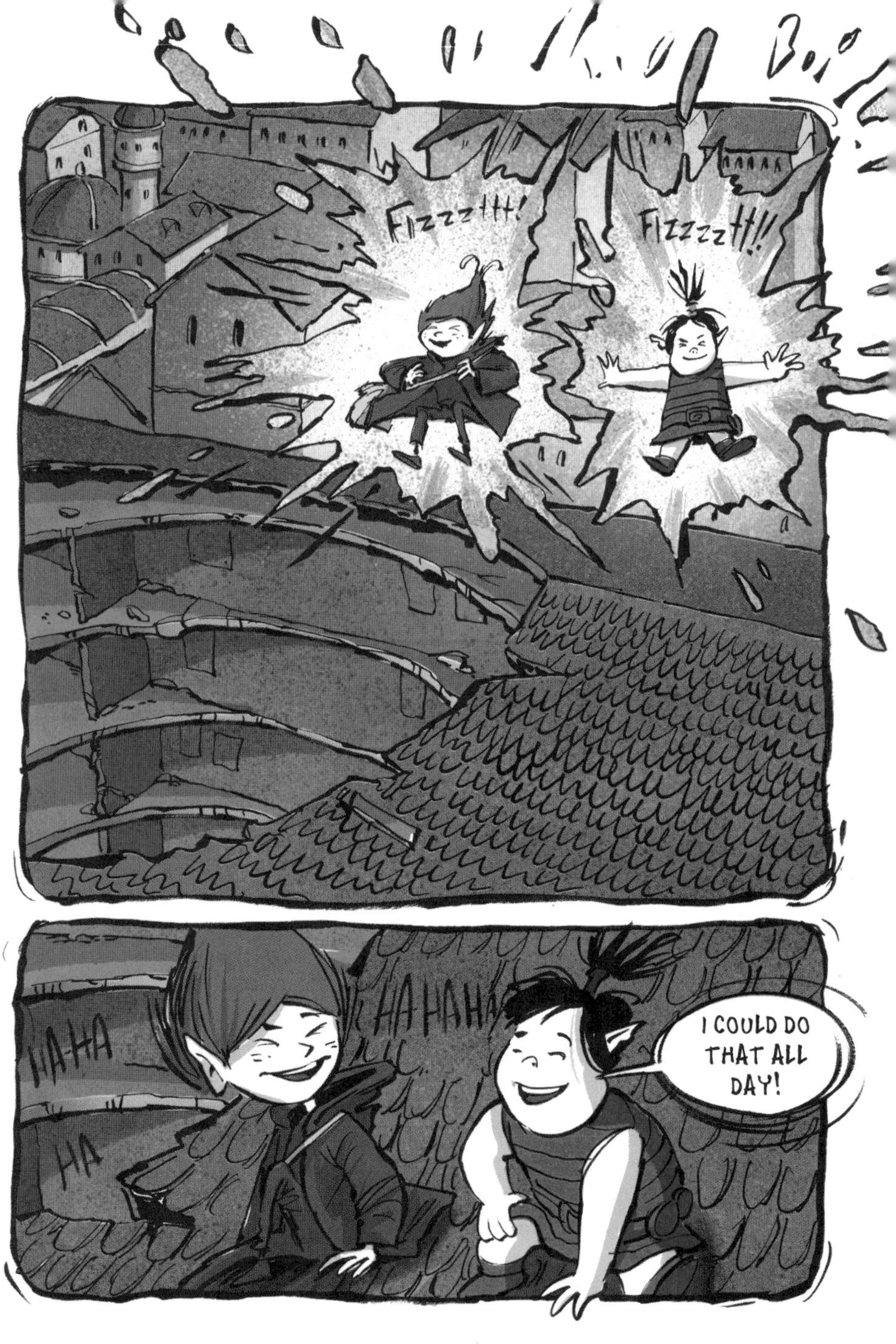
FIZZZZTTT!
FIZZZZZTT!!
HAHA
HA
HAHAHA
I COULD DO THAT ALL DAY!

Things didn't look good.

I picked myself up and unkinked my tail.

Firebane had dumped me on what was left of the town hall's roof. All that remained was a crumbling ledge around a dragon-sized hole.

A spider leg appeared from the hole and gripped the ledge.

"Hugo!" I dragged my friend to the safety of the ledge. "You're alive."

"And so are you," he said.

Above us, Firebane roared.

"And so is he." I hung my head. "Hugo, I dropped the stone."

"That's okay." Hugo raised an arm. "I found it."

He handed me something wrapped in web. I pulled off the sticky wrapping and held the familiar purple stone.

"The panzantium! How?"

"You had perfect aim when you dropped it." He pointed to the hole. "It sailed right down the shaft, and I found it in one of my webs."

"You caught that tiny stone in that hole?" I said.

"Sure." He smiled. "Catching little things in our webs is what we spiders do."

Lava Falls was living up to its name. From the top of the town hall, we could see fire folk marching through the streets, setting alight anything that would burn. Surprisingly, for a town surrounded by lava, that turned out to be a lot. Smoked filled the air, marking the fire folk's path.

Hugo adjusted a thick rope made of web he was putting around my waist. As he spun the web, he told me his plan to stop Firebane, and what had happened to Tank and Aleetha. My scales froze at the news.

"Are you sure they're gone?" I stared at the gaping hole in the roof. "We need to go down there and find them!"

Hugo shook his head. "We need to stop Firebane."

I couldn't think about stopping Firebane at that moment. I could barely think at all. My two best friends were gone, and so was my will to fight. I just wanted to curl up in a ball, wrap my tail around me and forget that I'd ever come to the Dark Depths.

"Fizz, snap out of it." Hugo tugged on the web tied to my waist. "We have to stop Firebane, or we'll lose more than just our two friends."

The dark shape of the dragon appeared in the distance just beyond the lava lake. He flew toward Lava Falls.

"He's coming back," Hugo said. "Just like you said he would, Fizz."

The sight of Firebane jolted me out of my misery.

"I knew that stone was sending out a signal to the fire folk and lagalanders," I said. "He has to fly over every few minutes to keep them under his control."

Firebane soared toward the town hall. Hugo stepped to the edge of the roof. In one hand he held the end of the length of web tied to my waist. The spider waited until Firebane roared over us.

"Hang on!"

Hugo leaped from the roof. The web around my waist snapped tight, and I was pulled into the air after him. Using his front legs, Hugo spun new strands of webbing and swung from building to building, following Firebane's path. I whiplashed through the air after Hugo as he chased Firebane. Hugo gained speed and I gained momentum, swinging wildly behind him, moving twice as fast.

Then, just as we came within reach of the crown, Hugo gave me one last whip and sent me into the air. The plan was to sail toward the crown so fast that Mr. Older Than the Mountain wouldn't even notice.

We nailed the moving-fast part. The going unnoticed? Not so much.

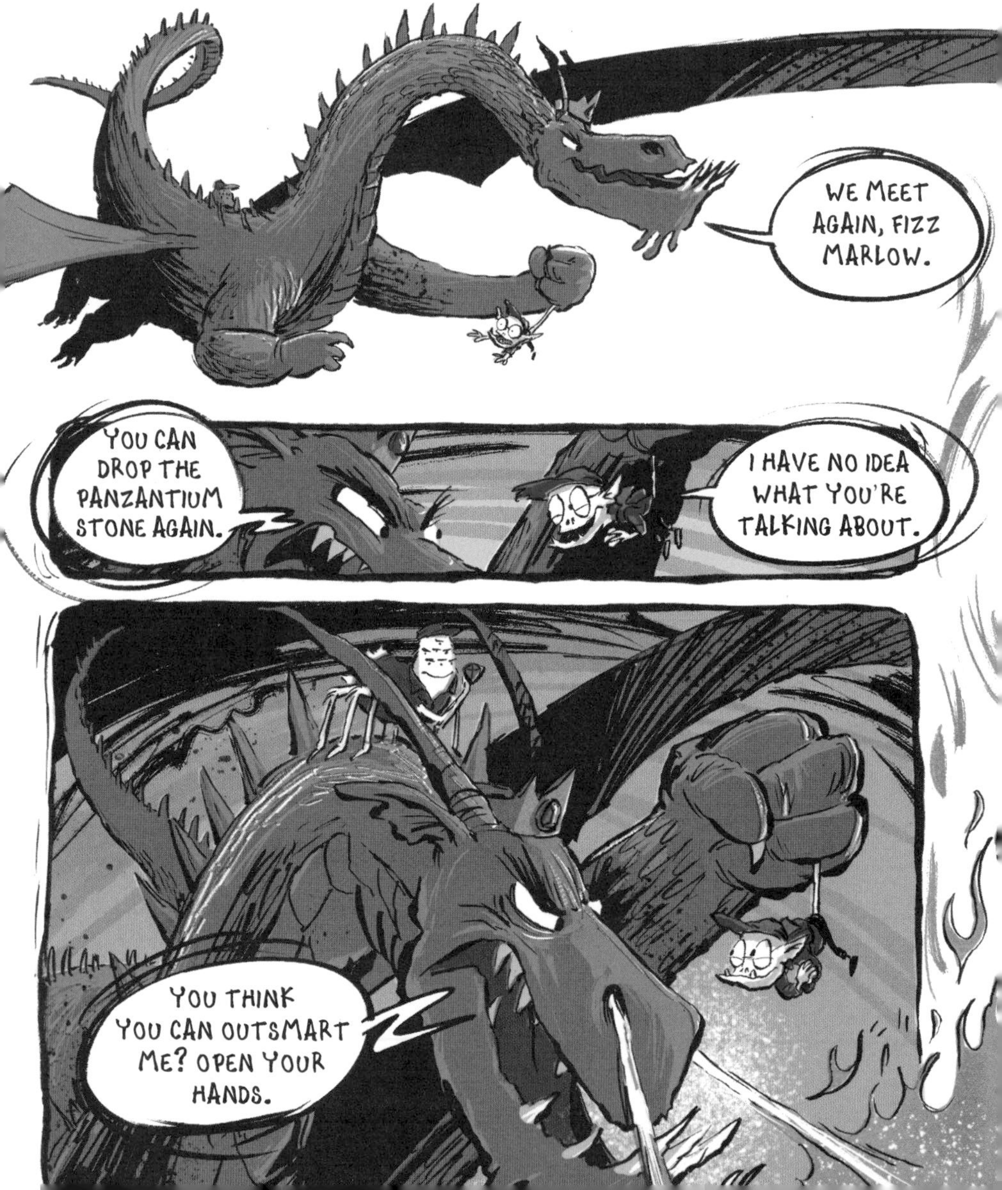
WE MEET AGAIN, FIZZ MARLOW.
YOU CAN DROP THE PANZANTIUM STONE AGAIN.
I HAVE NO IDEA WHAT YOU'RE TALKING ABOUT.
YOU THINK YOU CAN OUTSMART ME? OPEN YOUR HANDS.

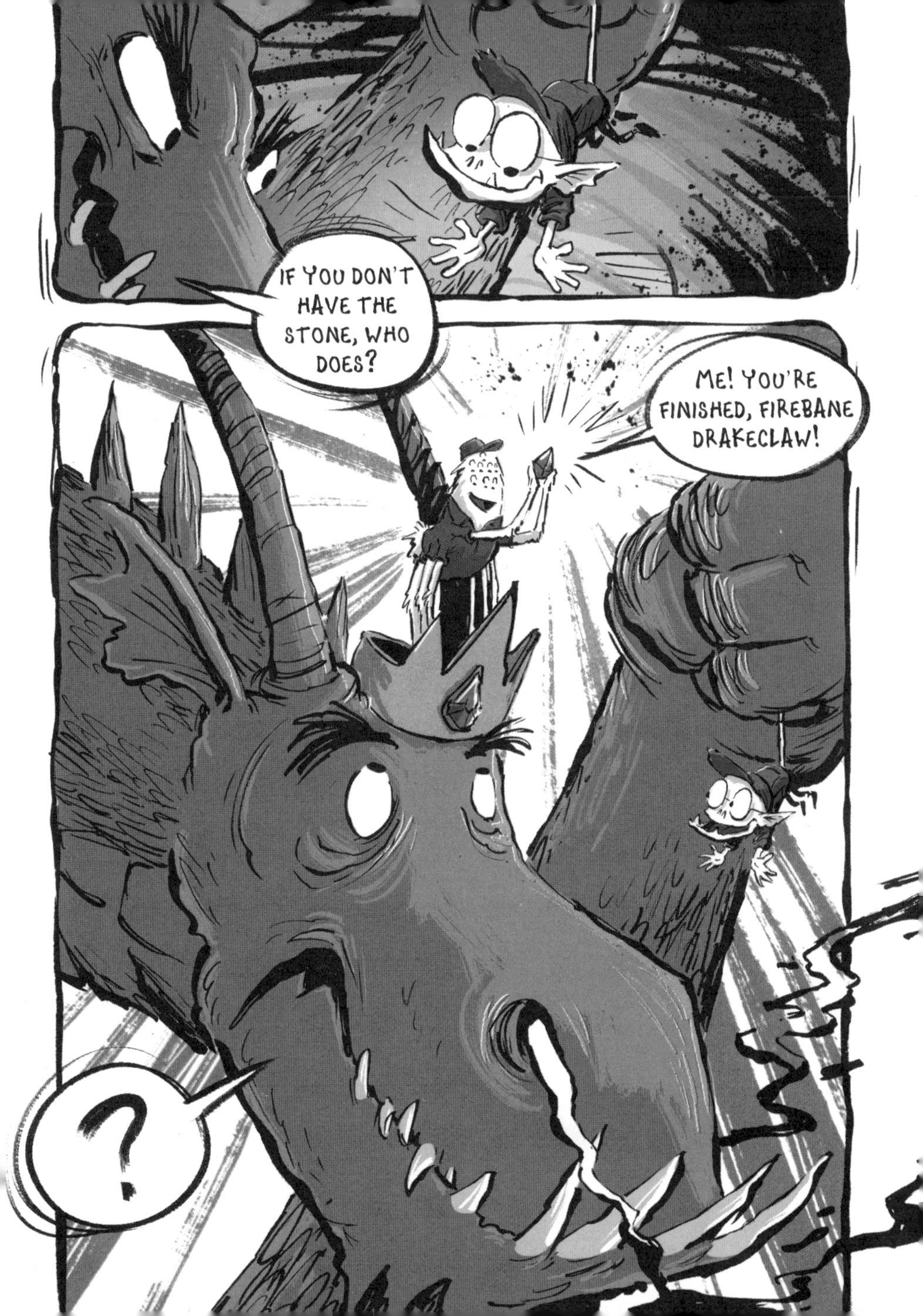
IF YOU DON'T HAVE THE STONE, WHO DOES?
ME! YOU'RE FINISHED, FIREBANE DRAKECLAW!
?

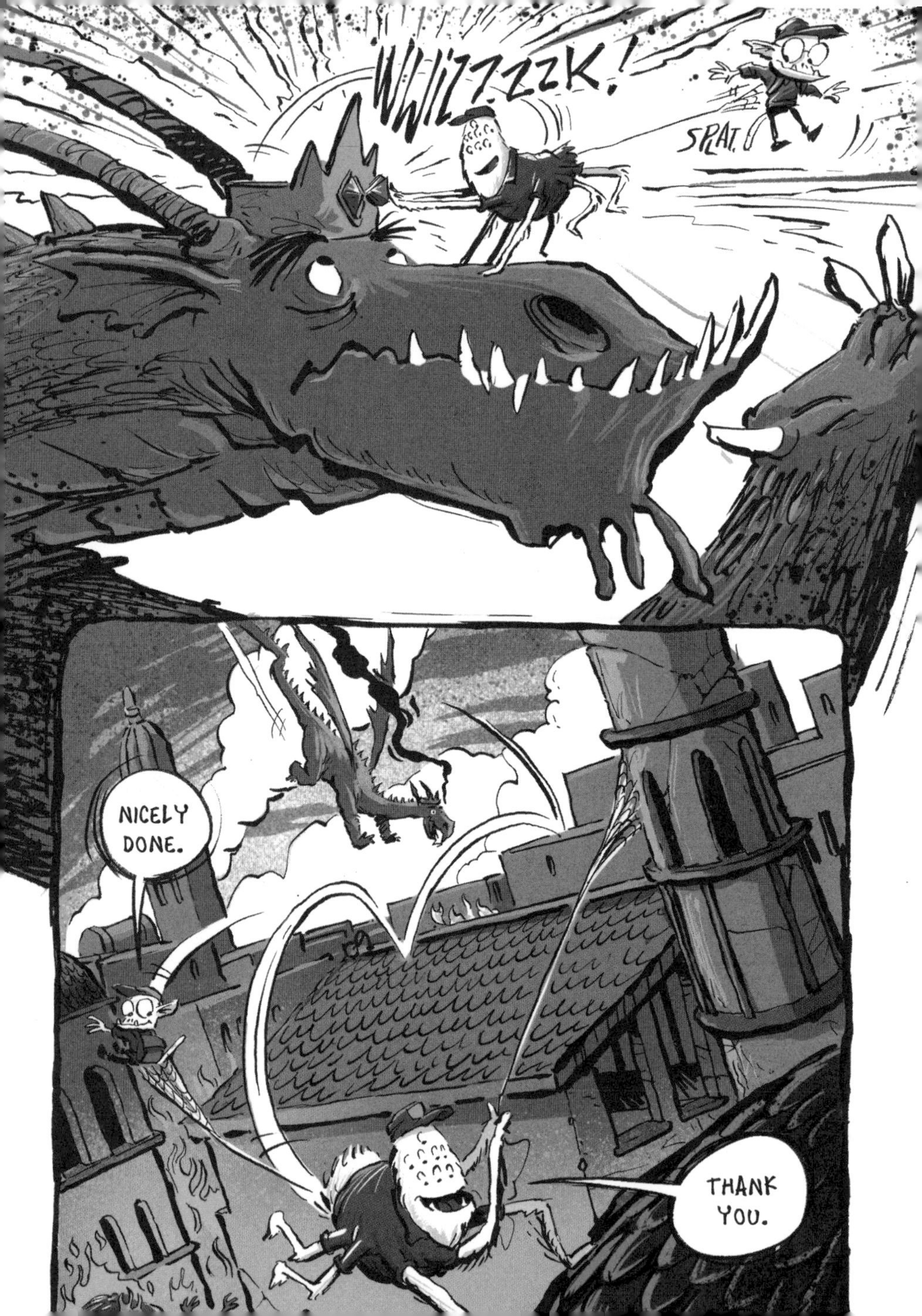
WWIZZZZK!
SPLAT.
NICELY DONE.
THANK YOU.

Firebane crashed into the town square and didn't get up. He lay there like a fallen building, with his scales cracked and his head scorched. We had outsmarted the king of smarts. The most fearsome monster in the mountain was down for the count. The crown lay beside him, dented and smoking. The two panzantium stones had fused together to become one very unstable stone. The glow from the stone grew brighter by the second, until it exploded in a flash of blinding purple light.

Captured monsters poured out from the stone as its power burned away. Queen Azelia, Principal Weaver and Lord Dunhelm burst from the panzantium and into the town square. They stumbled around, dazed from their ordeal, as more spiders and dwarves poured out of the stone. Hugo and I watched from a distance until my spider friend spotted the one monster he'd been hoping to see.

"Father!" Hugo rushed to where Captain Scorn staggered around the square. He wrapped him in an eight-legged hug.

My tail warmed to see Hugo reunited with his father. I thought of Tank and Aleetha, and the warmth vanished. My friends were gone. There'd be no reunion for us.

"There he is!"

The shout came from the other side of the square. Two shapes pushed through the crowd of monsters. I stood stunned as troll and lava elf rushed across the square.

"Nice shooting, little goblin!" Tank gave me a scale-crushing hug.

"I knew a goblin in a slingshot would do it!" Aleetha jumped in and made it a reunion to remember.

"How? Who?" was all I could say when Tank dropped me to the ground.

Before she could explain, a commotion broke out around Firebane. The dragon was waking up from the blast the stone had given him. His tongue hung out through his fangs like a wet towel.

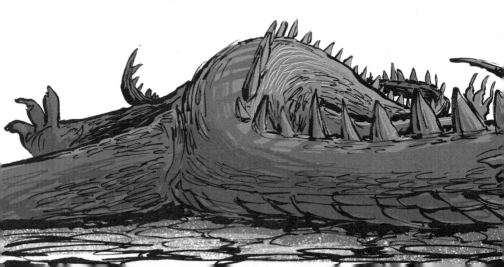

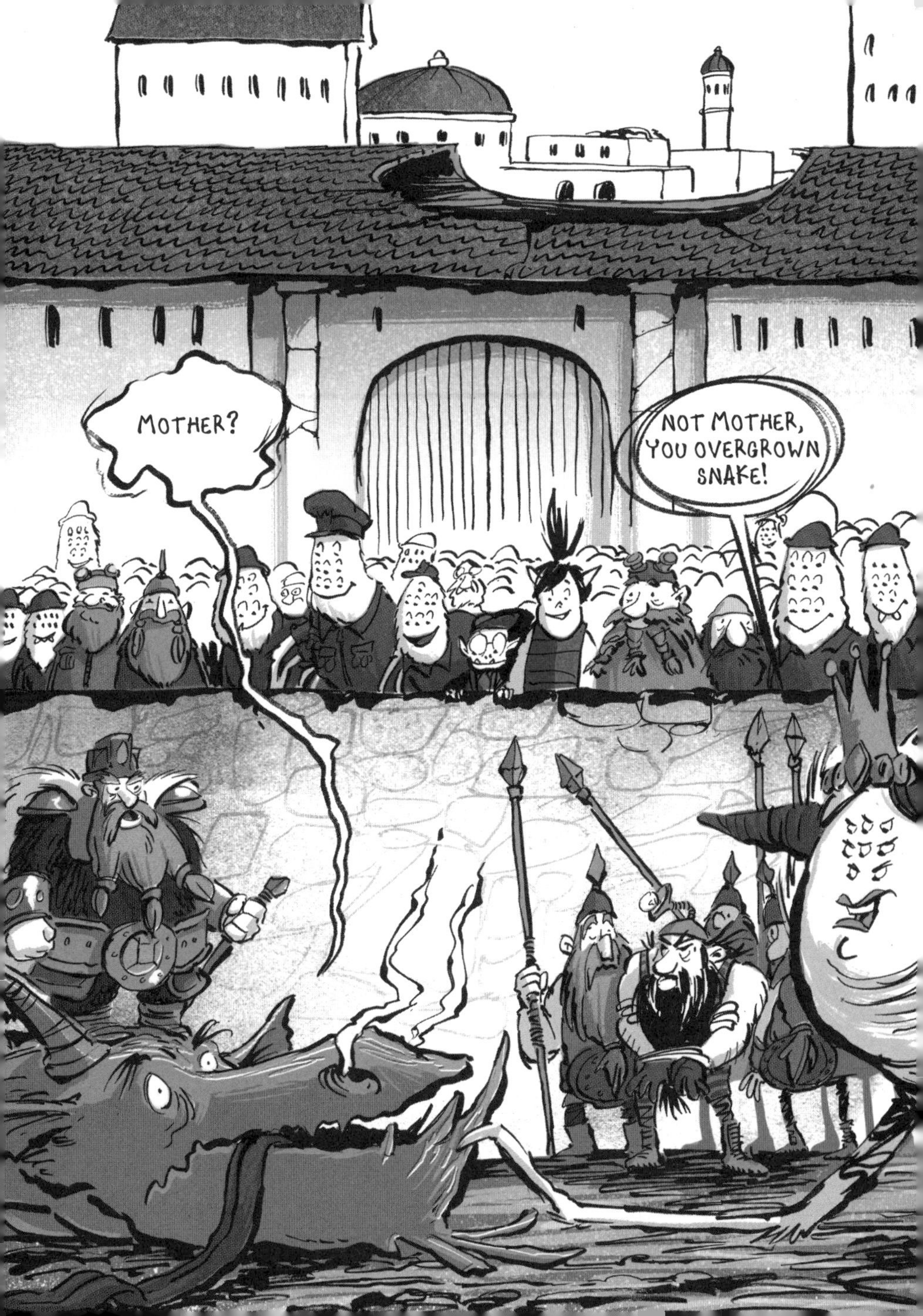
MOTHER?
NOT MOTHER, YOU OVERGROWN SNAKE!

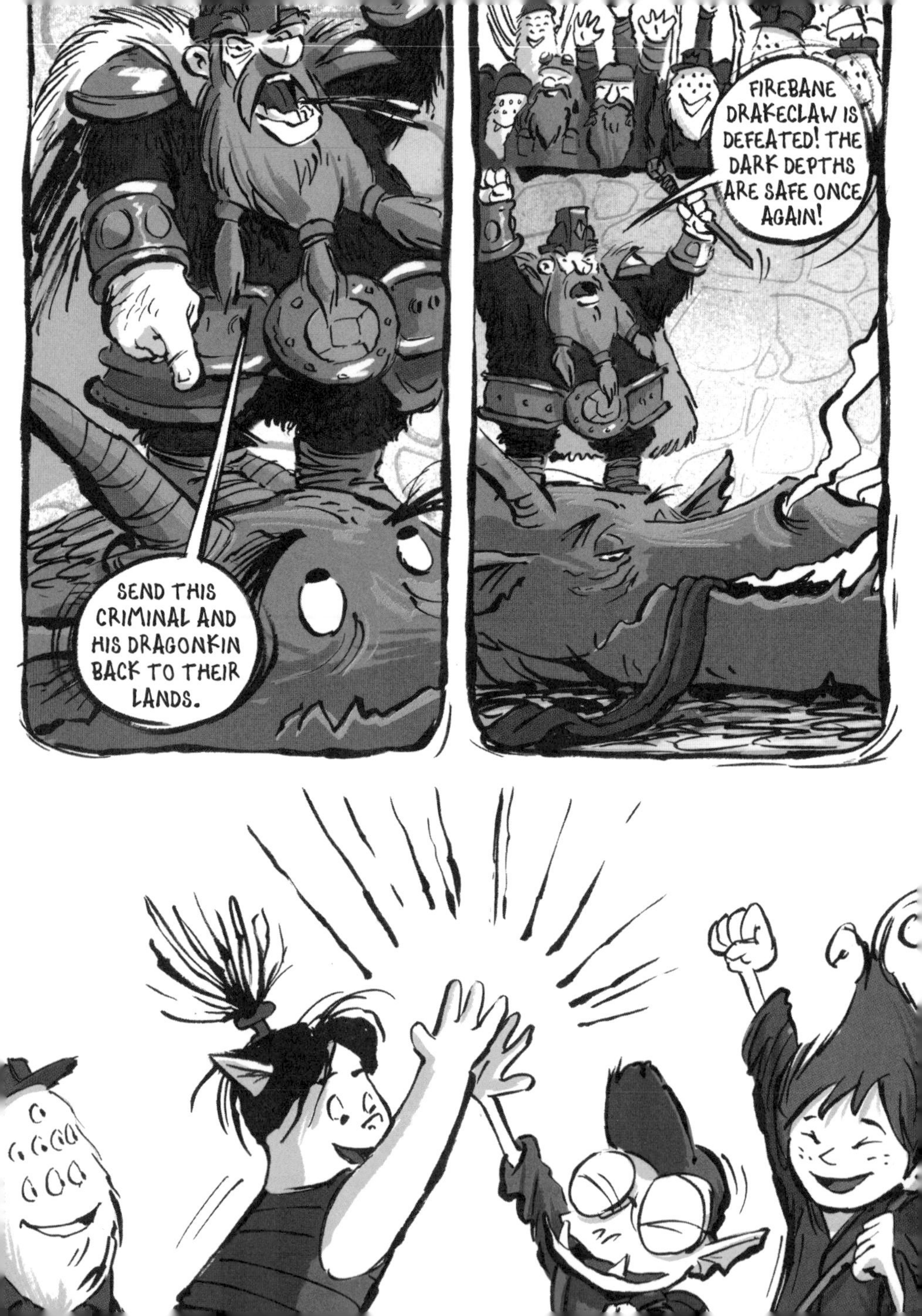
SEND THIS CRIMINAL AND HIS DRAGONKIN BACK TO THEIR LANDS.
FIREBANE DRAKECLAW IS DEFEATED! THE DARK DEPTHS ARE SAFE ONCE AGAIN!

CHAPTER TWENTY

Dancing in the Dark Depths

I t was party time in the Vale of Webs.

With Lava Falls still smoldering, Queen Azelia invited us all back to her web for a feast. And, as a special treat, the students of Gravelmuck were *not* the main course. Even Henelle was happy to hear that.

The queen's royal web was alive with music, laughter and swinging spiders. All monsters from the Depths were invited to the party. For the first time in the history of the dark region, spiders and dwarves mixed with lagalanders and fire folk (who turned out to be very good at not burning stuff like cities made of spider-webs). A dwarven brass band blasted out the tunes while spiders jigged with their new fish-head friends.

High above, young spiders swung through the webs with my classmates in tow. They slingshotted my schoolmates through the air like Hugo had me. From the sounds of Rizzo Rawlins's delighted barks, everyone was having a good time. I sat with my friends in a quiet corner and watched the fun from a distance. I'd had enough web swinging to last me a dragon's lifetime.

Hugo dropped down to us, dangling from a silky strand.

"Congratulations, detectives!" The spider had not stopped smiling since we left Lava Falls. "You solved another case and saved the day!"

"You're the real hero, Hugo," Tank said. "You're the one who defeated Firebane Drakeclaw."

"I had help from my friends."

"Yeah," Aleetha said. "Nice swinging up there, Fizz. Tank and I saw it all from the ground."

"I'm always happy to be a dragon distraction!" I said. "But I still don't understand how you survived a fall into the Abyss."

"It's simple, really." Tank took a deep breath, and I knew what was coming was going to be anything but simple. "The Abyss is really a regenerative energy system that swallows stuff, breaks down its energy components and then reassembles them at a spot directly above it. They are extremely rare but a totally natural wonder of the mountain."

"But it was eating the mountain," I said. "We all saw it chewing up the rocks like it was an all-you-can-eat buffet."

"True." Tank's ears wiggled. "But it also spat the rocks back out again. We didn't see that because the rocks reappeared about halfway up the mountain, far above the braces."

"So the Abyss has been eating rocks and spitting them back out all these years?" Hugo said. "The mountain has never been at risk of getting swallowed?"

"Nope," Tank said.

"Tank and I think Firebane knew that the whole time," Aleetha said. "He made up the story of the dangers of the Abyss and built the braces to try to win control of the Depths all those years ago."

"Instead, the spiders and dwarves made him share," I said. "And he's been mad about it ever since."

"Dragons can sure hold a grudge," Tank grumbled.

They can hold secrets too. Before the spiders and dwarves dragged him away from the town square,

Firebane called me over to where he lay on ground. He was still dazed from his fall, but his eyes shone with knowledge.

"Well done, Fizz," he croaked. "You refused to give up. Your mother will be proud."

My tail curled at the dragon's words.

"Did you know my mother? You said her name when you dropped me on the ground."

"I knew her when she was just a baby." A smile crossed Firebane's snout. His eyes still danced, but now they looked beyond me and far from the Depths. "I was good friends with her mother, your grandmother."

"You knew my grandma?"

Firebane chuckled. "Let's just say you and I could have held the panzantium stone to unlock its powers."

The spiders hoisted Firebane into the air and carried him away before I understood what he meant. I'm still not sure I get it.

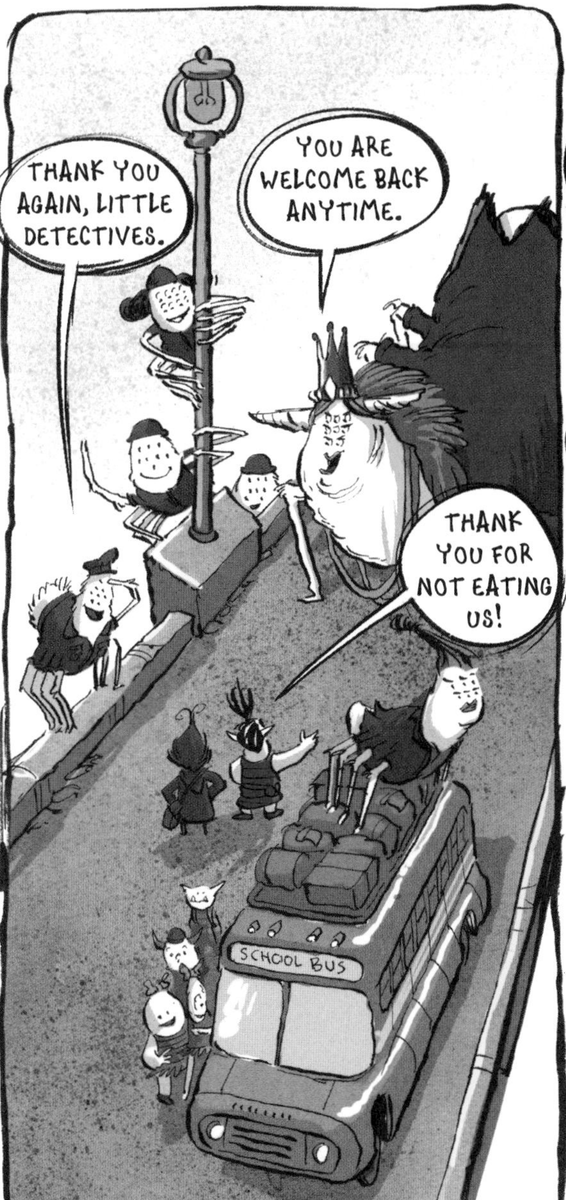
THANK YOU AGAIN, LITTLE DETECTIVES.
YOU ARE WELCOME BACK ANYTIME.
THANK YOU FOR NOT EATING US!
SCHOOL BUS
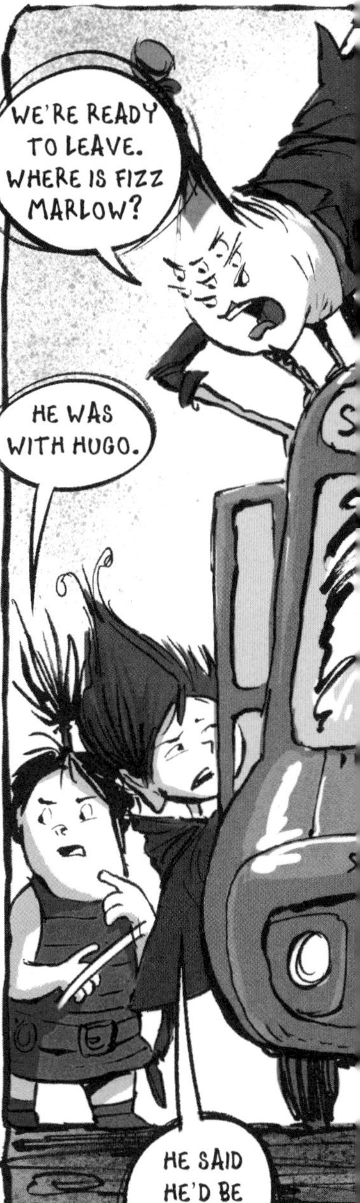
WE'RE READY TO LEAVE. WHERE IS FIZZ MARLOW?
HE WAS WITH HUGO.
HE SAID HE'D BE HERE.

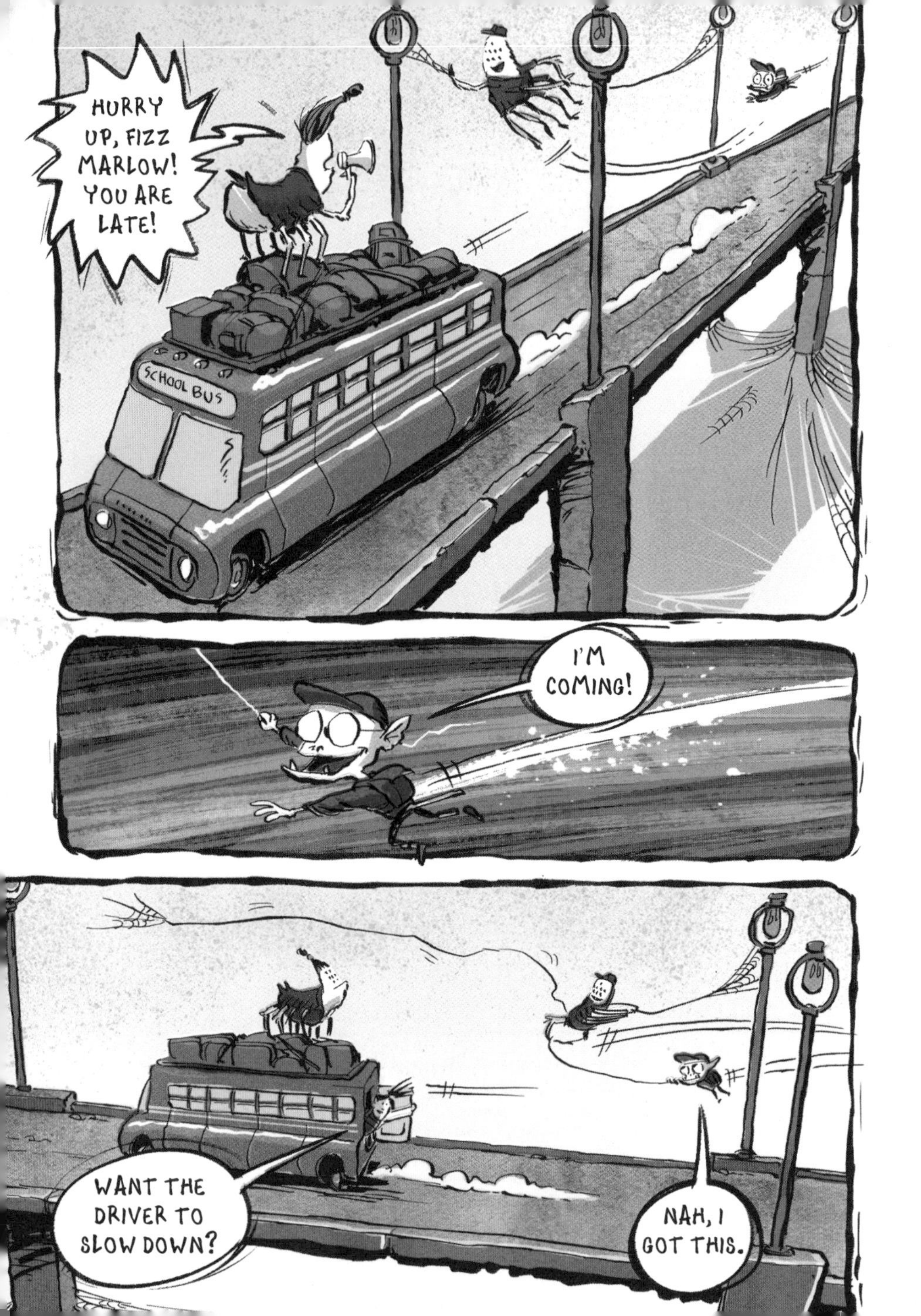
HURRY UP, FIZZ MARLOW! YOU ARE LATE!
SCHOOL BUS
I'M COMING!
WANT THE DRIVER TO SLOW DOWN?
NAH, I GOT THIS.

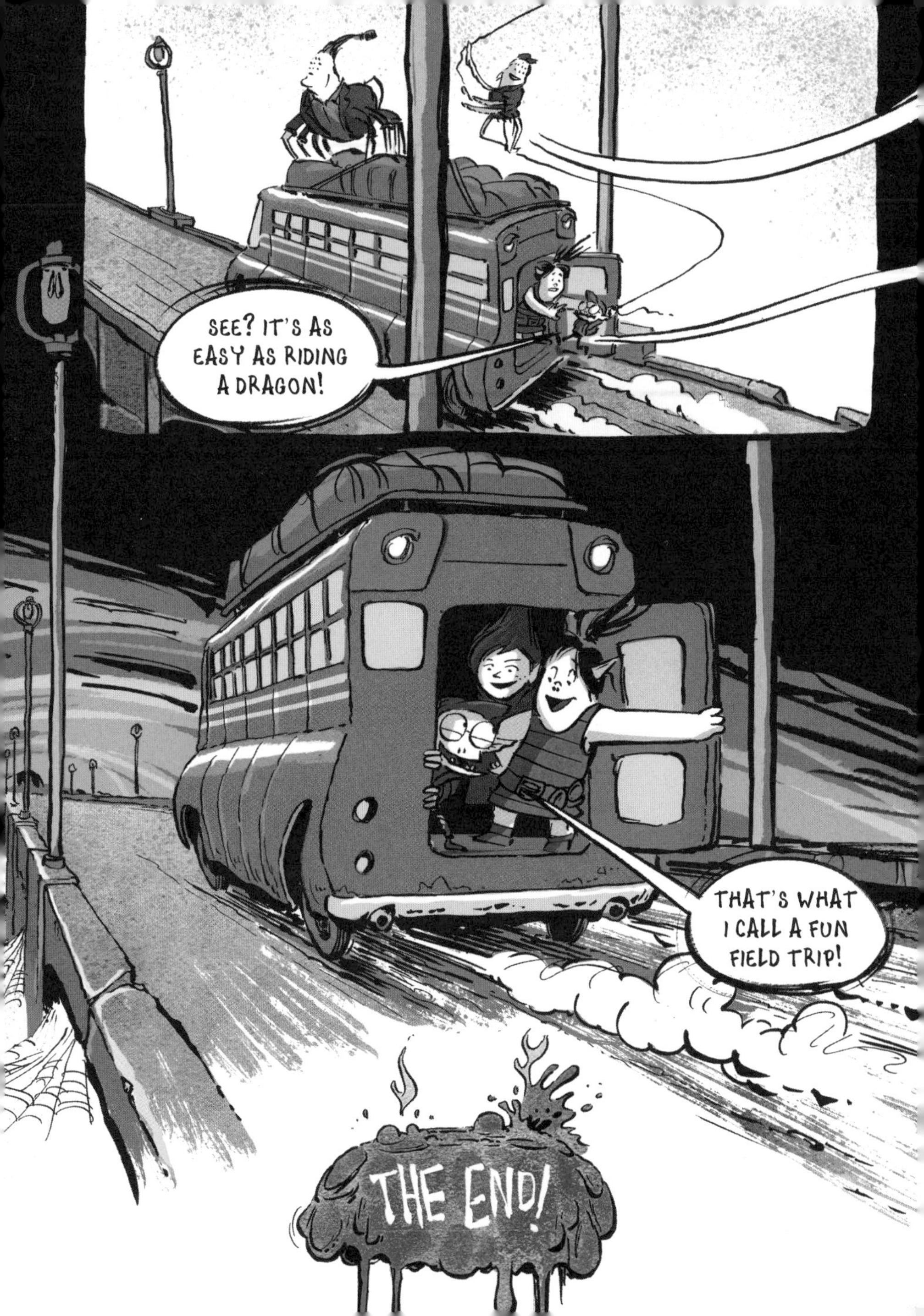
SEE? IT'S AS EASY AS RIDING A DRAGON!
THAT'S WHAT I CALL A FUN FIELD TRIP!
THE END!

LIAM O'DONNELL is an award-winning children's book author and educator. He's written over thirty-five books for young readers, including the *Max Finder Mystery* and *Graphic Guide Adventure* series of graphic novels. Liam lives in Toronto, Ontario, where he divides his time between the computer and the coffeemaker. Visit him anytime at www.liamodonnell.com or follow him on Twitter @liamodonnell.

MIKE DEAS is an author/illustrator of graphic novels, including *Dalen and Gole* and the *Graphic Guide Adventure* series. While he grew up with a love of illustrative storytelling, Capilano College's Commercial Animation Program helped Mike fine-tune his drawing skills and imagination. Mike and his wife, Nancy, currently live in sunny Victoria, British Columbia. For more information, visit www.deasillustration.com or follow him on Twitter @deasillustration.

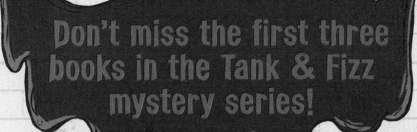

Don't miss the first three books in the Tank & Fizz mystery series!

LIAM O'DONNELL   MIKE DEAS

TANK & FIZZ

THE CASE OF THE SLIME STAMPEDE

LIAM O'DONNELL   MIKE DEAS

TANK & FIZZ

THE CASE OF THE BATTLING BOTS

LIAM O'DONNELL   MIKE DEAS

TANK & FIZZ

THE CASE OF THE MISSING MAGE

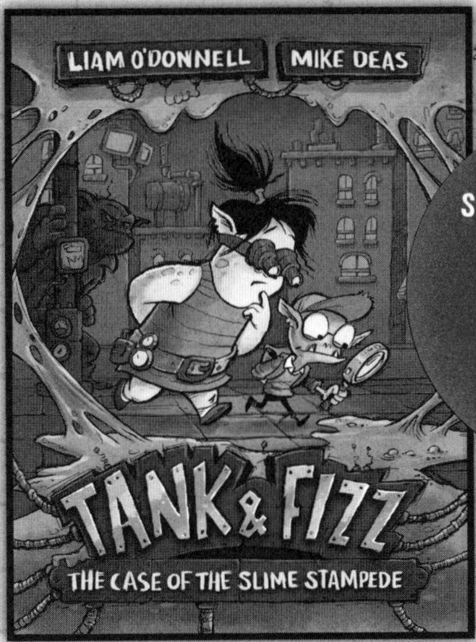
LIAM O'DONNELL
MIKE DEAS
TANK & FIZZ
THE CASE OF THE SLIME STAMPEDE

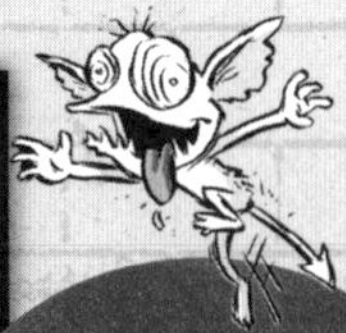

Silver Birch Express Award nominee

Hackmatack Children's Choice Book Award nominee

Tank & Fizz: The Case of the Slime Stampede
9781459808102 • $9.95 • Ages 8-11

The cleaning slimes have escaped, leaving a trail of acidic ooze throughout the schoolyard. Can detective duo Tank & Fizz solve this slimy mystery?

"Young readers will slurp up the gumshoes' gooey first exploit with relish."
—Kirkus Reviews

"Something slimy is running amuck in Rockfall Mountain and it isn't the cleaning slimes. This chapter book brims with reader appeal."
—School Library Journal

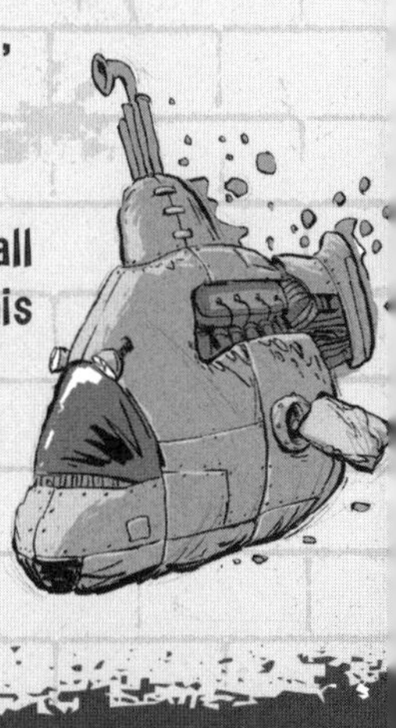

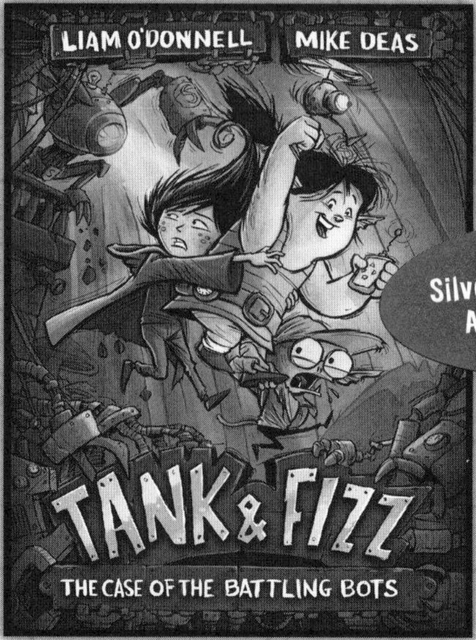
LIAM O'DONNELL
MIKE DEAS
TANK & FIZZ
THE CASE OF THE BATTLING BOTS

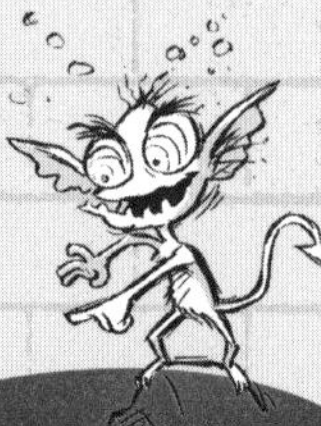

Silver Birch Express Award nominee

Tank & Fizz: The Case of the Battling Bots
9781459808133 • $9.95 • Ages 8-11

For monster sleuths Tank and Fizz, proving Rizzo Rawlins intends to cheat in the upcoming Battle Bot Cup should be a piece of cake. But a trail of corrupted computer code soon leads the detectives all the way to a mysterious hacker known only as *the Codex*.

"High-energy high jinks in a multicultural, or at least multispecies, setting."
—Kirkus Reviews

"A perfect mix of monstrous and silly."
—The Bulletin of the Center for Children's Books

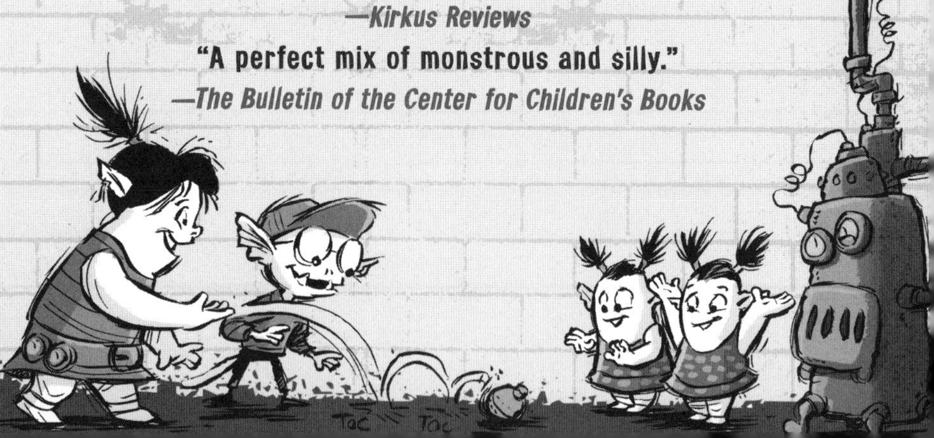

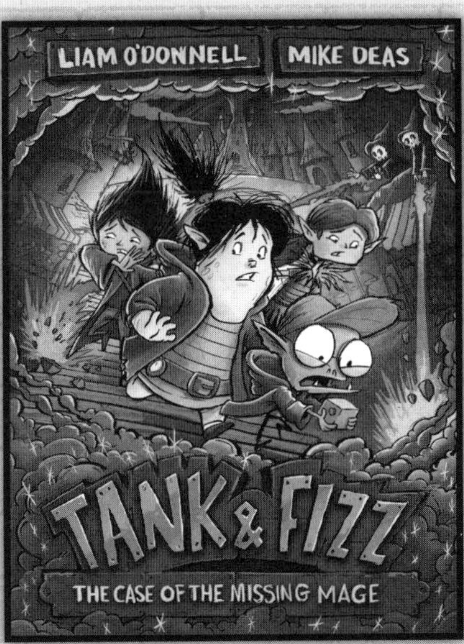
LIAM O'DONNELL
MIKE DEAS
TANK & FIZZ
THE CASE OF THE MISSING MAGE

Tank & Fizz: The Case of the Missing Mage
9781459812581 • $9.95 • Ages 8-11

When mysterious figures start making off with the professors at Shadow Tower, wizard-in-training Aleetha needs the help of supersleuths Tank and Fizz to find the missing mages. Using their detective skills, a pinch of magic and a trickle of technology, the friends explore Shadow Tower and stumble into a battle that's been brewing for decades.

"An action-packed detective story set in a land of monsters and magic."

—School Library Journal

"Fast paced and fun to read."

—School Library Connection

www.tankandfizz.com

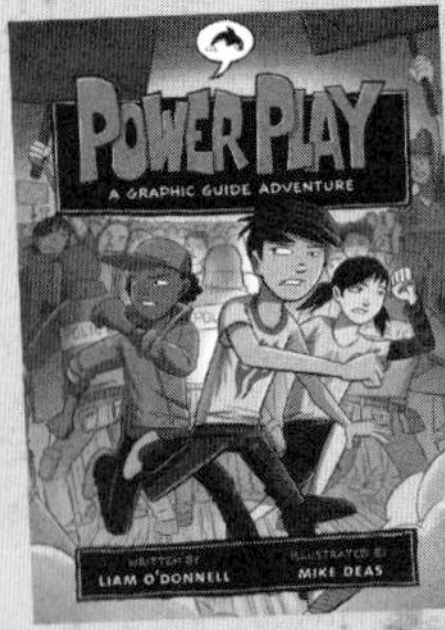
POWER PLAY
A GRAPHIC GUIDE ADVENTURE
LIAM O'DONNELL
MIKE DEAS

9781554690695 • $9.95 PB

"Rich in detail and chromatic with atmosphere."
—*Kirkus Reviews*

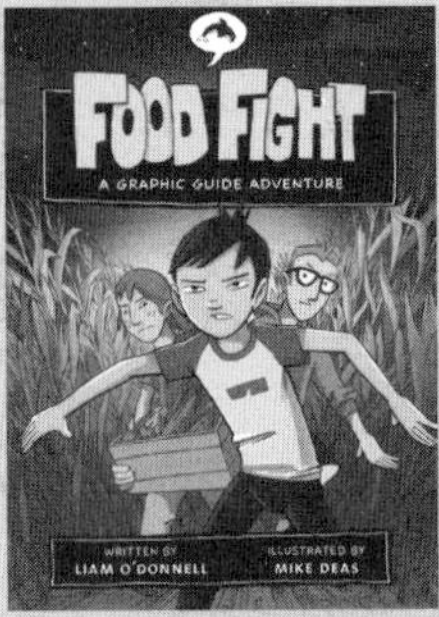
FOOD FIGHT
A GRAPHIC GUIDE ADVENTURE
WRITTEN BY
LIAM O'DONNELL
ILLUSTRATED BY
MIKE DEAS

9781554690671 • $9.95 PB

JOE SHUSTER COMICS FOR KIDS AWARD NOMINEE

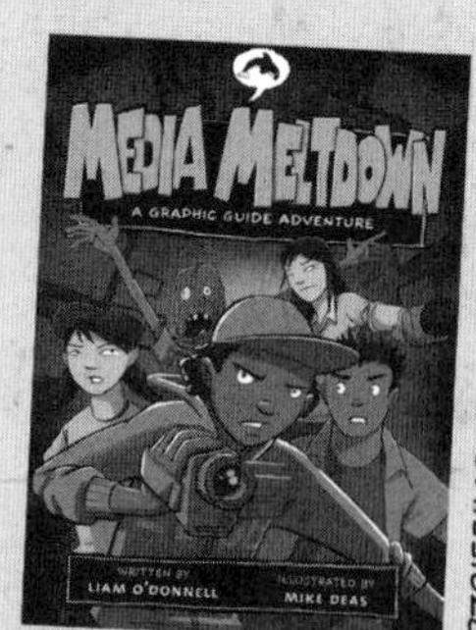
MEDIA MELTDOWN
A GRAPHIC GUIDE ADVENTURE
WRITTEN BY
LIAM O'DONNELL
ILLUSTRATED BY
MIKE DEAS

9781554690657 • $9.95 PB

"Colorful and fast-paced."
—*School Library Journal*

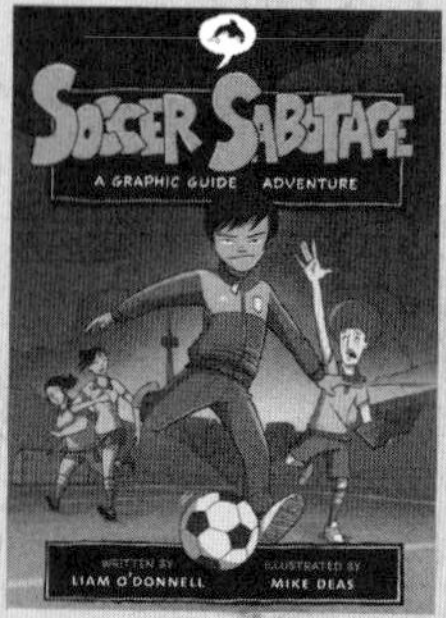
SOCCER SABOTAGE
A GRAPHIC GUIDE ADVENTURE
WRITTEN BY
LIAM O'DONNELL
ILLUSTRATED BY
MIKE DEAS

9781551438849 • $9.95 PB

JUNIOR LIBRARY GUILD SELECTION

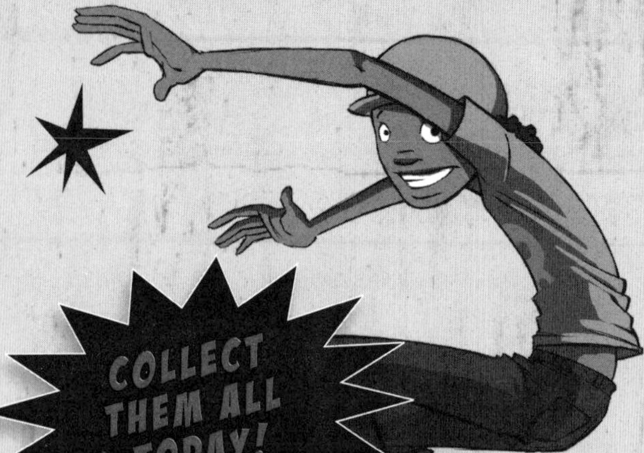
COLLECT THEM ALL TODAY!

ORCA BOOK PUBLISHERS

www.orcabook.com